The Black Regiment

by

James Odell

Published by James A. Odell

Text Copyright © 2016 James Odell

All rights reserved

Printed by CreateSpace

Table of Contents

The Black Regiment...1
   Chapter 1 5
   Chapter 2..29
   Chapter 3..72
   Chapter 4..93
   Chapter 5..128
   Chapter 6..175
   Chapter 7..201
   Chapter 8..216
   Chapter 9 256
   Chapter 10..286
   Chapter 11..325
   Chapter 12..340
   Chapter 13..364
   Chapter 14..396
   Chapter 15 424
   Chapter 16..449

contents reverse

Chapter 1

Introduction

Quebec, December 1851

The committee meeting in the governor's residence had lasted a couple of hours and the men sitting round the table were getting impatient.

They knew that the winter had brought supply problems for the Yankees. They had been forced to abandon their siege lines around Montreal and withdraw to the frontier.

But everyone knew they would be back as soon as the snows melted.

The governor in Quebec, Sir Humphrey Waite, had a fine set of salt-and-pepper mutton-chop whiskers.

The governor's secretary was an English official who expected to return home in a few months. "Agenda item six. The Colonial Parliament has complained to the Governor about number of black refugees seeking work in the colony."

The governor was puzzled. "Why do America's blacks want to come here? Why are there so many?"

The secretary looked up. "It's this Fugitive Slave Act of 1850. Canada is the only place where blacks are safe from southern bounty hunters. Blacks still want to escape. And some get through."

The official for internal affairs smiled. "Some officials in the Canadian government are eager to recruit blacks; they keep wages down."

But other men round the table grumbled. The

majority of them were afraid of a tide of refugees.

"I agree. We need to stop them," the governor said.

Debate was lively. This was more interesting than listening to reports. They decided to issue a statement that would deter any refugees.

The secretary crossed out a line and read the final draft.

"Take notice. Any refugee who reaches Canada is unlikely to find employment there. He is likely to be reduced to begging, with no sympathy from the populace. He is likely to starve to death. All we can promise a runaway is that he will die a free man."

The governor smiled. "I like that last bit."

"Yes, sir."

"No other business? The meeting is adjourned, then."

The secretary went downstairs and showed the statement to a clerk, a second generation immigrant. The clerk was shocked. "You can't publish that!"

"Why not?" the secretary said. "Remember, I'm from England. What's wrong with the wording?"

"The blacks will read this as a promise. This says they will achieve freedom. This will encourage desperate men."

The secretary read it through again. "Well, I'm not going to go back and tell the governor that."

London, Guild of magicians, April 2, 9pm

The fog had descended upon London. That made navigation difficult for pedestrians.

Lieutenant Henry Griffin, of the Royal Navy, walked along the west side of Berkeley Square to the College. He climbed the steps and knocked on the door.

The door opened at once. The doorman was surprised at seeing a naval man. "Good evening, sir."

Henry gave the man one of his visiting cards. "I would like to see the Earl. Urgent.

"Have you visited us before, sir?"

"I spent eighteen months studying here. Five or six years ago."

"Ah! So you aren't qualified, then, sir."

"No."

The doorkeeper shook his head. "Lord Edward is on a visit to Culham. But the Master of the College is here."

Henry sniffed. "Is Archibald still Master of the College?"

"Yes, sir." There was no need to say any more.

Henry knew that the Master was responsible for the apprentices' studies. He was also a martinet who shirked any task that was not directly related to his duties.

"Is it urgent, sir?"

"Yes. Very. It concerns Lord Palmerston's visit to the United States."

"Oh. As bad as that." The doorkeeper was taken aback. "Or there's the chatelaine, sir. Lady Samantha."

"But – I thought the Chatelaine kept the College's accounts."

"Yes, sir. But we have a new Chatelaine, now. She does a bit more than keep the accounts, sir. She knows everybody who's anybody. If she can't help you, then she can introduce you to somebody who can."

"Very well. Please take my calling card up."

A maid led Henry upstairs to the guest accommodation. She showed him into the morning room. A lady was sitting back in a comfortable chair, reading. She was accompanied by a girl in a maid's uniform.

The lady looked up. "Good evening, lieutenant."

Henry was surprised at the Chatelaine's youth. He guessed that she was about eighteen. "Good evening, madam. Perhaps I should explain. My wife is one of the guild's weather observers. She's studying, as an apprentice. She hopes to qualify some day. She used her telepathic skills to send weather reports to London."

"I remember that, yes, lieutenant." Please, sit down."

"Thank you, madam. I met my wife when she was in New York. Her father was the British Consul. She went back to stay with her parents when I was with the fleet. And then the war broke out."

She was confused. "Is that important?"

"Mr. Abernethy was chosen to accompany Lord Palmerston to the peace conference in New York. My wife accompanied her father."

"And something went wrong? Was Palmerston attacked?"

"You must understand that I'm a Talker too. I spent eighteen months here. Then my uncle said that he would pay for my naval training."

She nodded. "You can establish rapport with your wife."

"Yes. My wife tells me that the airship was diverted to a place called New Jersey. It burst into flames on final approach. There were many casualties."

"How horrible! Is - is your wife all right?"

"She waited until the gondola was just above the ground before she jumped out. She was shaken, that's all. But her father landed badly and broke three ribs. He is expected to recover."

"I hate to seem callous, but – Lord Palmerston?"

"The authorities have told Edith that they cannot find him. They have assumed that Palmerston is dead."

She looked shocked. "If your wife is an apprentice, then she is one of us."

"Yes, madam. But you have to see that I have no legal authority. My direct superior has no knowledge of my Guild training. I had hoped that by coming here I could cut corners – and save time."

She thought this through, reluctant to make any hasty decisions. Henry knew that her role was an honorary one. She had no authority. Her main task was to put on a fine dress every evening and preside at dinners. She had no power – except when things went wrong.

She stood. "Follow me." She led Henry to the guest room that was devoted to old Oswald.

Henry remembered the lectures he had received here. Oswald had suffered an accident, decades ago, and had been stuck in a wheelchair ever since.

He smiled as Lady Samantha walked in. "Good evening, my dear."

"Mr. Jackson, this is Lt. Griffin. A Talker. He received a message from the United States. His wife was in Palmerston's diplomatic party. There was a fire and Palmerston is assumed to be dead. But our informant was not there in an official capacity. She's the daughter of a diplomat."

Oswald blinked. "I see. Where's Lord Edward?"

"At Culham. I told him first. He's waiting for a train."

Oswald glanced at Henry. "Did you tell the foreign office?"

"Yes, sir. I handed in a routine report. But I don't have the authority to go to Downing Street."

"Of course, of course. Can we ask this girl to speak to the Yankees? Ask them to confirm that Pam is dead."

Henry shook his head. "She cannot make a request. She has no authority."

"Well – can her father ask?" Oswald said. "The PM will blame the Guild if we pass on false information. We must get it right."

"I see, sir."

"This is a Guild matter until we can get official confirmation." Oswald shifted in his chair. "They'll laugh at us if we get it wrong. We must get confirmation."

"Yes, sir."

New Jersey, Lakehurst base, April 3

The sick bay had never had so many casualties at once. Paul Abernethy, however, had the luxury of a private room. The medical orderlies ensured that he was kept quiet.

Now Edith sat at his bedside and watched as her father slowly recovered consciousness. She held his hand. She knew he was close to waking when he became agitated.

He complained of the pain.

She squeezed his hand. "I am sorry, father. But I need your help."

"Edith? I can't think."

"You have been given laudanum, father. You have three cracked or broken ribs. Don't try to move. Do you remember the crash?"

"Is that why I hurt so much?" He was lucid now. He was concentrating on the problem, not the pain.

"Yes. But – Lord Palmerston is assumed to be dead."

"Ah. Yes." His keen intellect was fighting the laudanum - and the pain. "Don't they know? How can they be uncertain? Perhaps he's on laudanum. Or is he in the morgue?"

"No, father. Algernon checked for us."

"Perhaps he fell on his head and he's lost his memory. But – I apologise, my dear – It is most likely that his body is in the wreckage and they haven't found it." He was abrupt. "Send that Yankee official in here. With Palmerston – out of touch, I'm the senior member of the diplomatic mission."

"Algernon says that you're unwell and he's senior."

"Does he, indeed. Well, if he's in charge, he can take responsibility when things go wrong. If the war starts up again, he'll get the blame. Tell him that."

"Yes, father." She stood and walked out.

Half an hour later, Edith led a US naval official into the hospital room.

Raphael Semmes was the commander of the naval air field. He was a southern gentleman, holding the rank of naval lieutenant. He had explained to her that he had gained temporary, wartime, promotion to commander.

She had mentioned that she was married to a naval officer. That improved her status in his eyes.

Mr. Abernethy turned his head so he could face the commander. Edith introduced them.

"Commander, you must check for his remains," Mr. Abernethy said.

Edith was shocked his tone. She thought that her father was quite bullying.

Semmes spoke formally. "We have checked the airfield, sir. My men were diligent. We found nothing."

"Then you must extend your search beyond the airfield perimeter."

"I have no authority over civil authorities," Semmes said.

"Then ask your president. Send a telegram. I am the senior British diplomat in the country. The president can ignore my request. But you can't."

Semmes was annoyed. "I have no authority to send telegrams to the White House. Who would I address it to?"

Mr. Abernethy smiled. "I can remember name of your Secretary of State."

"I can say with confidence that he would he ignore a telegram from an obscure naval officer."

Edith spoke up. "I can remember the name of the minister's aide."

Mr. Abernethy brightened up. "Yes. Send it to him. He'll read it."

"You've been to Washington?" Semmes was fascinated.

"No. I was the trade attaché in New York. But I had to learn the correct men to contact."

"I see, sir. Very well." Semmes left the room.

"You were rude to that poor man, father."

Mr. Abernethy's worries distracted him from the pain. "Will the talks continue? Who will replace Palmerston?"

Edith asked, greatly daring: "Could you?"

"Not flat on my back, dear."

Montreal, April 3

George Eastman and the thirty men of his platoon were stationed in Fort Longueuil, across the river from Montreal. All of them came from the Abenaki tribe.

He had joined the Sixty-Second Regiment, the Royal Americans, at the start of the war. Until then he had been a drifter with a low opinion of himself. He had joined up in the hope of proving his worth. Then things had taken an unexpected turn. He had received a commission and then brevet promotion to captain.

The fort had a perimeter of two miles and was defended by the biggest guns in Canada. Things had been quiet ever since the Yankees had hinted at negotiations. The worst enemy was the weather. The night before, they had been surprised by another snowfall. The view, looking across the battlefield, was desolate.

George and his men had the task of maintaining the fortifications and preventing sneak attacks. Any damage caused by enemy shelling had to be repaired promptly. They could never relax.

The Yankees had big guns of their own and the fort was just within their range. At one time, the Yankee artillery had pounded the fort without mercy, but now they merely fired a shell at the fort every hour, to remind the defenders of their presence.

George knew that the Yankees had been unprepared for winter. Hoping for an early victory, they had not issued winter clothing. Snowstorms had caused devastation. The enemy gunners needed a trainload of supplies every day, and snow had blocked the track for days at a time.

To make things worse for them, another platoon of Abenaki, experienced in winter conditions, was operating behind enemy lines, disrupting the railroad.

George left his shelter and walked along the main street of the fort. This was narrow, with frequent sharp angles. The most secure bombproof in the fort, more important than any officer, housed the telegraph equipment.

Early in the war, the colonel in charge had demanded that a telegraph cable should be laid under the St Lawrence river. He was fascinated by modern inventions and wanted his orders to be sent without any interference from the enemy guns.

George ducked his head as he walked through the doorway. He found there were two men in the bombproof. A burly sergeant in signals blue was bent over a charcoal stove. His companion was a thin private in a red jacket.

On the desk stood the single-needle telegraph instrument. For the moment, the needle was motionless.

George recognised the private. "Have you joined the signals, Tommy?"

"Detached duty, sir. The signallers are undermanned. So the sergeant asked me to volunteer."

George did not ask how the sergeant had induced Tommy to volunteer. "Is it usual for the sergeant to make the tea?"

The sergeant grinned. "If you've spent two hours watching a dial, then making tea is a relief, and that's a fact."

"Is there anything for me, private?"

Tommy looked up from the instrument. "Yes, sir. A message arrived from battalion HQ, fifteen minutes ago. I was going to bring the message up when I went off shift. I have the note here."

"Yes?"

"Your company is being withdrawn, sir. To Trois-Rivieres. The top brass seem to think that the Yankees might launch a sneak attack there."

"Right. Thank you." His men would be glad to hear of this move. They hated the overcrowding in the fort as much as they hated the Yankee artillery. George was aware that a single hit from a high-explosive shell could wipe out his entire platoon.

"The news from the US is terrible, sir. D'you think the war will start up again?"

"Here, do you mean?"

"Yes, sir." On several occasions the Yankees had attempted to take the fort, and on each occasion they had been thrown back, with great loss of life.

"They won't attack soon. Everyone knows they're short of supplies," George said. "Will Miss Grace get to know about this transfer?"

"She probably knows already, sir."

New Jersey, Lakehurst base, April 4

Edith paid regular visits to her father's room, to comfort him. Sometimes she took a book and tried to read. The doctor had reduced his dose of laudanum.

Her father was sleeping when the station commander came to see her.

Edith closed her book. "Good afternoon, sir."

"Good afternoon, Mrs. Griffin. I have come to advise you that the civil authorities have found Lord Palmerston. Or they say they have. He's in the county hospital in Lakehurst. They say he's very confused, the result of a blow to the head. He also has minor burns."

"But - how did he get to Lakehurst, commander?"

"I think he jumped from the airship gondola and fell badly. Then he picked himself up and ran. Men who have been injured are sometimes capable of running a fair distance. Particularly if they have been frightened or shocked or something."

"I see. But why did nobody spot him?"

"Well, when the hydrogen envelope collapsed and fell, everybody ran. Two of my ground crew ... didn't run fast enough. The burning fabric fell on them. I believe that another running figure could have passed unnoticed."

She nodded. "Go on, sir."

"He reached a farmhouse and collapsed. But he could not tell them who he was."

"Ah. I see."

"The farmer took him to the county hospital. Finally the matron realised that our hospital here was a body short and guessed what had happened."

"Yes. Thank you, commander."

He looked embarrassed. "Madam, we need someone to identify him. We can't afford another misunderstanding. And we cannot ask your father to do it."

"No." She guessed the next step.

"Can you go, madam?"

"Very well, commander."

"Excuse me, madam. But we have another problem. The Secretary of State went to New York. to greet your party. He's angry that you diverted here."

"But there was a thunderstorm. We were ordered to divert. Surely he can't blame us for that?"

Father interrupted. "Of course he can."

Semmes grimaced. "And now he's blaming me for keeping your party here. He went back to Washington. Your diplomatic party will have to join him there."

"Of course," Father said.

"I get the impression that the mood is changing in Washington, sir."

"I see, commander."

Montreal, April 5

Charles Lloyd, of the Guild of Magicians, waited at the Mont Royal airship field. The airship making its approach had his wife and child on board.

The wind was cold. Fortunately, the aviators had built a row of huts for their offices. The veranda provided shelter for civilian travellers.

The airship turned into wind and descended. The ground-crew were ready. The crew in the gondola dropped the landing ropes.

The ground-crew seized the ropes and, with a lot of shouting, pulled the craft down. They attached more ropes to secure the airship. The propellers stilled at last. The passengers descended from the gondola and walked across the grass.

Three businessmen led the way, followed by two army officers. His wife followed. She was thin, with her rich black hair hidden under a neat hat. Her maid was carrying a child. Behind them, porters carried two bags.

Charles stepped forward. "Welcome to Montreal, my dear."

Alice kissed him on the cheek. "Don't tell me I shouldn't have come here."

He kept his peace. "I already have, as I recall. And you ignored me."

"My place is by your side."

His daughter, in the maid's arms, was shy towards him. As if he was a stranger, he thought.

"Are you going to say that you're too busy, Charles?"

"No. I act as go-between for the general in Quebec and the colonel here. It can be tiresome but it isn't time-consuming."

"It sounds most – prestigious."

He grunted. How could he answer that? "I have acquired a reputation for getting things done. So when a problem comes up, I'm the first name that the powers-that-be think of."

"I promise not to get in your way."

"You must go back, as soon as I can arrange it. Canada isn't safe. Have you heard about this crash in the United States? Palmerston is in no state to open the discussions. There are all sorts of rumours about his disappearance."

"I heard when my ship reached Nova Scotia. Do you think it will destroy the peace talks?"

"It may. Each fresh rumour gives a different story. But never mind that. I have a Hackney carriage to take you to the hotel. Just two bags?"

"Yes. They told me, in London, that I would have to travel by sledge from Nova Scotia. So I decided to travel light. It was just as well – the airship has a weight restriction."

The army had taken over part of the Hotel Versailles as its headquarters. But the foyer was still open to hotel guests. The child looked round. "Indians? No Indians?" She sounded disappointed.

"What's that?" Charles said.

Alice looked embarrassed. "My father's been telling her the most absurd stories. She expected to meet Red Indians. She expected you to be attacked."

Charles smiled. "I can take her to meet some."

"Really, Charles?" Alice seemed astonished.

"Yes. It's not too difficult, here. I would like to introduce you to Captain Eastman. He's an Abanaki Indian."

She was dubious. "Is he a gentleman?"

He thought this over. "He's a bit of a rough diamond - promoted from the ranks. He hates the formal regimental dinners. He's bright, talented. The newspapers like to report his exploits - and he hates that. What can I say? He's fond of quoting Shakespeare."

"He sounds intriguing."

He led the way to their room. "And - I would like to introduce you to Miss Abenaki. She's bright too. She prepares the punched cards that are fed into the Analytical Engine."

Alice was as angry as he had ever seen her. "You intend to introduce me to your mistress?"

He was surprised. "Miss Abenaki is *not* my mistress. Is that why you came all this way? She's abstemious. She was educated in a convent. So she's uncomfortable in social conditions. Uncomfortable around anyone, really. She's more comfortable around that Engine than she is with people."

His wife was still suspicious. "And how did you meet this Indian maiden?"

"Oh, she's a natural Talker. And I had to recruit Talkers."

"Oh. I see. I think."

Montreal, April 6

Charles and his family met George Eastman in the hotel lobby. The soldier was wearing a tailored red jacket and dark uniform trousers. He was holding a glengarry bonnet.

Charles was carrying his daughter. He and his wife were followed by their maid. In her opinion, wealthy parents could only tolerate their children for fifteen minutes at a time.

His daughter was fascinated by the lieutenant's hair style, shaved at the sides of the head. "Indian."

George smiled. "Yes, miss. The real reason we do it is because everyone expects us to do it." The child laughed.

George spoke in an undertone. "I was surprised when you suggested this, sir. Are you sure you want a formal introduction to your wife?"

"Of course. I would rather introduce you than Lord Cardigan."

George grinned. "That's not saying much."

Charles gestured for his wife to step forward. He spoke formally. "My dear, may I introduce to you Captain Eastman of the Royal American Regiment?"

They shook hands.

Alice smiled. "I did not realise you were such a high stickler, Charles. An earl isn't good enough for you."

Charles was serious. "It isn't his social rank that I'm worried about. The man's a disaster."

His daughter was insistent. "Me, me, me."

Charles sighed. "Very well. "My dear, may I introduce to you Captain Eastman of the Royal Americans?"

George smiled and shook the child's hand. She was suddenly shy.

"You have to be careful what you say in her presence," Charles said. "If I said that Cardigan was a bounder, she's likely to tell him so."

George grinned. "They're not likely to meet, are they? Surely you wouldn't let your daughter associate with a man of such uncertain character?"

Charles' eyes widened in shock. then he laughed. "Yes, you're quite right."

"This is absurd," Alice said.

"Not at all," Charles said. "If my daughter were sixteen rather than three, I would be worried that she would want to meet such a dashing character."

"Is a bad man?" the child said.

"Let's say he's accident prone."

"Tumble down stairs?"

He grinned. "Something like that, yes."

"Feather, feather. Indian."

"I must apologise, lieutenant," Alice said.

"If it was only children, madam, I would not mind."

George's glengarry bonnet had a feather stuck into the badge.

"Want, want, want," the child said.

"It's too big for you," George said. To prove his point, he held the hat so that it came down over the girl's eyes. This amused her.

"You would have to have one made especially for her," he said.

"Is Lord Cardigan here? Resident in Montreal?" Alice said.

"He's supposed to be on campaign, south of Quebec. But he visits the hotel regularly, madam," George said.

"I don't particularly want to meet him, if he's of such uncertain character," Alice said.

Charles turned to his wife. "Yes. You could refuse to meet him. Not too bluntly, of course."

George was surprised. "Could she do that? Wouldn't that cause a scandal?"

"Well, yes," Charles said. "The rules of society are tiresome, and sometimes they restrict your actions. But they're all designed to prevent ladies from being insulted by bounders. If my wife thinks that Lord Cardigan would insult her, she's entitled to avoid him."

Alice smiled. "My mother would be shocked if I did that. But my father would be delighted. The idea that his daughter was too proud to meet an earl ..."

"In England, this would not be a problem," Charles said. "We would never meet. But here, in army headquarters, with a war on ..."

"I see," George said.

Fort Ticonderoga, April 7

The twenty redcoats waited in the woods until nightfall. These woods were small and tame compared to the northern forests of home. They provided little shelter. The scouts had kept watch all day, but no-one had come to disturb them.

"Sunset. Time for you to go," the lieutenant said. "Have you got your map?"

Five of the men, all Mohawk volunteers, helped each other put on their haversacks. They said farewell to their comrades and set out for their destination.

They tried to keep to the woods. But this far south, the woods were surrounded by cultivated land. Avoiding all the farms was tricky.

They met no opposition and made good time. The moon provided enough light to avoid obstacles in their path. They reached the edge of the wood and stepped out onto the gravel track.

"We turn east," the sergeant said. They had been told there was no farm traffic on this path. It led only to the fort.

The sergeant, Joseph Thayendanega, knew that this is was a suicide mission. They could not win this fight and the US army was said to shoot Mohawk prisoners.

"It was built by the French. That shows you how old it is. The US army took it from the British but they didn't need it, so they sold it. To someone in New York. But then the war started and they kicked the owner out ..."

"But how can you be so sure it's empty?" Thomas said.

"Well - the army didn't want the fort but they wouldn't let the owner back in. The owner was annoyed. He wrote a letter to the newspapers, complaining about it. That's how the captain learned about it. So, unless things have changed since then, it's probably empty."

They came to a bend in the path and caught their first glimpse of the walls. They were built of stone and brick.

"Where's the way in?" Thomas said.

"On the east side," Joseph said.

The men had to walk right round the fort to reach the gateway. If the fort had been manned, they would have been caught in a crossfire. But they saw no-one.

The double door was made of wood, with metal bands. Joseph pushed, but the door did not move. "We'll have to climb up. Where's the rope?"

Next to the door was a bell-pull. It looked like a stirrup dangling on a chain.

"What's this?" the private said. He yanked the handle down.

The bell tolled. Joseph was exasperated. "Idiot. What did you do that for?"

"I just wanted to know," the private said. They heard footsteps inside, walking across cobblestones.

"Is that you, Thomas?" the person said.

The private grinned. "Yes, it's Thomas here."

Thomas was surprised. "How did he know it was me?"

"There must be plenty of men called Thomas in the US army," Joseph said.

"Oh."

They heard the heavy bolts being pulled back. A small door within main door opened. A man peered out. "You're not Thomas."

The private pushed open the door but then fell, obstructing the doorway. The sergeant climbed over him and grabbed the watchman.

"The rest of you, get in, quick."

They climbed in and helped the fallen man to his feet. They looked round. They were in a rectangular courtyard. On three sides were tall, narrow houses.

"Where is everybody?" Thomas said.

"You're Indians," the watchman said.

Joseph realised the watchman was alone. "There's only him. I told you that the place was empty."

Fort Ticonderoga, April 8

At sunrise, Joseph opened the side-door and chased off the night-watchman. "Our orders are to cause confusion. We can't do that if no-one knows we're here."

They raised the flag. Thomas sounded the bugle. They climbed to the battlements and settled down to wait.

Half an hour later, five Yankees approached across the grass. They wore the uniform of the militia.

"Stop right there," Joseph said.

"Why are you trespassing on federal property?" the militiaman said.

"I am Sergeant Joseph Thayendanega, K Company, Sixty-Second Regiment. The Royal Americans. I claim this territory for the British crown." The captain had made him memorise that. He had never expected that he'd get a chance to say it.

"You're Canadians? Stop being childish," the Yankee sergeant said. "You'll have to surrender. Let us in."

Sergeant Thayendanega spoke to his colleagues in an undertone. "I suppose we'll have to. Our orders were that we could surrender if we were outnumbered."

"No. There's only five of them," the corporal said. "So they don't outnumber us."

The militiaman was growing impatient. "They're redskins. Halfwits."

That irritated Joseph. "We can only surrender to a superior force."

"Well, how many of you are there, then?"

Joseph was angry. "Do you think I was born yesterday? I want to see a hundred of you death-or-glory boys in that field. Then I might think of surrendering."

The militiamen were annoyed. Joseph threatened to use his musket, so they withdrew.

All morning, the impasse continued. Joseph and his men patrolled the battlements.

Joseph was surprised that no-one attacked. Twenty men with a ladder could do it. What were they waiting for?

They searched the fort and found a kitchen. There was a store-room full of tins of food.

Thomas was frustrated too. "Why don't they get it over with?"

Montreal, April 8, noon

Charles took his wife and daughter to see the Analytical Engine. It was housed in its own fireproof building. The boiler that provided the steam was next door.

The Engine dominated the room. It was twenty feet long and four feet high, the iron frame painted red and green. The delicate inner workings were protected by a gauze screen.

The young woman sitting at the desk wore a blue bodice to her grey skirt. Her white lace cap was held in place by ribbons, fastened by a brooch under the chin She was thin, with dark features. She stood as the visitors approached.

Charles turned to his wife. She nodded. Charles stepped forward. "My dear, may I introduce to you Miss

Grace Abenaki."

Grace smiled and the two women shook hands.

"Miss Abenaki is listed in the records as a civilian auxiliary, attached to the Royal Corps of Signals. Her official task is to send despatches, written in Abenaki, to the Abenaki company operating behind enemy lines."

"And your real task, Miss Abenaki?" Alice said.

"Well – the Engine, madam. We use it to process our weather observations," Grace said. "Of course, the men on campaign need our weather prediction too."

The child was fascinated by the noise of the engine. She was disappointed that it was hidden behind a gauze screen.

Grace smiled and pushed one of the screen panels to one side. The complicated array of iron and brass cogs and carry-arms gleamed.

Charles held his daughter back when she tried to get close. She pouted.

"It's too dangerous. If you snagged your dress, we would have to cut it off."

"Oh."

"I have to be careful too, of course. My cravat."

"You too?" She subsided.

Grace explained to Alice that the Engine was second-hand. "There wasn't time to make a new one for us."

"Yes, I see," Alice said.

"The Engine is used mainly for weather prediction. We receive weather reports four times a day."

"From Guild members?" Alice said. "It's more complicated in London. Many of the observers are overseas."

"Most of the reports come in by telegram. But the telegraph system isn't reliable. Unless the messages are delivered exactly on time, they're worthless. Sometimes the telegraph operators are overworked."

"Yes, I see," Alice said.

Charles had timed his visit just right. Sergeant Chard and signaller Asher brought in the telegrams. Charles did not introduce Asher.

"We have to keep out of the way," Charles told his daughter. "Their work comes first."

The child watched, fascinated, as they used the telegraph messages to prepare the punched cards.

The craftsman pulled on a lever and the current calculation was halted. The cards were fed into the Engine, the craftsman pulled on the lever and the cogs and carry-arms resumed their rippling dance. Charles thought his daughter would soon get bored but she was fascinated by the Engine.

An officer in an engineer-blue jacket came in and watched the others. He had lost his left arm. Charles introduced him as Lieutenant Eathorpe. "He writes the weather algorithms."

He shook hands with Alice. "Delighted, madam."

An hour later, the Engine produced its result. Grace used the numbers to prepare the synopsis and prediction.

This was double-checked by Lieutenant Eathorpe. "Good. That's not contentious."

He gave the document to Sergeant Chard, who nodded and hurried off to the telegraph room. "The list just keeps getting longer," Grace said.

Signaller Asher was given a copy of the document. He had the task of establishing rapport with the Talkers behind enemy lines.

"Is that the only task you use the Engine for, lieutenant?" Alice said.

"No. We use the Engine to solve problems for the engineers or gunners. Ballistics. But the weather takes priority."

Fort Ticonderoga, April 9

At dusk, the men on the battlements heard a train arrive from the south. "Taking ammunition to the front," Joseph said.

But, instead of continuing on its way, the train stopped in the town. They heard sergeants shouting.

"Disembarking. A hundred men, do you think?" Thomas said.

"Yes. That sounds about right," Joseph said.

Half an hour later, Thomas noticed a pair of enemy scouts. "Regulars, not militia. There's bound to be more. Look."

The scouts kept themselves under cover, but they were easy to spot. The Yankees could not keep still.

"To the west and the north. Everywhere except the lake side," Joseph said. But we could get past them if we had to."

"They'll attack in the morning, sergeant."

"Yes," Joseph said.

"What do our orders say, sergeant? Are we asked to fight to the last?"

Joseph knew his orders by heart. "I was told to bring confusion to the enemy."

"Well - we've done that, haven't we, if that's a troop train. And - there's a boat down by the lake," Thomas said.

It took Joseph a moment to realise what Thomas meant. "Are you suggesting we run away?"

"You said we should confuse them. And what would be more confusing than if we vanish without trace?"

Joseph had to admit he was right. "It'll be difficult ..." He glanced round at his companions.

They all agreed to make the attempt. "I hate this place," the senior private said. So they hauled down their flag and Thomas played the bugle, just like a normal day in the garrison.

They could not make their attempt until full dark. So they took a tin of stew from the owner's stores and cooked a meal.

Joseph felt guilty about the stew. It had come from the civilian owner. So he wrote out a promissory note.

The Yankee sentries were watching the walls to the north and west. Joseph and his men sneaked out the eastern gate. There was a steep slope down to the beach.

"Tricky. That's why the defences are weaker on this side."

But there were no boats in sight. "We'll have to go back. I don't want to be trapped in these woods. Surrender in the morning," Joseph said.

There was a wooden shack on the waterfront. "Perhaps they stored boats in there," Thomas said.

They looked inside. Instead of upturned boats on trestles, they found a sort of jetty. Two boats were moored up. One was a steam launch.

Thomas wanted to take the steam launch, but they had to abandon the idea. They did not know how to get steam up.

The rowing boat had oars, so they climbed in and pushed it out.

They set about the task of rowing across the lake. None of them had rowed a boat of this size before.

They had to learn as they went and the task took them all night.

They landed at last and looked up at the mountain peaks. "This is the Green Mountains. Vermont," Joseph said.

They started their walk north. "We must get away from the shore. That's where they'll look first," Joseph said. They were soon climbing steeply.

Chapter 2

Montreal, Hotel Versailles, April 10

Charles led his wife, Miss Grace, and Signaller Asher down the stairs to the basement of the headquarters building. The long room had been fitted out as a firing range.

Charles was carrying an elegant wooden box. He placed the box on the table and opened it to reveal two duelling pistols. Miss Grace was fascinated. "I've heard about those things, sir."

"This was a gift. I never use them. But I brought them as an excuse, to justify taking over the range for an hour."

He loaded one pistol and turned to face the target. "I hope you don't mind loud noises." He aimed and fired in one fluid gesture. He just nicked the target. "This is useless as a defensive weapon. It goes off too easily." He put the weapon down. "I prefer magic. Watch."

He held out his arm, with his palm towards the target. He created a fireball and sent it racing down the range.

"You hit the target dead centre." Grace was impressed.

Charles smiled. "That's because I practice this more often. But this is really two spells. First you create the heat, then you push it." He nodded to Asher, who raised his arm and sent his own fireball down the range.

Charles showed Grace the first spell, creating heat. "Each spell has its own shape. You already know how to create light. Don't get the two mixed up."

Grace nodded and concentrated. She created the fire easily, but it flickered and dimmed. She was disappointed. "I'll try again."

"No. Close the spell. You mustn't exert yourself for too long." Yet Charles was pleased. "That's very good for a first attempt. Some apprentices take an oath - to only use violent magic to defend the weak and helpless."

"I don't need violence. I'm not a soldier."

"What if the Yankees got across the river?" Alice said.

Grace cheered up. "Well, yes, if that happened, it would be right to use violent magic."

"Try again," Charles said.

Grace held her hand out, opened her palm, and created a ball of heat. This time she kept the ball intact for several seconds.

"Well done. Now kill it. Wait a minute, then practice doing it again."

Charles and Asher alternated sending balls of fire down the range. Charles got a very close grouping.

Then he demonstrated the push spell to Grace. "Did you feel that? I shall demonstrate again ..."

"Yes, sir."

Then Charles loaded and fired the second pistol. He turned back to Grace. "You must practice pushing. It could be used as a weapon in itself."

He cleaned the pistols and put them away. "Let's go."

Green Mountains, April 13

The five Mohawk soldiers of the Sixty-Second regiment were woken from their sleep. Joseph realised that he had a knife to his throat. His assailant whispered. "Give me one word why I shouldn't kill you, white man."

"Ah - Victoria. Ah - God save the Queen."

His attacker had not expected that. He drew back. "What?"

"Royal American Regiment. And don't call me white,

half-breed," Joseph said.

"How much white do you have in you, Mohawk?"

"One quarter. And you, Huron?"

"That's Wyandot to you. One quarter English, one quarter French."

"Ah. What unit are you?"

"Company J; Royal Americans." The Huron sergeant sat back on his heels. "Where do you come from?"

Joseph was reluctant to admit the truth. "Fort Ticonderoga."

"That was you? Where are the rest of you? Were they killed?"

"No, we all got away. Just us five."

"But the Yankees said – the newspapers said -."

One of Joseph's Mohawk privates grinned. "You mustn't believe everything you read in the newspapers."

"Yes. You get newspapers here?" Joseph said.

"Three days late." The Wyandot sergeant scowled. "I can't deal with this. I'm taking you to the lieutenant."

All that morning, they climbed higher up into the mountains.

Just before noon, they reached a bivouac in the woods. This looked temporary. Joseph guessed that they probably moved every day.

The Wyandot sergeant introduced him to Second Lieutenant Brent.

The lieutenant was blond, and Joseph thought that in formal uniform he would look dapper. But in a sack-jacket, he looked comfortable.

He listened to Joseph's story in silence. "So you took the fort, just like that?"

"We just walked in, sir. There was only a night-watchman."

"The newspapers say you massacred the garrison, except for one man."

"There was only one man, sir. The watchman."

"I see. The newspapers say there were a hundred of you."

"No, sir. Only us five."

"Yes. The newspapers are saying we sent in a hundred men by airship and then airlifted you out again."

Joseph grinned. He could not help it. "You can't do that silently, sir. The airship took us to Essex County and we walked the rest of the way."

"But after you took the place you just left?"

"We heard a hundred men get off the train, sir. With their sergeants shouting. So we thought – I thought, we should leave. Our orders were to cause confusion to the enemy, and I thought that leaving would cause them more than by fighting to the last."

"You may have been right about that. They searched all along the Vermont shore. Captain Eastman will be jealous of you. Well, I'm going to ask them to send an airship to lift you out. I don't want you to confuse *me*. And the general wants to know what happened."

"Oh."

Green Mountains, April 14

At breakfast the platoon's Talker, a Wyandot, told the lieutenant that an airship would come that day. "Mid-afternoon, sir."

"Today?" Lieutenant Brent was surprised.

"It's good weather for an airship, sir. Light winds."

"True. But either they had an airship prepped and ready to go or the general wants you very much indeed."

All that morning they climbed higher up the mountain, away from habitation. They reached an open meadow. The scouts told Lieutenant Brent there were no soldiers within five miles.

"Right. Prepare the recognition signal."

An hour later, they spotted the airship approaching from the north. It was very noisy. Joseph hated that. And the things were so fragile.

"We'll have to be quick, there'll be a hundred Yankees here in an hour's time," the lieutenant said.

"Yes, sir."

The airship descended, the propellers straining to push the airship down. Half a dozen Wyandot soldiers rushed forward and grabbed the gondola.

The rear half of the gondola was open to the sky. The commander leaned over the guardrail. "Is this them?" He had to shout.

"Yes." Lieutenant Brent grinned at the commander. "You can tell everyone that you airlifted the entire Ticonderoga attack force."

Joseph was reluctant to get aboard. But his men enjoyed flying and were eager to climb in.

"Let go," the commander shouted, and the Wyandot soldiers stood clear.

The sergeant-engineer pulled the lever that disconnected the propellers from the engine. Immediately, the craft rose up into the air.

Joseph, looking down, could see that Lieutenant Brent's men had already left the meadow.

Montreal, April 14, afternoon

A staff sergeant met Joseph's team at the airfield and escorted them down the hill to army headquarters.

"Have you been here before? They've taken over a hotel for themselves."

"Yes, staff. But I don't like Montreal, any big city."

"So you know the drill." The staff sergeant led them to the rear of the hotel and then along the corridor to the scullery. "Get a quick wash. Then dust your jackets."

The water was cold, so they hurried. They pulled their jackets back on and pulled them straight

"Belts level? There's no time for any more." The sergeant led them upstairs.

This part of the hotel had luxurious furnishings, delicate tables and pictures on the walls. Joseph knew that he did not belong here.

The staff-sergeant knocked on a door and led them into a large room. "Sergeant Thayendanega, sir."

Three men were sitting behind a wide desk. Joseph recognised them and came to attention.

The general with the sideburns was Sir Reginald Trevor-Roper, c-in-c Canada. Colonel Grimwood, sitting to the general's right, was the commander of the Sixty-Second Regiment. The third man was Captain Eastman, who had become famous operating behind enemy lines.

"What the hell happened down there, sergeant?" the general said.

Joseph was terrified. Was he on trial?

Captain Eastman spoke more gently: "What were your orders, sergeant?"

Joseph had memorised this. "Oh. To advance as far south as I could. To try and reach the fort. Then to reconnoitre. Find out if the place was occupied. If not, move in. Raise the flag. And then hold out as long as I could."

"And then you ran away!" the general snapped.

Again, the captain intervened. "Were you ordered to die a hero's death, sergeant?"

Colonel Grimwood - Joseph's colonel - was indignant. "Of course he wasn't!"

The captain smiled. "Were you ordered to fight to the last man, sergeant?"

"No, sir. I was ordered to surrender to superior numbers, if, if that was possible. And to - bring confusion to the enemy, sir."

The general spoke in a level tone. "And then you just left?"

"I thought I could achieve more confusion by leaving than by staying, sir," Joseph said. The general glared at him.

"I agree with the sergeant's reasoning, sir," the captain said. "If he had surrendered, the Yankees would have forgotten by now. As it is ..."

Joseph was emboldened to speak up. "We were not ordered to fight to the last, sir." The general merely glowered.

"I thought they had a fifty percent chance of reaching the fort, sir," Colonel Grimwood said.

The general nodded. "I see. In that case, I cannot fault your decision-making, sergeant."

Joseph tried to hide his relief. "Thank, you, sir. Beg pardon, sir, but what are the newspapers saying now?"

Captain Eastman turned to the general, who nodded. "They're saying that the townsfolk imagined the whole thing – the flag, the bugle, the lot. They want the townsman put on trial."

"That's not right, sir."

"No," the captain said.

"You may go, sergeant," the general said.

"Yes, sir. Thank you, sir."

Lake Ontario, Brant's Ford, April 14

Sergeant Chard of the Corps of Signals travelled by train to the little town of Brant's Ford. He asked the stationmaster for directions and made his way to an address in a leafy suburb. Spring had not arrived yet. There was a dusting of fresh snow on the ground.

He counted house numbers. His destination was a prosperous house with three broad steps leading up to the doorway. A label in the window read 'Army Headquarters'. Chard wondered whether the whole thing was an elaborate joke.

Full of doubt, he knocked on the door. A perfectly ordinary housemaid in a pinafore asked his business, then let him in. She had a broad face and was rather dark. She showed him into a cramped morning room. Four men were sitting round a table. The table held an atlas.

Chard realised by their colouring that they were all Mohawks. Two were wearing enlisted men's red sack-jackets, but with collar and cuffs in dark green.

One man wore a buckskin jacket over army shirt and trousers. The last was a fussy man, older than the others. He wore a suit. Chard guessed that the civilian was the most important.

One of the redcoats wore the rank-badges of a colonel. "Welcome to Brant's Ford, sergeant. I am Colonel Hendrick Teyonhehkwen. Most white men call me Hendrick. You can call me Colonel Hendrick if you wish."

"Yes, sir." Should he salute? But they were not properly dressed.

"My companion here is Major Peter Theyanoguin." He indicated the civilian. "And this is Mr. Brant."

"Good afternoon, sir."

The maid returned, bearing a tray with a coffee-pot and five cups.

"Sit down, sergeant. There is no need to be formal today," the colonel said.

Chard was uncomfortable. A sergeant did not sit in the presence of officers. Not in the British army, anyway. "Yes, sir. Thank you, sir."

"We are members of the Mohawk nation," Colonel Hendrick said. "That sounds grand, doesn't it? But it is a farce. It's the result of a promise that King George made to one of my predecessors. A fairytale."

"George the Third?" Chard ventured.

"Yes, the mad one. Because we are called an independent nation, we deal with the governor's Foreign Secretary.

"Another legal fiction is that we are members of the Mohawk army. That sounds grand too."

"Is that a fairytale too, sir?" Chard said.

"In peacetime it is. We're not part of Canada, so we can't join the colony's militia. We have no equipment. Some of our muskets date back to the war of 1812. Our headquarters is – here."

"I see, sir."

"They didn't give us any uniforms, so we had to make our own. But when we made our own buckskin jackets, they complained. They sent us some red coats and told us to get rid of the buckskins."

Chard noted that the captain had disobeyed the order.

The colonel was rather young. Chard guessed that he was well-educated. Sharp. He seemed easygoing, but Chard knew that if he stepped over the line the colonel would slap him down. The trouble was, what was the line for this Mohawk officer?

"Then the war started, sergeant. Suddenly, we were valuable. We had trained more than the white militia. We thought we would be sent into battle, at Montreal, and be wiped out. Instead, we were sent to a backwater – the Lake Erie coast."

"The coast? Last spring, sir, everybody said the smart move would be for the Yankees to attack by boat, across the lakes," Chard said. "Nobody would have called it a sideshow then."

"Perhaps so." The colonel pointed at the atlas. "We were ordered to guard this stretch of coast. The northern shore of Lake Erie. The Yankees could land unopposed, march on Toronto, and sack it."

Chard remembered that Captain Eastman had said that Iroquois could be a bit slow on some subjects, but on strategy nobody could teach them anything. "Yes, sir."

"We're the only troops under arms between Fort Malden and the regulars at Fort Niagara."

"What's at Fort Malden, sir?"

"Two regular regiments and the black militia. The blacks came north along the Underground Railroad. When the war came, they volunteered for the local militia. *They* know what they're fighting for."

The captain in the buckskin jacket spoke poor English. "The campaigning season is about to begin. The Yankees could attack at any time." He gestured to the atlas on the table. "They could attack anywhere."

"Yes, sir," Chard said. "The obvious place is Portland. We're trying to defend it. And our forces there are weak."

"The obvious place is not always the wisest," Colonel Hendrick said. "It would be better to attack somewhere along the Great Lakes."

"Portland would make a good diversion," Major Theyanoguin said.

"Never mind that," Colonel Hendrick said. "When we were ordered to defend the coast, we set up observation points. Our orders said, if we saw any ships, we would order our men to stand-to. Then we would send a warning to the British. A call for help."

"Yes, sir," Chard said.

"In the last war, if we spotted the enemy, we were supposed send a horseman to the general, asking for help. These days, we're supposed to send a telegram -."

"Ah," Chard said.

"Yes. Very advanced. But the railroad is a couple of miles inland." He pointed to the map.

"So we've still got to send a courier to the station. And,

here, the railroad is twenty miles inland. Worse, the stations, and telegraph offices, are few and far between. What I want is a telegraph wire from our beach lookout posts to the nearest telegraph office."

The major smiled. "The Mohawk Military Telegraph."

The colonel was solemn. "Yes. We need your help, sergeant. We need signallers. But can you do it, organise it, sergeant?"

Chard considered this challenge. "Well. We need materiel. And the workforce."

"The ministry of the interior has promised me all the wire we need. There is no shortage of tree-trunks. We have the construction force. Untrained, but still ... What we need is someone to pull everything together."

"Do you have distribution skills, sir? For example, can you get food to the workers?"

The major glanced at Colonel Hendrick.

"Yes. I know how to organise that. It would not be a problem."

"Very well, sir. We will need a team to put up the telegraph poles and rig the wire. And telegraph operators to send these reports. I doubt if the Telegraph Company will loan you any?"

"No," Hendrick said. "So we asked for military operators."

"But your Lieutenant Eathorpe said no," Major Theyanoguin said.

Chard felt the need to explain. "We have less than twenty Army telegraph operators in all of Canada. We have to rely on civilian contracts. We can't spare six men for posts that will probably never see a battle."

"If there is a battle, we will need those operators very much indeed." Hendrick was decisive.

"Yes, sir." Chard tried to think of an answer. But he was only a sergeant. This problem needed an officer. Or a lawyer. "You said that you had an army. Infantry?"

"Yes. But it is a legal fiction. A fairytale. We have a battalion at most."

"Do you think the Yankees will attack soon?"

"As soon as the lake is clear of ice," the captain in the buckskin jacket said.

The major shrugged. "We cannot say for certain *where* they will attack."

"Yes, sir," Chard said. "My suggestion, then, is that the Mohawk army trains its own signallers. The only equipment you need is half a dozen telegraph instruments. I can scrounge those for you."

"I see," Hendrick said.

"I could train the men you need, sir. Can you find half a dozen literate men who could be trained as telegraph operators?"

"Six?" the captain in the buckskin jacket said. "We could find such men, yes."

"Set up our own Signals Corps?" the major said. "We can't do that. It would be illegal."

"A legal fiction, sir," Chard said. "Not the same thing. Have you ever been told that you cannot set up a Signals Corps?"

"It's absurd," the major said.

"If the Yankees don't attack, or they attack somewhere else, you can say it was all a mistake. And the men can go home. If the Yankees do attack, and your signallers save the day ... the British general will probably say it was all his idea."

The captain snorted. "These signallers – what uniform would they have?"

Chard shrugged. "Any you like, sir. They would be in you army. Green, yellow ..."

The major shook his head. "No. It must be blue. You wear blue. We want to be the same as you."

"I can get some, sir. Would you have any trouble recruiting more men?"

The captain smiled. "Not during wartime."

Hendrick nodded. "Because we are called an independent nation, we deal with the Foreign Office. They pay our recruits. So the *army* does not care how many recruits we have."

London, April 15

Mr Richard Cass had an appointment at the College of Magicians. The task was all very tiresome, but he had to admit that it was his own fault.

Back in Bermuda, he had tried to save himself some trouble, in the short term, by recruiting a girl. Now he was burdened with this long-term responsibility.

The day was cloudy. Smoke from London's chimneys could not escape upwards and instead was drifting towards the East End.

The maid who opened the door was polite. Richard wondered whether she came from one of the guild's orphanages. "My name is Cass. Here is my card. I have an appointment with Lady Samantha."

"Yes, sir, her ladyship is expecting you." The maid led him upstairs. This was ladies' territory. Richard was uncomfortable. He had never been allowed up here during his term as an apprentice. He reminded himself that he was qualified now, a gentleman, so he should be comfortable around ladies.

Lady Samantha was sitting in a comfortable chair. She had a chaperone, Miss Reid.

The third person in the room, Dido, smiled shyly at him. Her dark skin betrayed her mulatto heritage. Her wiry hair had been trained into fashionable ringlets. Richard calculated that she was now fifteen.

Dido had become his responsibility when he asked her to take weather observations for him. But Dido could not prosper in Bermuda. So he had sent her to London to ensure she received a formal education.

Richard spoke the usual pleasantries and then asked how Dido's studies were progressing.

Lady Samantha smiled. "Dido is doing well." Richard guessed that she was not put out by Dido's colour.

"But you must understand, Mr. Cass, that Dido does not study here in the college. She attends a few lectures but most of her studying takes place at home."

"Yes, I understand that, madam."

"The other female students meet in each others' homes or in hired function rooms."

"Yes, madam. But I thought you had found a home for her. She was staying with Mrs. Lloyd."

"Quite so. But Mrs. Lloyd went off to join her husband. I could hardly stop her. And Dido cannot stay at the college any longer. We have a few rooms for temporary guests, but there is simply not enough room for anyone to stay here permanently."

"I quite understand, madam. We have imposed on your hospitality enough."

"So I have arranged for Dido to stay with one of my acquaintances."

Richard could not really believe that Lady Samantha referred to the Dowager Viscountess Inismore as one of her 'acquaintances'. Richard hoped that the lady was not as intimidating as she sounded.

"The old lady needs a companion. She is living in the town-house of her son."

"Yes, my lady."

The maid brought the news that Lady Samantha's carriage was waiting. The ladies stood. Dido put on a bonnet and pulled an elegant shawl around her shoulders.

"Shawls are the latest fashion, you see, Mr, Cass. Ladies cannot wear coats because they will not fit over fashionable dresses."

"And you want to be fashionable?"

"Yes, Mr. Cass." Together, they walked downstairs.

Richard took the front seat of the carriage, sitting opposite Dido. They exchanged glances. Both of them were nervous. Would this work?

At Inismore house, a footman led them upstairs. The Dowager Vicountess Inismore had a suite of rooms on the second floor. She was still sprightly, with strong white hair. She told them to address her as Lady Forlaith. She seemed to disapprove of Richard but welcomed Dido.

Richard explained why he had arranged for Dido to study magic. "She established rapport with her aunt, in the West Indies, so they could keep in touch. She showed great potential. I felt it wrong to bury her talents because of her origins."

"I see, Mr. Cass. And is the girl diligent in her studies?"

"Yes, madam. She has studied Latin." Richard said. "I am prepared to act as Dido's mentor while I remain in London."

"Do you plan to leave?" Judging by her tone, Lady Forlaith did not approve.

"It's the war, you see, madam. I may be asked to serve the admiral again. The Atlantic fleet."

The dowager turned to Dido. "I hope you understand that you will not dine with the family. Unless we have no guests, which will not happen very often."

"Yes, madam. I understand. Male apprentices did not dine at high table, so why should I?"

"Quite so. You will dine in your room or with the family's governess."

"Yes, madam." Dido accepted this. Her treatment was not because of her colour, it was because of her age.

Lady Forlaith turned to Lady Samantha. "The mail-steamer from Halifax arrived in Southampton last night. It brought such dreadful news. Have you read the morning newspapers about Lord Palmerston?"

"Yes, madam. The story really is sensational."

"Some British newspapers and politicians have taken it badly. They blame an American plot – assassination."

Lady Samantha was appalled. "Where have their wits gone?"

New Jersey, Lakehurst Naval Base, April 15

Paul Abernethy was recovering. He was able to sit up. He bullied the doctor until he released Paul from the hospital.

The peace talks had been postponed while news of the accident was sent by ship to London. But then Washington asked whether it was now possible for the wounded gentlemen to continue their journey. The doctor had surprised everyone by saying yes.

Two medics carried Paul to the waiting carriage. The Commander Semmes accompanied them, as courteous as ever.

Edith smiled. "Thank you for your assistance, commander."

Paul and his daughter had a carriage to themselves. He was irritable. "This journey is a waste of time. I trust your discretion when I say so, my dear."

"Yes, father."

"Lord Palmerston is recovering, physically at least. But he's lost his nerve. He told me that he cannot negotiate for such high stakes." He stared out of the window. "What an appalling time for this to happen!"

"Can't you continue without him, father?"

"No. The other diplomats and myself were empowered to advise Lord Palmerston only. None of us have the authority to take his place."

At the railway station, the diplomats gathered in a corner and discussed whether Britain would send a replacement for Lord Palmerston.

"Hopefully a man with tact," Algernon said.

"We may not have that much time," Paul said. "I don't know how they'll receive this news in London." He glanced at his daughter.

Every day, Edith established rapport with her husband in London. He provided her with updates of the way the news had been received in London. She, in secret, told her father.

Paul was disappointed. "Conspiracy theories? Worse and worse."

Montreal, April 16.

Captain George Eastman and his company had been withdrawn from Fort Longueuil. They were given a tour of duty in Montreal.

Whenever he could, he visited Miss Grace at army headquarters. She was occupied producing weather predictions and then telegraphing the reports across Canada.

That annoyed him. It was not suitable work for a lady. But he had to admit that it was vital work. The airship people, and the warriors in the mountains, depended upon her.

Then Colonel Grimwood told his subalterns that the regiment was about to hold a formal mess dinner. George hated these events. But the colonel knew he was in Montreal, he had no excuse for staying away. Some of the young men grumbled quietly.

Colonel Grimwood smiled. "Gentlemen, my wife has asked me to say that she would like each of you to bring a partner. Our numbers are uneven."

George remembered that Miss Grace had spoken wistfully of attending parties. A regimental dinner was not actually a party, but ...

So after the colonel had dismissed the meeting, George asked for a word in private.

Grimwood smiled. "You're not married, are you, Eastman? Do you have a sweetheart?"

"Ah - I wondered whether I could bring Miss Abenaki."

"I know the girl. Rather dainty? She works on the Engine, doesn't she? Hands out the weather reports? Bit of a scholar, is she?"

George was caught out. "She tells me that she went to a convent school, but -."

"It all sounds fascinating. Well, she knows her table manners, of course. I'll ask my wife to send an invitation."

"Thank you, sir."

So George went to visit Grace in her office. "Good afternoon, Miss Grace. I've been told to attend one of these wretched formal dinners."

"Yes, captain?"

"I wondered whether you could accompany me. Although these things are an ordeal. You might hate it."

She pouted. "I'm sure it's not as bad as you say. And even if it is - I want to be able to say I've done it."

"Very well. I'll tell the colonel."

Her petulance was replaced by fear. "But - but - I have nothing to wear."

"So if you can find a dress, you can come?"

She was doubtful. So they visited Charles Lloyd, down the hall, in his office. He was sitting across the table from Signaller Asher.

"May I interrupt, sir?" George said.

Mr. Lloyd sat back in his chair. "We could do with a break. What is it, captain?"

George explained about the invitation. "Miss Grace would like to accompany me, but she doesn't have a suitable dress."

"That formal dinner? Yes, I understand. I think you could cope, Miss Abenaki. My wife and I have also received invitations. That sort of invitation is supposed to be a great honour. The sort that you can't refuse. So my wife has to go."

"I see, sir," George said.

"The bad news is that Lord Cardigan had been invited too."

"Will he refuse?" George asked.

"He *likes* these pompous affairs. He'll be there."

George nodded. "We'll just have to avoid him."

Charles considered Grace's request. "Your manners are good enough. Have you got an evening dress? No? Then you'll have to borrow or make one."

"Well, perhaps I could make a dress. But - must it have a low neckline?"

"For a formal evening, yes. There are strict rules about that. The lower the line, the higher the rank. A high collar would imply you were a servant."

She nodded her acceptance. "I've seen portraits. I'll have to make one. But what design?"

He glanced at George and smiled. "May I suggests a copy of an officer's mess jacket. Appropriate, don't you think? That way, you can use standard materials."

Grace nodded. "But I have nothing to talk about. What will interest these fine ladies?"

"You can talk about that convent school that you went to. Tell them how dreadful it was. But you can't tell them about your war work.

George smiled. "Mention the Engine."

Grace obtained a uniform mess-jacket and waistcoat. Mrs Lloyd was amused at her husband's idea and offered to help.

She laid out the jacket and drew a series of chalk lines across the front. "This pattern is fastened with a single button at the waist. You keep the buttons -."

Grace was shocked. "No, madam. It reveals too much."

Mrs. Lloyd smiled. "It's not just the jacket alone. The jacket is worn with a waistcoat. Have you got one? And then a fine white shirt, here. You can fake the collar and tie. That would come across here."

Grace nodded. "A bow tie? Yes."

"Besides the dress, you will have to find long gloves."

Grace did not believe this. "You say that it's barbaric to wear a leather skirt but it's civilised to wear leather gloves?"

Mrs. Lloyd nodded. "Yes. They have buttons at the wrist - you open the buttons and slip your hand out without taking the whole glove off."

"But I still need to know how to curtsey, madam."

Mrs. Lloyd stood. "Haven't you taken any lessons? Very well. Stand up straight, girl. Pull your stomach in. Stand up *straight* ... No. Stand on tiptoe. Hold your arms above your head. *Stretch*. Yes. Back down on your heels. That is how a lady stands *all* the time."

"Ah." Grace was dismayed.

"Now, I shall demonstrate a curtsey. Watch. You slide your right foot back. This is how you would curtsey to me."

Grace was fascinated. "I thought it would be deeper, madam."

"I'm not royalty, child. Now - show me."

Grace demonstrated a curtsey.

"Near enough. You'll need to practice."

Lake Ontario. Brant's Ford, April 18

Sergeant Chard made another visit to the Mohawk army's headquarters in the suburban house. A railway porter followed him, carrying a large case.

The maid opened the door for them. The same three officers were sitting round the table. Chard nodded and the porter gently lowered the case to the floor.

"Would you like some coffee, sergeant?" Major Peter Theyanoguin said.

"Thank you, sir."

The major nodded to the maid, who whisked away.

Chard opened the case and produced six wooden boxes with glass dials. "Here we are, sir. Army issue single-needle telegraph instruments."

"You may be just in time," the colonel said. "They could attack any day now."

"I see, sir."

"You will instruct our volunteers how to use these?"

"Of course, sir. Although they will be slow at first. How did the recruiting go?"

The captain in the buckskin jacket was amused. "Very well. We have our six operators. Three came from Toronto. They were living in exile. Outcast. But now they want to help their old country."

Montreal, April 19

George escorted Grace to the hotel where the Royal American Regiment were holding their formal dinner. Grace took off her shawl and was suddenly very shy. She was certain that her dress was too daring.

George was wearing his formal mess jacket. He had told her that the expensive silver lace decoration was really a cheap forgery. But it looked real enough to her.

They joined the other guests chatting in the ante-room. She observed the other ladies. Their dresses, all in extravagant fabrics, had similar low necklines. Just like all those books she had read. So Mr. Lloyd had not been teasing her.

"You will be sitting to my right. That's important," George said. "See the gentleman with all the gold lace? That's the earl."

Grace examined the notorious lord Cardigan with interest. He was middle-aged, but handsome still. She spotted Mr. Lloyd, wearing a civilian dinner-jacket, so he stood out in this room full of officers. Mrs Lloyd's dress was more daring than her own. She remembered Mr. Lloyd's remark about the neckline indicating your social standing.

George murmured in her ear. "I had a word with the steward. He'll serve both of us with lemonade. I hope you don't mind." She was inclined to be indignant. But if George was having the same as her ...

The steward made his way through the crowd and handed them glasses from a silver tray. "Your drinks, sir, madam."

"Thank you," Grace said. The lemonade looked just like the wine that the other ladies were drinking. Or was it champagne?

At the signal, the gentlemen led the ladies into the dining room. There were three tables. "This way," George whispered. He led her to the third table.

"Our places should have name – cards," George said. "Yes. This is it. Wait for the signal. These events are as bad as the parade ground."

"What signal?" she whispered.

"Watch the colonel's lady."

All the ladies sat at the same time. Each officer assisted the lady to his right in taking her seat. Grace was grateful that Mr. Lloyd had made her practice this.

She was sitting between two men. She knew that was usual. George was to her left. But, to start, she had to talk to the gentleman at her other side.

He asked a bland question about her daily routine. "Not too dull, I hope?"

She said that she did clerical work for the army. "It's the Analytical Engine. It requires an education. I prepare the punched cards."

He pretended to be interested. "The Engine? It's unfortunate that a lady such as yourself has to demean herself by earning a wage."

"I do not work because of the money, sir, but because it is important."

"I beg your pardon, madam."

"Of course, when the war ends, the work will go. Or a man home from the war will get it."

"Ah, I see, yes."

"I thought, with these negotiations ..."

"The news isn't promising, is it?"

The steward topped up her glass. She rather enjoyed taking small ladylike sips from her delicate glass.

One course followed another. Then the last course was taken away. She felt that she had done nothing to disgrace herself.

But the next stage might be more difficult. "Time for the ladies to withdraw," George said.

She watched the colonel's wife, sitting at the foot of the table. The grand lady gave the signal and the ladies stood.

George helped her stand, although she could have managed without him, and she followed the other ladies out to the withdrawing room.

Her hostess, the colonel's wife, asked whether she would prefer tea or coffee?

She asked for coffee and one of the stewards handed her a cup. The other ladies sat down, so Grace took her place on a sofa.

The old lady next to her asked what she did. Grace explained once more that she worked on the Analytical Engine.

The old lady sniffed. "I suppose that a lady doing 'clerical work' might be justified in wartime. But when the war comes to an end ..."

"Yes, madam."

"Do you come from a family of distinction?"

Grace wondered whether she should she tell the truth. "Yes. But I quarrelled with my mother. My grandmother supported me but my mother had the final say."

"That is proper."

Lt. Colonel Grimwood, at the head of the table, had a word with his senior guest. But Lord Cardigan was in no hurry to leave. He topped up his brandy glass.

Finally, Cardigan finished his drink. Grimwood and his guest stood to follow the ladies.

Charles Lloyd, who hated after-dinner banter, took the opportunity to follow them. He looked round and spotted his wife. Lord Cardigan was on the other side of the room, talking to Grimwood.

He relaxed. Perhaps he could avoid a confrontation after all. He moved to join his wife. She smiled in welcome.

Lord Cardigan stopped the steward. "Another glass of your port. Although it's not the best I have tasted."

The steward seemed unperturbed. "At once, my lord."

Charles overheard. "What appalling manners." With a bit of luck, he and his wife could avoid the fellow.

But Lord Cardigan took his glass of port from the waiter and crossed the room to intercept Charles.

Charles was in a dilemma. Should he introduce Lord

Cardigan to his wife? Or cause a scandal by refusing to do so?

"So this is the grocer's daughter, Lloyd?"

Charles was outraged. All of his doubts vanished. "Good evening, my lord."

Alice nudged Charles. He recognised this as a subtle message to show restraint.

Lord Cardigan did not notice. "I was disappointed when I heard, you know. Here's my friend Lloyd, letting the side down, marrying into trade."

"Yes." Charles was aware that several men and women were listening. The colonel and his wife were among them.

Lord Cardigan smiled. "Well, I'm sure the fellow's rich enough to provide a dowry. Aren't you going to introduce us?"

Charles barely hesitated. "No."

Cardigan's smile vanished. "What?"

Charles tried to keep his voice level. "I do not want my wife to associate with a man of your temper." There, he had said it.

Cardigan did not seem to be offended. "Too warlike, am I?"

"You are a successful leader, my lord. You are also reputed to be very successful with the ladies."

Cardigan smirked. "Jealous, Mr. Lloyd?"

"Not jealous, no."

Cardigan made a pretence of sipping his port. "Envious, perhaps?"

Charles said nothing. Let the man think what he liked.

Cardigan drained his glass, smirked and turned away.

Alice spoke in an undertone. "I was afraid. I thought he was going to challenge you to a duel or something."

"No. *I* behaved within the rules. But he insulted you. If anything, I should call *him* out."

She gripped his arm. No, you mustn't."

"Of course not. But if he did want revenge, he would have to act in an underhand way."

The colonel's wife moved across to console Alice. "I feel that I ought to apologise, madam."

Alice demurred. "You have done nothing to apologise for, madam."

George was burning with impatience. He wanted to join Grace in the withdrawing room. What was happening in there?

He murmured a polite apology to the man next to him and followed the colonel and the other guests into the withdrawing room. He spotted Grace, sitting primly on a sofa next to an old lady.

But Grimwood stepped forward. "Captain, I would like a quiet word."

"Yes, sir?"

"Some Abenaki soldiers of J company, in the Montreal barracks, have been saying that when the war is over they want a country of their own. They talk of a republic."

George was horrified. "That would be disastrous, sir. If they accomplished it, I mean. The Yankees would invade as soon as the war ended."

"I don't care about that. But this loose talk is embarrassing for me, Eastman."

"Yes, sir. I see that. But this is just off-duty gossip, surely?" He had no authority to silence the warrior braggarts. In the old days, men with a serious dispute would consult the matriarchs. But those days were gone.

"The civil officials have heard of this talk. Someone reported it to the police. Can you shut these fools up?"

He shook his head. "No, sir. This is a political matter. About policy after the war. I can tell them to be more discreet, but that's all."

"Do that, by all means. But if this is a political

question, can you find a political answer?"

Were they asking him to be a politician now? "I shall try, sir."

Montreal, April 20

The next morning, George thought through the implications of Colonel Grimwood's request. He decided that Grace might have an answer.

He waited until the morning weather-analysis rush was over, then went to the weather office at army headquarters. Grace was sitting at her desk, writing in a ledger. Lt. Eathorpe and Signalman Asher were there too.

Grace looked up and smiled. "Good morning, sir. I thank you for a pleasant evening."

He smiled back. "Good morning, Miss Abenaki. The colonel gave me a little problem last night. Do you know whether the old magistrate Melody is still alive?"

Grace jumped as if she had been stung. "Yes, captain. She is."

"Do you know where her family is?"

"The Black Mountain area. North of Moosehead Lake. Aroostook headwaters. Why?" She seemed frightened.

"I need to ask an augury – just like the old days."

Asher was staring at him in astonishment. Lt. Eathorpe merely looked puzzled.

"I need a volunteer for a very unusual mission. To deliver a request."

Quebec, April 21

Signaller Asher had been given his orders. The captain's request was placed in a sealed envelope. Miss Grace used that infernal Engine to print his travel papers. The lieutenant even gave him an official leather document case, with 'V+R' embossed on it. That, Asher thought, was more effective than any printed document.

He presented his travel permit at the station and asked about the next eastbound train.

The train crew bickered. Should they allow an Indian in a passenger car?

"I'm prepared to ride in the mail-van, sir," Asher said.

The train-captain glanced at the shiny leather document case and led the attendant and Asher to the second-class carriage.

"If it's full, he'll have to travel in the baggage car."

"Yes, sir," the attendant said.

But half the seats were empty. Asher smiled. They had no excuse for keeping him out.

He reflected on the change to his fortunes. A year ago, they would have told him to ride in a freight car. Now, with a blue uniform coat and coins in his pocket, he could take a seat alongside the white folks.

At Quebec he took the ferry across the river. At Levis station, he handed over another travel document. This train took him south to the mountains. From the terminus he walked.

Ontario, Port Stanley, April 22

The corduroy road to the lake ran south through the woods. Major Theyanoguin and Sergeant Chard travelled in a spring-cart. Their precious cargo required careful handling. The trees were still covered in snow.

The farms were isolated from each other and only small patches of ground around each had been cleared. Long stretches of the road ran through woods.

The major's men had cut a few branches off selected trees and then hammered pegs into the trunks. Iron wire

- Chard had specified no. 16 gauge - had been strung from the pegs. The effect was crude but serviceable.

The major waved a hand. "There was talk of building a railroad here. But the war put a stop to that."

"Yes, sir."

"I am worried about attack," the major said. "The snows are clearing, the ice is melting. It could happen any day. The colonel thinks that the most likely time for an attack is within the next ten days."

Chard nodded. He had heard all this before, but a sergeant could not say that to a major.

"Our task is to delay the Yankees until the militia arrives. So it is vital that we warn them as speedily as possible."

"Yes, sir. The peace negotiations seem to have stalled."

"It is all very ominous, sergeant."

The fishing town was small, with neat weatherboard houses. The major ignored them.

They left the cart and walked to the lakeshore. Chard noted a small stone breakwater and a couple of ship-repair sheds. He looked over the lake. It was desolate. "It's still frozen, sir."

"Well, yes, but not thick enough to walk on. The deepest parts melt first."

The Mohawk soldiers had built a miniature earthwork, twelve feet across, to protect their lookout point. The wind was cold. Ten observers were on duty, wearing army greatcoats and hats that covered their ears. They barely bothered to look south.

"The army gave us tents. Adequate in summer," the major said. "When winter arrived, the colonel sent most of the men home. The remainder were billeted in the houses here. The townsfolk were kind. They knew why we had come."

"I see, sir." Chard looked south. "Is there something

out there?"

The men turned to look. "There's something," the major said. "It's too small to be a ship, though."

The sentry studied the object through his telescope. "I can see it, yes. In the winter, a fisherman built a hut on the ice. When the ice melted, the hut floated."

The major nodded. "My nightmare is twenty ships each with a hundred men on board."

Chard was embarrassed. "I thought perhaps it was the army, walking across."

The sentry heard this and spoke at length. The major translated. "There's only one object and it isn't moving. In winter, fishermen cut holes in the ice. At this time of year they fish from the shore instead. The centre of the lake is ice-free. If the Yankee general tried to send an army across, they would have to walk round the edge. Why come this far?"

The soldiers laughed at this.

The major led Chard away. "My men suffered during the winter. Now they are glad that the days are warm. But the good weather will bring the Yankees."

"Yes, sir."

A fishing boat had been hauled up the slipway. Despite the cold, a team of men were painting it.

The major pointed. "They are looking forward to the good weather too. When the ice is gone they can start fishing. But if the war -." He shook his head. "Fishing isn't their only work."

"Sir?"

"Smuggling is rife. These days, the most useful item is newspapers. Rumours. In a few days, boats will start arriving again. So my coast watchers would see them coming."

"Would that cause false alarms?"

The major shrugged. "My men have learned what to look for. The ways of the white man are strange. We've been told not to interfere with the smuggling. We can't fight them and the Yankees."

"It sounds complicated, sir."

"It is. And when my men came here they had to learn all these rules."

They returned to the spring cart. The major turned it and drove inland a few yards. At the limit of the town, someone had built a new single-storey weatherboard house. Two men, wearing engineer-blue jackets, came out to greet them.

"This is the end of telegraph line," the major said. "It leads to the railroad line, where our signaller waits."

"Your men have worked very fast," Chard said.

The major shrugged. "They were bored. This is new for them. And they're grateful to be trusted with this work."

Chard and his volunteers unloaded the sand-batteries and the jars of dilute sulphuric acid from the spring-cart. He checked them for damage.

He gave his volunteers a brief lecture on the dangers involved in batteries. His team had heard it before, but Chard thought that a reminder would do no harm.

"You make those things sound very, very dangerous," the major said.

"They are, sir. But so is a musket. Mistreat it and it can kill you. But treat it with respect and it's reliable."

Once the equipment was safely inside, he and his volunteer technicians set about the task of connecting the batteries to the wire. Other army men clustered round to watch.

Chard checked the signal strength. "Good." He attached the telegraph instrument and slowly tapped out a message. Then he let each of his assistants send a message in turn.

He turned to the major. I would be grateful, sir, if you could send a courier to the other end to see if they received it."

"Why shouldn't he?"

"Perhaps he's asleep. Or perhaps I made a mistake when I attached the needle-instrument at the far end ... I wish you would allow me to send signals the other way."

"That needs more batteries, yes? There isn't time, sergeant. The Yankees could attack any day. The requirement to send a warning – that is what counts."

"Yes, sir."

Montreal, April 22

George Eastman walked into Mr. Lloyd's hotel room to find two men waiting for him. Lieutenant Eathorpe, with only one arm, was sitting an upright chair.

George was puzzled. "You asked to see me, Mr. Lloyd?"

"Yes, captain. My wife is worried. She thinks that Lord Cardigan is angry at the way I humiliated him. She fears that he may be planning my murder in revenge."

George was surprised. "Does he really think like that, sir? Beg pardon, but he's probably forgotten what Mrs. Lloyd looks like."

"Quite possibly. But he has not forgotten that, in his view, I betrayed my class by marrying a plebeian."

George considered the problem. "He wouldn't do it himself. Wouldn't get his hands dirty. Unless he's a fool, he wouldn't ask his own men. They're not *that* loyal. And if he paid a couple of 'em, they'd likely get roaring drunk and blab the news. I assume he wants to avoid blame?"

"Yes, most likely."

"The safest way would be for him to hire outsiders. Some Yankee bushwhackers. They would do the deed, slip back across the border, and no-one would see them again. But does he have that sort of contacts? I doubt it.

"If he asked the wrong question, the story might leak out. Or if he asked the wrong man, he might end up dead. It would be safest not to try."

Mr. Lloyd? Was irritated. "He doesn't have a reputation for being cautious, captain."

"No. I could detail some of my men to escort you, but they would ask why. They might talk. You want it kept quiet?"

"If the story leaked out, he might sue you for libel, Charles," Lieutenant Eathorpe said. "A revenge of a different kind."

George nodded. "I could ask Signaller Asher to escort you home. He's discreet. And I could escort you myself from time to time."

"I want to tell my wife something to reassure her, captain."

"Well, you could change your patterns, Mr. Lloyd. If you normally arrive home from the north, approach from the south or east. Change every day. Arrive home late. Take a trip to Quebec."

"My wife would hate that. The governor's wife's functions are boring."

George frowned. "You may say I've been reading the wrong sort of novels, sir, but might he take his revenge on your wife instead of you?"

"What do you mean?"

"Might he try to seduce her, sir?"

"You go too far, Eastman."

"Steady, Charles," Eathorpe said. "The captain is asking what Cardigan thinks your wife might do."

George nodded. "The fellow has a reputation as a skirt-chaser. He might think your wife could be persuaded."

"Just to get his revenge on me?" Mr. Lloyd asked. "Would he stoop that low?"

"You know him better than any of us," Eathorpe said.

Mr. Lloyd thought this over and grimaced. "He might. Forewarned is forearmed."

"Well, sir, if you do go to Quebec, could you have a word with the general? Get Cardigan and his unit transferred?"

"Ha. You don't like him either."

"No, sir, I don't."

Washington, April 24

When the British delegation arrived in Washington, they had been greeted politely. The officials of the State Department had hoped to resurrect the negotiations. They had been dismayed that Lord Palmerston was still languid and indecisive.

Active negotiations would have kept the war-party at bay. Paul Abernethy despaired at Lord Palmerston's failure to act.

He was already aware of pro-war sentiment in Washington. He wondered whether the delay had allowed the war party to gain ground. He knew that several factions had benefited from the war.

Paul - and everyone else in Washington – had been counting the days. The mail-ship, with its news of the airship disaster, should have reached London ten days ago. Surely the decision-makers in London would have responded at once? Everyone was waiting for the mail-ship bearing London's reply.

Then the mail-steamer, flying a white flag, sailed up the Potomac and into the Washington Channel. It carried news of the conspiracy theories circulating in London. Soon everyone in the capital was talking about the allegations.

Paul was dismayed that no-one in the delegation had

been authorised to act in Palmerston's place. If the Foreign Office had sent a new diplomat to replace Palmerston, Paul would have served him gladly. But the Foreign Office had assumed Palmerston would recover.

Many of the senators were indignant at the apathy of the British government. Those from Northern industrial states claimed to be shocked at the allegations in the British newspapers.

This indignation spread to the State Department. Paul was summoned to the Treasury Building, where the Secretary of State informed him that the majority in the Senate were no longer prepared to support negotiations. The peace talks were scrapped.

Paul, and Palmerston, were appalled. Paul encouraged Palmerston to protest at this irrevocable step. But Palmerston did not complain. Paul was forced to follow his lead.

Both men were fit to travel. They and the other members of the delegation were informed that they would be sent under flag of truce to New Brunswick.

Paul's daughter said that was the quickest way to get back home.

Depot Mountains, April 26

Asher left the French Canadian farming communities behind and continued his climb into the mountains. The hike lasted several days. But the nights were getting warmer and he had an army groundsheet and bedroll.

On the morning of the third day, he felt he was being watched. He grinned to himself and made coffee for four. He had brought spare tin cups.

A year ago, he had suffered pity from his cousins. He had tried to escape by joining the army. But he had failed the medical examination. Then Mr. Lloyd had turned up, with the offer to teach him magic. Asher had not believed his talk. He had accepted the offer only because it allowed him to join the army. But the magic had turned out to be real. He could talk to Miss Grace, a hundred miles away. Mr. Lloyd said it was dangerous, but Asher did not care. True, he had joined the signallers and wore a blue coat rather than a red one, but the engineers prided themselves on being brighter than the typical redcoat.

Now he was carrying a message of a different kind. His guess about his watchers had been right. The men came out of hiding. They looked sheepish.

When they had finished their coffee, they led him up the hill to the village. This was a traditional longhouse.

Asher showed his orders to the headman. He said that he must deliver the sealed envelope to the matriarch.

The headman summoned a couple of men who could read French. The entire village gathered round. Together, they introduced Asher to the matriarch.

He was intrigued. So this was the famous Melody - Miss Grace's grand-mother. Her dress was store-bought but her traditional hood was richly ornamented. Her face was lined with age and responsibility. But she was, in the white man's inelegant phrase, as tough as old boots.

Asher handed the sealed envelope to Melody, who opened it and handed it to the French-speaker. They were astonished that anything could be written in Abenaki. They read the request out loud, struggling to decipher Miss Grace's quaint spelling.

The letter set out the options for their nation that had been discussed by the warriors in the city.

The old woman frowned. "You know that I cannot issue a judgement? I cannot decide what the tribe can do."

"Yes, madam. The captain only asks your views.

Which alternative is best?"

The matriarch considered the request. "A republic? Madness. Don't they remember what happened to the Cherokee? They sent a letter to President Jackson, saying they had set up a republic. He kicked them out and sent them to the Indian Territory. If we tried it, that's what they'd do to us."

"Yes, madam."

Melody said she would give her reply in the morning. Then she withdrew to talk the problem over with her companions.

The next morning the villagers assembled and Melody explained her conclusions. She stated that a republic was a pleasant dream, but it was madness. The Yankees would destroy it. Best would be an Abenaki colony, subject to the British, reporting to the palace in England. Second best would be a county, part of Quebec.

The headman produced a villager, one of the French-speakers, who wrote this down.

The letter was handed to Asher with great formality. He thanked them for their hospitality and put the letter in his leather bag.

The young hunters escorted him to the edge of their territory and he began the journey back to Montreal. He knew that the young warriors in the army would accept the matriarch's ruling. And, with a bit of luck, they would stop bitching.

He realised that his mission would probably boost Captain Eastman's standing among the soldiers too. He had shown respect for the old traditions.

Michigan, April 26, Sunset

Commander John Winslow, USN, was in his cabin, on board *USS 'Patriot'* in Detroit harbour, reviewing his plans for an attack.

The week before, Washington had asked him to consider an attack on the enemy. So he had drafted his contingency plans and advised the governor.

If the peace talks failed, Washington would probably ask him to attack immediately. He wanted to be ready.

His thoughts were interrupted when a messenger from the telegraph office brought a sealed envelope.

The message that it contained outraged him. The governor had ordered the militia to cross the river and capture the Canadian Bois Blanc Island. Tomorrow they would attack Fort Malden and needed his support. The governor ordered him to sail at once.

He knew that unless he helped them, the militia would be wiped out. He stormed out of his cabin and handed the note to the engineer. "Mr. McTavish, how long will it take you to get steam up?"

The engineer blinked. "Six hours, sir. I had better give the order at once."

"Yes. Do that."

He left his ship and strode through the town of Detroit to the telegraph office. His marine escort had to increase their pace to keep up. That walk allowed him to put his thoughts in order.

There were two smaller ships in the port of Gibraltar. His first telegram ordered them to get steam up.

His second telegram was to the Colonel of regular infantry. "Colonel, we discussed our plans a month ago. I intend to put it into effect at once."

He hurried back to his ship. He was bursting with impatience. But he could not allow himself to show it.

He explained the problem to his second-in-command, Lt. Thornton. Why had the militia invaded a Canadian island? The place had no strategic value.

Lt. Thornton suggested that the governor felt obliged to attack something. The island was enemy territory and within easy reach.

He had sent copies of his attack plan to the other commanders. Now he hoped that they worked. And would the fools listen to the orders they had been given?

He was not happy. To defeat the British, they need a fleet. Ten ships, each with ten cannon. And at least five regiments.

But it would take weeks to fit out the warships. The British would have noticed and would have raided Michigan. The British were said to have spies everywhere. If it wasn't blacks, hoping for freedom, it was Indians, eager for revenge.

There was an answer to a British threat – build forts to protect the ships. But that would take months. The politicians – and the newspapers – wanted a swift victory.

So he had decided upon speed and secrecy. How many ships could they assemble before the British noticed and attacked? His answer was three.

The fact that the he had fitted out these ships without being attacked meant that he had achieved surprise. A success of sorts.

It would be hours before the engineer had built up steam. He decided to get some sleep.

Michigan, April 27, dawn

The engineer knocked on the door to his cabin. "We have enough pressure to make way, sir."

"Thank you, Mr. MacTavish."

Winslow pulled on his coat, climbed up to the bridge. The wind was cold and the open bridge gave no shelter.

He gave orders for the steam schooner *USS 'Patriot'* to leave the dock. "Half speed ahead, Mr. MacTavish."

They approached the harbour entrance. Were the

British waiting for them? The *Patriot* left the shelter of the harbour. He looked round the horizon. No, they were alone. He gave the helmsman a course to steer. He lifted the cover on the speaking tube. "Full steam ahead, Mr. MacTavish."

"Full steam ahead, sir."

Winslow turned to his first lieutenant. "You have the watch, Mr. Thornton."

"Thank you, sir."

They picked up speed, the funnel belching out black smoke.

They headed south, following the coast to Gibraltar, Michigan. Were the other steamships ready?

He was relieved when two small steamships came out of the harbour. They exchanged signals. The vessels held the governor of Michigan, along with a detachment of 200 militiamen. The regulars from Gibraltar would follow them, in slower sailing boats.

Winslow was pleased. That part of his plan had gone all right. The smaller steamship continued signalling.

His signalman read it off. "He says, sir, that a contingent of the militia crossed to the island during the night, in small boats."

But Winslow knew that already.

The flotilla headed south. This part of the journey was out of range of the British guns.

The three steamships continued on to the end of the Canadian Bois Blank Island and turned towards Fort Malden on the Canadian shore.

Winslow turned to his gunnery officer. "You may fire at will."

"Thank you, sir." The *'Patriot'* fired a salvo at Fort Malden.

"Mr. Thornton, we must get closer to the shore. Improve our aim -." Then the Canadian artillery opened fire.

The first shot missed. The *Patriot* returned fire, scoring a couple of hits on the fort.

"Good shooting."

The little fleet continued on towards the town of Amherstburg. The intention was to get the US Army ashore and into the town.

Winslow had hoped for complete surprise. But somebody was awake over there. The Canadian militia were already advancing, taking up positions in the town. Winslow had heard that some militiamen were black.

Under cover of the *Patriots*' cannon-fire, the Michigan militia moved the 300 men on Bois Blanc Island to a position opposite the town.

Winslow thought they were doing very well. Then the lookouts spotted the Canadian steamer *HMS Alliance* advancing south to intercept them.

"They've got Canadian militia on board the steamer, sir," the lookout said. "Mebbe a hundred of 'em."

"Very well." Winslow told his gunners to open fire as soon as the British ship came within range. They obeyed with enthusiasm.

The *Alliance* did not respond. Winslow realised that the *Patriot*'s modern cannon had a longer range than the Canadians' improvised warship.

But he fretted that this distracted them from their main target – Fort Malden.

A shot from the *Patriot* carried away the *Alliance's* fore-mast. She turned about and withdrew. Winslow's men cheered at this display of cowardice.

He was encouraged. Perhaps this would work after all. If they could keep this up, the sailing boats full of infantry would be able to get ashore at Amherstburg. They could attack the fort and put it under siege. But he had to distract the Canadian gunners from firing on the troopships.

The Canadian shore artillery fired at the *Patriot* again.

The shot struck home, damaging the mast and rigging and injuring several of the crew.

Winslow felt a moment's panic. But this damage was not a disaster. The *Patriot* was powered by an engine below the waterline, not her sails.

"Cut that wreckage away. Gunners, maintain your fire. Aim carefully. Make every shot count."

The *Patriot* fired another salvo. But then the Canadians fired again. Winslow tensed, but it was a near miss. The shell landed just astern, and exploded, sending up a huge plume of spray. The planking shuddered.

"Are there any casualties?" Winslow shouted.

But then the helmsman cried the alarm. "The explosion crippled the rudder. I can't steer a straight course, sir."

The ship turned in a circle, drifting towards land. Winslow told his first lieutenant to make repairs.

The men tried to rig a makeshift rudder but they did not have much time. The shore was close.

The ship drifted until it ran aground. The artillery in Fort Malden seized the opportunity and fired a couple more shells. Winslow felt helpless. The '*Patriot*' was unable to return fire.

Then the Canadians turned their attention to the infantry in their sailing boats.

The steamer *Alliance* turned south again. She ignored the '*Patriot*' and instead headed for the sailing ships.

The two smaller US steamships bravely advanced to protect the troopships. But their cannons were no match for those on the *Alliance*. They suffered several hits.

The troopships, deprived of their naval support, promptly abandoned the attack and turned south.

The artillery in Fort Malden switched their aim to the *Patriot*. They scored a few hits. Losses mounted.

Winslow knew there was no hope of escaping. He

decided that further losses by his men would achieve nothing. He put out a white flag.

The gunfire stopped. A unit of the Canadian militia waded out towards the *Patriot*. Some of Winslow's crew wanted to open fire but he said no. He realised that the approaching militiamen were coloured.

The first of the militiamen boarded the *Patriot*. They encountered no resistance so they helped their officer to climb on board. Winslow remembered there was a tradition for this situation and offered his sword in surrender. The blacks were cheerful but courteous.

The militia officer accepted his sword. "Your men are injured? We have a sick berth attendant with us."

"Thank you."

"Do you have a small boat? You can get ashore without getting wet, captain."

"Thank you."

Winslow turned to watch the battle. The artillery at Fort Malden were now shelling the remaining US forces on Bois Blanc Island.

The militia must have decided the situation was too hot for them. As Winslow watched, they quit the island for the safety of the American side of the river.

Chapter 3

Portland, May 1, dawn

The snows had melted; the mud had dried. The men of the British regiments defending Portland were bored. They had seized the town in a daring attack during the winter. They had expected a counter-attack, but the Yankees had been unable to mount a major attack while the roads were covered in snow.

Lt. Warwick commanded a unit of the Third Bermuda Militia. His challenge these days was to keep his men alert.

They had volunteered to serve overseas. They had hoped for adventure. Well, some of them had found more adventure than they wanted. Now they were bored and wanted to go home.

They were billeted in the academy building overlooking the small town of Gotham. But the territory around them was a wilderness, with more woods than cultivated land. Warwick's men, from cosmopolitan Bermuda, hated it.

They got up at first light as usual to prepare breakfast. Then, at dawn, they heard artillery fire to the north. Every man looked round.

"North of here. Two miles. Perhaps three."

"Sounds as if the Yankees are attacking Fort Hill."

"Yes. It's the middle of our line."

Lt. Warwick had been expecting an attack, but it was still a shock. He ordered the drummer to sound the assembly. But there was no need for a warning. The men were already checking their equipment.

Sergeant Priddy was on top of the situation. "Pack your kit. Prepare to march. Is your ammunition ready? We may have to abandon anything we can't carry." He was middle-aged, below average height. He was about one quarter white, which was important in Bermuda. He also had a good education.

Warwick's task was to guard the crossroads from an attack from the west. He made certain that the men at the strong-points were alert. But thirty minutes went by and nothing happened. The only sound was that constant artillery barrage, three miles to the north. The sergeant made sure that the men remained alert.

Then the artillery fell silent. But nobody believed the Yankees had given up. The blockhouse must have been destroyed or captured.

"Our turn next," one infantryman said.

"But where are they?"

Warwick straightened his jacket, for the tenth time that morning. Then he checked that his belt was level.

One man volunteered to climb to the roof of the academy building. The sergeant gave the go-ahead and everyone turned to watch.

The man reached the roof and turned to look north. "I see 'em! The five-acre field. The Yankees are pouring through the gap. Heading east. Flags flying."

"Cavalry? Horses?" Warwick shouted.

"None, sir."

"Anything to the west?"

The man turned. "Nothing, sir."

"Right. Get down." Warwick turned to Sergeant Priddy. "My guess is that the infantry plan to advance east, then wheel round, to take our unit in the flank."

"But how can they do that, sir? Those woods to the north of here are as good as a fortress. There's no roads through it. No clearings, even."

"There are Indian trails. Hunters' tracks. We've

checked them out. And the trees aren't that close together."

Warwick realised that the Bermudians had become the right flank of the defending army. "Sergeant, we have to retreat east, along the Bridge Road, and turn to face north. We must block every track through the forest that leads south."

"Yes, sir." The sergeant passed the order on. "At the double!"

Warwick's worst fear was that cavalry, moving faster than his own men, would outflank his unit. But his lookout had said that the Yankees only had infantry.

He summoned a runner. "Private, you are to go to Major Montpelier of the Quebecois Fencibles on our left. Tell him that I am pulling out of my position and am moving east. Do you understand that?"

"Yes, sir. But what if the major says no, sir?"

"I'm not asking his permission, I'm advising him what I'm doing. By the time you deliver the message, I'll have done it. Understand?"

"Yes, sir." The man ran off.

Sergeant Priddy was shouting. "Go, go. Along Bridge Road."

Over the next quarter-hour, the sergeant stationed his men at intervals along Bridge Road. This was a corduroy track leading through the woods to the river. The track was crossed at intervals by footpaths, barely wide enough for two men to pass one another.

Warwick put five men at the end of each path. He knew that there were not enough men to defend the line. But he had not expected to carry out this the task.

The men, encouraged by their sergeants, set about improvising barricades from fallen branches and anything else they could find. There was an anxious pause. Sergeant Priddy snarled at them to keep busy.

Warwick began to worry that he had misjudged the

situation. What if they attacked from the west after all?

He stood at the western end of the track. It was straight, so he could see several of his detachments.

Then the men guarding the nearest track shouted the alarm. Yankees were advancing towards them. Warwick's men yelled at them to stop. The Yankees took no notice so his men began firing.

Warwick ran to the spot. The barricade, of thorn bushes, hid the defenders but provided no protection from bullets. His men were kneeling down. Warwick peeped over the barricade.

The trees on each side of the footpath were very close together. There was barely enough room for two men to pass. Two Yankees had tried to advance together and had been shot down. The men coming behind them had tried to take cover.

"Get back, sir!" the Bermudian private said.

Warwick did as he was told. He checked his pistol. A vicious firefight developed. His men kept under cover as much as they could.

One of his men was killed. But the Yankees suffered casualties too. Several were injured.

Warwick realised that the result was a standoff. If the Yankees tried to advance along the track, they were easy targets. But it was impossible for them to push their way through the undergrowth on either side of the track. To do that, they would need men with axes. Had they anticipated that?

Then the shooting stopped. The Yankees withdrew, leaving their dead. They had suffered enough.

Warwick's men were jubilant. Sergeant Priddy growled at them to reload their muskets.

"Build those barricades higher. All of 'em." He walked along the line, telling the men to stay alert. "Dig deeper!"

A runner arrived with news from Major Montpelier.

"Yes?" Warwick said.

"He says that the Quebecois to our left are moving up in support, sir. They've put some men into the academy building."

"Good."

The Yankees did not attack along that road again. But, half an hour later, one of the sentries shouted that they were attacking along the bridle path further east. Warwick knew that this was wide enough for a rider. He guessed that they were still attempting to outflank him.

There was another firefight. Warwick's men had dragged a series of logs across the bridle path and were now sheltering behind this barricade. But it was inadequate.

The Bermudians were surprised when the Yankees backed off without really trying.

Warwick guessed that the Yankees would make another attempt further east. This forced him to move his men. "They have to move from further west to guard the eastern tracks."

Sergeant Priddy disapproved. "You're taking an awful risk, sir. If they attack from the west instead ..."

"I know. I hope that Major Montpelier will deal with that."

His hunch proved correct. The Yankees kept moving east. It was a battle of anxious waiting and then a short, intense firefight.

Each time the Yankees advanced along one of the tracks, Warwick was forced to reposition his men further east to stop them.

Another runner arrived with a note from Major Montpelier. The runner knew the substance of the message. "He sent to tell you, sir, that he has moved all of his Quebecois north to hold the crossroads, sir."

"Good." One less thing to worry about, he thought.

Maine, Nonesuch Marshes, 10am

'H' company of the Sixty-Second Regiment, the Royal Americans, was a mixed unit of Mohawks and Hurons. They had been deployed in the southern marshes. They were acting as skirmishers in front of a detachment of Royal Marines.

The Mohawk sergeant, Joseph Thayendanega, knew that their task was to guard against any attack from the south-west. This terrain of streams and ponds was totally unsuitable for line infantry. The only clear route through the marsh was the railroad track, but that was exposed to any sniper.

Their lieutenant had Huron blood in him, but the sergeant regarded him as a priest-educated French-Canadian.

Their first warning of an attack was the sound of cannon-fire to the north. The men were alarmed. They had been expecting an attack for days. The lieutenant ordered the bugler to sound assembly and stand-to.

But no attack came. The cannons fell silent. "Perhaps they've given up," a private said.

"Fat chance," Joseph said.

The lieutenant told them to stay put. "There's a river between us and them."

Joseph agreed and passed the word to his men. "Nothing's going to happen anytime soon. Cook your breakfast."

Then a runner brought the news that the main force, the unit of marines, was withdrawing. "But only a couple of miles, sir. Back towards the city."

The lieutenant was annoyed. The retreat was not necessary. Joseph knew that he wanted to criticise the marine commander. But he could not do that in front of his men.

"Sergeant, tell the men they can finish their breakfast.

Then give the order for them to withdraw towards the city. We must maintain contact and avoid being cut off."

"Yes, sir,"

Presumpscot River

The Yankees called off their attack along the logging path. Lt. Warwick was certain that they would move to the east and make an attack along another track. He felt obliged to order his men to move east.

"Build another barricade, sergeant. You know what to do. We must stop them."

He sent another runner to Major Montpelier to his left. "Tell the major that I am moving east. I want him to deploy his men to fill the gap."

"Yes, sir."

But the sergeant of the leading squad sent word that they had reached the bridge across the Presumpscot River.

Warwick was annoyed. He should have remembered that. He had explored the river over the previous weeks and knew it was fast-flowing. There were many waterfalls. And there were very few bridges.

An army, laden down with firearms and ammunition, would find it difficult to get across. "That barrier will protect our right flank. But we'll have to defend the bridge."

Sergeant Priddy asked the obvious question. "But what if the Yankees change their plan and attack from the west?"

"That's Major Montpelier's problem now. My guess is that the Yankees have orders to march east and outflank us." That would make sense in open countryside, but was folly in these woods. If the Yankees attacked in the west, as his sergeant feared, his men would be crushed.

Priddy nodded. "Yes, sir. It'll take them an hour to march north to the next bridge. And another hour to march down the River Road on the far side." The sergeant sounded pleased. "Perhaps you should send word to the major."

"Yes. What's our casualty list, sergeant?"

"Three men dead, sir. Two seriously wounded, sent back to the hospital. Two walking wounded, unable to fight."

"I see."

An hour later, a mounted courier, a lieutenant, rode along the Bridge Road from the west. Warwick stepped forward to greet him.

"Lt. Warwick? Commanding the Bermudians? Are you holding on here?"

"Yes."

"Major Smythe is confident that the Yankees will not attack head on. Instead they will cross the river further up and then march south along River Road."

Warwick nodded. "Outflank us, yes."

"Major Smythe has decided to send several units east to pre-empt this. The Bermudians are to march east to defend the eastern railway bridge."

He was shocked. "But what about the line here?"

"The major has arranged for the Quebecois to advance east to cover it."

Warwick was annoyed but he passed on the order. "We're being pulled out of line and sent further east."

His men complained, but not loudly enough for him to object. "We've done all the fighting so far."

The sergeant told them to shut up and fall in.

They pulled on their backpacks and shouldered their muskets. They marched fast, all through the afternoon. There were no horses to spare so Warwick had to march too. They got to the railroad bridge by mid-afternoon.

Warwick was afraid that the Yankees would reach the bridge before his men. But he found that the scene was peaceful.

Both sides of the riverbank were densely wooded. This stretch of the river was fast-flowing. It was just as much an obstacle as the northern section.

The men were exhausted from the march but they could recognise the danger. They complained that the Yankees could approach through the woods unseen.

Warwick had no time for this. "They can't push their way through the forest. And they can't wade across. They'll have to use the bridge. Concentrate on that."

The men set about the task of digging trenches on each side of the railroad track to give themselves cover.

They could hear firing to the north. Sergeant Priddy knew what that meant. "The Yankees are pushing the Quebecois south, sir."

"Yes. The major didn't get enough reinforcements."

But the Yankees made no attempt to approach the eastern bridges.

Evening saved them from the threat of further attacks. They set about the task of preparing their dinner. Each man asked himself the same question - if the Yankees attacked in the morning, could they hold on?

Fort Hill blockhouse, evening

General Winfield Scott, commander of US forces in Maine, was an imposing figure. Over six feet in height, he was taller than any of his subordinates. He was stout, but that did not bother him.

Scott had been taken prisoner in the war of 1812, exchanged for another prisoner, and then promoted to brigadier general.

He insisted on military appearance and discipline in

the Army. His liking for regular parades and smart uniforms had earned the nickname of 'Old Fuss and Feathers'. He did not let that bother him either.

His army consisted mostly of regulars. For his own campaigns, Scott preferred to use a core of Army professionals whenever possible. Militiamen were badly trained and their officers were often political appointees, with little care for their men. Scott despised them. He perennially concerned himself with the welfare of his men.

The fall of darkness had brought fighting to a close. His subordinates reported back to the captured village. The blockhouse was badly lit. All they had to light the room was a set of candles.

He sat upright in his chair as an aide described the tactical situation as it appeared at close of day. "We've pushed them south of the river, sir. The land east and north of the river is free. Tomorrow we can advance east and cut the railroad."

Scott was appalled. "I don't care about the railroad, major. I had hoped that we could break through their line and 'roll up' the enemy. Instead they appear to have retreated in good order." He turned to the infantry colonel.

The man was in no mood to apologise. "My orders, sir, were to advance east as fast as I could. Except that you can't advance particularly fast along country lanes. And every time my men turned south, those blacks stopped us."

"What's that?" the major said, startled.

"My men said that they were stopped by a regiment of blacks -."

"Nonsense. Our intelligence reports that the British had a single company, from Bermuda."

"That may be so, but when my men advanced along those Indian trails, they were stopped by blacks. Until they pulled out."

"Ran away, you mean," the major said.

"It is equally possible, major, that they fought to the last."

Scott was tired of this squabbling. "Gentlemen." He did not raise his voice, but his tone was enough to make the two officers step back.

"Beg pardon, sir," Colonel Grant said. "If we had cavalry, sir ..."

Scott had heard this complaint every day. "Bah. We have to work with what we've got. If the British are allowed to build fortifications, they could hold out for months. The Royal Navy controls this coast. The defenders can be supplied by sea."

The major was unhappy. "But the railroad -."

"That is a side issue. While the enemy holds Portland, Maine is cut in two. And that means we cannot advance on Canada." His orders had been clear on that point. They had to invade Canada. And to do that they needed Maine.

He looked at the map. "I want to reach the harbour. Deprive it to the enemy. Yes ... attack from the west."

"Yes, sir." The aide opened his notebook.

"New orders. Tomorrow, a fresh regiment will attack Eight Quarters. Along the road, you understand. They will be accompanied by artillery. Then we advance until we can get our cannon within sight of the harbour. Sink their ships."

"Yes, sir. Even the threat will be enough. They dare not risk their ships."

"I hope so, major, I hope so."

Portland, May 2, Dawn

Sergeant Joseph Thayendanega and his mixed force of Mohawks and Hurons were still positioned in the southern marshes. They were woken by the sound of cannon fire to the north.

"Closer than yesterday," a private said.

"They're still on the other side of the river," Joseph said. "Cook your breakfast."

The lieutenant spoke to each of his sergeants in turn. "We may have to leave in a hurry. Get your men ready."

The men speculated on what they could hear. "They're attacking the French-speakers from Quebec."

Joseph turned to listen to the cannon. "Yes. The lieutenant was right. When you've finished your breakfast, pack your kit. Get ready to march."

As the morning wore on, one man after another said that the gunfire sounded closer. Joseph guessed that the attack was succeeding. He could not see anything moving. Blueberry Hill, on the other side of the river, blocked their view. But he guessed that the Canadiens were being pushed back.

His men had the task of defending Portland from any attack from the south-west. But the Yankees had attacked due west, on other side of stream. The railroad, raised above the marsh, was deserted.

"They're attacking Eight Quarters, sergeant," the lieutenant said. "We're wasted here."

"Yes, sir."

Then a runner brought news that the marines had retreated back to Portland. The lieutenant was angry.

"That means that we're isolated. We'll have to withdraw, sergeant. Pass the word."

"Yes, sir."

"Something moving on Blueberry Hill," the sentry said. "They're hauling cannon up there."

Joseph dismissed this idea as absurd. But then they heard the unmistakeable boom of a cannon.

"They're firing at us," Joseph bellowed. "Get under cover!"

But some of them did not move fast enough. The Hurons lost their lieutenant.

Joseph knew that he was senior to the Huron sergeant. Until they could find an officer, he was in command.

"Should we stay and fight, Sergeant Thayendanega?" the Huron sergeant said.

"But who are we defending?"

The Huron sergeant nodded and Joseph gave the order to retreat eastwards. They marched along the southern side of the railroad embankment to the bridge.

As they drew closer, they saw that the Marine detachment was holding the eastern end of the railroad bridge.

Joseph and his men scuttled across the bridge before the Yankee artillery could destroy it.

He reported to the marine lieutenant. "Should we stay and guard the bridge, sir?"

The Marine lieutenant looked harassed. "But my marines are doing that. No, move north to guard next bridge."

Joseph exchanged a glance with the Huron sergeant. "Yes, sir."

They made their way north along the riverbank. They found chaos in the town. Lots of soldiers were milling around, in detachments of various sizes.

After walking north for half a mile, they were stopped by an army lieutenant. "What regiment are you?"

"Sixty-Second, sir."

"There's nothing for you to do here. You should never have come here. Report to the dock area."

"Yes, sir."

They moved back through the city to get to the docks. The chaos was worse here.

Someone said that the Bermudians were holding the right flank, but they could not hold on forever.

This made no sense to Joseph. The Bermudians had been holding the centre.

He realised that the chaos had some sense to it. The soldiers were all moving in the same direction. Joseph could see that ocean-going ships were tied up alongside the docks. Smoke was drifting from funnels.

The Hurons, deprived of their lieutenant, kept close to Joseph's Mohawks. The throng of soldiers forced them along to the dockside.

He noted with approval that everyone still had his musket. So there was no panic.

They were pushed along to the north end of the dock. An ocean-going paddle-steamer was waiting. Smoke was rising from its twin funnels.

An officer was questioning each detachment. "Who's in charge here?"

"I am, sir. The lieutenant -."

"Never mind that," the officer said. "What regiment are you?"

"Sixty-Second, sir."

"Right. Get your men on board."

"But we want to stay and fight." In truth, Joseph wanted to get back home.

"Get on board, soldier. You're holding up everyone else."

Joseph glanced round. The mass of waiting soldiers made movement impossible. There seemed to be no option. He led the way on board.

Presumpscot River, eastern railroad bridge

The men of the Third Bermuda Militia, expecting trouble, were awakened at first light. The sergeant told them to get an early breakfast. They might not get another chance. Captain Warwick expected a dawn attack.

Then they hear artillery to the west. Warwick sent his men to their trenches. But no attack came. He and his Bermudians had nothing to do. The fighting was elsewhere.

At 10 am, a mounted courier brought a written order. "Read it. Hurry. You are to withdraw to Portland to be evacuated."

Warwick read the note. It repeated, in more formal terms, what the courier had said. "We have to leave?"

"The tactical situation is deteriorating, lieutenant. We're trying to get everyone out." The courier wheeled his horse and rode off.

Warwick, who understood ships, knew there were not enough ocean-going vessels in harbour to take the entire garrison. Was there any other escape route? Perhaps they could retreat to the beach?

He turned to Sergeant Priddy. "All of the men understand boats. Could we evacuate?"

"There's some boats on the river, sir, further downstream. I had a look. Sea-going boats, I mean. They couldn't cope with a hurricane, though." They both glanced east. But the sky was clear.

"Good enough." Warwick decided to ignore the order.

Portland, dock area

Soldiers kept filing on board the paddle steamer until the deck was crowded.

A naval rating shouted at them. "There's no room in

the cabins. You'll have to stay on deck. It'll be cold."

"We'll be better on deck," Joseph told the others. "I don't want to be trapped down there."

A bridge had been built across the ship from one paddle-box to the next. A naval officer was standing up there, speaking-trumpet in hand. He walked to the shoreward end of the bridge and shouted an order.

Stevedores on the dock cast off the mooring ropes and dropped them into the water. Teams of sailors hauled the ropes on board. The steamer was belching smoke.

The officer shouted another order. The paddles thrashed the water and the ship moved forward. They cleared the end of the dock, turned east, and headed out to sea.

Joseph had crossed the river at Quebec, on a steam-ferry. But he had never seen anything like this.

He turned to look behind him. He could see another ship manoeuvring to take the paddle-steamer's place at the wharf. Men began filing on board. He realised that they were planning to evacuate the entire army.

As the ship came clear of the harbour, they got their first glimpse of the fort. "The marines said they blew it up. But it looks all right from out here," the Huron sergeant said.

"Have the Yankees moved back in?" a private asked.

Joseph wondered whether the fort's cannon would fire on the ship. Then he realised that the gun-ports were empty.

They continued east, past a series of islands. Out at sea, they turned south. The waves were bigger outside the protection of the islands.

The Mohawks were surprised. This course would not take them to Halifax. Joseph asked a seaman what was going on.

"Och, didn't anyone tell you? We're going to Bermuda, not Nova Scotia." He smiled "We're cooking a meal for you all. Get your men in line."

Joseph was dismayed. He passed this news along. Some of the men took this badly. They were being forced away from home.

"I don't like it either. But there's nothing that you can do about it. So you might as well get in line for dinner."

Mouth of Presumpscot River, May 2

The Bermudians, guarding the railroad and the right flank, heard the renewed cannon-fire, away to the west. But there was still no sign of the enemy. Some of the men were digging their trenches deeper, just to have something to do.

Far to the south, they saw the smoke of a paddle-steamer. "Heading out to sea." Warwick said.

Then a sentry cried out that he could see the Yankees advancing to their left.

Warwick turned to look west. A knot of Yankees, a quarter of a mile away, were running south, carrying a flag.

"Hundreds of 'em. Must be a whole regiment," Priddy said.

"Have the Yankees forced the bridge to the west?"

"Perhaps they waded across."

Warwick realised the Yankee attack had cut them off from the town. But the Yankees ignored them and headed for their main target, Portland.

The Bermudians were at risk of being surrounded. Warwick did not hesitate any further. "Retreat. Back to the river."

"You want us to abandon the bridge, sir?"

"There's no point in defending it, is there? The Yankees have crossed by the road bridge."

"Should we go back, sir? Get to the port? We could get

home from there."

Warwick glanced at the advancing Yankees and their flag. "The port will be occupied by now, sergeant. We'd be walking into a trap."

The southern railway bridge marked where the river widened. "Did you say that there were ocean-going boats south of the bridge, sergeant?"

"Yes, sir."

"Let's take a look."

They turned to see a train with empty boxcars steaming out of town towards them. The Yankee skirmishers were moving west, toward the city. They ignored the train.

The train slowed as it approached the bridge. The engineer leaned out of his cab.

Warwick saw his chance. "Get on board."

The engineer waved to them and slowed further. They scrambled aboard the boxcars. Warwick instead chose the footplate. The train rattled across the bridge.

The engineer opened the throttle. Warwick discovered that the locomotive crew were all coloured.

The engineer was eager to talk. "There's eight of us, sir. We're from the US – New York. We left 'cause of the Pursuit Act. In Portland, we were taken on by the Grand Trunk Railroad. Oilers and fitters."

"But what are you doing here?"

"When this fight started, we didn't want to be enslaved. So we fired up the loco and lit out. Did we do the right thing, sir?"

"Yes," Warwick said.

He wondered whether they were being pursued. He leaned out of the locomotive to look. It was difficult to make sense of the situation.

No. There were no other locomotives behind him, no cavalry. The Yankees were concentrating on Portland.

The railroad led north, away from the coast. Ahead lay the mountains and the frontier. The Bermudians expected to be held up. But they did not encounter any opposition.

Almost an hour went by. Then they saw some houses ahead. They were approaching the town of Auburn.

Warwick was anxious. He knew that the town had a small garrison of French-speaking Quebecois. Had the Maine militia overwhelmed them?

But the town was quiet. The black engineer said that he would like to stop to take on water.

The locomotive slowed to a stop and the commander of the Quebecois garrison hurried up and asked what was going on. "We heard the cannon-fire." He was suspicious. "Are you running away?"

Warwick's men were leaning out of the boxcars, curious.

"Portland is being attacked," Warwick said. He remembered his written orders. "I have received orders to withdraw. The rest of the garrison is being evacuated by sea."

"As bad as that?"

"Yes. You can stay if you want. Die a hero's death."

"What would that achieve?" The lieutenant told his men to seize the locomotive waiting in the siding.

He turned back to Warwick. "It already has steam up, you understand."

The station manager was sour. "Why should I give you Limeys any assistance?"

The black locomotive engineer intervened. "We know how to get this other locomotive moving, sir. There's enough of us to keep both of them moving."

Warwick turned to the station manager. "If your men here do not co-operate, the garrison will be trapped. When the US Army arrives, they would fight. The town might be wrecked in the fighting."

"The army's on the way here?" This made the station manager more sour than ever. He told his team to do everything they could to get the locomotives under way.

The Quebecois lieutenant became anxious. "We've got an hour at most. Hurry, hurry."

Warwick expected the Yankees to turn up, but the trains got under way before any interruption arrived.

Together, the Bermudians and Quebecois retreated north along the railroad. The Quebecois lieutenant said that his men were cheerful. They were going home.

The Bermudians were more troubled. Every mile they travelled took them further away from home.

The map told Warwick that this line went several miles west of the town Brewer. This caused him further anxiety. Did the town have a militia? And would they move across to intervene?

The Quebecois lieutenant said that the town had no military value and had been ignored by the Maine militia, but Warwick could not relax.

As the train approached the station, they could see that a few men were waiting. Warwick's anxiety grew.

But the men were not armed. They turned out to be curious onlookers.

Once again, the locomotives stopped to take on water. The task seemed to take for ever. But the place remained quiet. There was no sign of pursuit behind them.

The black engine crew selected a spokesman. He approached Warwick and asked to be taken to Canada.

"No," Warwick said. "You have families in Portland, right? If you cross the border, there will be no going back."

Maine, Sebago Lake, May 2

Thirty Abenaki of 'K' Company and an equal number of Royal Marines were holding a blockhouse by the shore of the lake. This was the northern end of the defence line. All morning, they had heard the artillery fire to the south.

For most of the day they were ignored. Then a company of Yankee skirmishes marched up the road. The defenders took a few shots at them and the skirmishers took cover.

The marine sergeant watched the attackers from the firing slit of the blockhouse. He said that escape was impossible. He suggested that mounting a sally to drive away the attackers was better than staying cooped up in the blockhouse.

The Abenaki sergeant detested foolhardy heroics. He suggested an alternative. "We could retreat north, all the way to Canada, sir. Steal a boat and get across the lake. And north of the lake is a river. It takes you all the way to the mountains."

"Escape? Live to fight another day?" The marine captain said. "That sounds like a good idea."

Some of the marines were reluctant. The sergeant said they were afraid of the wilderness. "They would rather fight it out here."

The captain told his sergeant to select ten men and hold on until nightfall.

"Yes, sir."

The Abenaki and the remaining marines made their way to the lakeside. They found two rowing-boats, climbed aboard, and began their voyage north.

Chapter 4

Upper Canada, Brant's Ford, May 4

The train pulled into the little railroad junction of Glencoe. Sergeant Chard stepped down and found a porter. "I want to hire a trolley."

His baggage included a set of eight sulphate cells, known to insiders as sand batteries. There were also several jars of dilute sulphuric acid. He loaded those onto the trolley himself. "Now I want to take these to the railway freight shed."

The man grinned. "This way, sergeant."

He was met by the militia major, Peter Theyanoguin. "Ah. Good morning. We were glad you could make this inspection, sergeant."

"Good morning, sir. I hear you're making good progress."

"Yes. But you may be just in time. You've heard about Portland?"

"Yes, sir." Everybody knew the Yankee attack had started. They had retaken Portland and the railroad in a couple of days of fighting. Their success had been complete. But where would the Yankees attack next?

The major was amused. "A week ago the governor's secretary was asking why we needed so much wire. Now he's asking why we aren't working hard enough."

"Yes, sir. Everyone is feeling the heat. That's why I'm here." He had hoped to relax for a few days.

A hand-car was standing on the tracks. The footplate had been freshly painted. Then someone had painted 'Mohawk Rail Road' round the edge of the footplate.

Four Mohawk infantrymen leaned on the handles, watching him.

Chard asked the men to lift the batteries and the jars of acid up from the trolley onto the handcart. "Careful, careful."

He tipped the porter. "Who wrote that, sir?" he said, pointing to the graffiti.

The major shrugged. "I have no idea. It was probably meant as a joke – or an insult."

The major walked across the freight yard to the signal box. He had a word with the signalman, then climbed on board. "Let's go."

The men grinned and pushed on the handles. The hand-car began moving east. This was a branch line that took them within two miles of the coast. Chard knew that it did not see much traffic.

The men worked the handles with enthusiasm. The major smiled. "The men thought that if they met a locomotive coming towards them, they could just jump off. Then they realised just how fast this thing could go. So we have to treat this as a real locomotive. We have to obey the signals and all that sort of thing. Bill here memorised the timetable."

Chard realised the major was right, they were going fast. The major told his men to slow down. "We're reaching the switch."

They rounded a bend and Chard could see a linesman standing next to a switch-lever.

The men had stopped working the handles but the hand-car was still going fast. The major pulled on the brake handle but it did not seem to have any effect.

They reached the switch-point and were diverted on to the spur line. The little vehicle rocked wildly. Chard thought it was going to jump the rails.

But instead it settled down. The major leaned on the

brake handle and the little car slowed to a stop. The linesman hauled on the switch lever. The semaphore-signal now showed that the through line was clear.

A road crossed the track here, but the spot was no more than a cluster of houses – there was no station.

Five minutes later, a locomotive thundered past. The engineer leaned out of the cab to give them a wave.

"This the northern end of the wire to Port Stanley," the major said.

"Yes, sir."

The major exchanged a few words with the switch operator, who turned out to be the Mohawk telegraphist.

The telegraphist and his companions were living in a tent. Chard knew that the man spent all his time waiting for a signal from the coast. Over the last few days, that no longer seemed a pointless exercise.

The major spoke in an undertone. "We don't need five men here, you understand. His friends' real job is to talk to him and stop him from going crazy."

"Yes, sir."

Chard turned his attention to his mission. He and the soldiers lifted two of the batteries down from the flatcar and across to the tent. Then he lowered two of the jars of acid.

"Careful, there, careful." With luck, this would give them two-way working.

Chard told the others to stand back and poured the acid into the battery. Then he wired up the battery to the instrument. He tapped out a message. "Now we will find out whether they can receive your signals."

A minute later, the needle instrument flickered out a message. The telegraphist grinned. "Now we're really in business."

Chard sent another message. "I asked the operator in Port Stanley to send a message to us every hour, to check the wire and to stay in practice."

"Yes, sergeant. They arrive regularly. It was annoying that I could not reply. But when the wind blows, the branches tap the wire. That confuses the signal."

Chard nodded. "We may have to cut a few trees down and replace them with poles."

The major intervened. "We wanted to run the wire from here to the next station. So our fellow doesn't have to stay in a tent. But the telegraph company's manager refused."

"Yes, sir. I have experienced their ways before."

"They said they wouldn't allow our people on their premises. Their excuse was that our people were untrained and ignorant."

"It isn't just you, sir. They obstruct everyone."

Chard used his equipment to test the strength of the signal. Then they said farewell to the telegraphist and climbed back on board the hand-car.

They continued eastward to Tilson. This was the northern end of the more ambitious twenty-mile wire to Port Burwell.

"This wire is not complete yet," the major said. "If the Yankees attacked now, the men on the coast would have to send a rider to summon aid."

Tilson was a small town. But it was big enough to have a station and a telegraph office.

The Mohawks parked the hand-car in a siding. Townsfolk paused to stare at the men in uniform. But no-one moved to intervene.

"The telegraph company is being obstructive here too." The major lowered his voice. "The stationmaster gave us a linesman's hut, so we wouldn't have to keep our equipment in a tent, but we mustn't tell his boss."

"Yes, I see, sir." Chard stowed the last sand-battery and jars of acid in the hut.

Chard and the major hired a spring-cart. They started

out along the coast road. It was wide enough to allow carts to pass. This section of the wire was attached to telegraph poles.

"We're working from both ends," the major said. They haven't met yet."

"Still, they're working very fast, sir," Chard said.

They reached the work-crew, digging a pit for another telegraph pole. They stopped their work to greet their commander.

Chard used his kit to check the section of the wire between them and Tilson. "Fine."

"Another couple of days and they'll have linked up," the major said. "But - the telegraph company won't allow their telegraphists to relay messages for us. They won't even allow our telegraphist to sit in the station building. The operatives themselves help out, but the top brass are stubborn."

"Yes, I see, sir." Sergeant Chard had tangled with the telegraph company before. "In theory, you could relay the wire all the way to Brant's Ford. Bypass the telegraph company. If only you could get enough wire."

"Could you do that? Set up a receiving station at headquarters?" The major was astounded. "Let me get this clear. You say we can set up a *telegraph* office?"

"Not a commercial station, no. You couldn't cope with messages arriving from all over. But messages from these three observation posts? Yes. The difficult part would be getting the wire."

"No, no. I think the colonel could manage that," the major said. "The governor is eager to encourage us just now."

"Yes, I can understand that, sir," Chard said. "Well, if you can get the wire ... Could you recruit some operators at Brant's Ford?"

The major was full of enthusiasm. "Oh, yes. I can find them."

"You will need batteries, of course. I can get those. But - you won't have to put up any telegraph poles. You can use the company's. If they try to stop us ..." He grinned.

Depot Mountains, Railroad pass, May 5

Five hundred men of the US army advanced along the line of the railroad. They reached the gap in the mountain range. The colonel's orders were to cross the frontier and advance to the St. Lawrence. He was then to cross the river and take Quebec, as fast as possible. Then the British would have to concede defeat.

They found that the pass was heavily fortified. The colonel noticed an airship hovering overhead.

The scouts reported to the colonel that an entire regiment of highlanders was stationed there. They were supported by a regiment of heavy artillery.

The colonel and his men came under fire from a long-range gun. He glanced up at the airship.

"Those bastards are watching how accurate the firing is," his adjutant said.

"I wish we had one," the colonel said. "Get the men under cover. Into the trees. Get them out of sight of that thing."

He realised that he did not have enough men for an assault against the highlanders. On this mountain, the defenders had all the advantages. He hated the thought of squandering lives. Should he send a report back to Portland, then wait for reinforcements and artillery? Or should he try another route?

The telegraph wire had been taken down. Nobody had thought to bring a repair team. If he sent a courier for orders, he might have to wait a week before a reply came.

New Brunswick, May 6, morning

Fredericton, situated eighty miles inland from the Bay of Fundy, was the capital of the colony of New Brunswick. The streets of the centre were graced by elm trees and genteel single-storey villas. The biggest building in the town was the three-storey barrack block. The two hundred men of the garrison were British regulars, with the task of protecting the colony from American invasion.

The town also contained the residence of the Lieutenant-Governor, George Perkins. The building was modest in size, but carefully proportioned, to match the neighbouring buildings.

The governor was in his study reading a sermon when he was interrupted by his secretary. He looked up, annoyed. "Yes?"

"Beg pardon, sir, but a courier has arrived from Quebec. He says he has brought a message from the governor."

Perkins had been dreading this. He closed his book. "Show him in."

The secretary opened the door for the visitor and then stepped back, waiting for further orders.

The governor's aide was young, very self-assured and wore an expensive frock coat. "Good morning, sir. I am an aide of Sir Humphrey Waite. I travelled here by airship."

"I see. Those things are very efficient," Perkins said.

"Yes, sir." The aide stepped forward and laid an envelope on Perkins' desk. "I am fully conversant with the contents of the message, sir."

Perkins opened the letter. He ignored the long-winded introduction and read the short central paragraph. The news was dire. The Yankees had retaken Portland -

which he already knew - but they were advancing north. They had crossed the mountains and had reached the territory of Quebec.

Lieutenant Governor Perkins was ordered to create a diversion before the US Army could reach the St. Lawrence, organise a river crossing and attack the city of Quebec.

"I must protest," Perkins said. "There are only two hundred regular troops in New Brunswick. And the militia cannot be expected to defend the colony unaided. Those regulars are needed for the defence of the colony."

"The defence of Quebec is considered more important than New Brunswick, sir," the aide said.

Perkins bristled. "I was entrusted with the defence of this colony by Her Majesty and ..."

His secretary intervened. "We have all these black refugees here, sir. From the United States."

"Absurd. They have no training," Perkins said.

The aide straightened up. "Sir Humphrey asks you to do *something*, sir."

"Sending untrained blacks across the border would be no more than an empty gesture. The Yankees would slaughter them."

"A gesture is all that Sir Humphrey expects, sir."

"Are things that bad?" He thought through the problem. "Very well. But most of these black refugees are runaway slaves. The only skill they have is farming." Another problem occurred to him.

"But we have no officers to spare. Can the governor provide any?"

The aide nodded. "Of course, sir."

So Perkins sent the young man back to Sir Humphrey, with a letter asking if the army in Lower Canada had anyone experienced in commanding blacks.

Montreal, May 6

Tommy Adams' real name was Alexandria Thompson. For almost a year she had served as a private in the Sixty-Second regiment. She had expected to be discovered in a matter of weeks, but the continual transfer of the regiment from one place to another had given everyone other things to think about.

But then her luck had run out. The day before, they had discovered her identity and she had been arrested.

She had been kept overnight in the barracks' jail. She sat on her bunk, her back to the wall. She could not sleep. They had taken away her red jacket and her boots. Her feet, without them, looked small – dainty.

She was humiliated by this spell in prison. She realised later that she had been imprisoned because they were embarrassed to have a woman in the barracks. There were no private rooms so it had to be the jail.

The turnkey brought her breakfast, which she ignored. Then she heard footsteps outside. She looked up. She recognised the platoon sergeant. He was wearing his best red jacket. He carried a cloth bundle in his left hand.

"Adams – on your feet. Time for your meeting with the colonel." Two other redcoats stood behind him. They were grinning.

The sergeant opened the door. She flinched. "No."

He stepped back. She realised that he was embarrassed.

"You going to haul me out?" Tommy asked.

"I could. But let's do it soldierly, shall we?" the sergeant said. "They've got some female nurses at the hospital. I could get a couple of 'em to drag you out."

She considered her options and then stood. The sergeant handed her a dress. "Put this on and get decent."

She was still defiant. "You gonna watch while I take my pants off?"

The sergeant was nonplussed. The second man spoke. "Put the dress over your pants. It's cold out there."

"Oh. Right."

The sergeant handed her a pair of summer moccasins.

"You know the way," he said. He escorted her along the corridor to the colonel's office.

The sergeant knocked. "The prisoner's here, sir."

"Enter," a deep voice said.

They walked in. Lt. Colonel Grimwood of the Sixty-Second was sitting behind his desk. He had black hair with a white streak.

Alexandria had expected the colonel to be angry, but he merely looked tired. She looked round. "Oh. I thought there was going to be a court martial."

"No. We could hold a trial and have you flogged, but that would bring the entire regiment into disrepute. You've caused us enough embarrassment already. So the doctor has agreed to give you a medical discharge."

"Medical? How, sir?"

A single sheet of white paper lay on the desk. Grimwood pulled the sheet towards him, dipped his pen in the inkwell and wrote his signature at the foot of the document. "You are not a healthy male. You are free to go, Adams. Your friends are waiting for you."

She wanted to protest, but the sergeant gave a meaningful cough. If she tried to stay, she would be dragged out. Her shoulders slumped.

The sergeant stood aside to let her pass. She walked along the corridor and stumbled down the stairs into the street. She recognised Sergeant Chard and Miss Grace. Both were wearing heavy coats. The sergeant had a greatcoat over his arm.

Sergeant Chard spoke gently. "I'm here to take you home."

Alexandria was close to tears. "I'm not going with you. If you try to force me, I'll scream."

Chard nodded. "That's why Miss Grace is with me. You act girlish, she gives you a slap. All very girlish. The passers-by will just be embarrassed. Do you have a home to go to? Friends to take you in? Thought not. Come on then." He draped the greatcoat over her shoulders.

At the signallers' office in army headquarters, they gave her some tea. Lieutenant Eathorpe gently asked how this all started. She was still close to tears.

Mr. Lloyd told him to stop. "I'm as curious as you are, Daniel. But we shouldn't bully the woman." He turned to Tommy. "You pulled your weight in this team, but we're now a man short. And now the Yankees have attacked."

"We're short-handed," Lt. Eathorpe said. "There's no-one with your knowledge about the weather. Are you prepared to work as a female auxiliary? You're a valuable member of this team. You know how to read those weather reports. And you can get results out of the Analytical Engine."

Tommy gripped her cup. "But you're not allowed to hire women, are you, sir?"

Mr. Lloyd answered this. "I can hire civilians. Anyone who has the necessary skills or expertise." He smiled. "I could even take you on as an apprentice. Although the pay is meagre."

"No," Tommy said. "Everyone in this building knows me. They would laugh at me."

Lt. Eathorpe nodded his understanding.

Mr. Lloyd glared down at her. "I suppose you intend to join another regiment. But it won't work. Not until this fuss dies down."

Miss Grace interrupted. "We need a weather observer in the Adirondacks, sir. And - Tommy's brave enough."

"That?" Lt. Eathorpe said. "No. We can't send a civilian. If he was caught, the Yankees would shoot him as a spy."

Tommy realised what he meant: the task had to go to somebody in uniform.

She considered this. She would be in the army. Home. "Yes."

"Eathorpe, I shall have to take her on as an apprentice," Mr. Lloyd said. "If that doesn't work the whole plan falls apart."

Lt. Eathorpe sighed. "I'll have to perjure myself then."

Sergeant Chard straightened up. "We could share the burden, if you get my meaning, sir. I shove an order under your nose and you sign it without reading it."

"I'll need new name," Tommy said. "An' stop saying 'she'. That destroys the trick."

They debated the matter and decided upon Alexander Thompson.

After Tommy had signed the papers, the lieutenant smiled. "I am promoting you to sergeant. A private can't act independently."

She was indignant. "It's not right."

The lieutenant grinned. "Shut up and soldier."

Bermuda, May 6

Sergeant Joseph Thayendanega stood on the foredeck of the paddle-steamer as Bermuda came into sight. He was not impressed by what he saw. The island was no bigger than some mountains that he had climbed. His fellow Mohawks joined him as the ship drew closer.

The ship passed down the eastern shore. Joseph recognised cedar trees, although the palmetto was new to him.

A marine corporal named the forts as they passed by –

St. Catherine, Fort Albert, and Gates Fort. "All of them are manned by blacks - the Militia Coastal Artillery."

"Some of them served in Portland," Joseph said.

"That's a lot of forts," the Huron sergeant said.

"This is an important naval base. The Royal Navy's Atlantic Fleet is based here."

"So we'll see warships too."

"Most of them are in the Great Sound – that's at the western end," the marine said.

They passed Paget island and then turned west. There was another island to the south. "It's called Gunner Point. An' this is called St. George's Channel."

Finally, the ship reached the town of St. George's and tied up. Joseph, who had seen Montreal, was not impressed.

The purser told the men to disembark. Joseph and his men were left to last. They picked up their backpacks and their muskets.

They were resigned to their fate. There was no way to get home.

They followed the marine corporal down the gangplank. He waved a hand. "This is King's Square."

To the north was the stone town hall. The other buildings, also of stone, were painted white.

Half of the people wandering across the square seemed to have some African in their ancestry.

"Are any of them slaves?" Joseph asked in an undertone.

"I think they were all freed, fifteen or twenty years ago," the Huron sergeant said.

The soldiers filed into the dock office. "Join the end of the queue," the corporal said.

The port officials, sitting behind a desk, struggled to cope with this sudden influx of men. The army men were sent to the barracks. The marines were detailed to take a coastal ship to the port of Hamilton.

One of the port officials, in civilian clothes, stopped the sergeant. "You can't keep your muskets."

Joseph was alarmed. Did this official have the right to do that? "If my men lose their muskets, it'll be deducted from their pay. And if the weapons are stolen, I'll have to report it."

The marine corporal grinned. "He's got you there."

The official was annoyed. "Where are you from?"

"Lower Canada. Quebec. And the Mohawk nation. It's complicated -."

The official's assistant grinned. "They're Mohawks? Indians? Send them to St. David's Island."

The marine corporal was annoyed. "That's daft."

"We've got to billet them somewhere. St. David's. Why not?"

Some of the onlookers found this amusing. Joseph wondered why.

The official wrote out a billeting request and handed it to Joseph. He turned to the corporal. "Show them the way."

"Pick up your kit," Joseph said.

The corporal led them outside and along the dock. A steam ferry, wide and squat, was moored up there. It had a ramp at one end so it could carry wheeled vehicles. Joseph's men filed on board.

The corporal turned to Joseph. "Good luck."

"Thanks."

The village on St. David's Island was simply called West Wharf. It consisted of a score of wooden houses each side of the carriage road leading inland. Joseph could tell that the village was poor. Four open boats were drawn up on the beach. Fishing nets hung up to dry displayed the profession of the villagers.

But the place was neat, tidy, and clean. The villagers had not lost their pride. The houses were built of wood, with palm-leaf thatch. Most of them had open porches where the owners could sit in the shade and take advantage of a cooling breeze.

Joseph thought it bizarre that each house had a stout chimney made of limestone blocks. He wondered why the villagers had gone to so much effort until, later, he learned of the destructive energy of hurricanes.

Joseph had expected blacks in a poor place such as this. But the people coming to meet them looked more American than African.

He was dismayed. How could a poor community like this feed so many new arrivals?

He asked to speak to the headman and introduced himself. He showed the billeting request. The villagers gathered round.

"So you soldiers are Mohawks?" the headman said. He grinned.

They explained the joke to him. "In the old days, the English would take slaves from all over. Not just blacks. Whites - Scottish and Irish rebels. And Algonquin."

Joseph nodded.

"We're descended from Indian prisoners of war. They called us Mohawks because that was the only tribe the English had heard of."

Joseph thought this over. "Not likely. The Mohawks live too far inland."

The headman shrugged. "We'll find room for you. Two or three men to each family."

"Thank you."

"Although in this weather you may find it more comfortable to sleep on the porch."

Joseph learned that education in this community was never a priority. The men fished and farmed to survive. Because of their isolation, other Bermudians always teased and embarrassed the St. David's Islanders whenever they left the island.

As a result, the Islanders did not discuss their heritage in public or among strangers, only around their kitchen table.

Quebec, May 7

Lord Cardigan of the 11th Hussars and Lt. Colonel Green of the Upper Canada volunteer Hussars had been summoned to the governor's residence, in the old castle.

Lord Cardigan was resplendent in his regiment's full dress uniform, which he had designed himself. His fur shako with the straight plume in the front was tucked under his arm.

Green was rather envious. He thought that his lordship outshone other officers in the antechamber. Green would have liked to discuss the strategic situation, but Lord Cardigan had indicated that he was not interested in gossiping with commoners.

The governor's aide stepped forward and invited the two colonels into the governor's office. Green was disconcerted to find that General Reginald Trevor-Roper was standing at the governor's side.

Lord Cardigan bowed and smiled. "Sir Humphrey, I am pleased to meet you again, sir."

Green realised that he was the least senior man in the room. Embarrassed, he murmured his own greeting.

The governor looked weary. "Gentlemen, the Yankees have crossed the mountains. We expect them to attack Quebec. You are ordered to take your regiments south and use delaying tactics."

Lord Cardigan nodded. "Very well. Exactly what hussars are trained for."

The general intervened. "This time, my Lord, I do not want to hear of any cavalry charges against prepared positions. We are short of experienced soldiers. I do not want to hear of any more men thrown away to no good purpose."

Lord Cardigan was annoyed. "Now look here -."

The general subjected him to a glower. "My lord, I believe you have already been court-martialed once. I do hope there will not be another."

"How dare you? I am a peer of the realm. You're a -."

"Upstart? Perhaps. But I would quite understand if you felt you were unable to take orders from a plebeian such as myself."

Green was shocked by the general's request. He realised that Lord Cardigan had not understood.

It took a few moments for the implications to sink in. Lord Cardigan was suddenly angry. "Are you asking me to resign, sir?"

"Only if you feel you are unable to take orders from an - upstart. I would be saddened to lose such an experienced officer, of course." The general smiled.

"Oh, you would, would you? Well, I'm not going to give you that satisfaction, sir. Do you hear me? The 11th Hussars are mine and I'm not going to give them up."

"I am glad to hear it, my lord. So there will be no newspaper reports of heroic cavalry charges."

Lord Cardigan gave an ironic little bow, turned and stormed out.

The governor was perturbed. "Sir Reginald, you've just made an enemy for life."

"That's no loss." The general shrugged. "I went to the military college, and he despises me for it. He thinks that because he's an aristocrat he was born knowing everything he needs to know about soldiering." He turned to Green. "Your orders are the same, colonel. To use delaying tactics. Slow the enemy down."

"Yes, sir."

"However, you are to operate independently of his lordship. Pick another patch of countryside. More than that: you are ordered to ignore any tactical orders that his lordship might give you."

Green was shocked. "I must request that you put that in writing, sir."

"Is that necessary, colonel?"

"I do not want to be court-martialled by his Lordship, sir. Or - challenged to a duel."

"He does have a point, general." The governor sounded tired.

The general nodded. "Given his Lordship's past record, I suppose he might. Very well."

Green was shocked. The implications behind this bizarre order were still sinking in. The general had doubts about Lord Cardigan's decision-making ability.

Even more shocking, in his view, was that the general thought that Green, acting alone, might have more success than if he followed Cardigan's lead.

"I can't afford losing both regiments in a single battle," the general said. "If one goes, the other has to take up the slack."

"Oh, yes, I see, sir."

Montreal, May 8

Charles Lloyd set about the task of training Tommy. He found it impossible to forget that Tommy's real name was Alexandria. He ensured that they were never alone together. Her usual training partner was Asher.

"One of the reasons that so few people know about magic is that it's very dangerous. Men who try to learn it on their own usually kill themselves. So most of my lessons will be about safety."

"Can women perform magic, sir?"

"Oh, yes. They rarely receive tuition, though. Some people say that the practice of magic causes miscarriages. Although I assume you don't have to worry about that."

"No." Her tone was surly.

Charles discovered that Tommy was able to establish rapport with him easily enough. She managed it with Signaller Asher too. But when she tried with Grace, neither could hear the other.

"I don't understand," Grace said. "I thought I could talk with everyone."

"It would probably become easy enough after a week's practice," Charles said. "But we don't have a week."

"Perhaps I can only establish rapport with men," Tommy said.

"I haven't heard of that one before. But it's possible. With magic, anything is possible."

So he suggested that she try to establish rapport with Lt. Eathorpe. The lieutenant looked embarrassed, which seemed to amuse Tommy. They were able to establish contact at the third attempt.

"You'd better exchange tokens, so the lieutenant can act as backup if anything goes wrong," Charles said.

"Yes, sir," Tommy said.

Charles had more urgent problems. He had access to military reports and less formal sources of information, including the latest Washington newspapers.

His acquaintance George Eastman had operated behind enemy lines and his Indian colleagues sent him interesting snippets of information.

So he knew that the US Army was sending a large number of men and supplies north along the railroad to the frontier with Quebec.

At the same time, a small Yankee force, estimated to be a hundred men, had advanced across Maine to the frontier with New Brunswick. They had occupied the frontier town of World's End. But they made no attempt to advance further.

The Maine militia unit at Fort Kent, guarding the northern tip of Maine, was said to be at full readiness.

Bermuda, May 9

The detachment of Mohawk infantry had been on St. David's Island for three days. The fishing village had a patch of bare ground and Sergeant Joseph had decided to use it as his parade-ground. He spent the morning leading the men through their physical exercises. He did not want them to go soft.

They had all taken off their red jackets, to avoid getting them stained. Some of the villagers, with nothing better to do, were watching from the sidelines.

One of the fishermen walked up from the landing stage. "Joseph, a visitor is coming. A fine lady with her own boat. I've heard of her. And she isn't coming to speak to *us*."

"But why should she want to speak to me?" Joseph told the men to rest and pulled on his red jacket.

A rowing boat was approaching the dock. Joseph had learned a lot about boats since coming to this island. This boat was big, with high sides, quite capable of coping with these Atlantic waves. There were six rowers. Joseph noted that they were all black.

Sitting in the stern was a white lady. She wore a broad-brimmed straw hat to protect her complexion. A coloured girl, as neatly dressed as the lady, sat beside her. She kept her hands in her lap.

The boat had a square stern, so Joseph knew it was steered by means of a tiller. He wondered who was steering. Was the lady doing it? Perhaps that was usual here, a place of islands. The most popular sport seemed to be racing sail-boats. All of the fishermen were enthusiasts.

The rowing boat approached the landing stage. The oarsmen, all at once, brought in their oars. The boat turned neatly, and stopped alongside the landing stage. Two of the rowers grabbed the jetty. Another stepped nimbly ashore and tied up.

Then he helped the lady to climb out. She managed to appear elegant as she did so.

One of the rowers helped the lady's maid to step ashore. She trailed behind her mistress.

Joseph straightened his jacket as he walked forward. The villagers tagged along behind. "Watch yourself, Joseph. She's a grand lady. Eccentric. Don't cross her," the mayor said.

"Right. Those rowers – are they her servants?"

"They're employed by her husband." He grinned. "But they're not just hirelings. If you offended her, any one of them would cut your throat."

"Ah." He nodded. *That* sort of servant.

The villagers drew up in an arc behind the sergeant, eager to listen. Two more of the rowers stepped ashore, as if to protect their lady in case of need. Joseph felt that they acted out of loyalty.

The lady ignored the villagers. "Sergeant. Your name and your regiment, if you please."

She was wearing a lightweight dress, perhaps to help her keep cool. Joseph wondered whether fine ladies did sweat. He judged that she was in her late thirties, but she had aged well. He fought the urge to salute.

"Good morning, madam. I'm Sergeant Joseph Thayendanega of the Sixty-Second Regiment."

"Sergeant, my name is Mrs. Warwick. My son was stationed in Portland. What can you tell me about him?"

Joseph recalled that one of these parishes was called Warwick. Did this lady own it? "Was your son commanding the Bermudians? Yes, madam. I know of him." He tried to remember where the Bermudians had been fighting. Oh, hell.

"You have news of him?" The lady's face crumpled into lines.

"No, madam. We were at the south end of the line. Guarding the flank, as you might say. The Bermudians, they were guarding the centre. The Yankees, they attacked the north of the centre. The marines were holding that. I heard it said that the Bermudians retreated to the river-bank."

"They retreated? You mean they ran away?"

"No, no. It was a fighting retreat, madam. They held the flank for us. That enabled us to get away. So the Bermudians, they might have got out, retreated along the railroad. Back to Quebec." Home, he thought.

"So he's alive?" the lady asked.

He shook his head. "Beg pardon, madam, but I don't know. The next ship from the north could bring good news, but it would be wrong of me to rise your hopes."

"I see. Thank you."

"He's well liked, madam."

"What's that?"

He wondered whether he had somehow given offence. "He's a good officer, madam."

"My son?" She seemed confused. "I see. Thank you. Is there anything I can do to help?"

"Well, we're billeted here. These people are supposed to feed us. But they struggle to feed themselves. Could you, er, have a word with the governor?" Joseph was getting tired of fish. And if the villagers gave their catch to him, rather than selling it, they would not be able to pay the rent.

"I am not that important. He would not listen to me. But I will see what I can do."

"Thank you, madam."

Montreal, May 10, first light

Lieutenant Eathorpe escorted Tommy to the airfield. Not, she felt, to prevent her from running away, but out of companionship. She reminded herself that she had to think of herself as Thompson, *Alexander* Thompson. And Alexander was a sergeant.

Things had moved fast. They had given Alexander an engineer-blue jacket, to wear under his standard-issue grey greatcoat. Alexander had a backpack that contained a barometer, in addition to his usual kit. But he did not have a rifle or ammunition. That felt wrong.

Alexander climbed aboard the airship. The commander introduced himself as Sergeant-major Horace Osborne. He was dour, of country yeoman stock. He wore a close-trimmed beard. "Your name, sergeant?"

"My name is Thompson. But everybody calls me Tommy." He had to think of himself as Tommy.

"The fighting Tommy?" Osborne gave a series of orders. The ground crew cast off their mooring lines and the airship rose into the air. The wind up here was cold. The engine speeded up, making talking difficult.

"South-south west a half west, helmsman," Osborne said.

"South-south west a half west it is," the helmsman said.

Osborne turned. "You can go down to your cabin if you want. Nice and warm. Read a book."

"No, thank you." Tommy was queasy. "I'm surprised they let sergeants command these things. I thought that was restricted to officers."

"They wouldn't allow it in peacetime. They offered me a commission, but I refused to take it."

"Ah. I see." Tommy guessed that Osborne had a low opinion of officers. He understood that mentality.

Osborne was prepared to talk with a fellow sergeant. "We're carrying supplies for the Abenaki. Tins of stew and packs of desiccated vegetables. And despatches. Written in code."

"Code? Yes, I heard about that." Grace Abenaki had been writing those despatches for months.

"When we land, I won't be able to linger. You'll have to be sharp about it."

Tommy, looking down, was appalled at the mountain forest they were flying over. Most of the trees were still covered in snow. "I couldn't understand how the scouts could hide from the Yankees for so long. But, seeing that wilderness, it makes sense."

"Yes. They tell me that homesteaders cut roads to their farms, but then they give up. The roads are soon overgrown."

"I see. When do we cross the frontier?"

"We already have." An hour went by.

The lookout spotted a mark on the hillside. This was two letters, 'V-R', trampled into the grass.

"That tells us they're confident that there are no Yankees within five miles," Osborne said. "Bring us into wind, helmsman."

The airship turned in its ponderous fashion. Osborne gave a couple of orders and the airship began to descend. The propellers were now pushing the airship down, not forward. The engineer opened the throttle. The noise was terrible.

As they neared the ground, the reception committee ran forward. Most wore scruffy red sack-jackets.

When the gondola was a foot above the ground, Tommy scrambled down. "Careful, there," Osborne said.

An airman handed down the kitbag with its delicate contents. "Thanks."

The infantry leader was Sergeant Thomas Francis. There was also a man in blue – the unit's Talker. Tommy guessed that most of the men were Abenaki or Mohawk. Most were wearing standard-issue greatcoats and hand-made woollen hats that covered their ears.

They were scruffy, but undeniably soldiers. Tommy guessed that these airship visits kept the unit from disintegrating.

The airship crew unloaded the food. These were mainly tins of stew and packets of vegetables. A few packets of tea were added on top.

Sergeant Francis explained to Osborne that he wanted the airship to take an injured man back. He handed over a heavy envelope containing his report. Tommy assumed that it was written in Abenaki - the code they used. "It includes an explanation of the man's injury."

Osborne had an envelope of his own. "Right. And here's your new orders."

In just a few minutes, the task was finished and the airship rose into the sky. Tommy watched as it turned north.

"Let's go," Francis said. "If the Yankees send a search party, I want to be somewhere else."

"Of course, sergeant."

Francis explained that they would not make any attempt to attack the railroad. "Not this time. They told us that you and your mission were too important."

"My task is important," Tommy said.

"The Yankees are searching for us, but I'm sure that we can avoid them." Francis sounded confident.

Lake Ontario, Brant's Ford, May 10

Sergeant Chard made another visit to Colonel Hendrick of the Mohawk army. At the station, he rented a spring cart. His cargo was delicate.

That little suburban house still served as the colonel's

army headquarters.

He found that the pioneers from the Coloured Corps were laying a cable. They had dug a shallow trench the length of the street. Halfway down the street was a handcart with a loop of cable on it. The pioneers were unwinding the cable from the cart and laying it in the trench. As the handcart moved forward, a squad of Hendrick's militiamen shovelled the dirt over the cable and trampled it down. The local residents stood watching.

Chard walked up to the sergeant of pioneers. "Good afternoon, sergeant. You should have waited until I arrived."

The sergeant waved a hand to indicate the onlookers. "These good people said the sooner we started, the sooner we'd finish. So the lieutenant told us to start at once."

Chard glanced down at the cable. "The army will want their cable back when the war's over."

"Yes. But we could set up in business after the war - setting up telegraph links."

Chard grinned. "Sounds good. I'll connect the end of the cable to these instruments."

One of the prosperous local residents walked over. "Are you setting up as a rival to the Telegraph Company?"

Chard risked a joke. "I can't take on them *and* the Yankees, sir."

The man was amused. "True, true."

Chard told some of Hendrick's men to unload his instruments from the hired cart and carry them into the house.

The maid in the pinafore opened the door and led him into the parlour. He found that the colonel and the major were waiting. "Good morning, sir."

The men accompanying him placed the three single-needle telegraph instruments on the table. Chard thanked them.

"The men can take them down to the basement later," the colonel said. "Our traditional houses don't have basements, so my mother refused to use it."

"How did it go, sir?"

"Well – the telegraph company in Brant's Ford refuses to keep somebody on standby waiting for our signals. Not unless we pay them," Major Theyanoguin said.

Chard had experience of the Telegraph Company. "You could offer to supply your own operators to receive the warnings."

"No. The company would not allow our people on their premises."

"Ah. So you decided to bring the wires here."

"Yes. But – we cannot find enough men," Peter said.

"Really? It is that bad, sir?"

"The fighting men think that scholarship is – womanly. They refuse to do anything that is *only* writing. The men who are both warriors and scholars want to be leaders, not clerks -."

The maid in the pinafore brought in a pot of coffee.

"Thank you, miss." Chard was convinced that this household was run by a woman with a strong personality. These maids would not be so demure in an all-male household.

"And if those recruits are stuck here, safe at home -."

"I don't understand, sir. I thought the government had set up schools -."

"Those schools are useless. They're *worse* than useless. So every parent who can afford it sends his children to a private school."

Chard recoiled. He remembered all those stories about Iroquois atrocities. "Well, sir, could you find two woman scholars to work here to receive the signals?"

"Girls?"

"They don't have to be young. They could be widows, so long as they can read and write. Or wives whose husbands are serving in the army. I do not know what your rules are."

"Why two?" Peter said.

"So they can guard each other. Here amongst strangers - men. That is one of our rules."

Montreal, May 10

The train entered the station and slowed to a stop. A porter shouted that this was the evening train from Quebec.

Charles was waiting on the platform with his wife and daughter. He was annoyed. His wife was upset, his daughter was being difficult, the Yankees had crossed the border, and now Lady Forlaith, the Dowager Viscountess Inismore, had come to Canada to see him. Well, not just to see him, admittedly, but he was top of her list.

The train captain helped the dowager step down. She thanked him, looked round, and recognised Charles. She was gaunt. She moved aside to allow her companion to step down beside her.

Charles stepped forward. "Good evening, my lady. I apologise for the presence of my daughter. But she hasn't seen me for months. Now she throws a tantrum whenever I leave her."

"You're spoiling her, Mr. Lloyd."

Charles hid his annoyance. "I have arranged a hotel room for you. I have a hackney carriage here."

"Very well." Behind her, the porter handed down two heavy cases. "We have two items of luggage."

"That's all?"

"Yes, Mr. Lloyd."

Charles realised that the viscountess was used to travelling light too.

Grace Abenaki was nervous. The old dowager, who had come all the way from England, had demanded to see her. Mr. Lloyd had explained that the old lady was an aristocrat. That was what viscountess meant. And her son, the Viscount, was one of the most powerful men in England.

Grace walked into the lobby of the Hotel Versailles. The Army had taken over most of the building as its headquarters. But part of it remained in commercial use and the old lady had hired a couple of the rooms.

She began climbing the grand staircase. Mr. Lloyd had said he could not prevent this interrogation. He and the lady were both in the Guild. He had said that the old lady was annoyed with him, not her, and trying to put it off would make things worse. She knocked on the door.

"Enter!"

Grace entered the room with reluctance. Was the old lady powerful enough to harm Mr. Lloyd?

The lady had a companion. She was young, with dark skin and a serious expression. The two ladies were sitting at a low table. It held an elegant tea service.

The lady was the only female aristocrat in Canada, Mr. Lloyd said. Socially, she outranked the governor, who was only a knight. She was newly arrived from England to carry out an inspection. And the girl at her side was a lady too, a real companion, not a servant.

The lady was old and gaunt, but her back was straight and she held her head high. Grace was suddenly ashamed of her own slouch and straightened up.

"Sit down, child." The lady spoke severely.

"Yes, my lady."

"We were quite shocked when we heard that Mr.

Lloyd was recruiting girls."

"I'm not a child, madam." She was eighteen.

The lady sniffed. "Mr. Lloyd should not have recruited an innocent country girl as a Guild Talker."

Grace was offended at being called an innocent country girl. She felt the need to defend Mr. Lloyd. "He needed a Talker who understood Abenaki. And – the airship was due to leave in a couple of days. He was in a hurry."

"That sounds familiar, madam," the young companion said.

The lady changed tack. "Are you well-treated? Is Mr. Lloyd polite? Are the army officers?"

Grace could guess what the old lady was hinting at. "Yes, madam. I have a room of my own. In a respectable apartment building. Mr. Lloyd selected it. He said it would be quite improper for him to visit me there. Because, if he did, everyone would assume the worst."

"So he has a care for your reputation, does he? And the army officers? Other ranks?"

Grace stroked her blue jacket. "I'm on the payroll. I have official duties. Everyone understands that, and respects it." She smiled. "Oh, yes. I enjoy my work here."

The old lady stopped being condescending. "Tea, Miss Grace?"

"Thank you, madam." She tried to be equally polite.

The companion poured out the tea into three delicate cups. "Is it stressful Talking to soldiers? On the battlefield?"

"They only Talk at a bivouac. They're in the mountains. I am determined to do my duty."

The viscountess snorted. "Duty!" She looked up. "What's that noise? It isn't thunder."

Grace was surprised. "Didn't anyone tell you, madam? It's the Yankee siege guns. They're trying to knock a hole in the earthen embankment. That's on the far bank. And the pioneers try to fill the gap in again."

"You're very blasé about it, young woman."

Grace shrugged. "It's been going on for months. It's not as bad as it was."

"Do you have any children?" the viscountess said.

Grace was irritated. How dared the old woman ask that? "I am not married, madam. My mother sent me to a convent. I hated it. I went home. But -."

"Why did you leave your home?"

Grace was annoyed at this impertinence. "There was a famine. Not enough food for the little ones. I thought, if I left, there would be more food for the others. I hoped to make my fortune."

The viscountess snorted. "I've seen enough of famine. And you ended up in a kitchen, earning a pittance."

"The cook would have given me more, but I asked her to teach me instead. I preferred learning and books to ... dresses and things. But -."

"Yes?"

"When I came here, Charles – Mr. Lloyd - gave me a new dress. And this jacket. Was I right to accept?"

"Interesting question," the viscountess said. "Did he offer it as a gift from him, or from your superior in the Guild?"

"He said it was a uniform, not my property at all."

"Devious of him." The viscountess seemed to approve.

"But what uniform is that?" the companion asked.

"The signals company of the Royal Engineers. It doesn't have any rank-badges, of course." Grace summoned her courage. "Should I get lessons in elocution? Would it help me here?"

The viscountess considered the question. "You could, but - no. You don't need any lessons. Where did you learn English?"

"I went to a convent school. They taught me French and a little English."

The lady's companion smiled. "Some unkind people might say that your accent is better than Lady Forlaith's."

Grace was astonished. "Why would anyone say that?"

The old lady's smile had little humour in it. "Because I have an Irish accent, child. It would be a bad idea for you to mimic my accent. You might need lessons in deportment, but no elocution."

"Oh, yes. Deportment." Grace was not enthusiastic. But if the old lady said it was necessary ...

The young companion was puzzled. "Why does it matter so much? I don't suppose your father was a king or a war leader or anything?"

She smiled. "No. The men in my family were all peaceable ... my grandmother was a magistrate. Is that the right word?"

"A magistrate?"

"Among the Abenaki, men are regarded as hot-blooded. War-leaders. Women are calmer. Older women, that is. They make better judges. My grandmother tried to arbitrate a peace, with ... But it didn't work."

Montreal, May 11

Lady Forlaith, the viscountess, asked Charles Lloyd to join her in the hotel foyer. It was voiced as a polite request, but he knew that he could not refuse.

When he walked into the foyer, carrying his child in his arms, he found that Lady Forlaith had taken over a quiet corner for herself. As always, her mulatto companion sat beside her.

He walked over. "I apologise, my lady. I will have to postpone the interview. My child refused to leave me."

"The child deserves a thrashing."

Charles shook his head. "A punishment cannot be justified unless the child knows shy she's being punished."

Lady Forlaith turned to the child. "Well, child?"

The child turned to stare at the old woman, but merely blinked.

Lady Forlaith sighed. "Come here, child."

Charles was surprised. But his daughter was already holding out her arms. He handed her across.

He expected an outburst, but his daughter squirmed round so she could look at him. Charles was indignant. These two females had just conspired to embarrass him.

"I suppose you're angry with your wife for giving you a daughter?"

He was annoyed. His daughter understood everything that was said in her hearing. And she remembered everything that was said about her. He did not want her remembering the old lady's comments.

"Not at all, madam."

"What can she do with her life, except marry? Sixteen years from now, you'll have to find a husband for her."

His daughter's stare was expressionless. But he was not deceived. "I hope she'll study at Bedford Square college."

"That place is ambitious. But it has problems."

"I'm sure they will be sorted out by the time my daughter is ready to go there."

"You may sit down, Mr. Lloyd," Lady Forlaith said. "Let us begin."

"Thank you, madam." Charles was worried. Lady Forlaith outranked him socially. She was acting on behalf of the chatelaine in London. He knew that he would have to treat her with tact. And he *had* bent the rules by recruiting women.

"I am most unhappy about your conduct, young man."

"Yes, madam. But Miss Grace is a natural Talker. She

hears voices inside her head. That distressed her. I taught her how to shut the voices out."

Lady Forlaith was not impressed. "You could have done that without recruiting her, young man. That lady needs a companion."

"So she is a lady?"

"She conducts herself like one. Do you realise that she has been given an officer's responsibilities? And operating that Babbage Engine! You should never have allowed it."

He was embarrassed. "I didn't plan it that way. I took her on as a Talker. She simply took on more and more tasks. Her official work is equal to that of a telegraph operator. Quite plebeian."

Lady Forlaith refused to be diverted. "She has been doing more work than you asked."

"Yes, madam."

Lady Forlaith shook her head. "Miss Grace is surrounded by men. She needs a female companion. I trust you to see to it."

"Yes, madam."

Charles retreated to the weather team's office. Miss Grace and Lt. Eathorpe were waiting.

"How did it go, sir?" Eathorpe asked.

"I survived. But Lady Forlaith says that Miss Grace can only stay on if we find a companion for her."

"We're overworked, yes ... But can we justify hiring a female?" Eathorpe said.

Miss Grace was annoyed. "Why do I need a chaperone? Don't you trust my honour?"

"It's not like that," Charles said. "I didn't understand it until my wife explained it to me. A woman's testimony in court is rated as half that of a man."

"Ah." Grace's ill-humour vanished.

"But if she has a companion, and their testimony agrees, they can challenge their attacker."

"The viscountess has a companion too," Eathorpe said.

Chapter 5

New Brunswick, May 11

The passenger airship carried a couple of businessmen and Captain Warwick's team. He was accompanied by one white lieutenant, Harrington, three white sergeants and four black sergeants. Two of the blacks came from the Coloured Corps, two from his Bermudian unit. Sergeant Priddy had been promoted to sergeant-major. Together, they almost filled the passenger quarters on board.

They felt out of place. Mostly it was bureaucrats and businessmen who make the trip. Merchants would travel to the port of Halifax and then onward to Britain. The airship was never used by junior officers or sergeants.

General Trevor-Roper had offered him temporary promotion, on full pay, to captain. This generous treatment made Warwick nervous.

The two civilian passengers gave them the cold shoulder. They began grumbling to each other. "Are things so bad that we have to share this table with enlisted men?"

Sergeant Priddy made his excuses and went out on deck for some fresh air. He looked down and studied the terrain. "Will we be fighting over that?"

"All of New Brunswick's like that, sergeant," the airship commander said.

"Beg pardon, sir." He watched the ground pass by for a few minutes and then went back inside. "It's endless forests down there, sir."

"Yes. Their main crop is logging," Warwick said.

The commander bobbed down into the cabin. "We're

flying over Fredericton, the capital of New Brunswick. We will be descending shortly."

"Thank you, commander," Warwick said.

The commander went back on deck. The airship turned into wind and began its approach.

The two civilian passengers watched as the soldiers packed their kit. They were going on to Halifax.

At the landing field, the soldiers disembarked and walked to the edge of the field. Warwick spotted a lieutenant of the regular army waiting.

"Captain Warwick? I have a carriage here. I am to take you and your second-in-command to the commander's office, sir."

"Very well." A carriage was rare for him. They had limited use in Bermuda.

"There's a wagon for your kit and the sergeants."

Warwick had a word with Sergeant Priddy and then he and Harrington climbed into the carriage.

The carriage rattled over the cobblestones. "We're going to the Garrison District on the riverside," the lieutenant said. "This is Officers' Square. The commander's office is here. The barracks hold two hundred troops."

"Not many, to defend a colony," Harrington said.

"They would be supported by the militia, you see. But we're only prepared for self-defence."

"Yes, I understand," Warwick said.

The carriage stopped and the lieutenant stepped down. "This way, sir."

Warwick descended from the carriage. He was nervous. He should never have volunteered for this.

The lieutenant led the way inside and along a corridor. He knocked on a door and pushed it open. He introduced Warwick and Harrington to the colonel of the regulars.

The colonel stood and shook hands. Warwick realised

that this man was nervous too. "You have experience in commanding coloured troops?"

"Yes, sir. The militia in Bermuda, and now the expeditionary force here."

"I see. We have over two hundred black refugees here. There's a similar number in Nova Scotia, they tell me. The runaways wanted to go on to Montreal. They claim that they want to enlist."

"I see, sir."

"They've been arriving all winter. The authorities in Hamilton couldn't cope so they sent half of them here. They couldn't go further because the St. Lawrence river was frozen. The civil authorities put them in a riverside warehouse.

"These men assumed that if they reached Canada they would be allowed to enlist. Most of them are desperate. Death in battle is the best they can hope for."

"I see, sir." Fanatics, Warwick thought. And the general wanted him to lead them.

"I made a mistake. I told them that I could find jobs for them if they gave up this absurd idea of joining the army. But they refused ...

"Your orders are to invite these black refugees here in New Brunswick to enlist in the army. Personally, I think that, if you're lucky, half of them will take you up on it."

"Yes, sir." A hundred men. That might not be so bad.

"We want you to take as many of these runaways as you can and mount a raid on the nearest town across the border. World's End, they call it. It's heavily defended."

"I see." To Warwick, this sounded like a suicide mission.

"You are to create a lot of noise. Distract the Yankees from their attack on Quebec."

And get a lot of men killed, Warwick thought. But he kept that thought to himself. "Very well, sir."

He went downstairs to the square and looked round.

He found that his sergeants had caught up with him.

"I put your kit in the officers' quarters, sir. They've allocated you a room. Do you want to go there first, sir?"

"No. There's no point in delaying this. Follow me."

He led the way to the riverside. Most cargo arrived in Fredericton by river, so there were extensive docks. The black detainees had been sent to an empty warehouse.

A high brick wall separated the compound from the street. There was only one sentry at the door. He saluted. "The blacks don't give us any trouble. Except that they refuse to leave town, sir."

Warwick suspected that the governor would be pleased if the blacks *did* run away. He opened the door and led his companions into the compound. The runaways were sitting down around the walls, listless.

The office building was on the far side. As he and his sergeants walked across the compound the runaways barely looked up. They seemed to be apathetic.

"More redcoats," one man muttered.

Then they noticed that four of his sergeants were coloured. Warwick could hear their comments. "They're black. The ones with him."

"The sergeants, they're black. They're soldiers."

The men got to their feet. A few stepped forward. Suddenly, they had hope. Warwick was embarrassed.

He reached the warehouse office. There were two steps up to the doorway.

He squared his shoulders and stepped up. Those two steps became his podium. The blacks had gathered round. He turned to face them. They were waiting, expectant, hopeful.

"Listen! I have been sent here to invite you to join the British army. I have the authority to recruit any of you who wish to join up."

"Yes, sir, we accept," a man at the front said. "That's why we came."

Several men at the front took a step forward. There was a commotion as men further back moved forward too. Warwick realised, with surprise, that they had all accepted.

"Very well." What should he do next? Perhaps some of them were unfit. He decided to improvise a medical inspection.

He told Sergeant Priddy to lead them on a run around the compound. "That'll sort them out."

"They all look fit to me, sir. Army rations all winter."

"Yes."

The men were puzzled by the request, but eager enough. Warwick was not surprised when most of the volunteers passed the simple medical test.

Warwick was appalled by this. He did not have the authority to command such a large force.

Eight men dropped out during the tests. They lacked the stamina. "The poor fellows are heartbroken, sir," Priddy said.

"We need a couple of medical orderlies. Have any of them any experience? Are they prepared to learn? And I need a servant."

"I think they came north to escape that sort of thing, sir."

"They would be soldiers ... wear red coats. Their duties would be different, that's all."

"I'll ask them, sir."

"And my servant would do that on top of his military duties. He'd be paid a bit extra, remember. Not much, of course."

"No, but that gesture would mean a lot. I'll ask, sir."

"And we'll need drummer-boys."

"It was only grown men who came north. An' I'm grateful for that, sir."

"Well, perhaps a couple of these medical drop-outs would be prepared to take it on. It's an important task.

They wouldn't carry muskets, though."

"Dangerous work on the battlefield, sir. I'll ask."

"Good."

Warwick went to his quarters, sat at his desk, and set out a list of his requirements. Uniforms, firearms, other kit. He would have to see the quartermaster. Then there was the paperwork. He sent his sergeants on various tasks.

An hour later, Warwick and his team returned to the compound. Two privates were pushing a heavily-laden handcart. He sought out Sergeant Priddy.

"I had a word with the quartermaster. He found sixty-one full dress jackets, mostly oversize. Eighty-six sack-jackets. They look graceless, but they're more comfortable on a route march. Fifty jerseys, intended for fatigue duty."

"I see, sir."

"It's the best the quartermaster could do at such short notice, he said."

"Yes, sir. But the men would prefer full dress jackets."

"Tell 'em that as soon as I've got things sorted out they'll get one of each."

The sergeants set up a desk in the compound and told the volunteers to form in line. He had a pile of uniforms, red sack-coats rather than full-dress jackets. Next to them were a pile of pay-books.

Sergeant Priddy started. "First man, step forward. Name? Surname?"

"Harry. Don't want second name. One good enough for me."

"In the army, you must have a surname. Your mother's name? Or the name of your old master?"

"No, sir. I don't want *his* name."

Warwick decided to help out. "May I suggest Freeman?"

Harry smiled. "I like the sound of that, sir."

Priddy sighed and filled out the pay-book.

Some of the men already had surnames. The next time a man said he had none, Warwick suggested Newman.

The next man said that he did not have a surname but that he came from Wycombe county. "That's good enough for me."

"Wycombe it is, then," Priddy said.

The task took them all afternoon. They ran out of pay-books. Warwick had to arrange a work detail to fold a hundred sheets of card to make some more.

Fredericton, evening

Late in the day, the sergeants divided up the recruits into platoons. They started drill.

Wycombe found himself in the platoon of one of the white sergeants, Benjamin.

For an hour, each platoon was drilled individually. Then the platoons joined together and sergeant-major Priddy took over. He was tougher on them than the white sergeant had been.

Then one volunteer referred to Sergeant-major Priddy as "Sir."

The sergeant glared. "You do *not* call me sir!" That is because 'sir' is an epithet reserved for *officers*. And I am *not* an officer, I am a *sergeant*. Got that?"

Wycombe recognised his cue. "Yes, sergeant."

"Louder!" Priddy said.

"Yes, *sergeant*."

"All of you!"

"Yes, sergeant."

"Good. Never forget that."

"You obey the captain and the lieutenant because they're your officers, an' they've got the rank tabs to prove it. You salute officers from other regiments, but you don't have to obey their orders. Well, you can if you have a moment to spare." Priddy smiled. "And I'm going to make sure you never have a moment to spare."

Priddy's next lesson was how to salute. "You salute officers from any regiment, but only if they're properly dressed -."

"Sergeant ... does that mean we'd have to salute US Army officers too?"

"Yes. If you ever meet a Yankee officer, you should salute him too. You salute the rank, not the person. But - you don't have to salute on the battlefield."

For Wycombe, the rules were bewildering. Priddy emphasised that they should not salute an officer who was not properly dressed. "Because he can't return your salute, and that would embarrass him. So if he isn't wearing his hat, don't salute. So it isn't simple at all. You've got to think about it."

Montreal, May 12

Lt. Daniel Eathorpe walked across Montreal to visit a female cousin. It was a long way, but the weather was fair and he needed the exercise.

The lady was older than him, and matronly. When he walked in he found that she was sitting in an armchair, sewing a dress. Her daughter, Branwen, sat at her side. She was sewing one of those absurd winter hats, and had the air of a prisoner set an unpleasant chore. She had been a bit of a tomboy when she was younger. Daniel wondered whether she had outgrown that. He hoped not.

His cousin invited him to sit down and asked whether he would like some tea.

"Thank you, madam." He sat back in the chair.

"I hope that your wound does not trouble you, Daniel," his cousin said.

The stump of his left arm twinged. He wished that people would not keep reminding him of that. "Not at all, madam. I am still in the army, you understand, working in the Signals Corps. We're overworked. One member of the team writes letters in Abenaki for the airships to take to Indian soldiers behind enemy lines."

Branwen let her work fall into her lap. "I read about that. I thought it was very clever."

"The person doing that is a girl. Did the newspapers say that? But she's overworked. She needs help." Both women looked puzzled.

"And, and, a girl working alone -."

His cousin went off in a whoop of laughter. "You want my Branwen to be a chaperone?"

Branwen tried to ignore this mockery and retain her dignity.

Eathorpe sympathised with her. "I wondered whether you could join the team, miss, and take on some of Miss Grace's work."

"It sounds fascinating," Branwen said.

"I warn you, the work is repetitive and it requires great care. But a mistake could get men killed. Are you up to it?"

"It would be better than this," Branwen said. She held up her needlework.

Adirondacks, May 13

The scouting party led Tommy west for two days. They had thought of putting Tommy in an Iroquois village. But if the US Army had found her, they would have punished the villagers.

Finally, they reached the Yankee millionaire's Great Camp. To Tommy, it looked like an extra-large log cabin, stuck in the wilderness. All of the windows had been boarded up.

"I don't know why they built it here, so far from any town. They had to build their own road, miles of it," Sergeant Frances said.

All of the trees around the cabin had been cut down. The grass was almost waist-high. "And when the war started, they just abandoned it."

"In England, they would call it a Folly. He did it to show how wealthy he was," Tommy said.

"This meadow isn't natural," Frances said. "Give it a couple of years and saplings will begin to grow. But the war will be over by then."

Most of the team remained in the shelter of the woods. They said that open ground was dangerous. Only Francis and his Talker accompanied Tommy to the building. They walked in single file to minimise the track through the grass.

Francis was relieved when they reached the shelter of the porch. "I hate being out in the open." He picked the lock on the kitchen door.

"The owner abandoned it when the war started. My men regard this place as a trap. There's open ground all round it, you see. They're eager to leave. But one person alone might escape detection."

The place was empty, echoing. The rooms were dark because of the shuttered windows. "Makes you think of ghosts," the Talker said.

"But no-one has ever lived here," Tommy said.

Tommy thought it was luxurious. She moved in.

New Brunswick, May 14

Smith was a sergeant in the New Brunswick Fourth Black militia company. Family tradition had it that an ancestor had fought with the British in the American

Revolutionary War and had then fled north when the Yankees won.

Another ancestor had served in the militia in the crisis of '38. The community of blacks had grown in size as runaways had fled north from the States.

Now there was another crisis and he knew what he had to do. He explained the situation to his wife. She did not like his decision but she understood his reasons.

So he said his farewells and trudged the five miles to Fredericton. He was surprised to find fifteen men gathered in Officers' Square. They were all black. Then he realised that most were from the militia.

"What are you lot doing here?"

One man grinned. "Why, the same as you, sergeant."

He grunted. "I figured it wasn't right, staying behind while those refugees went off to fight."

"Yeah, me too."

He found himself nominated as spokesman. He went indoors and explained his request to the white desk sergeant. The sergeant must have realised he was out of his depth, because he called for the officer of the day.

Smith went back outside to wait.

The headquarters building had three broad steps up to the door. Fifteen minutes later, a young British officer appeared in the doorway. Judging by his expression, he knew he was out of his depth too. "Go home. This is a civil disturbance."

"We want to fight, sir. To defend her majesty's domains." Smith had despised those pompous phrases in the past. He quite enjoyed using them now. "You can't call us deserters. We want to fight."

A man at the back jeered. "What you gonna do, sir? Call out the militia?"

Smith was angry at this interruption. He half-turned. "Silence in the ranks, there."

The officer accepted defeat and sent a messenger to

the governor's mansion.

The crowd settled down to wait. As time went by, their numbers grew. In ones and twos, they trickled in to volunteer. All of them were surprised to find that so many other blacks had made the same decision.

Just before noon, one of the governor's aides arrived. He wore a fancy staff-officer's uniform with a cocked hat. He stood at the top of the steps and looked them over. "I'd like to hang the lot of you for mutiny."

"You can't do that, sir," Smith said. "Right now, the colony needs every fighting man it's got."

"We need you to stay here and defend the frontier. And your homes."

Smith chose his words carefully. "All my life, men have said that blacks can't fight. Now you're asking these untrained refugees to fight. If we stay behind, everyone will sneer at us. And – I'll be wondering whether they're right."

The aide glared at them. Then he gave up and went back to the governor's mansion.

Once again, they settled down to wait. Some of them thought they had won and thanked Smith for his fine words. He was less confident.

A few more men joined them. Smith noticed that less than half of them were militiamen. But all of them were determined to prove themselves. He guessed that there were almost a hundred black men in the square.

A couple of hours later, the governor's aide returned. He climbed to the top step and looked them over. Smith guessed that the young man was angry. He began to hope.

"Pay attention! Firstly, the governor is prepared to consider your request. However, there is a warning. Once you cross the border into the United States, different laws apply. Any black who is taken prisoner is likely to be taken south and sold."

A man at the back spoke up. "That's not true, sir. Any slave who takes up arms against his master will be struck down. That's the US law, that is. If they get their hands on us, they'll hang us."

"Just so long as you know all that," the aide said. "One last thing. If you decide to go back to your homes, the governor will forget what happened today. This colony needs every fighting man we've got."

Smith shook his head. He spoke for them all. "It's too late for that, sir. If we back down now, we'll be wondering whether we're truly fighting men."

"Very well. The governor will have a word with the commander of this unit."

Fredericton, May 14, Evening

Captain Warwick went to the headquarters building and asked for an interview with the colonel of the regular army unit. A captain was not supposed to do that sort of thing, but for once he did not care. He was harassed.

"There were two hundred men in that courtyard, sir, and every last one of them signed up. All two hundred of them. The sergeants have been putting them through the mill but none of them has quit.

"That number is way beyond my authority, sir. I ask for a superior officer to be put in command. I'm only a captain. Promoted a week ago."

The colonel was annoyed. He placed his hands palm-down on the desk. "I cannot produce experienced officers just like that. None are available."

"Surely - ."

"The news is worse than you thought, captain. We have a couple of hundred black labourers in this area. They arrived over the years and found themselves jobs.

But they've heard the news and a hundred have come forward. If you're recruiting, they want to join."

Warwick felt a moment's hope. "Do they have experienced officers, sir? Captains?" Perhaps one of those captains was senior to himself.

"None of their officers has come forward, captain. They have experienced sergeants, though."

"But - that makes three hundred, altogether." He was shocked. "But that's the task for a major. And several experienced captains."

"You will have to cope."

"But -."

"Don't worry too much. In the first battle, you'll lose half your men. Many will just run away. After that, your unit will be a reasonable size."

"That is no comfort to me, sir. I need time to train them."

"Well, yes. If you had more time, you could turn them into a useful team. But your orders are to cause a diversion, now, before the Yankees reach Quebec."

"But how can we equip that many? Can we even feed them?"

The colonel smiled. "Yes, of course. We can do that. We have a supply depot here."

"I see, sir."

"Have you given any thought about your target? There's Fort Kent, up north. A key Yankee stronghold."

Warwick shook his head. "It would take too long to get there. And I'd need a thousand men to have any hope of success. No, I'll just advance across the frontier. The place has no military value, but I can get there soon."

"Very well, captain."

Quebec May 16

The troop of Upper Canada Volunteer cavalry rode along the farm track. They were alert, looking for the enemy.

The rain fell steadily. They were soaked through. They and their horses were miserable.

But there was no infantry nearby. There were neat fields on both sides of the road, so an ambush was impossible. A marksman, hiding in the woods, could take out one man before he was ridden down. Everyone was tense. But no shot came.

Lieutenant Roberts was suspicious. Where were they? Over the last few days, his patrol had skirmished with enemy infantry patrols. Now they had vanished.

"Perhaps they're sheltering from the rain," his sergeant said.

"Bah. They're probably doing something clever while we're wasting our time here."

Then, in the distance, they noticed a team of Yankee soldiers in a field. They were clustered round an object. Roberts pulled out his telescope. They were trying to push an object along. "It's a cannon."

"Are they bait for a trap?" his sergeant asked.

Roberts gave this serious thought. These days, he could not take a step without weighing up the odds first. "No. They wouldn't use a cannon as bait. Too valuable. The woods are too far away for an ambush. Let's go."

He was concerned that the ground was very soft from all the rain. They might cripple their horses. He would have to trust the skill of his men.

As they galloped forward, the artillerymen saw them coming. They turned and ran.

"I want prisoners!" Roberts shouted. His men obeyed, ignoring the fastest runners and rounding up the three slowest.

They turned back to the cannon and found that it was stuck in a shallow stream. It was mired to the axles.

Roberts dismounted and walked forward. The cannon was surrounded by the tracks of the men and horses who had tried to pull the gun free. He could see that both men and horses had slipped. What had happened to the horses? Maimed? Or merely sent to safety?

He turned back to his colleagues. The captured artillerymen were sullen but prepared to talk. One explained that the retreating British had blown the bridge. "So we were forced to use the old ford."

"Where are the other cannon?"

The man spat. "We don't have to say. You can't make us. Rules of war."

"Can we pull it out?" the Volunteer sergeant asked.

"Where they failed? No." He decided that they would have to leave it there. They could not move it until the rain stopped and the ground dried out. "Getting these prisoners back to the colonel is more important."

Colonel Green had taken a farmhouse as his headquarters. Early in the campaign, the advancing Yankees had forced him to move every day. But then the rain began, the advance had slowed, and he had been stuck here for three days.

The farmer was a French-speaker and did not like the English. Green would have been glad of an excuse to leave, but the Yankee advance seemed to have stalled.

He went out onto the porch. The rain showed no sign of easing up. Perhaps the Yankees were bogged down. He would have liked to go for a ride, despite the rain. But his men needed to know where to find him. If the Yankees attacked, they would need direction. Unfortunately, couriers from the general also knew where to find him.

He saw a group of men tramping along the road

towards him. He was annoyed. Why were so many men neglecting their duties? Then he realised that three of the men were wearing blue.

He stepped back so that the men could get onto the porch and out of the rain. Lieutenant Roberts was enthusiastic. In civilian life he had run a tailor's shop or something boring. But he had turned into an enterprising officer.

"We found these artillerymen, sir. Ten men. Their cannon was trapped in the mud - mired to the axles. We ambushed them. No casualties ourselves. We took these prisoners. Five of them ran off. We let them go. I thought that bringing these men in for questioning was more important than chasing down the fugitives."

"Yes, lieutenant." He realised that the notion that they were capturing Yankees, rather than the other way round, would give his men a tremendous boost. The Yankees were professional soldiers, while his men were volunteers, given only a few days' training before the war started.

He looked at the prisoners. They were soaked through, dispirited. "We don't want these men dying of consumption. Dry them off. Give them clean shirts. Put their jackets in the farmhouse laundry to dry."

The Yankee corporal was surly. "I hear you've recruited Indians. Mohawks. You going to torture us?"

"No. Where did you get that idea?"

Roberts smiled. "They've read too many of those despicable instalment novels, sir."

"And they believed what they read? Shocking."

The prisoners were led off. Green thought for a moment of threatening to torture them, then smiled. He turned to his orderly. "Tea and biscuits for five, please."

Half an hour later, the prisoners were led into the dining room. They had been given fatigue trousers and white knitted guernseys. Green and Roberts stared at them across the table.

Green was worried. The British were losing this battle. These prisoners might provide vital information. And this would be his only chance.

The Yankee corporal stared at the biscuits in disbelief. "This all you got to eat? You're worse off than us."

Green smiled. "No, this is just a civilised afternoon snack. Dinner is much bigger." He wondered whether the Yankees were on short rations. That was more useful than the names of regiments. "Do you take tea?"

"I'd prefer something stronger. Sir."

Green considered getting these men roaring drunk and then squeezing information out of them. He decided he would only try it if all else failed. "I'm surprised. I thought the US Army had better supplies than us, better logistics."

The corporal held his cup in both hands, as if he was using it to warm him up. "We haven't got no railroad. We tried to advance west, but your highlanders blocked us. So our general thought it a good idea to advance due north, over the White Mountains."

"Yes. It worked in the revolutionary war."

"Back then, we had hundreds of men. Now we have thousands. Can't feed them. When we marched out, each of us was given ten days' rations ..."

"Hard rations?" Green tried to sound sympathetic. He was sure there was more to this story.

"Yes. We were told we would reach Quebec before we ran out. Then we'd have your rations. Instead, our supplies have to come over the White Mountains. There's no railroad that way, not even a decent wagon-road."

"I see." Green tried to hide how pleased he was at this news. As the British retreated, their supply problems decreased. But every mile that the Yankees advanced took them further from the railhead. He took a sip at his tea.

The corporal copied the gesture. "They said we could live off the land. Requisition stores." The corporal's tone was bitter.

"I see." Green said. He knew that the Yankee foragers were now hated by the French-Canadian farmers.

"And the number of desertions is growing."

Green was surprised. He had expected low morale and desertions amongst his own men. But the Yankees seemed to be suffering worse.

A courier had brought him a summons to headquarters. It was a symbol of British defeat that he could travel from the front line to headquarters in a couple of hours. In the past, he would have been flattered by such an invitation. Now he felt that he had more important things to do.

The four officers stood in the lounge, holding their pre-dinner drinks. General Sir Reginald Trevor-Roper was polite, which was flattering. The French-Canadian militia colonel standing next to him listened carefully and said little.

Lord Cardigan, the famous cavalry commander, was part of the group too. But today he was being awkward.

He sneered at Green's colonial volunteers. "I've heard that you've taken to wearing fatigues on the battlefield. Your men no longer wear their hussar uniforms. Saving them for a victory parade?"

Green was stung by this criticism. "If the Yankees keep making mistakes, perhaps there *will* be a victory parade."

The infantry colonel was surprised. "But they outnumber us. How can we possibly stop them?"

"They've run out of food," Green said.

"A good cavalry charge will stop them," Cardigan said.

Green was annoyed. "Well, true, but you can't charge

properly in this mud."

The infantry colonel looked alarmed at this deliberate provocation.

Green realised that he disapproved of Cardigan's policy. He no longer trusted the aristocrat's advice.

"Our task is to delay the enemy. We're doing it. The enemy aimed to reach the St. Lawrence and take Quebec. So far, they have failed."

Lord Cardigan merely sulked.

The mess steward murmured something to Sir Reginald, who announced that dinner was ready. As they walked into the dining room, Sir Reginald had a word in private with Green. "Your regiment is doing a better job than Cardigan's. Keep it up."

"Better?"

"You seem to suffer fewer desertions. And you lose fewer men to disease. Always a good sign."

"All of my men were wealthy enough to buy their own horses, sir. They would make terrible peacetime soldiers."

"You keep out the plebeians, eh?"

Green thought of Lt. Roberts. Did a tailor count as plebeian? "My men come from all walks of life, sir. They're used to making decisions, adapting to new problems. But in this situation ..."

"Well, whatever your secret is, keep it up."

Quebec May 16, After dark

A detail of men from the pioneers had been sent to salvage the barrel from the stranded Yankee cannon. The rain had stopped but the field was still muddy. A company of Highlanders in skirmishing order provided cover for them.

The Yankees guessed they were up to something and

began shooting at them. But in the dark they missed consistently.

The pioneers rigged a portable crane over the stranded cannon. The sergeant checked that everything was ready. They hauled on the ropes. "Steady, there." The barrel lifted a couple of inches.

But the feet of the crane began to sink into the mud. The pioneer sergeant was worried. Would his crane sink faster than they could lift the gun? "Pull it across."

The second team hauled on their rope and pulled the barrel sideways, over the sledge. "Lower it. Gently, now."

The first team paid out the rope hand over hand and slowly lowered the barrel onto the sledge.

The sledge creaked under the strain but did not break. But it began to sink into the mud.

The sergeant felt close to panic. "Pull! Before it sinks too deep."

The infantry officer shouted. "Leave the crane. Let it drop. Everyone pull the sledge."

The men grabbed the ropes and the sledge began to move across the mud. "Keep going, keep going!"

The Yankees, alerted by the noise, intensified their musket-fire.

The highlanders shot back, trying to upset the Yankees, but the sergeant thought they were wasting ammunition.

The pioneers dragged the sledge and its cargo free of the soft mud. One man fell and then another.

The pioneers kept going until they were out of range of the Yankee musket-fire. The officer told the infantry skirmishers to retreat.

The pioneer sergeant was upset. "That crane was worth more than this iron barrel, sir."

"Not in military terms, sergeant."

New Brunswick, Fredericton, May 17

Warwick's sergeants were putting the black volunteers through their basic training. Sergeant Priddy reported that they were making good progress. "Eager to learn, sir."

Warwick, encouraged, paid a visit to the major and asked whether his men could be given firearms. The major agreed and sent him to the Quartermaster, a plump, cheerful man.

"You're lucky, captain. The regulars have just switched to rifles. We've still got stocks of the 0.75 inch Pattern 1842 smooth-bore musket. Two hundred of them. And I found fifty Minnie rifles. And fifty British 0.702 inch rifles."

Warwick was dismayed. "Three different calibres?"

"I'm afraid so, captain."

He realised there were not enough firearms for everyone. A hundred men would have to make do with pikes. They would hate that.

The men were summoned, thirty of them at a time, and were given their muskets and their ammunition.

The sergeants showed them how to load their weapons and how to fix bayonets. Each man spent a few minutes practising.

"Not good enough. Let's try that again." Sergeant Priddy smiled. "You have to be able to do this in the dark."

He showed them how to make straw bales, then how to use their bayonets. The men enjoyed attacking the objects. But the straw bales did not last very long.

On the fifth day, they formed up in squads and marched out of the town to the shooting range. Sergeant Priddy tried to teach the first squad a marching song, but the attempt was a failure.

They were shown how to load their firearms. They were allowed to fire five shots each. Giving each man more would have taken too long.

They also practised dry firing, but the men soon learned the routine and hated it.

Montreal, Fort Longueuil, May 17

The defenders in Fort Longueuil had been given advance warning by men in the mountains. The New York railroad had been busy for days as the Yankees brought up more ammunition.

Now the Yankees launched their attack. Three battalions of men in blue followed their flags across the barren ground.

Lt. White, in the East Bastion, despaired. His long-range artillery fired again and again. But the Yankees kept on coming. And they were heading straight for his position.

Then the Yankee artillery fired a shell over the heads of their own men. It was a risky stratagem, but on this occasion it worked perfectly. The shell scored a direct hit on the earthen embankment, north of White's position, and blew a gap in it. The men defending that stretch of wall were blown aside.

The Yankee gunners caused damage to the embankment regularly, of course, but in the past the pioneers had been able to repair the gap.

White knew that repairs would not be possible this time. The attackers were drawn to the gap like iron filings to a magnet.

The attackers were now rushing past his position, not towards him. His gave orders for his main cannon to be trained round until it was facing sideways at the attackers. His men loaded their piece and fired again.

But nothing seemed to deter the attackers.

The Yankees reached the gap and climbed through. One man was carrying the regiment's flag. The survivors among the defending infantry rushed to stop the attackers. White could not see clearly but he guessed that the defenders were pushed aside.

The alleyways inside the fort were narrow. White's fear was that Yankees would advance along those alleyways towards his position. Instead, a group of redcoats, pushed aside by the attackers, retreated towards the bastion. Their insignia showed they were a company of Iroquois militia. Their rearguard kept reloading and firing back at their attackers.

The action was now far too close for White's liking. His own men were suffering casualties. But they stuck to their guns.

The infantry lieutenant shouted in his ear. "We had no intention of standing up and being targets. We'll take cover and try and protect your guns."

White had a notion that the infantry had been ordered to stand and fight to the last man. But he was not going to mention that now. "Yes. Good."

But the Yankees ignored the guns in the bastion. With singe-minded determination, they headed towards the centre of the fort.

"The Bastion should have had a wall on both sides," the infantry lieutenant shouted.

"Yes."

The interior of the fort was a warren of alleyways. By intent, the alleyways did not go straight, so the impact of a bursting shell would be stopped at the first corner. Those winding alleyways now provided protection for the defenders.

White relaxed slightly. The Yankee artillery had fallen silent. For the moment, no-one was shooting at them.

"But keep your heads down. The biggest danger now

is stray shots. I don't want to lose you to a British bullet."

His sergeant made his report. "We're running low on black powder, sir."

"Then we'll have to spend it wisely, sergeant."

Peeping between the crenellations, out over the approaches to the fort, White could see the Yankee second wave approaching.

The infantry lieutenant joined him. "Why so slow?"

"They're carrying portable boats. To get across the river."

"They're that confident? Can you fire at them as they pass by?"

"That'll attract their attention."

"That won't matter if they get across the river."

"True." He pointed out the attackers to the sergeant and told his men to load with canister. He depressed the cannon as low as it could go. He waited for the best moment.

"Stand clear." He pulled the lanyard and the cannon roared out. He risked took another look. The boat-carrying crew vanished. "Reload! Before they can reach shelter."

The Yankee infantry within the fort responded by subjecting them to a hail of musket-fire.

"Steady, there," the infantry lieutenant told his men. He turned to White. "Will they give up now they can't get across?"

"They'll just send more boats."

Montreal, May 17

Grace was sitting at the telegraph operator's desk. This particular instrument was connected to the underwater cable that led to the fort. The artillery bombardment had continued all morning. She had heard enough stories from men who had served at the fort to imagine what was going on.

Now the bombardment ceased. Had the defenders won? Or were the Yankees preparing to cross the river? But the telegraph needle did not move. Sergeant Chard was on duty at the other end. She knew him well and liked him.

She could bear the suspense no longer. She reached for the dedicated 'Fort' telegraph instrument that sent messages by underwater cable to Fort Longueuil. She tapped out a message. 'Are you all right?'

The reply came back promptly. 'Do not obstruct the wire with unnecessary signals. Report to follow.'

Somehow, she got the impression that he was irritated rather than afraid. She smiled and went to make some tea.

Grace did not particularly like British black tea. Her own people made better herbal infusions. But it was better than nothing. She took the mug back to her desk and resumed her seat.

"You can stop for tea at a time like this?"

Grace jumped with surprise. She turned to see her accuser. She was terrified. Colonel Dalhousie, CMG, responsible for the defence of Montreal, was breathing down her neck.

He was tall, plump, with brown hair and mutton-chop whiskers. Grace was more afraid of him than she was of the Yankee guns.

"What's a girl doing in military headquarters, eh?"

She noticed Lieutenant Eathorpe, standing at the colonel's shoulder. He looked as terrified as Grace felt. But he found the courage to come to her defence.

"She normally just sends weather reports, sir. Civilian work. Not military at all." That was not true, but just now Grace was not tempted to contradict him.

"Are no male telegraphists available? Proper soldiers?" Dalhousie growled.

"All of them are at the other desks, calling for reinforcements, sir." The lieutenant spoke in an undertone. "I could send the message if you wish, colonel."

"An officer to do a menial task while the enlisted men can see you? Don't be a fool." He raised his voice. "What's happening over there, girl? Ask."

"Yes, sir."

Grace tapped out her message. 'The colonel wants to know what's happening over there.'

The telegraph needle flicked in reply. 'You've got the colonel there? I'm glad I'm over here. I'm caught in a crossfire. Bullets coming at me from all directions.'

Grace reported the last part of this to the colonel. "The telegraph equipment has its own bombproof, sir."

"Crossfire, eh? What's the intensity of the fire? Ask him."

Grace dutifully sent this query and reported the reply. "He says about one a minute, sir."

"Bah. And he's hiding in a bombproof? Ask him to look outside. Find out how close the Yankees are."

"Sir -." Lieutenant Eathorpe was agitated. "Colonel, he's the only telegraphist we've got over there. If he pokes his head outside and gets a bullet through it, we won't get any reports at all."

The colonel glowered. He was reluctant to admit that Eathorpe was right.

"We could ask him to report if the situation changes, sir," Lieutenant Eathorpe said.

Grace turned to face them. "We could ask him to send a report every five minutes, just to let us know he's alive. If the messages stop coming ..." She was quite fond of the sergeant.

"Very well. Do that," Dalhousie said.

That afternoon, a train arrived at Montreal docks carrying six companies of the Sixty-Second regiment. George Eastman's platoon was among them.

He and the other officers were summoned to a briefing at Hotel Versailles. They sat round a table while a steward handed out cups of tea. It all seemed unreal.

Colonel Dalhousie spoke with uncharacteristic bluntness. "The Yankees haven't reached the riverbank, but it's chaotic in there. The telegraph operator says the Yankees haven't reached him, but he can't tell us much else."

Everyone nodded. All of them had spent a tour of duty in the fort. They could hear the gunfire across the river.

"We don't have enough boats to get all your men across at once," Dalhousie said.

Lt. Colonel Grimwood, commander of the Sixty-Second, turned to George. "Captain, I would like you to go in first. I want to know whether it's safe to send the whole battalion across. Try and reach the telegraph operator and send a message back."

There was only one answer that George could give. "Yes, sir." He thought of the practical difficulties. "If I lead my men into that warren, no-one will recognise me. I'm likely to be shot by mistake. I need a recognition symbol." He clicked his fingers. "I need a piper."

"What?" Colonel Dalhousie was indignant.

"The Yankees don't have pipers, sir. So our men will know I'm with them."

The room fell silent. "I'll ask Colonel MacGregor," Lt. Colonel Grimwood said.

"Very well," Dalhousie said.

So George and his Abenaki marched down to the river-bank and climbed into three rowing boats. George had a piper beside him.

The rowers were pioneers from the Coloured Corps.

"Just tell your men to sit still, sir, and let us do the clever stuff," the black sergeant said.

George was happy to comply. "Very well, sergeant."

The boat reached the landing stage on the far bank and George climbed ashore. He was met by panicked men from a militia regiment.

"Thank God you're here, sir. The whole fort has fallen to the Yankees. Take us back. There's no point in anyone staying."

"Are there any wounded here?" George said. "Put them in the boats, then." He turned to the pioneer sergeant. "Tell the colonel that I got across and that the bank is safe."

"Yes, sir."

"Let's go, piper," George said.

"What tune, sir?" the piper asked.

"Bonnie Dundee." It was the only marching tune that he knew.

He detailed ten of his men to lead the way. He followed, with the piper and his remaining men behind him. The defenders, crouching in the doors of their bombproofs, told him to stop – it was too dangerous.

The piper ignored them. He kept on marching.

A sniper fired at them. Everyone ducked, sheltering behind the bombproofs, except for the piper, who kept on playing.

George wanted the piper to get out of the way. "Piper, "I want you to retreat fifty yards, then turn around and come back."

The man did not reply. Still playing, he performed a neat about-turn and marched down the hill.

George turned to the militiamen. "I need a marksman."

One of the militiamen came forward. "Yes, sir."

George peeped up and spotted the sniper. "There," he said, and pointed him out to the marksman.

The marksman popped up, saw the sniper, and fired. The sniper vanished. George did not know whether the man had been hit, but at least he kept quiet.

They continued their advance, hunched over, with the piper playing. Occasionally they were shot at and George would point out the sniper's position to one of his marksmen. A growing number of the fort's defenders were following behind George's platoon.

The survivors would say afterwards that Captain Eastman strolled up the road like an unconcerned gentleman in Hyde Park. But in truth, he spent most of his time poking his head up like a gopher, a most ungainly posture.

More and more of the fort's defenders joined him him. A couple more marksmen volunteered to help. Somehow, the piper escaped injury.

Grace watched the dial of the needle instrument. She was concerned about Captain Eastman. And Colonel Dalhousie had returned and was breathing down her neck once more.

"What's a girl doing in military headquarters, eh?" He seemed to enjoy asking that question. "What's the world coming to?"

His orderly brought him a huge mug of tea. "It's hot, sir."

"Thanks." He turned back to Grace. "Are no male telegraphists available? Proper soldiers?"

The other clerks did not look up from their instruments. For a moment, the only sound was the clacking of telegraph keys. Someone coughed.

Grace found the courage to answer him. "All of them are at the other desks, calling for reinforcements, sir."

"Enough of that. How is Eastman going, girl? Ask, damn it, girl."

She reached for the telegraph key and sent an urgent

message. She had never expected to do that. 'Rush rush rush. Can you hear the piper?' For a moment, the needle remained motionless.

Then the answer came back, click-click-click. 'Who would be playing the pipes here?'

So the wire was not cut. She hid a sigh of relief. 'Captain Eastman.'

'He can't play the pipes.'

'He has his own piper.'

There was no reply. Grace was about to send a reminder. Then the needle clicked. 'Yes I can hear them.'

She turned to the colonel. "Captain Eastman hasn't reached the telegraphist, sir. But they can hear the piper."

"Good man. Wasn't that fellow breveted captain? I must confirm it."

"Yes, sir."

George's platoon reached the bombproof shelter that held the telegraph equipment. Everybody was stooped over, because of the snipers.

He told the piper to stop playing. "Take cover in one of these bombproofs. Perhaps they can get you some coffee."

"I would prefer a drop of the hard stuff, sir."

"I can't allow that." George had learned that a simple word of praise meant a lot to these men. "But I won't say you don't deserve it, piper."

"Thank you, sir."

He ducked into the bombproof. "Hello, Chard."

The sergeant looked up. "Good afternoon, sir."

"Tell the colonel that I've arrived. Send 'The section of the fort between the telegraph bombproof and the shore are clear. Please send reinforcements. Eastman'."

"Right, sir."

"Do you know what's going on?"

Chard was busy at his telegraph key. He did not look up. "That's for the officers to say, sir."

"You're the only man I've met who still has his wits about him, Chard."

"Well – the Yankees hold most of the eastern half of the fort. And the north, I think. You can still hear gunfire from the East and South Bastions, so they can't have taken those."

He thought this over. Judging by what he had seen and heard, Chard was right. "Where's Colonel Wallace?"

"They say that his bombproof took a direct hit. But I didn't go to look."

"Right. Send a new message. 'My estimate is that the East and South Bastions are still holding out. Eastman'."

He watched as the telegraph needle in its glass dial flicked in reply. "What's it saying?"

Chard wrote down the message on his pad as calmly as if he was in Montreal. "It said, 'Go and take a look. Dalhousie'."

George decided to try and reach the South Bastion. He summoned the piper and advanced a bit further through the maze. He knew that three alleyways led in the general direction of the south bastion.

He pushed forward and found that the direct route was blocked by the Yankees. He backed off and tried another route. But that was blocked too. So he withdrew again.

But the western approach, closest to the river, might still be open. He found a man to lead the way through the warren of alleyways. His men were hampered by sniper-fire all the way.

He turned one corner after another. This section of the alleyway was only wide enough for three men. He turned another corner and was met by a three-man reception committee. The two men on each side had bayonets fixed but they were wearing red jackets. The lieutenant, standing between them, smiled. He belonged to a French-Canadian militia regiment.

"We thought it might be the Yankees attacking. But the Yankees can't make a noise like that."

"That's why I brought him. Are you the defenders of the bastion?" Have I reached it?"

"Yes. And, yes, you are now in the bastion." The lieutenant turned and led him to the heart of the bastion.

One bombproof, larger than the rest, served as the company headquarters. George found the fort's second-in-command, Major Farquhar, sheltering there.

The major's face was lined. "Lieutenant-Colonel Wallace is dead, captain. I thought it best to stay in the South Bastion, conserve our strength, and hold out until help arrived."

"I see, sir." George thought this lacking in initiative at best. He tried to keep his voice neutral.

"The Yankees hold the eastern half of the fort, captain. Although we stopped them advancing any further. I think they're waiting for reinforcements before advancing further."

"I see, sir."

"I'm glad you've brought reinforcements, captain."

George had no intention of staying cooped up here. "I have strict instructions from Colonel Dalhousie to send reports back to him. I must return to the telegraph operator."

Farquhar bit his lip. "The colonel? I see."

George retreated along the alleyways until he got back to the telegraphist's bombproof. He was still pestered by snipers. He ducked under the low doorway. "Hello, Chard."

The sergeant looked up. "Glad to see you back, sir."

"Tell the colonel that we still hold half the fort. We've

stopped the Yankees for the time being. If we can get reinforcements across the river before dark, we may be able to push the Yankees out."

"Yes, sir." Chard reached for his telegraph key. "Colonel Grimwood says he's already ferried one company across."

Then the Yankee artillery opened up again. Everyone dived for cover.

George was astonished. "Do you know what that means?"

Chard looked up. "They must have assumed their attack has failed. They're softening us up for another attempt."

"Yes, yes. But don't you see? They can't send reinforcements while that's going on. And their men here are trapped."

"Yes, sir. But, even if we push them out, this time, they'll attack again." Chard was bleak.

New Brunswick May 18

Captain Warwick gathered the sergeants together and told them that there was no hope of getting any more officers. "I will take Company 'A'. I want each of the sergeants to take direct control of fifty men."

They hated the idea. They would have to play the role of junior officers. They went away, grumbling.

An hour later, one of the sergeants, a white from Upper Canada, called at his room. "Beg pardon, sir, but I'd like a private interview."

"Come in, then. Yes, sergeant?"

The sergeant held his hat in his hands. "I think the runaways are crazy, sir. The blacks. I feel they're out to get me."

"Get you?" Warwick wanted to say that the man was a

fool. "Well, they are a bit crazy. But they came here to enlist."

"They escaped so they could kill Yankees, sir. Whites. And we're training them how to kill. I ask to be sent back to Montreal, sir." The man was terrified.

Warwick thought the man's fears were baseless, but he knew that he could not persuade the man. "I can't let you walk away. "But I can make you quartermaster."

"Very well, sir," the sergeant said. "I've spotted several troublemakers. And they say that clever troublemakers are potential leaders. The army copes with troublemakers by giving them authority."

"Yes, I've heard that too." Warwick was sour.

New Brunswick, May 19

The volunteers were told to pack their kit. Fifty men at a time, they formed up in the road and marched down to the railroad station.

With a great deal of confusion and shouting by their sergeants, the men were put into boxcars. The train was fully loaded a last and pulled out of the town, taking the line west towards the frontier.

Most of this territory was forest, so there was not much to look at. Warwick had been told, several times, that logging was the main industry.

"The Maine logging companies tried to grab our land in '38," the militia sergeant said. "The governor sent the state militia up to the frontier. We glared at each other for a few weeks, but they backed down. We stopped them."

They reached the frontier town of Victoria. Across the frontier, barely visible, was the small town known as World's End.

Warwick told the men of his company that they would

attack the strong-point in the morning.

"Canada is under attack. Our task is to create a diversion. We must force the Yankees to send reinforcements here. The town is heavily defended by regular troops. They are veterans of the Mexican war. Heavy casualties are likely."

Warwick assumed they would resent this, but they took it calmly.

"One important order is that we must *not* cut the telegraph wire. We want them to call for reinforcements."

That evening, the militia sergeant led the officers and senior sergeants forward and showed them the lie of the land.

The man was overweight. "The frontier itself isn't defended. The main road leads straight up to the town. An alternative is to advance along the lanes on either side. There's one there, sir. Do you see it? There's a couple of farm gates to your left. But you ignore those. Take the first lane on the left."

Warwick was impressed. This plump sergeant had been scouting. "Isn't there a fort? A blockhouse?"

"They built a barracks in the crisis of '38, but after the peace treaty was signed they abandoned it."

"So there's no blockhouse?"

"They didn't think it was worth the trouble."

"I see."

"They built a series of barricades, but they aren't much, not really. The local people are annoyed, sir. If the US Army hadn't arrived, their town wouldn't be a military target."

"Yes, I understand," Warwick said.

The man grinned. "In the last war, 1812, the New Brunswick government sent the militia three barrels of gunpowder. The militiamen gave it to the Maine militia for their Fourth of July celebrations."

Warwick was shocked. "What happened?"

The militia sergeant was puzzled. "Happened? Oh. The townsfolk used it for their Fourth of July celebrations. What else?"

Warwick smiled. "Oh. That's all right then."

Sergeant Priddy was disgusted. "That's not the way we do it in Bermuda."

"Hush, sergeant."

Warwick asked the militia sergeant to draw a map. Then he told his own sergeants to study it. "I want to attack at dawn. So we'll have to walk there in the dark. Memorise the route you will take. Don't just study it. Make your own copy."

World's End, May 20

Wycombe had been allocated to a small team, led by one of the white sergeants, Benjamin. The sergeant led them to a barn and told them that they could sleep until just before dawn.

He had not expected to get any sleep. So he was surprised when the sergeant shook him awake at first light. "No noise, now."

They were each given a ration of hard tack but most of them could not eat it. There was very little talking. They had assumed the volunteers had been given this task because casualties would be high.

Wycombe shrugged this notion off. That was what they had come for.

Sergeant Benjamin explained that the plan was to attack the target from several directions at once. Their target was a barricade, reached by a minor road from the north-west. Benjamin described this as the least significant point. They had the furthest to go so they started out first.

They crossed the border, marked only by a wooden sign, and walked along the lane. The moon was partially obscured by cloud. Sergeant Benjamin stopped. "It's too dark for me to read my map. But I reckon I know it by heart anyway." They reached a side-road and turned left.

Benjamin was worried that the sentry might sound the alarm. But there was none.

They approached the town as quietly as possible. To Wycombe, their boots sounded noisy on the path. All they could see were trees and fences. Wycombe wondered whether they had taken the wrong turning. But he dared not ask.

No. They saw the first houses, white, ghostly in the dark. They were made of wood, with a cladding surface, surrounded by neat gardens. The sergeant ignored them. Then they saw the barricade, set up between two brick buildings. There was no sign of the defenders.

Wycombe strained to make out more detail, but the barricade was in the shadow of the buildings on either side.

They halted. Wycombe could smell tobacco. So somebody was awake.

Wycombe was close to Benjamin. He whispered. "Should we wait for the others to attack first?"

"They said we had furthest to go. Perhaps they're waiting for us."

This was not what Wycombe had expected. He had imagined a huge battle, attacking thousands of enemies, perhaps with him carrying a flag.

"Come on," Sergeant Benjamin said. They ran forward.

Then one of the defenders shouted in alarm. "Who's that out there?"

The first volunteer reached the barricade and started to climb. He reached the top of the barricade. "Freedom!"

A shot rang out, loud in the quiet. The man was hit, and fell back.

Wycombe was shocked. Then he thought, he's free at last.

One of the defenders popped his head up for a look. A volunteer behind Wycombe fired his musket. The shot went wild but the man ducked down.

Benjamin shouted to the others. "Move to the side - out of the line of fire." He began climbing up. "Follow me."

Wycombe began climbing, his musket in his right hand. He thought Benjamin would be shot too but the sergeant reached the top, aimed and fired at a defender.

Then Benjamin was shot. He cried out, slipped and fell back.

Wycombe pulled himself up. "Go, go!"

He reached the top, grabbing the timbers with his left hand. He expected to be shot too. He realised he was carrying his musket at the point of balance. His hand was too far from the trigger.

The two defenders turned and looked at him. One was re-loading his rifle. A third man was lying on the ground.

The second defender shot at Wycombe. But he missed. He yelled and ran away.

Wycombe jumped down. Another man followed. He could hear others climbing up. The third Yankee held up his hands. "I surrender."

Wycombe realised there were no other defenders. That was it.

He and the others were surprised. They were not dead after all.

Wycombe went looking for Sergeant Benjamin. He had a superficial flesh wound. But he had broken his leg when he fell. "Leave me here. You must carry on. Help the captain."

Wycombe straightened up. "Right."

He led the other men into the town. They moved at a jog. It was dark, there were no lights, and the street surface was in shadow. The streets were empty. What should he do?

They heard a shot. "It's not over yet." He told himself there was still a chance for him to die a hero.

They ran forward, down the narrow street. They reached a crossroads. A man came round the corner and turned up the street, straight towards him. He did not have time to dodge and they collided. Wycombe fell on his backside. He realised the other man was wearing a uniform.

"Grab him! Take his rifle." Three of the volunteers grabbed the enemy soldier and his rifle.

"Thanks. Two of you - take him back to the sergeant." He climbed to his feet.

They ran towards the shooting. This road was far wider, with three- and four-storey brick buildings on either side. They could see another barricade. It was heavily defended, but they had a longer line to defend. Ten men were shooting or reloading. Three men were lying on the ground.

Wycombe did not hesitate. "Go, go." He and his men charged. They took the Yankees in the rear.

The Yankee sergeant turned towards them and cried alarm. One of Wycombe's men shot him and he fell.

The remaining defenders turned to face the new enemy. Two raised their weapons and were shot down. The remainder realised they were outnumbered.

Two of Captain Warwick's men climbed over the barricade and jumped down.

The Yankees surrendered. "Where did you come from?"

"Yeah, why'd you come *here*?"

But the Yankee soldiers in their billets were running

into the street. Wycombe turned to face them. He was afraid his men would be outnumbered.

The leading Yankee looked at Wycombe and stopped. He was not angry. He spoke as an adult to a child. "Put down that musket, boy. Everyone knows Negroes don't fight." He had an Alabama accent.

Wycombe was angry. He raised his musket.

"Put that down before you hurt -."

Wycombe achieved complete surprise. The soldier was so smug, so certain in his prejudices, that he did not realise Wycombe's intentions until it was too late. The musket-stock hit him on the side of his head and he toppled.

"Who's next?" Wycombe snarled. He swung his musket at the next enemy. He missed. But his colleagues stepped up beside him. Together, they used their muskets as clubs. They advanced down the road, swinging their muskets. One of their opponents fell, then another.

The Yankees stepped back. One of them brought his rifle up to his shoulder and pulled the trigger. Wycombe did not know where the shot went.

Behind him, Captain Warwick's men climbed the barricade. More of the black volunteers were joining the fight.

Wycombe could hear shooting on the other side of town. He had no idea who it was.

More Yankee soldiers were leaving their billets and running into the street. But they were still half asleep and did not know the nature of their enemy. Their leaders were missing.

More and more black soldiers climbed the barricade and joined in. The defenders realised they were outnumbered. They were forced back to the crossroads.

The third team, Lieutenant Harrington's, arrived,

taking the Yankees in the rear. "Drop your weapons," Harrington said. "Stand against that wall."

Sullenly, the Yankees obeyed. Then Sergeant Priddy led his own men to the crossroads. "We've captured the Yankee commander, sir."

The wretched man had been taken in his nightshirt. The man next to Wycombe whispered. "An officer? Do we salute him?"

"Nah. He isn't properly dressed."

"Well done, sergeant," Captain Warwick said. The volunteers realised there was nobody left to fight. They had won.

The Yankee commander whined. "Why did you come here? This place isn't worth fighting over. Your sergeant wouldn't let me get my clothes. Can you fetch my clothes?"

Captain Warwick was flustered. "Send somebody to go and fetch the captain's clothes, Sergeant Priddy."

"Yes, sir." The sergeant and his platoon hurried away.

Captain Warwick was baffled. "We need to help the wounded. Are any of you any good at nursing?" He turned to the prisoners. "Do any of you know where the doctor lives?"

One of the prisoners raised a hand. Captain Warwick sent him off, accompanied by one of his own men, to summon the doctor.

Sergeant Priddy came back with the Yankee officer's orderly, who was burdened with a pile of clothes. The sergeant carried the officer's sword as well. "Present for you, sir."

Captain Warwick did not look grateful. "What do I need a sword for?"

He turned to Lieutenant Harrington. "I've just realised. We weren't supposed to do this. We've won. We were supposed to let him send a telegram calling for help ..."

"You could send a message for him, sir," Harrington said.

The captain looked blank. "What do you mean?"

"Well ... 'We are surrounded. We are outnumbered ten to one. We will fight to the last. When the wire goes silent, assume the worst. Long live the republic.' Something like that."

Captain Warwick glared. "What sort of garbage do you read, lieutenant?"

"Sorry sir."

"You could sign it yourself, sir," Sergeant Priddy said. "What about 'We are coming. Today, World's End, tomorrow Washington?'"

The captain merely glared. The sergeant wilted.

Wycombe coughed. "Beg pardon, sir, but I've heard that if you send a telegram, all of the operators along the line can hear it. So if you send a message east ..."

"Is that true, Harrington?" the captain asked.

"Even if it isn't, sir, the telegraph operator won't sit on his hands," Harrington said. "As soon as your back's turned, he'll call for help."

"Right, I'll do that," the captain said. "I shall have to send a report to the colonel."

Harrington nodded. "This place has a telegraph office, sir."

"I'll need an escort, sergeant. Ten men."

Wycombe thought the task sounded interesting, so he straightened up. Priddy must have noticed. "You to start with. And ..." he nominated nine more.

The captain led the way down the street. Wycombe and the others trailed after him.

Then, out of the hearing of Priddy, the captain stopped. "Where will I find the telegraph office?"

Wycombe tried to be tactful. "In these small towns, it's usually in the station building, sir."

"Ah. I know where that is. Come on." They walked

down the hill to the railroad.

The man behind Wycombe spoke in an undertone. "He doesn't know how to find the telegraph office?"

"Shut up, you fool." Wycombe looked up, but the captain did not seem to have heard. "He's from Bermuda. Small island. Doesn't need a telegraph. I think they mainly send messages by boat."

The station was a dainty single-storey wooden building. Wycombe thought the telegraph office might be shut at this hour, but a light showed inside. The captain climbed the steps and pushed open the door. Wycombe and the others followed.

A grille separated the telegraph operator from customers. Wycombe knew enough about telegraph offices to guess the contents. To the left of the table was the battery box, which supplied local power for the station. On the table were the telegraph register, for recording incoming signals, a cut-off switch for disconnecting the line during storms, and the telegraph key for sending messages.

He realised that the telegraph operator sitting behind the grille was female. She had red hair, held in place by a neat lace cap. She sat back, frightened by the arrival of so many men. "All that shooting - so that was you, was it?"

Wycombe felt like apologising.

"Yes, madam." Captain Warwick was courteous.

"What are you going to do now, sir?"

"Well - it's over now. I sent for the doctor ... They put a woman on duty here? At night?"

"That's quite usual in country offices. I always get the early-morning shift. The men hate it."

"I see," the captain said. "I want you to send a message to army HQ in Fredericton, New Brunswick."

She followed the normal routine and reached for a receipt slip. "That will be five dollars, sir. Payment in advance."

"Five dollars?"

"Yes, sir. It's an international message."

The captain was outraged. "Government messages are free of charge. Don't you know that?"

"I know the rule-book, sir." She refused to be intimidated. "I cannot send messages without payment."

"Now look here. I am acting as representative of the government. I can send official messages free of charge."

She shook her head. "You do not represent the US government."

The captain grabbed the message pad and wrote out a message. "Have taken control of World's End. Eighty prisoners taken. Minimal casualties. Request instructions, Captain Warwick, commanding black volunteers.

"Send that. To army HQ in New Brunswick."

"No. I can't."

Wycombe noticed that she had stopped calling the captain 'sir'. He was alarmed at the intensity of the dispute. He tried southern charm. "We're just doing our duty, ma'am. Just as you are. May I know your name, ma'am?"

The girl seemed to welcome this interruption. "Miss Montgomery."

"Well, Miss Montgomery, I would pay in coins if I had any."

She stared at him as if the statement was a trap. "You haven't got any money?"

"I've got a couple of British coins. I didn't think I'd need any US money where I was going, ma'am."

"Ah," the captain said. "This gives me an idea. Have you any writing paper. Miss Montgomery? And carbon paper?"

This mundane request seems to calm her. She found a writing-pad and pushed it towards him.

"Thank you, miss." The captain took a pencil and started writing. "This is a requisition chit. If you or your company presents this to a bank in New Brunswick, the government will honour it. My name, rank, regiment and signature."

She read the note through. "A promissory note? Yes, sir, I can accept that."

Wycombe coughed. May I suggest, sir, that the note should be for several messages, not just one?"

"Yes, good idea," the captain said. He amended the document and pushed it across the counter to Miss Montgomery.

She turned to her telegraph key and started sending the captain's message.

Captain Warwick led the way back to the town square.

The wounded were being tended to. Stretcher-bearers were taking the worst of the wounded to hospital. Some of the townsfolk had gathered to stare.

Sergeant Priddy reported to the captain. "I've collected the Yankees' weapons, sir." He sounded pleased. "The M1842 smooth-bore 0.69 inch Springfield. Not as good as Enfield manufacture, of course, but better than nothing. Eighty of them."

"Another calibre, sergeant?"

"I'm afraid so, sir."

An hour later, one of the male telegraph operators walked up. He was carrying a standard telegraph company envelope. "Message for Captain Warwick. Is that you, sir? It's the reply from Fredericton, captain."

Warwick opened the envelope.

To Captain Warwick, World's End. There must be more Yankees out there. Put a guard on the prisoners and lead a reconnaissance of the remainder of your men westwards. O/C, Fredericton."

Warwick paid a visit to Sergeant Benjamin, in the town hospital. The man was lying on a bed in a quiet corner of the ward. His leg had been put into splints.

He looked up. "Good afternoon, sir."

Warwick sat in a ladder-back chair. "Good afternoon, sergeant." He continued in an undertone. "I need to know. Did one of your men shoot you? Because they hate whites?"

The sergeant laughed, then winced. "No, sir. It was a Yankee who shot me, fair and square. Then I fell. It was the fall that put me in here. They're good boys. Make good soldiers some day."

"I see."

"The one they hate is Sergeant Priddy. When he says. 'If I can do it, you can do it', they know it's true because he was a slave himself once."

"I see. Thank you."

"That boy Wycombe might make a good non-com, sir."

"I'll bear it in mind, sergeant."

Chapter 6

Maine, May 21

Captain Warwick had received clear orders that his unit was to advance. He passed the word to the sergeants to get the men up early. His sergeants were competent, but the men were disorganised and it was almost two hours before they had cooked their breakfast and were ready to march.

Warwick tried to hide his frustration. His sergeants were doing their best in a difficult situation.

The two volunteer medical orderlies were given a buggy to ride. They objected, saying they could walk.

Sergeant Priddy told them the buggy was for the men who dropped out. "And, believe me, they will."

Warwick ensured that his orderly was given a place in the buggy too.

The men were ready to march at last. Warwick followed immediately behind the leading group, which he placed under Sergeant Priddy's eye.

For all of that day, they marched along the country road. The experienced sergeants tried to teach the men a marching song, but all they could achieve was a chant of *'left – right – left – right'*.

There was dense forest on each side of the road. Mile after mile of it. The farmsteads were so far apart that each was treated as a landmark and named on the map as worthy of comment.

At first, they expected to encounter opposition. The men were tense. But they met no soldiers at all.

The civilians that they met were surprised to see a large body of men on this road. They offered no resistance. Each time, Warwick stopped to question them, but they said there were no troops nearby. The nearest militia unit, they said, was in Fort Kent.

There were many delays. Several men fell out, ill. Some had forgotten to drink from their canteens. They all had to be cared for. The two medics found they were far more useful than they had expected.

The sergeants expected the men to march at a regular pace and were frequently angry at their malingering.

It took them most of the day to cover ten miles. Late in the afternoon, they reached the edge of a small town, Marshville.

Warwick told the men to halt in a field. "Lieutenant Harrington, I'm leaving you in charge. I intended to find the telegraph office and send a report to the colonel."

"You mustn't go alone, sir."

"No, of course, not." He looked round. "Wycombe. You and your men can accompany me."

"Yes, sir."

They found the telegraph office easily enough. The operator this time was male. He gaped at the intruders, but offered no objections to sending a message.

"Yes, sir, they explained about your promissory note."

"Good." Warwick wrote a message to be sent to New Brunswick.

"To O/C, Fredericton. Have reached Marshville. No US forces between here and next town. Captain Warwick, CO expeditionary force."

The men marched into the town and bunked down in the railway freight shed. When the men were preparing their evening meal, Warwick called his sergeants together. They were all exhausted.

"We're going to have to lie to the men. I'm going to tell them that now they've seen combat, we know we can trust some of them with a bit of authority."

Sergeant Priddy nodded. "Most of them arrived too late to see any fighting. But it has to be done."

One of the white sergeants grimaced. "My best prospect got himself killed."

"I did say it was a lie, sergeant. But we need more NCOs. I can name a few likely prospects. Can you nominate anyone?"

"I've had my eye on a few," Sergeant Priddy said.

Warwick received a list of twenty men. That evening, he summoned each of the men in turn, praised their performance, and offered them temporary promotion to sergeant.

One of the men who accepted was Wycombe.

Wycombe sat on his bedroll, sewing his new stripes onto his jacket.

Freeman was angry. "Have we got to call you 'massah' now?"

Wycombe was concentrating on his task. "Sure. You can call me anything you like."

Another soldier had been lying on his blanket, face up. Now he rolled onto his side, facing Wycombe. He was grinning. "No, you can't do that. Remember what Sergeant Priddy said?"

Wycombe was confused, "No, what?"

"Don't you remember?" He tried to mimic Priddy. "You do *not* call me sir, because 'sir' is an epithet reserved for officers. And I am *not* an officer, I am a *sergeant*."

Wycombe grinned. "I remember that. Well, there you go, Freeman. If you call me 'sir' or 'massah', Sergeant Priddy is going to jump on you."

Freeman grinned. "I'll be careful."

Maine, May 22

Early in the morning, the men assembled in the station yard. The sergeants were eager to get the men ready sooner than they had the day before.

The preparations were interrupted when the telegraphist walked across the yard. He was carrying a sheet of paper. "Captain Warwick?"

"Yes, that's me."

"I've received a telegram from New Brunswick, for Captain Warwick."

Warwick read the message. The colonel in Fredericton had ordered a train to pick up the infantry. The colonel was sending a telegraph operator with mobile equipment. Warwick was ordered to advance as far as he could.

Warwick dismissed the telegraphist and told his senior sergeants that there was no rush. "We'll be travelling by train. And get the new sergeants to pass the word on to the men."

The train arrived an hour later. Immediately behind the locomotive were two passenger carriages, with boxcars behind. The sergeants told the men to climb into the boxcars.

Warwick walked along to have a word with the locomotive engineer. "This mission could be dangerous."

The man leaned down from his cab. "Yes, sir. They told me. I'm in the militia, sir."

"Well, I want you to stop just short of the next town down the line. And if we run into trouble, I want you to put this thing into reverse and get us out of there."

The engineer looked back at the volunteers milling round in the yard. "I thought these blacks were death or glory boys."

Warwick smiled. "They're fussy. They want to die on

the field of battle, not in a trap. So if things go wrong, get us out of it."

"Right you are, sir."

Sergeant Priddy told Wycombe to get his men into the first boxcar. Wycombe passed the order on. "You heard him. Get your kit into the boxcar, then climb in yourselves."

"They said we would march twenty miles a day," one man said.

"You complaining?" Wycombe said. "If you ask politely, perhaps Priddy will let you walk."

"Funny."

Warwick checked that all of his men were on board, waved to the engineer, and climbed into the leading carriage. The train got under way.

A mile outside the next town, Duckpond, they stopped. Captain Warwick ordered fifty men to de-train and scout north and south of the line.

The telegraphist climbed up a telegraph pole with his portable telegraph key and sent a report back to Fredericton.

Warwick explained to the sergeants that the signal for the scouts to withdraw was three blasts of the locomotive's steam whistle.

Sergeant Priddy was ordered to take twenty men as a scouting party towards the town. He chose Wycombe as his subordinate, with his ten-man squad.

Wycombe guessed that the town was undefended. "This is a waste of time."

"Orders are orders," Priddy said.

They passed a couple of wooden houses, set back from the road, with plots of vegetables. Once again, the local people were astonished to see soldiers marching by.

They came across a farmer working in his garden patch between the road and his house.

When he saw them coming, he stopped his work and leaned on his spade. Wycombe realised that their arrival was the most interesting thing that had happened all week.

Priddy stopped. "Good morning, sir. Are there any US Army troops here?"

"No," the farmer said. "I know who you are. You're blacks from the South. I saw some in a minstrel show once."

A private behind Wycombe snarled. "We are not minstrels."

The farmer smiled. "No, of course not. But blacks, in red coats, asking where the US army is? That's better than any minstrel show."

Wycombe was annoyed. But he had to admit that the man was right. "Where *is* the US Army, then, sir?"

"Well ... I would say that the nearest regular troops are in Portland."

"So there's no militia here, sir? The town is undefended?"

"The militia are defending those precious logging camps on the frontier. Fort Kent. They won't defend the likes of us. And the militia won't move unless the governor himself authorises it."

"Thank you, sir. Where's the way to the telegraph office?" Sergeant Priddy asked.

The farmer pointed along the road to the town. "That's the way."

"Thank you." They walked through the town to the telegraph office. People stopped to stare.

Sergeant Priddy was uncomfortable. "Straighten up. We're soldiers. Act as if you're proud of it."

The telegraph office had a male operator. He tried to look unconcerned as Priddy and Wycombe walked in. "I guessed you'd be here before long."

Priddy stepped up to the counter. "Good morning.

Can you send a telegram to my colleagues? They're listening, a mile down the line."

The man grimaced. "No. I can only send messages to official addresses. But ... if you send a message to an official address every operator will hear you."

"Official address?" Sergeant Priddy was annoyed. "There's New Brunswick. But I don't know the address of the HQ. The captain didn't tell me. Wycombe, do you have any ideas?"

"Let's see," Wycombe said "Can you send a message to the telegraphist in World's End? I believe her name is Miss Montgomery."

The telegraphist was suspicious. "You've met her?"

"Yes, sir. Very nice lady. We had a bit of an argument. She defied the captain. Refused to send a telegram until we paid for it."

The operator smiled. "Good for her."

Wycombe started writing. He read out loud. "To Miss Montgomery. I trust you are well. I hope you were not discommoded by our exchange of words. I have reached Duckpond. The locals say the nearest US troops are in Portland ..."

The telegraphist sat up. "Who told you that, I wonder?"

"Is it true?" Sergeant Priddy asked.

"Well - yeah. The only troops between the frontier and Portland are you lot."

Wycombe added a footnote. 'I am awaiting instructions.'

He showed it to Sergeant Priddy, who nodded. The telegraphist counted the words and began sending the message. He finished and sat back.

"Do you think they got the message?" Wycombe asked.

"Well, somebody's playing the fool down there," the telegraphist said.

They expected the captain's telegraphist to send a message. Instead, the locomotive sounded its whistle.

"He's on his way," Priddy said.

Sergeant Priddy and his little team watched as the train pulled into the station. Captain Warwick climbed down from the carriage. "No problems, sergeant?"

"I felt rather foolish, walking through a peaceful town, sir."

"I see."

"Do you want us to go through that rigmarole at the next town, sir?"

"I think not," Captain Warwick said. He walked forward and explained the change of plan to the locomotive engineer.

The man nodded. "We'll need to stop, to take on water, sir."

"Right."

As they approach the next town, Waukeag, the locomotive began to slow down. Everybody tensed, but nothing happened.

The locomotive engineer continued to the centre of the town and then stopped to take on water. The townsfolk turned out to stare. "This won't take long, sir," the engineer said.

Sergeant Wycombe complained that this was not what he expected war to be like. "I thought there'd be a battlefield, you know, with cannons belching smoke and thousands dead."

"There's going to be a battle soon," Newman said. "Before the day is out. You'll see."

Captain Warwick used the opportunity to call together Lieutenant Harrington and his senior sergeants. "I think we can get all the way to Portland before nightfall. But it will be heavily defended. Should we stop?"

Sergeant Priddy shook his head. "We would look foolish if we turned back now, sir." The others nodded agreement.

"Very well. Our original orders still apply. If we're outnumbered, if we suffer heavy casualties, we retreat."

"All the way to Brunswick?" Lieutenant Harrington said.

"Yes. I don't want to see losses for no good purpose."

The locomotive got under way again and they continued their advance towards Portland.

A couple of hours before nightfall, their line crossed the Trunk Railroad line. Then the train slowed and clattered over a long bridge.

"The Royal River, sir," Sergeant Priddy said.

"Yes. I never expected to be back here so soon," Captain Warwick said.

The men took turns to keep a lookout, standing on the platform of the leading passenger carriage. Wycombe noticed something on the track ahead. He could just make out ten men standing on the track. They had a large white flag.

The locomotive engineer had seen them too and began slowing down. Wycombe made his way back inside the carriage to make his report.

Captain Warwick was worried. "Why are we stopping?"

"Yankees, sir. They're showing a white flag. It's not going to be simple after all."

Warwick was incredulous. "That's absurd. If the Yankee commander surrenders to us, he'll be put on trial."

Wycombe was hurt. "There is a flag there, sir."

"Yes, yes." Warwick sighed. "Go back and tell Sergeant Priddy to get the men ready. I need four men. They must look soldierly. Tell him to be prepared for anything ...

No, I can't tell him that."

Wycombe made his way back to the second carriage. "Sergeant, the captain says you're to get the men ready. And four men who look – soldierly."

"Anything else?"

"He said you're to be prepared for anything. Then he changed his mind."

"Be prepared for anything? No, I can't do that. That's his job," Sergeant Priddy said. "Go and tell him I'll find his four men."

The locomotive had slowed down to a crawl. Wycombe returned to the leading carriage.

He found that Captain Warwick had taken off his jacket and handed it to his black servant for a quick brush-down.

"I don't believe it," Lieutenant Harrington said. "He can't surrender. They'd court-martial him for it."

One of the white sergeants spoke up. "Perhaps him and those ten are all he's got."

Lieutenant Harrington snorted. "Nonsense."

Wycombe felt emboldened to intervene. "Perhaps he was ordered to send his best men north, sir. To take part in an attack, mebbe. And now we've turned up and he's sent a telegram north, saying I told you so. And asking for reinforcements."

Lieutenant Harrington frowned at this interruption, but Captain Warwick nodded. "That's the best reason I've heard. I thought he held all the aces. But perhaps he has four deuces and he's bluffing like crazy."

The train came to a stop. Sergeant Priddy joined them with four men. "These are the smartest, sir."

Wycombe looked the men over. He guessed they had been chosen because they had acquired smart red full-dress jackets and not the comfortable sack-jackets. Their buttons were polished. They carried muskets rather than rifles but they too were clean and polished.

Wycombe decided that if he was feeling unkind, he might almost have called them pretty.

The captain looked them over. "How good is their drill, sergeant?"

"Adequate, sir. They're rotten shots, though."

The captain nodded and turned to the four. "You've got to look smart. That might help us win today."

"Yes, sir," the tallest said

"You've got to be sharp. Wide awake. That officer might pull out a pistol and plug you."

"Beg pardon, he's more likely to plug you, sir."

Wycombe thought this might work after all.

The black servant helped the captain put his jacket back on. Then he fastened the captain's belt and holster. "Belt has to be level, sir."

"Yes. Good."

"Muskets loaded?" Priddy said.

"No. If things go wrong, four loaded muskets won't make a difference."

"Bayonets?"

"Yes. Certainly."

"I'd like to accompany the captain," Sergeant Priddy said.

"No." Captain Warwick was decisive. "I can't risk you or Harrington.

"This is the drill. Sergeant Wycombe climbs down. If no-one shoots him, the four privates climb down and form a line facing the Yankees. Then I will climb down and take my place in front of you. Then we all walk forward."

Lieutenant Harrington was unhappy but he nodded. "Yes, sir."

"Priddy, take thirty men, cover our line of retreat. Harrington, if anything happens to me, your task is to get the men back to Victoria."

Sergeant Priddy was shocked. "What if we're

attacked? Superior numbers? Can't escape?"

"Then fight until you're the last man standing. Perhaps I'd better put that in writing." He turned to Wycombe. "Let's go."

Wycombe climbed down the steps. He stepped clear of the carriage and turned to face the Yankees. A hundred yards down the line, the officer stood at parade rest. The ten soldiers standing behind him remained motionless.

The locomotive engineer glanced back at Wycombe, then turned back to watch the Yankees. The officer and his soldiers continued to ignore Wycombe's existence.

"Come on," he said.

The four privates climbed down. They formed a line. "An arm's length apart, just like the drill," Wycombe said.

He looked back. Men were leaning out of the boxcars, trying to get a glimpse of the action.

Captain Warwick climbed down. He managed to look dignified. He straightened his waist-belt and took his place in front of his men.

"You must act as if you're three-year regulars. But don't watch the officer. Watch the men behind him."

"And behind us, sir?" Wycombe asked.

"You can leave that to Sergeant Priddy."

Captain Warwick, Wycombe and the four men walked forward. The trackbed made this difficult.

The locomotive engineer waved as they passed, but the soldiers ignored him.

Behind them, Priddy was bawling at the men to get out of the boxcars and form a line. Wycombe was comforted by this small piece of normality.

The US Army officer waited in silence. Behind him the ten men of his escort stood, impassive, the butts of their muskets resting on the ground.

"He's a major," Captain Warwick murmured, to himself.

They stopped and Captain Warwick saluted. The major ignored this.

Wycombe was offended. He realised that Captain Warwick was better turned out than the major. One point to our side, he thought.

He murmured, "Squad - ground arms."

The four men carried out the procedure neatly. He was relieved.

The major glared. "So it's true. I didn't believe it. The British army really is recruiting blacks."

Wycombe recognised the accent immediately. Alabama. Perhaps Birmingham County?

"Desperate situations require desperate measures, major." Captain Warwick was bland.

"It's a mistake that you'll regret," the major said.

"I don't suppose you plan to surrender, major?" Captain Warwick said.

"No."

"And I hope you're not going to insult me by asking me to surrender my command?"

"No," the major said. "You have a lot of blacks in Canada, have you?"

Wycombe tensed. Had the Alabamian guessed where they were from?

"Oh, yes." Captain Warwick said.

"And you put them in uniform?"

"Haven't you heard of the Canadian Coloured Corps? No, I suppose not. A lot of coloured men and women have fled north since that Pursuit Act was pushed through Congress. They fled from free states, you know."

Wycombe realised that Captain Warwick had implied that his men had fled from New York.

"It seems that any southerner can claim that any coloured man is a runaway …"

"What of it?" the major said.

"The only evidence that is required is that a southern

gentleman makes a statement. So some of these southerners perjure themselves and a poor free black man is dragged off south -."

The major was angry. "You impugn the honour of southern gentlemen, sir."

Captain Warwick ignored this. "So it's not surprising that some cautious free blacks have fled across the border. Then, of course, they join the militia. In peace-time, they were laughed at. Why do all that musket drill when war is never going to happen?

"And then, you see, war broke out and we had these trained men, very eager to defend their liberty."

Wycombe wondered whether this tale was pigwash or whether there really was a Canadian Coloured Corps.

"So all these blacks were born free?" the Major's tone was contemptuous.

Warwick waved this aside. "I didn't ask. It's very bad manners, you know. If a man's on British soil, then he's free. No Canadian would be rude enough as to ask about a man's history."

The major looked annoyed, possibly at this repeated reference to bad manners.

Wycombe realised that Captain Warwick was needling the major on purpose.

The major squared his shoulders. The Yankee soldiers tensed.

The volunteer closest to Wycombe shifted his weight from one foot to the other. He, too, was ready for action.

"Your men are very neat, captain," the major said.

"Why, thank you." The captain smoothed down his red jacket.

Maycomb realised that his care over his appearance had not been vanity.

"Anyone would think they'd never fought a battle."

One of the privates gave a moan. "Shuddup," Wycombe snarled, as quietly as he knew how.

"Oh, they have, sir, they have," Captain Warwick said. "We wouldn't be here today if they hadn't. The British army prides itself on being neat. Even after a battle." His mocking tone vanished. "Your men at World's End didn't give up without a fight, you know. I assure you of that. It was quite a desperate fight for a while ... But your men were outnumbered and my men were determined to prove themselves. I would write a commendation if I could."

"Thank you for that, sir." The major's tone was dry. He shrugged. "Surely you will admit that the Black man is inferior to the White man?"

"I assume that your question has some purpose?" Captain Warwick said. "One of those Greek philosophers said that some free men had the souls of slaves, while some slaves had the souls of free men."

The major glared. "How dare you, sir. I demand that you apologise. Immediately."

Wycombe and his four men straightened up.

Captain Warwick spoke in a tone of wounded innocence. "I merely quoted one of those clever Greeks. It was not aimed at anyone. How could you assume such a thing?"

The major glared.

They heard a locomotive whistle, to the south of them. Wycombe looked round, but the locomotive was hidden from view by the woods. He recalled that two railroads ran parallel here. The other one was two miles to the south-east, out of sight. He guessed that a train was heading out, north along the Grand Trunk Railroad.

The major relaxed slightly.

Captain Warwick stiffened. "This is monstrous, sir!"

The major smiled. "There will be another train at five this afternoon." He sounded smug.

Wycombe assumed the cargo would be munitions, bound for the Yankee invasion of Canada.

Captain Warwick must have made the same assumption, because he was angry. "Isn't that a violation of this truce, major?" He pointed at the white flag.

The major shrugged. "That is solely a promise that no-one will shoot at you. I did not promise to close down the railroad."

"That train was taking munitions north," Captain Warwick said. "Do you deny it? Upon your honour as a gentleman?"

The major pursed his lips and said nothing.

"No. I will not have it," Warwick said. "You can send a train west, back to Boston, but not north to reinforce the attack on Canada."

The major grimaced. "You have no right ..."

Captain Warwick half-turned. "Private Jones, go back to the train. Tell Lieutenant Harrington to take a hundred men south to block the other railroad track."

The major protested. "We are negotiating."

The black private hesitated.

"Sending munitions north would be a breach of good faith." Captain Warwick said. He turned to the private. "Tell Harrington that he's my most trusted lieutenant. You got all that? Go."

"I get you, sir." The private ran off.

"Captain, I must protest," the major said.

Captain Warwick pointed to the flag. "That's a promise that we won't shoot at you, major. Nothing more."

The major seemed to accept this. "Very well" He turned to one of his men. "Go back to town. Tell them no more trains north." He spoke to the man in an undertone for some time. Then he got the man to repeat the message back.

The man did so, also in an undertone.

Wycombe watched, fascinated. What were they hiding? He wondered whether this delay was the whole purpose of the truce.

The soldier ran off and the major turned back to Captain Warwick. "I have been ordered to protect Portland from harm. The citizens and their property."

"Yes, major?"

"If there is any fighting, Portland will be destroyed. The British burnt it down once before."

"Very likely. Regrettable, of course."

The major squared his shoulders. "Captain, I offer to withdraw my men south-west of the city – if you will promise that the city and all its buildings will be spared. You will also have to maintain law and order. And ..."

Wycombe was astonished. The major was going to give up Portland without a fight?

Behind them, Wycombe heard shouting. Sergeant Priddy was telling a hundred men to get out of the boxcar and line up. Wycombe tried to ignore the commotion. His task was to watch this southern major.

"Go on, major," Captain Warwick said. He sounded unperturbed.

"And - you must not cross the Fore Bridge until you receive written orders from your general to the contrary."

Captain Warwick thought this over. "I give my word to protect the town from harm. But for you to withdraw across the bridge is not enough. My men will be in full view of your snipers. And your men will be in view of mine. You must withdraw south of the Nonesuch Bridge."

The major thought this over. "No. I can't allow you to advance west of the Fore River."

"I promise not to send armed men across the bridge," Captain Warwick said.

The major inclined his head. "Your word on that? Very well, I agree." He turned and walked away.

Captain Warwick waited a moment, then turned. "Let's go. Back to the train."

Wycombe was determined to retreat in style. "Shoulder arms. About turn. Good. Now, walk back, don't try marching."

Wycombe realised that he was the hindmost. His shoulders itched all the way back to the train. But he refused to turn to look.

Then he realised that Sergeant Priddy was standing next to the locomotive cab, watching him. The sergeant did not look worried, so Wycombe assumed the Yankees were not doing anything.

"What happened out there, sir?" Priddy asked.

Warwick explained the negotiations to Priddy and the other sergeants. "We have to assert our authority in Portland. So we have to bluff. Walk in there bold as brass. Act as if we have a thousand regulars at our backs. Act as if we are three-year veterans.

"But - if the town surrenders, we'll have to protect the civilian population." Sergeant Priddy was dismayed. "You want us to act as policemen now? Crazy. But we can do it, sir."

"Good."

Portland, evening

The troops formed up on the road. The sergeants got them into columns, four abreast, and they made a reasonable job of marching towards the town.

Wycombe still had his fears. Would that southern major keep his word? Or would they be ambushed?

But, at the first house, they were met by the mayor and the police inspector. Plenty of townsfolk had turned out too.

"Company - halt," Sergeant Priddy said. His men

came to a stop, stamping their feet in unison. The other sergeants repeated this order in turn as their companies closed up. The column came to a halt.

"Good evening, gentlemen," Captain Warwick said. He repeated his promise to protect the town from harm.

"Do you want a us to set up a curfew patrol, sir?"

The mayor turned to the inspector, who nodded. "That would help, sir."

Sergeant Priddy led the men through the streets to the railroad freight terminal. Several men expected the townsfolk to turn hostile, but the crowds merely watched in silence.

The sergeant arranged for the men to bunk down in a railroad warehouse.

The men grumbled at the bare building. They wanted comfortable billets. "Like the Yankees at World's End."

Captain Warwick arrived and put a stop to the grumbling. "No. I don't want to be captured in my nightshirt. We all stay here."

This got a laugh from the men. They were impressed that he would share their hardships.

Portland, May 22, After dark.

Captain Warwick had several more tasks to accomplish. He asked Wycombe to find two volunteers for a special night-time mission. "Scouts. It will be dangerous. Challenging. They'll have to operate alone and then explain what they have seen."

Wycombe was dismayed, but promised to do what he could.

Warwick led twenty men through the town to the bank of the Fore River. Eight of the men, in uniform, carried rifles. "Quietly, now."

The two scouts kept close to Wycombe. They wore disreputable sack-jackets rather than the elegant red tunics that most of the men preferred.

Warwick reached the eastern end of the railroad bridge. They paused in the shadows. He could make out the outlines of a couple of houses and neat trees on the far bank.

Sergeant Wycombe spoke in an undertone. "No sign of movement, sir."

"There's only one way to be certain," Warwick said. "Go."

The ten skirmishers, with no weapons apart from the bayonets in their scabbards, ran across the bridge. They reached the far side and took cover in the shadow of the trees.

Everyone waited, tense, but there was no opposition. No challenges, no shots. The sergeant turned and waved.

Warwick turned to the first of Wycombe's volunteers. "I want you to go south, follow the railroad. Try to reach the next bridge. Check whether that Yankee major retreated south of the bridge as he promised."

The man nodded. "Yessir."

Warwick turned to other man. "I want you to check that the fort on the point is still abandoned."

"Yes, sir."

"Don't take risks, either of you. If you see any soldiers, any at all, turn back. You must report back. If you don't, I'll assume you're dead and send out two more."

Both men nodded, trotted across the bridge, and vanished into the darkness.

"Sergeant, I want those ten skirmishers relieved every hour."

"Yes, sir."

Portland, May 23

Wycombe reported to the captain's office. "You wanted to see me, sir?"

He knew that the two scouts had reported back. They confirmed that the Yankees had indeed abandoned the territory east of the Nonesuch River.

Captain Warwick was sitting in a ladder-back chair. "Yes. We're out on a limb here, sergeant, far from reinforcements or supplies. For the moment, we outnumber the nearby US forces ..."

"Yes, sir." Everyone knew that would not last. Captain Warwick needed help. But how to get it?

"Sergeant Wycombe, the townsfolk tell me that a British warship is loitering offshore, blockading the harbour."

He wondered where this was going. "Yes, sir."

"I cannot send any of my experienced sergeants on this mission. But several of you volunteers have proved to be versatile. I want you to take a message to that blockading naval vessel."

He was dismayed. But there was only one answer to give. "Yes, sir."

Captain Warwick led the way down to the dock area and asked the harbour-master a few questions. "I want a sea-faring vessel."

Captain Warwick wanted a pilot boat, while the harbour-master said a victualling vessel was available. It seemed there were several vessels that met Captain Warwick's requirements.

Then he asked about crews. "Did you know that Portland had a community of free blacks, Wycombe? Any citizen who helps us risks being put on trial. But blacks here aren't citizens."

He walked along Commercial Street, asking questions, and found a team of local blacks who were prepared to charter their sailing-boat.

"Let's see it," Captain Warwick said.

The sailing boat was open, without a cabin. The captain asked a few technical questions about the vessel that baffled Wycombe but which impressed the crew.

"Gaff rigged? Does she yaw when the wind's on the quarter?"

"No, she's well-behaved, sir."

He was pleased. "Yes, she looks seaworthy."

They sealed the bargain. Captain Warwick gave Wycombe a sealed letter.

The skipper of the boat told Wycombe to dress up warm. "It's cold out there." The crew gave him a tarpaulin jacket. "You sit in the middle of the boat and you won't come to any harm.

"Your captain knows something of boats," the skipper said.

"He comes from Bermuda. Are you fishermen?"

"No. We take stores out to anchored ships. When there are any anchored ships, that is."

They hoisted the sail and pushed away from the wharf. The sail flapped in an alarming fashion until they turned towards the harbour entrance. One of the crewmen hoisted a white flag. It was the largest they could find.

They sailed past the moored ships. The skipper said, without any prompting, that his men were born in New York. They had moved north to escape southern bounty hunters. "I was born in Maine, though."

"I heard about that," Wycombe said. "They were born free, then?"

"Yes."

"Yeah, you don't sound like southerners."

The boat left the shelter of the harbour. The waves were bigger out here. They sailed past Fort Preble. Wycombe could see that it had been reduced to a shell.

"The British marines blew it up, last winter," the skipper said. "They set the magazine off. Killed half the garrison. The Yankees made no attempt to rebuild it."

"You know all these islands?" Wycombe asked.

"Yes." The skipper smiled. "And the rocks that only show at low tide. I know them like the back of my hand, sergeant."

"Good."

They changed course again, then won free of the islands. The skipper pointed to a speck on the horizon. "There's your Royal Navy blockading vessel. Two miles offshore."

Half an hour later, they were almost within shouting distance.

Wycombe could see that the naval vessel was a paddle-steamer with a row of gun ports. She had two masts, with a small sail set on each. The flag at the masthead, white with a red cross, was as big as a sheet.

"Those sails aren't very big," Wycombe said.

"They're not trying to go anywhere. The sails stop the current from pushing the ship off position," the skipper said. "They don't have enough coal for long journeys. They only fire up the boilers when they have to."

Wycombe was worried that the ship might fire on him. But his boat drew closer without any action on board. And it was flying the white flag too.

Then a man on board shouted. "Boat, there! No closer. State your business."

He took off his tarpaulin jacket and stood up, to show red jacket. "Ship, there! I have a message from Captain Warwick, Sixty-Second Regiment, British army, in Portland."

The man shouted back. "What's the name of the regiment?"

It took Wycombe several seconds to guess what the man meant. "The Royal Americans."

"Good. Come on board."

"Can you do that?" Wycombe asked the skipper.

"Of course." The skipper gave an order to his men. The crew brought their boat alongside the warship.

"There's a rope ladder. Wait until a wave lifts us up," the skipper said.

Wycombe thanked them, grabbed the ladder, and climbed on board.

The officer of the watch glared at him. "You have a message?"

"For your captain, sir. We have retaken Portland and need your help."

"Retaken it, you say?" The officer eyed his red jacket and summoned a junior officer and two marines.

Wycombe noticed that the warship had two very large swivel guns, pointing fore and aft.

The young officer escorted him below deck and then aft to the captain's cabin. He explained his mission to the marine sentry.

The officer opened the door and ushered Wycombe inside. The cabin had a fancy stern window. The captain was sitting behind a desk. Wycombe noted that his peaked cap lay on the desk. So he was not properly dressed.

"Messenger from the shore, sir," the young officer said.

The captain subjected him to a glower. "Yes, sergeant?"

Wycombe stepped forward and handed over his letter. "I was sent by Captain Warwick of the Sixty-Second, sir. We have retaken Portland. He is asking for marines. It is safe to go in. Fort Preble is not occupied."

The captain took the letter and read it. "Why did Mr. Warwick send a – coloured man?"

"Well, sir, I'm evidence that the story I carry is true."

The captain read the letter again. Wycombe guessed

that he was unhappy. And he could not discuss his doubts with anyone.

"Very well." He sent a runner to fetch the lieutenant of marines. "But I'll send the open boats. Not my ship."

"Yes, sir."

The warship came in close to Portland head and lowered its longboats. An hour later, they rowed through the harbour entrance. Wycombe, sitting at the stern of the leading boat, could see men staring down at them.

They reached the dock and tied up. "Sit still," the marine sergeant said. "You wait till last."

The marines climbed the ladder to the wharf. The marine sergeant gave his permission at last and Wycombe scrambled up after them.

Captain Warwick and some of the coloured volunteers were waiting on the dockside. The volunteers gave a cheer as the marines formed up.

The lieutenant of marines saluted Warwick. "Captain Thorpe said that we must get news of this development to the admiral in Bermuda. They could be able to send us reinforcements."

"Of course," Warwick said. "I have already made enquiries. Portland harbour has several ocean-going vessels lying idle."

"I see, sir."

"I will have to ask Captain Thorpe to provide a navigator."

"Of course, sir."

Sergeant Priddy led the new sergeants into a dockside bar. The barman looked appalled.

It occurred to Wycombe that his dismay might be caused by the arrival of rowdy soldiers, not blacks.

"I'm paying," Priddy said. "A pint of beer for each man."

Some of them objected to this charity. Priddy waved these objections aside. "You can buy me one when you get paid. If you live that long."

Wycombe wanted to change the subject. He asked about Bermuda. "Is it really true that all blacks are free there?"

Priddy sipped at his beer. "We're free, yes. They wouldn't allow us in the militia, else."

"And do you have the vote?" Wycombe asked.

Priddy looked sour. "No. There's a property qualification."

Freeman nodded. "I get it. Whites can vote and blacks can't."

Priddy took another sip at his beer. "I meant what I said. You can only vote if you own property. What you Yankees call real estate. Money in the bank isn't property and neither is a pile of gold coins." He put down his beer-glass. "Only about a quarter of whites can vote. Mr. Warwick is rich enough, but because he doesn't own any property he doesn't have the vote."

Wycombe was surprised. "The captain doesn't have the vote? I see."

"And only eight blacks on the entire island have the vote," Priddy said.

"What? Blacks can vote?"

"Yes, but only if they own property. Eight of them, like I said."

Wycombe tried to grasp this. "Oh."

Freeman grinned. "That's more than any southern state."

"That's a weird way to run things," Wycombe said.

Priddy smiled. "It makes perfect sense to us."

Chapter 7

Maine, Augusta, May 25

The town of Augusta, the state capital of Maine, was located on the Kennebec River at the lowest bridgeable point. The river forced the coastal railroad to make a long detour to the north.

The governor had an unwelcome guest, the president of the state's logging interests. They glared at each other across the table.

"The regular army refuses to help," the governor said. "The general only listens to Washington. So I want to bring the militia down here, to protect us."

"This is outrageous," the businessman said. "I'm keeping my men up north. This is just a diversion. The Limeys are waiting for the chance to invade. If they do, I'll make sure you lose the next election."

The governor let his anger show. "Absurd. What are the redcoats going to do? Chop down all your logs and take 'em home?"

"They'll occupy my forests and hold on until the peace treaty. Then they'll redraw the frontier to include the land they're sitting on."

"I don't care about your timber. The British sent a trainload of redcoats through here, do you understand? They could have burnt this place to the ground. They could have thrown me in jail ...

You're a colonel in the militia, right? If you and your boys stay safe up north while fighting's going on down south, I'll see you're court-martialled."

"If we move south, the Limeys'll grab my timber!"

"And if they send any more troops to Portland, they'll

be able to grab all of southern Maine. And if that happens, I'm going to lose my job. So bring that militia south, you hear me?"

Bermuda, St. George's, May 28

Mrs. Warwick borrowed her husband's coach and told the coachman to take her to the town's business district. Two of her coloured servants went with her.

The coach rattled over the cobblestones, turned a corner, and then drew to a halt. The coachman opened the door for her. "We're here, madam. This is as close as I can get."

"Very well." She stepped down and hesitated. The alleyway was wide enough, as the law required, to roll a tun-barrel. Usually she would never visit such a masculine place. But this was a reputable chandler's store, managed by a woman.

Mrs. Warwick went in, followed by one of her servants. Broad shelves covered all four walls. The place had a low roof and was spotlessly clean. A male clerk, stacking merchandise neatly on a shelf, stopped to gape at her.

Standing behind the counter was Mrs. Priddy. She was three-quarters black. Or, some said, half white and one quarter Mohawk Indian. Rumour said that Sergeant Priddy had volunteered to serve overseas just to get away from his wife. Looking at this grim woman, Mrs Warwick could well believe it.

"Good afternoon," she said. "A vessel has just arrived from Maine. The dock manager sent me news."

Mrs. Priddy nodded. "People like us are always the last to be told, madam."

"Yes. That's why I felt obliged to come. I have news that the Bermudian volunteer company is safe in

Canada. But my son has raised a new battalion of coloured refugees and has seized Portland."

Mrs. Priddy was scornful. "That is very nice for your son, madam, but what of my husband?"

"Well - your husband is with my son. As his sergeant-major."

The woman was incredulous. "Do you mean my husband is famous?"

Mrs. Warwick was annoyed. "No, of course not."

"But if these despatches mention him by name - did they?"

Mrs. Warwick realised that this woman was right. And her son would be famous too. The newspaper would probably want an interview.

"Sergeant-major Priddy!" The woman squared her shoulders. This was a garrison town. She had just realised that the wife of Sergeant-major Priddy had far more consequence than the wife of platoon-sergeant Priddy.

Mrs Warwick realised that the same was true of her. The mother of conquering hero Warwick had more consequence than the mother of idle-wastrel Warwick.

How had the two men done it? Neither man had any initiative.

"And they captured Portland, madam?"

Mrs. Warwick could understand the woman's confusion. She could not understand it either.

"They had five hundred coloured troops with them, it seems. Refugees from the United States. Your husband must have kept them in line."

"Yes ..." Mrs. Priddy could not believe it. "A battalion, you said, madam?"

"Over five hundred men, I believe."

"But that's a colonel's job! A major at the very least."

"Yes." She could not believe it either. Her son? Lt. Colonel Warwick? Absurd.

"They won't let him keep it."

Mrs. Warwick knew how the British army worked. If this unit was a success, some man with political connections would be given command of it. "No."

"Do you know anything else, madam?"

"Only that they reached Portland. The marines went ashore to help them."

"I see. Thank you for bringing me the news, madam."

Mrs. Warwick took the carriage back to her home, two miles west of St. George's, and changed her dress. She settled down to read.

Two hours later, her coloured maid interrupted. "There's a woman calling herself Mrs. Priddy at the front door asking to see you, madam. Shall I tell her to go round the back?" The girl was clearly thinking that working as a maid might be demeaning but it sometimes brought the most juicy gossip.

Mrs. Warwick was indignant. "That woman, at my front door?" Then she realised that Mrs. Priddy must have news of her husband. "Could you ask what message she has? No. Send her in."

"Yes, madam." The maid was surprised, and now more curious than ever.

Mrs. Priddy was shown in. Her dress was dusty. She must have walked the two miles from town.

She was wearing her best bonnet and a neat shawl over her shoulders. Despite her humble origins, she managed to look dignified.

Mrs. Warwick swallowed her pride. "Sit down, please, Mrs. Priddy. You have a message for me?"

"Thank you, madam. I have a letter from my husband, madam. A note, really."

"Does he mention my son?"

"Well - see for yourself. It makes no sense to me."

In haste
The bo'sun says that the ship is leaving in ten minutes whether my letter is on board or not.
We fought a battle at World's End and took the train to Portland. Young Mr. Warwick played his hand like a riverboat gambler. The major walked out and we walked in. We asked the Navy for help and they promised to send despatches to the governor. No time for more. ~

Mrs. Warwick said the first thing that came into her head. "You received a letter. And my son did not write at all."

"I got a note. Seven lines, an' my Priddy didn't even sign it."

"That might be the answer. My son took extra time to sign it and so he missed the boat. But what does it mean?"

"At least we know he's still alive, madam. They're both alive."

"Yes. They took Portland without a battle ... The major walked out? What does that mean? I want to show this to my husband."

"No. It's all I've got."

She bit her lip. "Can I at least copy it out?"

"Well – yes, madam."

She took her pen and copied the note. "I am beholden to you, Mrs. Priddy. One of my men can escort you home."

"Thank you, madam."

Mr. Warwick returned home an hour later. Everyone agreed that he was a plain man, dull. When they had married, her mother had said that he was just the man to dampen down her enthusiasm.

Mrs. Warwick explained the message. "It's baffling."

He read it with interest. "You think I can help? But

I'm as much in the dark as you are."

"I had hoped that a man's guess about the man's world would help ... Do you know Priddy?"

"In a way. We grew up together. You know what that means. As a child, he was always very polite to me. I was foolish enough to think we were friends. But that's impossible when one is born free and the other isn't."

"Do you think he's a friend to our son?"

"Of course not. An officer and a sergeant can't be friends. They could trust each other, though. Mutual trust can be more powerful than friendship." He read the note again. "And he's got a parcel of black runaways to help him."

"Runaways? Isn't that phrase insulting?"

"Then I'll use a worse insult. They're Johnny newcomes. Raw recruits."

"How do you know they're raw?"

He smiled. "They wouldn't have received any training in the US."

"Oh! Of course not. Foolish of me."

"Andrew was always awkward. When I wanted him to study accounting, he refused. When I suggested he join the Rifles, he joined the artillery and studied ballistics."

"Yes." Her fear had been that he would start roistering.

"I was always worried that if I pushed him too hard, he would turn to drink. Or go off to London."

"You said that a private in the Bermudian rifle militia had more status than an officer in the artillery."

"Not any more! They will be furious at this. They voted to stay at home. And now the coloured men who went overseas are heroes."

"Well, yes."

"I'm going to visit the governor tomorrow. I'll ask whether he knows anything more about our son."

"But will Sir Herbert see you?"

He waved the sheet of paper. "My dear girl, unless this is a complete fabrication, our son is the hero of the hour. Of course the governor will see me. I fact, our son may have included a letter in the official despatches." He smiled. "Sir Herbert may even invite us to dinner."

Portland, May 29,

The land of the Port District sloped markedly down to the south, and the east-west streets formed gentle curves.

Captain Warwick had commandeered a suite of rooms in a hotel as his headquarters. If the Yankees attacked from the west or south-west, he did not want to be trapped down on the docks.

The hotel was inland, to the north, at the top of the slope. It was decorated in the classical style, with pillars each side of the door.

He felt it was vital to impart discipline and self-respect to his men. He and Sergeant Priddy had established a routine of drills, with and without muskets, and physical exercises.

Warwick organised daily scouting expeditions south-west towards the enemy. But the scouts continued to report that they had not met any opposition. Warwick knew that situation would not last.

They had decided that Commercial Street, next to the docks, was wide enough for the exercises. The naval blockade had disrupted trade, so the street was empty.

In the morning, the men would drill in squads and platoons. The new sergeants would learn their craft at the same time. In the afternoon, they would drill as a company.

Some of the townsfolk came out to watch the drills and comment on the soldiers' performance. A few of the spectators were black, either free-born or refugees from the south who had travelled north along the underground railroad. The more persistent of these black sightseers were women.

Sergeant Wycombe was surprised how difficult giving orders on the parade ground was. You had to give the order at exactly the right time or the squad made a mess of it. And then they blamed you. The afternoon drills, taking orders from Sergeant Priddy, was simpler.

Some of the soldiers complained that the spectators laughed at their mistakes. The fact that some of them were pretty girls just made things worse.

Sergeant Priddy had no sympathy for them. He merely told them they would have to try harder.

At dusk, Captain Warwick strolled down to Commercial Street. The sky was overcast. It was getting dark early. He watched the men at their drill and tried to look unconcerned at their mistakes. Any reaction from him would put them off.

He noticed another spectator arrive. She was black, in her late twenties. Should he ignore her? She was rather pretty.

He strolled across the road. She looked alarmed at his approach.

"I hope you're not going to give us any trouble, miss."

"No, sir."

"You arrived late."

"I work in a dressmaker's workshop. The manager, she said it was too dark to see properly and we'd be making mistakes. So she let us go."

"I've seen you here before. In daylight."

"Yes, but she docked me an hour's pay. I couldn't do that very often."

"I see."

"I wish I could fight too. I enjoy watching them handle those muskets."

He shrugged. "I wish I could ask these men why they left home and joined the army. But an officer can't ask that sort of question."

She was silent for a moment. "Is it true that the blacks on Bermuda are free?"

He realised this was not a change of subject. "Yes. Ever since 1834."

"Those men - they don't want their children born as slaves. At least, that's why I came north."

"Ah."

"And I wanted to learn how to read and write."

"Can you?"

"I can now, sir."

St. George's Island, May 29, 2pm

Mrs. Warwick was surprised when a courier arrived at her home with a note from her husband.

"My dear girl,
As I predicted, the governor and his wife have invited us to dinner and stay overnight. No letter from Andrew but the commander of the vessel that brought the despatches has a tale to tell.
In haste, your loving, etc."

She considered her options. Her husband had taken their only carriage when he travelled to the capital that morning. Finding a hired carriage would cause delay. And then she would have to wait for the ferry.

"I'll take my boat."

"Yes, madam." Her maid enjoyed these nautical excursions.

"Please pack my overnight bag. And include my evening dress. And tell my boat crew to prepare the pilot gig."

The maid nodded. She was used to this.

Half an hour later, she walked down to the landing stage. Her maid carried her dress in a bag, a smaller bag for herself, and two waterproof capes, just in case. Her crew of six were already on board. They, too, enjoyed this break in routine.

She turned to face the wind. "From the south."

"It won't last, madam," the boat-captain said.

"No. But it will be a good sail down to Long Point."

"Yes, madam."

She stepped aboard, with the ease of practice, and took her accustomed place, just forward of the helmsman. Her maid sat opposite.

The crew rowed out to deep water and hoisted sail. The boat had two small sails, only useful for sailing downwind.

They cleared St. George's harbour and turned south-west, sailing inside the reef. The waves were of a respectable size. She loved the rise and fall of these waves. The helmsman had his work cut out merely steering a straight course.

She turned to face the wind. "If this picks up …"

"It isn't going to do that, madam."

They made good time and rounded the end of Hamilton Island. They altered course to the south and adjusted the sails.

But the wind was now against them. The helmsman decided that sailing was impossible. The crew took in the sails and got the oars out.

"Beg pardon, madam," the helmsman said, "but we'll go faster if I row too."

She put on a show of reluctance. "Very well." She moved round and took over the helm.

They passed Rushy Island and turned towards Black Point. The task only required half her attention. A mistake, though, would make things difficult for the rowers. They trusted her to get it right.

The rowers maintained a steady rhythm. She thought about the lies that other ladies made up about her. The accusation that she had obtained her own boat merely because she enjoyed the presence of these rowers. Of course, the men were perfectly fit.

"Madam?" the senior rower said, without stopping.

"There's a sail, fine on the starboard bow."

"Right, madam."

She made a slight alteration of course to avoid the sailing ship. Then, a couple of minutes later, the ship altered course towards her. She hid her annoyance.

"They've altered course. We may have to change course drastically."

"Right, madam."

The sailing ship was getting closer. She could make out faces peering at them. She braced herself for a change of course.

Then somebody on board shouted. "Yes, it's her. Now can we go about?" The sailing ship changed course, away from the rowing boat. The crew rushed to trim the sails.

"Give the lady a cheer," the man said, and a cheer rang out.

"Idiots," the senior rower said, without altering his stroke.

She merely nodded, concentrating on her steering.

They passed south of Mark Rock and changed course again. When they passed Saltus Island, the town of Hamilton came into sight.

A few minutes later, the maid moaned.

Mrs Warwick was annoyed. "What is it, girl?"

"The shore-front, madam. There's a crowd watching."

Mrs. Warwick realised that the girl was right. She

panicked.

"But why? They've never bothered before."

"It's the news about your son, madam, begging you pardon," the senior rower said.

She almost gave the order to turn back. Instead she mustered her courage and steered towards the dock. This would require precise timing. She did not want to mess up in front of this audience. "Ten yards ... In oars." She turned sharply. It was a perfect approach.

The rowers performed splendidly, bringing in their oars and grabbing the dock wall. There was a smattering of applause. The rowers stared at the crowd.

She had to remind the senior rower to climb out so he could help her go ashore. She could have scrambled out unaided, despite her skirts, but it would have been undignified.

"Stand back, there," the senior rower said. He helped the maid climb out and then took her bags.

Mrs. Warwick's fear of the crowd made her excessively dignified. She ignored the staring faces.

Then her husband's coachman pushed through the crowd. He smiled in a fatherly fashion. "Your husband has sent the coach, madam. It's waiting."

"Thank you."

The coachman escorted her along the dock to the coach. "Make way, there. Stand aside, if you please."

One of her rowers tagged along behind, carrying her bags. The crowd moved aside to let them pass.

The coachman opened the door and helped her climb inside. Her maid scrambled in after. "It's all very exciting, madam."

"I would prefer to do without." Her tone was sharper than she intended.

The coachman climbed onto the box and drove her to the governor's residence.

The journey was short, hardly worth the trouble of

using the coach, but she was glad to be free of the crowds. The coachman opened the door for her and she stepped down.

Her husband was waiting to greet her. "Good evening, my dear. You're just in time to change for dinner."

"Good evening. I don't know what the fuss is about. I haven't done anything."

"If your son was here, they'd chair him around the town. He isn't, so they cheer you instead. And, besides, you're the only lady on the island who's given a thought to those Mohawk refugees."

She hurried upstairs to change. When she came back down, the guests were milling around, waiting for the call to dinner.

The midshipman who had brought the despatches was one of the guests. Everyone wanted to hear his story. He was flustered to find himself the centre of attention.

The governor introduced him to her. She thought that he seemed absurdly young for an independent command. He felt that his task had been routine and was surprised by this enthusiastic reception.

He explained that her son had sent a proper report. But he had been too busy to write to her. "Harassed out of his wits, madam. It's a great responsibility."

"Yes." Her son, acting responsibly?

The governor smiled and showed her the footnote to the report. "Please let my mother know that I am well."

The midshipman explained that her son's black troops were completely untrained. "His orders were to create a distraction, not to take territory. But he took everybody by surprise."

"Including his superiors. And us," the governor said.

The midshipman nodded. "Yes, sir. There's no way for the general to reinforce him. So this situation is unlikely to last."

Mrs. Warwick was alarmed at this prediction. Any

change in the situation was likely to put her son at risk.

At dinner, the conversation naturally turned to the news from Portland. The governor's wife disapproved of masculine topics such as strategy, and usually forbade it at at her dinner table. On this occasion, however, she could not prevent it.

If the fighting was renewed, everyone on the island would be affected. Mrs. Warwick was not the only lady with a relative in the armed forces.

The admiral complained about the fuss. "Captain Thorpe at Portland has asked for reinforcements. So I'm sending a couple of warships."

"With a full complement of marines?" Mr. Warwick asked.

"Of course, sir," the admiral said.

Mrs. Warwick was still bewildered. "But I don't understand why the Yankees just walked out. Or was it more – complicated?"

The midshipman put down his fork. "There were just thirty army regulars in the place, madam. And their main task was to guard the gunpowder."

Everybody stared. "Gunpowder?" Mrs. Warwick said.

"Yes, madam. According to the townsmen, Portland is a major junction. The army was sending supplies to their troops on the frontier. And when your son turned up, there were three boxcars full of gunpowder in the town. If there had been any fighting, the town would have been blown sky-high."

"I see," Mr. Warwick said.

"The Yankees tried to negotiate with Captain Warwick while they sent the boxcars north. They managed to send one north, but then your son put a stop to it. So they sent the rest of the powder back south again."

"I see. Thank you."

The governor was unhappy. "Young Mr. Warwick is begging for reinforcements. But there's nobody that I can send."

"There's those Mohawks on St. David's Island," Mrs. Warwick said.

The governor shrugged. "It's too much trouble."

"Why is that, sir? The quartermaster regards them as a nuisance because he has to feed them. They want to go home, and my son needs help. Sending them would solve three problems at once."

She stopped, appalled. She had just lectured the governor on strategy. Ladies were supposed to be docile.

The governor's wife tutted her disapproval of this unladylike conduct.

But the other ladies did not seem to mind. "You've talked to them?" Mrs. Drake said.

"I asked their sergeant about my son. But he could not help." She glanced at her husband, but he merely looked amused.

Chapter 8

Portland, May 30

Eliza and her companion left work early and hurried down to Commercial Street. They wanted to watch Sergeant Priddy put one of the companies through their drill.

They found that this time, to make things more difficult, the men were carrying muskets. Eliza realised they were learning fast. She enjoyed watching them at their drill.

Other townsfolk, white ones, were watching from the sidelines. They were fascinated by the sight of black men carrying weapons.

Eliza and her companion stood at the corner, slightly apart from the other spectators.

The captain was standing on the far side of the road, watching the drill. He was careful not to distract the soldiers. Then he noticed her and strolled across the road towards her. Eliza felt a twinge of panic. She was tempted to run, but she summoned her courage and stood her ground. She had a companion, after all.

He asked a few questions. He was very polite.

She explained that she came from Baltimore and that her name was Eliza. She was an experienced seamstress.

The pay was low, but she felt safe here. There had been a free black community here for years. She had fitted in amongst them without any fuss.

She had been fascinated when the black soldiers arrived.

She enjoyed watching, the way they handled their muskets. "It's so elegant."

"They weren't elegant when they started out," the captain said.

Eliza's companion interrupted. "At first, I thought that the same company was kept on the parade-ground all the time. But as I learned their faces I realised that they took turns."

The captain shook his head. "The rest of the time, they guard the western bridges or patrol the farmland east of the river. And then there's the firing practice. Each company in turn marches down to the shore and fires their muskets out to sea."

"I've heard the men say they're grateful when their drills are interrupted by a bit of musketry," Eliza's companion said.

"I wish I could go and watch," Eliza said.

"I'm afraid not. But I'm heartened by their steady development," the captain said.

"But they don't practice their shooting very often, sir."

"No. We're short of ammunition. We dare not squander it. But we all know that this modest practice isn't enough. Well, don't stay too late," Captain Warwick said. He turned and strolled off.

Eliza liked the officer. Although she had to ask the minister where Bermuda was. He was so confident and self-assured. Well, Sergeant Priddy was confident too, but he was old.

Captain Warwick had just reached the hotel that he was using as his headquarters when a runner brought word from the docks. "Sergeant Priddy sent me, sir. A paddle-steamer is approaching the harbour entrance. It's one of those Nova Scotia packets. Ugly they are, sir."

He was curious, so he decided to see for himself. He strolled back down to the dock to watch the vessel approach.

The skipper handled the task quite neatly. Warwick

was impressed. Then he realised that the deck was crowded with men in red coats.

Reinforcements! Hopefully with experienced officers. As the ship drew closer, he could see that the soldiers on deck were all black.

He watched with mounting impatience as the deck-hands threw ropes ashore and the vessel tied up. Finally, an army lieutenant came ashore. He looked round, noticed Warwick's rank-badges, and saluted. "Captain Warwick?"

"Yes, lieutenant, my name is Warwick."

"My name is Dulles, sir. I've been transferred from the Nova Scotia regiment." He indicated the soldiers on deck. "These men were refugees from the United States. They arrived over the last twelve months. The fools wanted to join the army. They heard you had accepted the refugees in New Brunswick, so they asked if they could volunteer too."

Warwick thought that Dulles was rather old for a lieutenant. He wondered what had prevented the man's promotion.

"They're raw recruits?"

"Yes, three hundred of them," Dulles said. "All eager to fight for their freedom. So when you pulled off this coup, the governor asked them whether they were prepared to come down here. All of them said yes."

"But who's in charge?" Warwick asked.

"Well - I'm in charge of this contingent. My orders are to report to you, sir," Dulles said. "No regular officers want to touch this. They expect these blacks to desert as soon as they see the enemy."

Warwick was appalled. He was now responsible for seven hundred men. "You don't have anybody more senior?"

"Well, no, sir. I was told you had everything in hand. There are three other lieutenants, all of them promoted from the ranks."

"How many sergeants have you?"

"Four," the lieutenant said. "They're all white, of course. I don't believe that blacks would make good NCOs. I refused to promote any."

Warwick was annoyed at this attitude. He realised that he would have to transfer four of his most experienced sergeants to the new units.

Portland, June 1

Sergeant Priddy took one of the companies on a route-march. They were all carrying firearms and wearing backpacks.

They were singing "Victory or death." Over the last few days they had learned several marching songs.

Sergeant Priddy was in the lead, setting the pace. Now he turned around and walked backwards.

"You can do better than that! I want you to shout so loud, they can hear you in Kennebunk. This singing isn't for fun. When you're marching, you need to fill your lungs with fresh air. An' singing makes sure you do that. So let's do that again."

Portland. June 1, evening

The men gathered in the warehouse that served as their barrack-room. Sergeant Wycombe was brushing his jacket when a telegraph boy in a peaked cap caught up with him.

"Telegram for Sergeant Wycombe. You Sergeant Wycombe?"

"Yes." He realised that the other men had stopped to stare.

The boy grinned. "I have a telegram from Miss Montgomery in World's End. Official, like. Paid for, you see. She says that the militia has finally taken action. They've moved south and occupied World's End. And she says they're less polite than you were."

"Thank you." Wycombe opened the envelope. It confirmed what the boy had said. "Will she get into trouble for saying that?"

"Nah. Everyone says they're rowdy. But they've blocked the railroad. They're building a blockhouse. The Maritimes can't send any more troops south. You're cut off."

"No. We can send troops by sea. But - thank you."

Some of the men were not happy with the route-marches or the marching songs they had to learn.

"I came north to fight. Instead I'm in a minstrel show. And carrying a backpack while I do it."

Wycombe was irritated. "Don't talk bilge, Freeman. What minstrel-song ends with 'victory or death'? They'd string you up, down south, if you tried that."

Some of the men grinned at this, but Freeman was still unhappy.

Wycombe tried again. "You could write your own song. Something about conquering heroes or something."

"Before we've fought a battle? No. That wouldn't be seemly."

A young private leaned forward. "I liked the bit about the banners."

"What's that?" Freeman said.

"March ye men of Harlech bold, Unfurl your banners in the field, Be brave as were your sires of old, And ..." he stopped, embarrassed. "I wish we had a banner."

"Nonsense," Freeman said.

"White regiments have them," someone at the back

said. Why not us?"

"Well, I can't hang about. I've got a social visit," Wycombe said.

The hall was bare, without any decoration. During the day it was used as a schoolroom. The Baptist congregation rented it on Sundays. This evening, the mission society had taken it over for a special event.

The old ladies asked each other whether anybody would turn up. Eliza stood to one side, by the tea table. At the moment she had nothing to do except wait.

Reverend Tomkins had organised this event. He had persuaded the congregation to issue an invitation to the soldiers, to guide them towards the light and away from excess.

Eliza was bored. Unwanted, the old memories came back. She had travelled north unaccompanied. She had lost her child. The father had been white. The bitterness that she felt about that would never heal.

Now she worked as a seamstress. The pay was poor. But she felt safe here. No southern bounty-hunter would come this far north.

She had been fascinated when the black soldiers arrived. Everybody in town knew that they had defeated the garrison at World's End. But nobody knew how they had done it. And the soldiers did not boast about it. All they would say that they had taken the Yankees by surprise.

They frightened her. They were crazy, saying they hoped for death in battle. But she could understand how bitter they were.

Her landlady was a church member and had asked her to attend this evening, to provide moral support and to serve the tea. It had been more than a polite request.

Her thoughts were disturbed when the first soldiers walked in. She could tell that they made made an effort to look neat. She recognised the sergeant, Wycombe.

Conversation amongst the old ladies stopped. But there were only five soldiers.

Wycombe recognised Reverend Tomkins. "Good evening, sir,"

Eliza was disappointed that so few soldiers had turned up. But she was not surprised. The reverend had not made his invitation sound attractive.

To her, the soldiers looked shy. They were very polite. The old ladies were excited at their appearance, though.

The reverend and his wife stepped forward to welcome their guests. They acted as host and hostess, very polite, but they were prim. They were born free and did not understand southerners.

Eliza thought that this dour reception would put the soldiers off.

The sergeant, in his clear voice, explained that only one company was off duty at any one time.

"Ah. I see." Reverend Tomkins was mollified.

The sergeant moved on to take some tea. She smiled. "We have coffee too, sergeant."

He noted her accent. "You from the south?"

"Baltimore. Why did you go to Nova Scotia rather than Fort Malden?"

"Well ... It was the Canadian governor. I thought he would take me in. Train me as soldier. Instead, they expected us to find jobs, out on the farms. When we refused, they set us to construction work. They treated me as an outcast ... Until they got desperate."

"I see."

"We're eager to prove that blacks can fight." He smiled. "I recognise you."

Another soldier stepped up and asked for coffee. She poured him a cup and turned back to the sergeant. She decided to ignore his last remark. "Reverend Tomkins is disappointed that so few of you turned up."

He grinned. "If you want to encourage more men to visit, offer them home cooking. The army feeds us, but it's dull."

She shrugged. "Nobody here understands southern spices. All they have is local herbs."

"Better than nothing. You know, if you really want to help these men, teach them to read. Set up Bible classes."

"They want to learn? I see."

"I recognised you as soon as I walked in. You watch the drill."

"Yes. When I can get away." She enjoyed watching them at their drill. the way they handled their muskets. "The older women chide me for that." Most of them had been born free in New England. Three were runaways who had made their way north to join their husbands.

"I joined the church to find shelter, you see. Reverend Tomkins is a bit harsh for some … I teach the Sunday school."

"Really? The minister would get more attendees if he promised to teach them. It would be good for morale."

"We don't have enough teachers. Men with things to lose would be reluctant to teach redcoats."

"Could you help teach them?"

"A girl couldn't teach grown men!"

"No? Not even if they promised to be polite?"

Could she persuade Reverend Tomkins to treat it as a church activity? "It would be more interesting than needlework, I suppose."

Bermuda June 2

The men of K company were now receiving rations from the barracks at St. George's. Sergeant Thayendanega was convinced that Mrs. Warwick was responsible. The men had agreed to share their rations with the villagers. It made for a more varied diet than fish and oatmeal.

The men halted their morning exercises to watch the ferry from St. George's arrive. A white sergeant disembarked and strolled up the hill. The men guessed that he had news for them.

"Sergeant Joseph? There's new fighting on the Atlantic coast. So they're sending you back there."

Joseph straightened up. "Maine?"

The sergeant nodded. "Your ship will leave from Hamilton, not the port of St. George's. So your orders are to march down to Hamilton. Your ship should be ready in a couple of days."

"Right, sergeant."

Sergeant Joseph passed the word. The men were sad to leave their new friends but were glad to be going home.

He organised an inspection. The soldiers' uniforms were worn but carefully mended. Their muskets were polished and cared for. It was unfortunate that most of them had lost their hats, though.

Portland, June 3

A naval courier vessel, a fast paddle-steamer, arrived in the harbour with despatches from the general in Quebec. The courier asked for Captain Warwick's signature.

Warwick glanced through the documents and realised that the authorities had woken up at last. They had accepted that the volunteers were not going to fade away.

"Important news, sir?" Lieutenant Harrington said.

"Yes. The volunteers have been classified as an

independent battalion within the Sixty-Second Regiment.

"Captain Eastman has been given a promotion and appointed commander of the battalion. He's on his way." The news that he was no longer in command was a huge relief to Warwick. Yet he considered Eastman to be a strange choice.

"Do you know him, sir?" Lieutenant Harrington said.

"Oh, yes. We've fought together before. I admire him."

Warwick strolled down to the barracks and sought out Sergeant Priddy.

The junior sergeants were being given a lesson in the street outside. As usual, a few curious onlookers had gathered on the opposite side of the street.

Warwick interrupted the sergeant's lesson and told him the news. "The new battalion will need a sergeant major. I intend to recommend you for promotion."

For once, Priddy looked gratified. "Thank you, sir."

Priddy was instructing the junior sergeants in the responsibilities of the sergeant of the day.

"You and your squad have to guard the gate, and you can only allow in men with the proper papers.

"But if the captain here turns up without any papers, you have to let him through," Priddy said.

"Well, you *could* send a runner to the officer of the day, to ask whether I was acceptable, but he wouldn't be pleased," Warwick said.

The men were bewildered, and the observers were amused. Warwick noticed the girl, Eliza, among the audience.

Warwick, growing impatient, decided he needed a clear example. He pointed to Eliza. "You. Come here."

The girl was frightened at being singled out but stepped forward. Warwick shrugged out of his coat.

"Here. Put this on." The girl, indignant, refused.

Warwick ignored her protests and draped the garment over her shoulders.

She squeaked in surprise and some of the men laughed.

"Some poncy officers like to wear their coats as if they were cloaks," Warwick said. "Now. Sergeant Wycombe here has been on duty for hours. He's bored. He's wishing something will happen."

Wycombe suspected a trap. "No, sir, I wouldn't say that."

Warwick gave the girl a nudge between the shoulder-blades. He looked round at the men. "And now this person in uniform turns up. And suddenly the sergeant recognises trouble and wishes he could go back to being bored." The observers grinned.

"Now, the uniform is all right, so the first thing is for the sergeant to ask whether any of our officers are as pretty as that. Be careful how you answer that question, sergeant."

Wycombe grinned. "No, sir, none of em' are."

"Good. So this person is a stranger. You bid him good day and ask him what his business is."

"He might not like that, sir, him being a gentleman."

"Too bad. It's your duty to ask, sergeant, and it's the visitor's duty to answer. He might say he's brought urgent despatches from New Brunswick. Or he could say his mission is secret, and he won't tell enlisted men."

Warwick looked round. "That is fine. But he's got to say *something*. So you ask to see his papers." He looked at the girl.

"But I haven't got any papers," she blurted.

"Suspicious," Warwick said. "So the sergeant says that private Smith will escort him to the officer of the day, who will sort things out."

"Ah," Wycombe said.

"Now, our guest could say thank you. Or he could say

he knows the way and doesn't need any help."

Wycombe nodded. "I might ask two soldiers to escort him if he said that."

The girl overcame her nervousness. "But what if this fine white officer said, stand aside or I'll have you flogged?" This was met with a grim silence.

"That *is* a problem," Warwick said. "Because if the sergeant allowed this suspicious character to walk around without an escort, *I* would have him flogged."

"Could the sergeant say you said that, Mr. Warwick?" the girl asked.

"What? Certainly. The sergeant here can say that he'd like to be easygoing, but his captain is heartless and won't allow anyone to step out of line."

He looked round at the listening men. "All of this is in the rule-book. If an officer turns up here, a genuine officer, he'll have read the book. He'll have reprimanded his own men for being sloppy. He'll be wondering if you'll be sloppy."

Bermuda June 4

Sergeant Joseph called his men to attention. They were about to march down to the ferry landing. They would cross over to St. George's, then march down to the port of Hamilton.

One of the villagers attracted his attention. "That's Mrs. Warwick's boat approaching, sergeant."

They all turned to look. Yet the passenger in the stern was a black woman.

"What's that old biddy doing here?" the mayor asked.

The woman was carrying a parasol and looked very pleased with herself. The boat tied up at the jetty and one of the rowers helped the woman to climb out. They seemed amused by the whole thing.

The mayor took off his hat. "We are graced by your presence, Mrs. Priddy."

"Less of your sauce," the woman said.

Sergeant Joseph guessed that this was some sort of joke between them.

One of the rowers handed Mrs. Priddy a large parcel tied up with string. "Sergeant, this is a present for you and your men." She opened the parcel to show a pile of caps. "Sergeant, Mrs. Warwick noticed that some of your men had lost their caps."

"Well, yes ..."

"So she asked us to help her make some for you. She asked me to bring them. We decided to make glengarry caps because they were fairly easy to make.

"Highland soldiers always put feathers in their caps. Perhaps you could do the same. Would you like that?" She looked embarrassed.

"Thank you, madam," Sergeant Joseph said.

The men had their doubts. "Should we wear them? Our company wasn't issued with glengarry caps."

But Joseph approved. "The unit would look better if we all dressed alike."

The mayor thought it a huge joke. He rushed off and came back with a handful of seagull feathers. "I can get more if you wait a minute. Indians have got to wear feathers. Everyone knows that. These white folks will be disappointed if you don't wear feathers."

"They're big feathers. Impressive," Joseph said.

The mayor grinned. "Seagulls are big beasts. It's unwise to argue with them."

Joseph put on one of the hats. He checked once again that the men's muskets were polished. "Let's go."

Portland, June 5

Sergeant Priddy asked for a private interview with Captain Warwick. This had now become part of their routine. "Yes, sergeant?"

The sergeant stood to attention. "Every battalion had its own pair of colours, sir. One of them is the usual design, but the other is unique to the battalion. And the men ..."

Warwick could guess where this was going. "So the men want a pair of colours, sergeant?"

"Yes, sir. Now that we're a battalion, sir."

Warwick decided that Eastman would not mind. "You'll have to ask the other sergeants for suggestions.

"We've already talked it over, sir. The most popular idea was a design of broken chains - to show that we've won our freedom, sir."

"Very well." Warwick accepted this. "I'll see what I can do."

Warwick found a backstreet workshop that housed a team of seamstresses. He had remembered that the girl Eliza had mentioned this place. He decided that he would not like to come here after dark.

The manager, a woman, listened to his story with interest. All of the women in the workshop were black. Warwick noted that some of them had watched the men at their drill.

He explained that he had already experienced a couple of rejections. At the first establishment he tried, the manager refused to consider the request. He said that he and his employees were good patriots and would not accept orders from redcoats.

Warwick guessed that this workshop could not afford to be proud.

The manager agreed to take on the order. Her

employees would enjoy making a flag. She said that some of the women were runaways, but most were born free.

A deputation of junior sergeants, promoted from the volunteers, asked for an appointment with Sergeant Priddy. Wycombe was amongst them.

"Yes, Wycombe?"

"The regular sergeants have been telling us, about the ceremony where new regiments receive their colours."

"Yes?"

"All of us here agree. If we're going to receive our colours, we want a presentation ceremony just like a white regiment."

This had not occurred to Priddy. But he was eager for a formal ceremony. He felt it would improve morale.

"I'm sure we can arrange something. A ceremony would not be a problem. Perhaps the major could do it. But in England, it's usually royalty who makes the presentation. The colonel would ask a princess to do this. A duchess at the very least."

"A grand lady?" Wycombe said.

"Yes." He wondered who they could ask. The governor? Or perhaps the governor's wife? The general's daughter? Then he realised that no government official would visit a beleaguered town.

"I thought you could ask one of these local ladies," Wycombe said.

"Sergeant, we're a redcoat regiment. Wives of local citizens can't do it. They could even be accused of treason."

"Oh. I see. Yes."

"I promise to take your request to the captain. But you must be prepared to be disappointed."

Toronto, June 5

Colonel Hendrick Teyonhehkwen was young for his rank. He was not married. He had a reputation as playboy.

The selection committee had chosen him to lead the militia because he had the right family background; and because he had been to a good school. He could speak good English, passable French and a smattering of Latin. Just as important, he understood the white man's table manners.

He had been summoned to an interview with the Governor of Upper Canada, Adam Nightingale. He had expected to be kept waiting in the foyer, or even told to come back another day, but the governor's aide showed Hendrick into the governor's private office.

Nightingale greeted him and invited him to sit. "This is a military matter, colonel."

"Yes, sir?"

"The army in the east is in dire straits. Unless we do something, the Yankees will get across the St. Lawrence and into Quebec. Those raw recruits on Portland won't last a week. We need a diversion. Could you arrange one?

Hendrick was defensive. "My regiment would be acting alone, I take it?"

"Yes."

"I don't have enough men to hold territory. The most we could achieve would be a raid." Yet his men were bored. They wanted action. He reacted with boyish enthusiasm. "Have you got a map, sir?"

"Here. The obvious target is Detroit," the governor said.

"Yes." The war-leader Tecumseh had taken Detroit in 1812. If he could repeat that, his reputation would be made.

He dampened his enthusiasm. "Detroit? No, it's too well defended. The population is too high."

"A modest success would be better for my people. This requires thought."

The Governor told him that if he restricted himself to Mohawks, a defeat could wipe out the nation. So he decided to widen his appeal for volunteers.

Ontario, Brant's Ford, June 5

Thanks to the railroad, Hendrick was able to reach his home late the same day. He explained the governor's request to his companions.

"Ah, yes," Peter said, with boyish enthusiasm. Everything else was brushed aside. They pored over the map.

"We are agreed that Detroit is too well defended. The garrison is too large," Peter said.

"Then there's Port Erie. There's a naval base?" captain Jones said.

"Perhaps," Peter said. "There is a blockhouse inland, but it would be difficult for us to get to."

Hendrick was impatient. "Forget the blockhouse. Is the naval base manned, these days?"

"Yes. But there's a gun emplacement at the entrance. A warship would have to sail round the eastern end of the island. An attack there would very likely fail."

Jones scowled. "But canoes could land on the beach."

Hendrick nodded. "I can't believe it's not fortified. Perhaps they've abandoned it and we'll conquer an empty sandbank."

"I can make enquiries," Peter said.

"Worth the attempt?" Jones asked.

"Yes."

Ontario, Brant's Ford, June 6

Sergeant Chard paid another visit to the suburban town-house of Colonel Hendrick. He had come to ask a favour.

The politician in the frock coat, Brant, was there too.

"We are delighted to see you again, sergeant," Hendrick said.

"Thank you, sir."

"But what is the purpose of your visit, sergeant?"

He was nervous. "Well, you see, I was sent by the lieutenant with a special request. You see, the lieutenant need reports about the weather. So the Engine can process them. The lieutenant would like the telegraphist in your westernmost observation point to take weather observations and send the reports to the Montreal. Four times a day."

"Why is this?" Mr. Brant asked.

"Well, the more reporting stations there are, you see, the more reliable the results."

Colonel Hendrick was reluctant. "Four times a day? My men are infantry. How many burdens are they going to dump on us?"

Mr. Brant shook his head. "Cousin, the Yankees are likely to attack in good weather. If we send these reports to Montreal, can they send a warning back to us?" He turned to Chard and raised an eyebrow.

"Probably, sir. It seems a reasonable request. The lieutenant feels honour-bound to send the reports to anyone who asks for them."

Mr. Brant nodded. "I want us to be useful to the politicians. That will help, after the war. And I want our men to know they are doing something useful. That is better than waiting and waiting, hoping for the Yankees to attack."

"Very well," Colonel Hendrick said. "The men on the coast are bored. Perhaps they will be glad of this extra responsibility."

"It isn't just the men at the coast, sir. One of your telegraphist here will have to receive the reports and send them on."

"But we don't have enough skilled young men," Brant said.

"Sir, could one of the women take on the task?" Chard said. "The Telegraph Company have signed a contract with the government to send all of our weather reports. If they give you any trouble, I'll set the general on to them."

Hendrick was surprised. "It's that important to the government?"

"Yes, sir. Those airship crews need light winds to fly safely. So they need reliable predictions."

Maine, Portland, June 9

The ship carrying George Eastman steamed through the harbour entrance. He hated his stuffy cabin and chose to remain on deck. Two of his subordinate officers had chosen to stand on deck beside him.

George watched with interest as the skipper gave a series of orders. They were passing a series of docks. The vessel slowed and turned to a vacant berth. The paddle-wheels went into reverse and the ship came to a standstill. Sailors threw lines to stevedores ashore, who seized them and made the vessel fast.

George could see a reception committee standing on the dock. They were here to greet their new commander. He was not happy. He regarded this as a great challenge. He had been given temporary promotion to major and sent to command the new battalion. He knew he was not the best man for this task. Yet the better men, career officers, had refused to take it.

Standing behind him was a signaller - his own personal Talker. Mr. Francis Laval was young, tall and thin, with a brown complexion and Indian cheekbones. As he was a signaller, he wore a-blue jacket rather than a red one. Very few battalion commanders had a personal talker. That was a measure of how desperate things were here.

The telegraph wire could be cut at any moment. And he had to assume that any message he sent would be copied to Washington.

The sailors rigged a gangplank. George drew a breath and walked up.

A company of the new battalion was lined on the dock to receive him. George recognised Captain Warwick standing in front of them. As he stepped ashore, the black sergeant bellowed an order. "Present – arms!"

The men performed the task neatly. They seemed eager to get things right.

Captain Warwick stepped forward and saluted him with enthusiasm. George gravely returned the salute.

"Welcome to Portland, sir. I'm glad to dump responsibility for this onto somebody else, sir."

He smiled. "I can understand why, captain."

Warwick smiled. "I've commandeered the town's best hotel as my headquarters."

"I see, yes," George said.

Warwick turned away from the dock and George followed.

He heard the black sergeant speak in an undertone. "He's an Indian! They didn't send a white commander. They sent a red one."

George pretended he had not heard. "They promoted me to major, on full pay. They gave it to me because no-one expects this to last. When the Yankees attack your men will scatter. No-one expects untrained troops to stand fast."

Warwick nodded. "Yes, I understand, sir. But we could be attacked any day."

"I have brought six officers with me. All of them are no-hopers, in one way or another. If nothing else, they can do the paperwork."

"I see, sir. Ah - that will be a great help."

"One of the captains is a Jew. Name of D'Israeli. He hopes that a bit of combat experience will improve his career prospects. Personally, I doubt it. I can recognise discrimination when I see it."

Warwick led the way into the hotel foyer. "The bar's through there, sir. Do you want a drink?"

"I would prefer tea."

The other officers walked in. George led the way to a set of armchairs and they all sat down. Signaller Laval trailed behind them.

George leaned back. "Captain, I want to make you adjutant. I need your experience. You will remain the senior captain."

Warwick was startled. "Thank you, sir."

"And I've brought thirty Hurons from Lower Canada. At least they have some experience. They brought their own muskets.

"And a hundred black runaways from Upper Canada. They travelled along the underground railroad to Fort Malden."

"Do they have firearms, sir?"

"I'm afraid not. There wasn't time."

"The men have asked for a pair of colours, sir," Warwick said. "Do you approve?"

Approve?" George said. "Well, they're a battalion, so I suppose they need a pair of colours. I don't know how you get approval for that sort of thing." He shook his head. "I'm not going to ask the top brass for permission. Just go ahead and do it."

"Yes, sir." Warwick said. "And the men requested a presentation ceremony. In England, you would get a prince or a royal duke to do that. But of course we can't do that in Canada. Here, it would be the governor."

"But we can't ask the governor to come to Portland! If the Yankees attacked ..."

"Yes, sir. The sergeants said they wanted a proper lady. Not a gentleman."

George was surprised. "What, even if she's white?"

Warwick nodded. "Yes, sir. They want it done right. They asked for a grand lady."

"Did they, indeed?" George said. "Well, I might just have the answer."

The waiter brought a teapot and cups on a tray. The other officers took the opportunity to request their own drinks.

George half-turned. "Signaller Laval is my secretary. Where necessary, he will write letters in Abenaki. There's someone in Montreal who can translate them."

"I see, sir," Warwick said.

"Laval, I want you to send a message to Miss Grace. To pass on to Charles Lloyd in Montreal.

"I can contact Mr. Lloyd directly, sir."

"In that case, ask him to speak to the Viscountess. Ask whether she could visit."

Laval took this without a blink. "Yes, sir."

"Are the Yankees going to attack, captain?" George said.

"There's a rumour that three regiments of the US Army had been sent to Boston, to prevent the battalion from advancing south. I think this report is reliable. So we can expect an attack any day now."

"In that case, I want to see the construction of emplacements, facing west," George said.

Montreal, June 9, Evening

Daniel Eathorpe needed to find Grace Abenaki. But Sergeant Chard said she had swapped places on the roster so she could take the evening off.

"She said that she wanted to attend a 'function'. But she didn't say what it was, sir."

Daniel found that the 'function' was being held in a rather tatty hostelry in a side street that had a private room for hire. The hand-written sign at the foot of the stairs said 'Debating society members only'. He was surprised. He had not associated the country girl Grace with debating societies.

He found that the room at the top of the stairs was crowded. A man was giving a speech in French. Daniel could not tell whether the meeting was artistic or scientific.

The woman closest to the door handed him a crudely-printed flyer. It informed him that the topic of debate was 'la validite du roman gothique de l'age de la vapeur'. Daniel struggled and translated this as 'the Gothic novel in the age of steam'

He estimated that half of the audience was female. Most of the people were wearing cheap suits or dresses. A few - those wearing the cheapest fabrics - paid more care to their appearance and managed to look elegant.

He spotted Grace, sitting at the back. She managed to look neater than most. He waited for the session to end.

The speaker summed up and there was a smattering of applause. This was followed by a buzz of conversation.

Grace stood and walked over. "Good evening, sir."

"Good evening. Is this a literary event, Miss Abenaki?"

She smiled. "Well, yes. But some of the members are engineers. And they know I work with the Engine.

There's usually someone who asks me whether the Engine can solve his problem. And of course I don't know. But if they can describe the problem to me, I can sometimes guess how much machine time it will take."

"Well, the Engine isn't busy all the time. We usually have a quiet hour or so. I wondered what your connection with these people was."

"We share a love for scholarship." She introduced him to the lecturer.

Daniel noticed that the cuffs of the man's jacket were frayed. Didn't he care about his appearance? He was fluent in English, but Daniel guessed that his first language was French. At first, he was truculent.

"Are you a career soldier? Some of those aristocratic officers have a low opinion of French speakers ..."

"Not at all, sir. I work on the Engine."

"Ah. Not a regular." The man was less hostile. "We're all very excited here. Quebec has got a university at last. If them, why not us?"

"They have? I didn't know."

"The governor has sent a request to the Queen. She hasn't signed it yet, but ..."

"I see. Are these seminars organised by the university?"

"Well - most of the boys here are students. But this meeting isn't official. No. I'm not being paid for this."

Daniel nodded. "That would explain the presence of these ladies."

"Yes. They're eager to learn. That Miss Abenaki turns up a lot more often now. She says that her working hours are more flexible these days. She can ask someone to stand in for her." He smiled. "I wish she could give a lecture on that engine."

"You asked her?"

"She said she could discuss her work to ladies, but could not speak in public to a mixed audience. We're all interested about engineering developments. But we're also interested in how those changes will affect society. And how they are portrayed in fiction."

"I see." But Daniel needed to talk to Grace. They had a crisis, the Engine's predictions were not making sense.

They wanted observations from as far west as possible. That would improve their predictions.

Daniel and his team had found that the Engine did not improve their performance very much. Sometimes it was best to reject the Engine's predictions and go with intuition instead. He dared not say so, of course. Outsiders trusted the Engine so much.

"That Engine is a fascinating device," the lecturer said.

"Yes, indeed."

"Everyone assumes that it gives the British a great advantage in this struggle."

Daniel knew this was not true. But he could not say so.

"I have heard that the Yankees also assume it will tip the scales in the redcoats' favour."

Daniel grinned. "I shall not contradict them."

Toronto, June 10

Colonel Hendrick knew that he was a good organiser. He had played a key part in turning his people's war-band into a militia battalion. One of the reasons for his appointment was that he understood politics and diplomacy.

He had no combat experience. But, these days, nobody had any combat experience. The last war had been forty years ago.

He had asked for an interview with the Governor of Upper Canada, Adam Nightingale. These days, the governor was prepared to listen.

A secretary showed Hendrick into the governor's private office. Nightingale stood to greet him. "Good morning, colonel. Please, take a chair. "This is about our little military matter, I take it?"

"Thank you, sir." Hendrick said. "Yes. I have worked out a plan for a raid on the coast. Unfortunately, I cannot accomplish this without support." He placed a document case on the desk. "This explains my requirements."

The governor read the documents. "You've done your homework. You want a ship?"

"It doesn't have to be a warship. Anything will do."

"Ah. These requests are modest. Yes, I agree."

Hendrick was surprised. "As simple as that?"

"The army in the east is in dire straits. The Yankees are building up their reserves for another attack. The governor in Quebec has requested that the men in the west should arrange a distraction."

"I see, sir." He had his own reasons for an attack. His own men were bored. *He* was bored.

The governor leaned back in his chair. "I have received word that the president has asked the north-western states to send their militias to the east. The state governors are reluctant. I want to make them more reluctant."

"Yes, sir. I shall do what I can."

Adirondacks, June 11, afternoon

Tommy, in her log cabin, was bored. Her weather observations might be vital, but it was tedious, monotonous work.

Rain had fallen all night. That morning, she had gone for a walk. Her boots and trousers were wet from the damp grass, so she had taken them off. Now she had nothing to do until the 6pm weather observation.

The millionaire's 'log cabin' was far too big for her. She had ignored the over-large upstairs suites and had instead made her home in a couple of downstairs rooms. She assumed they been the office and bedroom of the housekeeper.

From time to time, the Abenaki sergeant had paid a visit, to ask about her well-being and to bring a newspaper. She was reading the latest one for the third time. The hysterical reports of New York journalists were entertaining, but after reading the same delusions week after week they became boring too.

Tommy pushed the newspaper aside, and glanced out the window. Could she go out again? But rain was falling steadily. She sighed and took out her Talkers' tokens.

She was able to establish rapport with several acquaintances in Montreal. But who should she choose? Not Mr. Lloyd. The lieutenant? No. She chose the Abenaki signaller, Asher.

'You're not on duty, are you?'

'No. Are you bored?' The young man wanted to know about London. Was it really bigger than Montreal?

She said it was. She hated the town of her birth but she was prepared to describe it. He wanted to know about the glamour, not the squalor. She enjoyed describing it.

'Is this safe?' Asher said. 'Mr. Lloyd said we shouldn't talk more for than five minutes.'

'I haven't got a watch here.'

Afterwards, she had no recollection of collapsing.

She found herself lying on the floor. She ached all over. She was too tired to get up. But the position was uncomfortable. She pulled herself up and sat on the bed.

She heard footsteps on the gravel outside. Who was it? Some enemy? She thought of running for it. But she was too weak to run.

She remembered that the Indian had described this place as a trap because the owner had cut down all the trees. Perhaps she could crawl through the long grass.

She grabbed up her trousers and boots and made her way down the hallway. But just at that moment someone burst open the kitchen door.

She leaned against the wall and looked up. The door swung open and three Yankee soldiers burst in. She felt foolish. She was wearing a shirt and long-johns.

"On your feet," the sergeant said.

Tommy straightened up.

"You're a spy. So we can shoot you out of hand," the sergeant said. The corporal grinned.

"How did you know I was here?"

The corporal smiled. "A homesteader spotted the smoke from your stove."

Seven more soldiers walked in. They half-dragged Tommy back to her room.

She realised they meant what they said. They were going to put her against a wall and shoot her. And they hadn't realised she was female. Should she tell them? Or would that be worse? "Can I have a last wish? To put on my good jacket."

"Not your trousers?" the sergeant said. "More dignified."

"Them too, but its the jacket I want. In that wardrobe."

The Yankee sergeant walked across and opened the wardrobe. Hanging up were two jackets. Both were engineer blue with sergeant's stripes.

"Ah. You claim to be a soldier, then?"

"Yes. I'm a specialist. I'm a weather observer. I'm taking records so we can improve our predictions. Every ten days or so I send the reports back by airship."

"Records? What sort of records?"

She showed them her leather-bound journal. "I note the barometer readings in this journal. Four times a day. It'll be published after the war. Scientific research. Available to everybody. Including US universities."

"That's a military task?" the sergeant sounded doubtful.

"It makes the airship rides safer."

"Weather reports? That explains a lot."

"So we can't shoot him after all?" the corporal said.

"No." What's your name?"

"Alex – Tommy. Alexander Thompson. People call me Tommy."

The sergeant scowled. "Pack your kit. And those journals. In the morning we'll take you down the hill to the railroad."

Adirondacks, June 12

The walk down to the railroad took all day. Tommy was not fit enough to carry anything. She tried to explain her stroke.

"Not a hangover, then?"

"No. Did you find any drink?"

She told herself that she was Tommy again. She must always think of herself as Tommy.

She was exhausted by the time they reached the station. She sat slumped in a chair while the sergeant sent a report by telegram.

The reply came back promptly. They stopped the next southbound train. It had a passenger carriage.

"Better than a boxcar," the corporal said.

The sergeant put Tommy, the corporal and a couple of privates on board.

They allowed Tommy to take a window seat. She watched, fascinated. The railway track was well guarded.

She wondered what they were protecting it from. Every bridge had a blockhouse. Every switch-point had a squad of soldiers. She guessed that a thousand men or more were guarding the track. She realised they were protecting it from those thirty Indians up in the mountains.

It was after dark when the train stopped at Ticonderoga. "There's an old fort here," the corporal said. "They're using it as a POW base."

Once inside the fort, a trio of officers questioned her. They examined her meteorological equipment with interest. They seemed to accept her claims about the scientific value of her research.

Then she was put with the other prisoners. The barracks-block was overcrowded. Tommy expected her secret to be discovered. But the prisoners reacted to their lack of privacy with an exaggerated politeness.

Tommy wondered what had happened to Asher. Had he suffered a spasm too? Were they worried that Tommy's reports had stopped? But she was too frightened to try using magic again.

Lake Erie, June 12

Colonel Hendrick had arranged with the governor to borrow a paddle-steamer. The vessel was unarmed, a pleasure boat.

The Mohawk expeditionary force had gathered at Port Stanley. The canoes that the governor had promised were waiting for them.

Sergeant Johnson was disgusted. "They call these things canoes?" He had traditional face tattoos in horizontal lines.

Hendrick had been ashamed to find that the Mohawk nation no longer had any canoes. He had been forced to ask the army to lend him some. They were crude and ugly, with canvas sides, but serviceable.

"What do you expect?" They carried the objects onto the deck of the paddle-steamer. "Just lay them down flat."

At dusk, the telegraphist walked down the jetty. He handed over a sheet of paper, just like a real telegraph operator. "I have the weather report from Montreal, colonel. It's favourable, sir. Clear skies. Light winds."

Hendrick would have guessed that anyway. But a second opinion was reassuring. And his companions were impressed that he could arrange a telegram from Montreal.

"Thank you." He showed the note to the skipper, who nodded.

The warriors dumped their equipment in the first-class lounge. The room was luxurious, with varnished wood and brass fittings.

The ship left Port Stanley just after sunset and headed south.

The skipper had agreed to use clean-burning fuel. He said it was called anthracite. "Developed by smugglers in Bermuda."

The men on deck were quiet now. Most of them had adopted the traditional hairstyle, shaved at the sides of the head. Their earlier enthusiasm had been replaced by determination. Hendrick thought this was a good thing.

He had thought that only young men would be prepared to join him. He was not popular with the older generation. But old warriors who despised his modern ways had begged to take part. Some of the older men, like his sergeant, had tattoos or even warrior scars.

Some of the men suggested warpaint but Hendrick squashed the idea. "We're soldiers now."

"This is a night action. We all look alike," his second-in-command, Peter, said. "How do we spot the sergeants? A stripe on their faces." So he made each of the sergeants in turn sit in a ladder-backed chair while he painted a downward-pointing red chevron across their faces. The men crowded around to watch, grinning.

"But I need to be recognised too," Peter said. He sat while a sergeant painted a vertical line down his face. Hendrick watched, amused.

Only when his cousin said, "The colonel needs two stripes," did he realise he had been set up.

But there was no escape. He took his place in the chair. "I'll get you back for this one day." But his cousin merely grinned.

The ship stopped when their target was just below the horizon.

Hendrick gave his men a last-minute briefing.

"Remember, we ignore any houses. Concentrate on the shipyards. Destroy military stores."

They all understood. "Right, sir."

They lowered the canoes into the water and began climbing down into them.

Peter, watched the first of the men descend. "This is crazy."

"You can stay behind if you want." It would be a tragedy for the nation if neither of them came back.

Peter grinned. "I wouldn't miss this for anything."

Hendrick had a brace of duelling pistols, a present from the British to his uncle. He tucked them into his waist band. They were loaded but not primed.

It was Hendrick's turn. He climbed down and took his place. He was followed by sergeant Johnson.

They paddled towards land. They had practised for this on the river at home. The men were fit. Hendrick was fit too. All those British school sports that he hated finally paid off.

He had a compass. But, after paddling for a few minutes, he found that he did not need it. In the starlight he could just make out profile of the town. He could not make out the low-lying sandbank, but it had to be in front of the town.

He knew that the fort in the centre of town was old. It had last been used in 1812. And it did not see battle then.

But they had agreed that the old fort was not a worthy target for them. The naval base was more tempting.

Their target was supposed to be a shipyard. He had expected to see masts on the far side of the island. But there was nothing. Had the Yankees abandoned the place?

As they drew closer, his doubts increased. Were the Yankees waiting for him? Had the townsmen got their guns ready?

"I can hear waves, sir. That's the beach," Sergeant Johnson whispered.

"Yes." His tension increased. But the landing was unopposed.

They climbed out, splashing in the shallow water, and pulled their canoes up the beach. There was a row of trees to mark the high-water line. Hendrick thought the noise was terrible, but there was no outcry.

For a moment, they could shelter in the shadows. "Quiet, now."

He told the older warriors to guard the canoes. "If everything goes perfectly you'll have nothing to do."

An old man with tattoos responded. "In war, nothing goes perfectly."

He could see the nearest buildings. There was a lot of empty space between the trees and them. While his men were crossing that ground, they would be sitting targets.

"All ready? Quiet, now. Go." He led his men across the open ground at a run. They reached the buildings on the far side without anyone raising the alarm.

He found that this building was empty. He felt a

trickle of dread. Was the place garrisoned by ghosts?

They split up, to go looking for rifles or valuable military stores. Hendrick and ten men reached a two-storey building that he guessed was probably the base headquarters.

He turned the door-handle and the door opened. The ground floor contained offices. He wondered whether he should he set it on fire. No. Later. Search the place first. He ran along the corridor. The place was empty. He found a rack, mounted on the wall, that looked promising.

But it contained swords, not pistols. He rejected them as worthless. Who needed a sword in the 19th century?

They heard shouting in the distance. Had the garrison woken up?

"Hurry, hurry, hurry." He moved along to a cupboard and opened the door. He found that it was not a cupboard – it held six rifles, stored vertically in a rack.

His henchman, Sergeant Johnson, was delighted. "Splendid." His smile distorted the horizontal lines tattooed on his face.

"Yes. Take those."

He came to the foot of a wide staircase and decided to try his luck up the stairs. His team followed him.

He ran along the corridor. He was looking for a store-room. His sergeant stayed close behind him. The first two rooms contained rows of bunks, but the mattresses had been removed and they were barren. "Check all the rooms."

He pulled open the third door. He almost collided with a man coming the other way, pulling on his blue jacket.

The man glanced at the painted stripes down his face. He screamed. "Indians! Savages. Help!"

Hendrick was just as frightened, but recovered first. He used his pistol to club the man down.

Then he saw this was a bedroom. The person sitting up in bed was a girl. She was wearing a voluminous night-dress.

He was embarrassed. He was about to apologise. Would the girl scream?

Instead, the girl spoke in a low tone. "Take me with you."

It took him a few seconds to realise she had spoken in Iroquois. "You're a half breed?"

"Mother was Western door. Seneca. Turtle clan."

So she knew her heritage. This was crazy. "No. Stay here. It's too dangerous."

"I'll follow you anyway."

He sighed. "Get dressed. Hurry."

His henchman, standing in the corridor, was appalled. "Boss!"

The girl ignored him. "He gave me a silk dress. I hate it. He made me burn my old woollen dress. He said it was only fit for a peasant."

"You can't wear a dress in a canoe. Take his trousers."

"Isn't that stealing?"

They heard shouting downstairs.

"Not in a battle. Spoils of war. Take his fancy ones. Gold stripe."

She ignored this. She preferred the fatigue trousers. She pushed the skirt of her night-dress under the belt. It made her look as if she had a paunch.

"Hurry, hurry, hurry." He shoved the fatigue jacket at her. She shrugged into it. On an impulse, he grabbed the silk dress and shoved it at her. "Carry it."

They heard shooting downstairs.

He rushed out into the corridor. She followed and squeaked in surprise at the sight of Sergeant Johnson with his face tattoos in horizontal lines.

"He's very traditional," Hendrick said.

"Ah."

One of his men fired his musket down the stair-well.

"Front door blocked. No way out," the sergeant said.

"Yes, there is," the girl said. She led his team along the corridor to another doorway. "This is the back stairs." They pounded down.

"And this is the back door. For deliveries," the girl said.

The alleyway between the two barrack blocks was clear. They ran back along the alleyway towards the beach. They stopped at the edge of the open space. The trees that marked the shoreline looked a long way off.

He heard more shooting in the distance. One of the empty buildings had been set alight.

He realised it was time to go. They could not accomplish any more. If they stayed any longer they would be trapped.

He shouted "To me, to me!"

He realised that Sergeant Johnson was carrying all six rifles. Hendrick took one. He handed another to the girl.

"Here. Make yourself useful. Carry a rifle." She was indignant but did as she was told.

They met men from other teams. Some were carrying rifles too. "Back to the beach!"

They would have to cross the open ground to the lakeside. The Yankees were awake and angry now. But there was no alternative. They would have to run and take their chances.

He led the way. "To me, to me!" His men followed. The firing intensified. One of his men fell. Then another. That row of trees looked a long way off. Hendrick knew he had to be ruthless.

"Keep going!"

They reached the trees. They did not provide any protection but the shadows they cast hid them from the Yankees. They squatted down. At least the Yankees did not come after them, not yet.

He grinned at the girl. "You're probably wishing you'd stayed behind."

"Never!"

The men waiting on the beach were indignant. "You said no looting."

The old warrior growled at them. "Shut up. He's got six rifles. More than any of us."

"He broke his own orders."

"Privileges of rank." Hendrick tried not to smirk.

The old warrior approved. "Traditional. Like old days."

"She's not a captive. She's one of us. Western door. Get into your canoes. Go, go."

Five men were too injured to paddle. Sergeant Johnson told the men to put one injured man in each canoe.

Hendrick took a flare out of his canoe and set it on the ground.

He glanced up at his men. "Don't look."

He set off the flare and averted his own gaze. The flare spluttered into life and the girl cried out.

He was irritated. "I told you not to look."

She was indignant. "What did you do that for?"

"To summon the Royal Navy."

"The navy?"

"We couldn't do this on our own."

"But you can summon them?" She sounded hugely impressed.

Two more teams got into their canoes. One man from each pushed it out into deep water and then scrambled aboard. Sergeant Johnson pushed the girl into Hendrick's canoe.

He knew that time was running short. "Go, go!"

He pushed his canoe out into the water. "I should do that, boss," Sergeant Johnson said.

"Shut up." He climbed aboard. He nearly capsized the

canoe but managed to keep his balance.

The rearguard, the old men, took shots at the Yankees. Then they climbed into the last of the canoes.

The men were paddling. But some men in the canoes paused to take pot-shots too.

The old warrior snarled at them. "Don't shoot. They're firing on your muzzle flashes."

They kept paddling. They suffered two more casualties. Then the survivors won clear.

Hendrick paused to draw breath. He saw that the girl was watching him. "Were you his wife?"

"His wife hated me. I suppose you will -. You're just as bad.

"I will take you to my mother."

"Your mother's house? You do not want me?"

The old warrior sounded tired. "A canoe is no place for a fight. We will overturn and drown."

Hendrick grinned in the dark. "You are full of good advice, old man. You keep a cool head in battle. And you can tell your family I said that."

They kept paddling north. The Yankees made no attempt to chase after them.

At dawn, the paddle steamer came to meet them.

"You did summon the navy," the girl said.

"That's what I said."

The crew lowered a rope ladder. "You go first," Peter said. "It's traditional."

Hendrick climbed up first, followed by the girl.

They were welcomed by the captain. "It sounded lively over there. I'm surprised any of you made it back."

"We'll need the surgeon."

"At once, colonel."

One at a time, the warriors climbed the ladder onto the paddle steamer. The sailors rigged a sling for the wounded. Then they lifted up the canoes.

"We've got to take them back to the army." Hendrick

said to the girl.

"Will the Yankees come after us?" she said.

"I doubt it. But it would be unwise to linger." He turned to the captain, who nodded.

The paddle-steamer turned north. The paddle-wheels beat the water and their speed increased. The lookout said that there was no sign of any pursuit.

Hendrick told himself that he could relax now. The rest of the journey was the responsibility of the navy.

At last, the warriors had time to take tally. They had eighteen rifles. Thirteen men were missing. Sixteen more were injured.

Hendrick thought the rifles they had won were not worth the loss. But his men were enthusiastic at this success. "We have humiliated them, sir."

"A coup," Peter said.

A crewman handed out mugs of coffee. "Careful, sir, it's hot."

Hendrick remembered something. He turned to the girl. "Did he have a revolver?"

"No. A pair of old flintlock pistols. He liked the silver decoration."

"We should have blown up the powder," Peter said.

The girl shook her head. "He said it was damp. Mouldy. It would not burn. He complained to headquarters but nobody listened."

Hendrick realised that she could provide useful intelligence. That might be more useful than the rifles. It would justify bringing her.

"Why was the fort half empty?" Peter said.

"All the troops had been sent east. To take part in the defence of Maine. He was glad he was not chosen."

Hendrick was thinking ahead. His mother would not approve of a mistress. She was saying it was time he married. His aunts had been bullying him. The best arrangement, they said, would be Western door. Turtle moiety. "No. It would not work."

His aunts had wanted a landowner's daughter. "Were you his slave?"

"Not in the way the white men mean it. But in the traditional meaning ..."

"Ah," Peter said.

Chapter 9

Portland June 14

Another fast warship was approaching the docks at Portland. An honour guard of ten men was waiting on the dock. Sergeant Wycombe was in charge.

He was baffled by the whole thing. Their new commander, Major Eastman, had said that a grand lady was coming to present their colours. She was a viscountess, whatever that meant.

The major certainly knew how to get things done. The lady had travelled by airship to St. Johns, then south by naval vessel. Of course, naval vessels were regular visitors now.

The major said that the battalion had to do the whole thing in style, which meant an honour guard. So the soldiers with the smartest uniforms had been told to clean themselves up. Captain Warwick had found white gloves for them.

The major had asked Captain Warwick to put a dependable sergeant in charge, so Wycombe had found himself in everybody's sights. Again.

The major and Captain Warwick were standing on the wharf, to the right of the honour guard.

The major had said that the lady was a dowager. Wycombe knew what that meant. Her husband had been the Viscount, he had died, and now her son had the job.

Where had this grand lady come from? Where had the major found her? And was she really as grand as the major said? Apparently, she outranked the governor's wife. To hear him tell it, her son was as grand as an American senator. He couldn't imagine an American senator's wife coming to Portland.

The Royal Naval vessel tied up. This ship had a small cabin amidships, behind the funnel. The sailors rigged a gangplank, with rope handrails. Four marines and a sergeant lined up on deck. A man in a fancy uniform - presumably the captain - appeared at the gangway.

A door in the cabin opened and a lady stepped out. She was wearing a black coat and a broad-brimmed hat. She had vigorous white hair. She walked forward and exchanged a word with the captain. She moved in a stately manner. Wycombe was impressed.

Everybody on shore was straining to get a look at her. But the lady ignored them.

Another lady stepped out of the cabin. She was far younger, with dark skin. She was followed by a gentleman in a suit and top hat. Together, they turned towards the gangplank, and the marines presented arms. Wycombe glanced at his own men. Yes, they were alert.

The ladies climbed the gangplank. Wycombe realised it was his turn. He waited for the older lady put her foot on the ground.

Now. "Present – arms!"

The soldiers went through their drill. They had been practising this for days. He was gratified that none of them made any mistakes.

Major Eastman saluted. The lady did nothing. Wycombe guessed that ladies were not allowed to salute. She turned towards the waiting coach and Wycombe recognised his second cue.

"Order – arms!"

"I have a carriage waiting, my lady," George Eastman said.

"Excellent, Major Eastman."

George guessed that the lady had been taught

deportment in her youth. He helped her to climb into the coach. Her companion followed.

It occurred to George that the lady's stateliness might be a symptom of old age catching up with her. But, if so, she hid it well.

George and the civilian, Mr. Lloyd, took the rearward-facing seats. George smiled. "We have commandeered a hotel as our headquarters. The manager says he has received millionaires before, but never a peeress."

She raised an eyebrow. "I don't think I'm more demanding than a Yankee millionaire." Her tone was astringent.

The carriage ride was short. George led the lady and her companion up the hotel steps and into the breakfast room. "Would you like some refreshment, madam? Tea? Coffee? Ah - something stronger?" Was she in pain?

"Earl Grey, if you please. The earl was such a charming man."

The waiter bustled off. He might be a Yankee but he was impressed by aristocrats too.

"I must say that I was surprised that you accepted our request, madam."

"Why, major? It is an honour."

"Coming all this way -."

"I have been given first class treatment, I assure you. In the past, I have often been treated as little better than a poor relation."

"Well, the officers at Montreal regard a posting to this battalion as career poison. Even if they are offered a promotion."

She smiled. "Why did you accept, major?"

He smiled back. "When this war is over, I shall resign. Life in a peacetime regiment is not for me."

"Well, if I were sixteen, looking for a husband, I might have refused. But I am too old to worry about that sort of nonsense."

"Will your family criticise your actions?"

"Do you know, my daughter-in-law might be jealous."

The waiter brought the teapot on a silver tray.

"Well – thank you again for volunteering."

"I have never done anything like this before. I'm worried that I am not elegant enough for this task."

"We can turn it into a drill – practice it. I want you to be haughty -."

"Surely not."

"Well - not friendly. Not informal. The men expect that - want that." He realised that he was floundering. "The men accept your condescension as a gift. The more condescension, the greater the gift. Does that make sense?"

"I think so. Although people usually complain I'm too distant."

He smiled. "On the day, that's what we want."

"I can see that this means a lot to them. I would hate to disappoint them." She sipped at her tea. "I would like to see the site of the ceremony."

George nodded. "I had hoped for a red carpet so you could wear a dress with a trail."

"You have been reading too many romantic novels, young man. I shall wear walking boots and hold my skirts clear of the dirt."

"Yes, madam." He realised that behind her sharp tone was a sense of humour. He relaxed slightly. "Shall I summon your carriage?"

"I have been stuck on that ship for five days. A walk will do me good."

Together, they walked down the hill to Commercial Road. Her companion and Mr. Lloyd trailed along.

Road traffic was very light. George pointed. "The men would form a hollow square here, facing inwards. You and your companions would stand somewhere here, with your backs to the warehouse. The honour-guard would then step forward."

Lady Forlaith looked round. "I see. Yes, that could work."

That evening, for the first time, the officers of the battalion dined formally. Lady Forlaith was naturally their guest of honour.

The battalion's musicians were doing their best to entertain the diners.

Captain Warwick had offered the men extra pay if they would volunteer to act as waiters. He had been surprised that so many had come forward.

Lady Forlaith avoided any discussion of strategy. "I don't understand why the US didn't recruit these men for their own army. Or am I asking a foolish question?"

George shrugged. "It's a very difficult question, madam. Well - the US has a strange attitude to blacks."

Captain Warwick nodded. "We wouldn't have recruited them ourselves unless we were desperate."

Lady Forlaith smiled. "Britain seems to get desperate every ten years or so."

Captain Warwick smiled. "So true. But – may I ask why you came to visit Canada."

Lady Forlaith glanced at Charles Lloyd. "I was asked to go to Montreal to inspect the condition of the female nurses. We heard rumours that they had been ill-treated. As it turned out, their condition was much better than I had expected."

"I see, madam." George was relieved. Lady Forlaith was not merely a war tourist.

Lady Forlaith frowned. "I don't want to ignore the enlisted men. That's why I'm here, after all."

I think we have the answer to that," George said.

The mess stewards whisked away the plates and served coffee.

During coffee George, in his role as the commanding

officer, asked the mess steward to bring the band director to him. George introduced the director to Lady Forlaith. The mess manager brought a chair for the band director. George invited the band director to have a drink.

The mess manager brought the drinks on a tray. The band director, warned in advance, had specified lemonade.

Lady Forlaith complemented him and his team. Captain Warwick had explained beforehand that the praise was for his entire team. The band director seemed embarrassed by his role in this little play.

After his drink, the band director asked permission to retire. They had practised this too. George granted his permission, the band director withdrew, and the extra chair was removed.

It was all very formal, but the staff seemed gratified by the praise.

Portland June 15

At breakfast, Lady Forlaith announced that she was going to visit the sewing girls who had made the flag. This surprised everyone.

"But the place is in a back-street," Major Eastman said.

But Lady Forlaith refused to back down. The major gave in and led the way. Lady Forlaith's female companion followed her, unperturbed.

The windows of the side-street workshop were small, so it was poorly lit, but it was scrupulously clean. It was not as bad as Lady Forlaith had expected.

The women were equally astonished at the lady's arrival. She noted that all of the women were coloured.

Lady Forlaith guessed that the manageress had been

born free and she had accepted runaways because they would work for a pittance.

She smiled, dismissed her male escort, and asked whether she could have some tea. She asked to examine the flag. One girl unfolded it and shook it out. In the upper corner, where it would be fastened to the staff, was the three superimposed crosses of the United Kingdom. In the opposite corner was a device of six broken chain-links arranged in a circle. The gap in each link of the chain was marked by a zigzag red stripe.

The manageress was eager to explain. "That red stripe shows that the link has been broken. We wanted the gap to be a dark red, to show rust. That showed how weak the bonds were."

"I see," Lady Forlaith said.

"But the men wanted bright red to signify their freedom had been bought by fighting."

"Let us hope that is not an omen," Lady Forlaith said.

The woman was puzzled. "What's that, madam – my lady?"

"Nothing, madam." She spotted a loose thread, got out her needle, and set about the task of repairing it.

The sewing-women were astonished that a grand lady would do such a thing.

She paused, needle in hand. "All English ladies learn how to do delicate embroidery, no matter how grand they are. But, you see, ladies are not allowed to do anything practical. We're only supposed to work at decorative things." She returned to her work. "I feel that it's very important that I make a contribution."

She finished, then asked her companion to do deal with another loose thread.

"I wish there was time to do more."

The girl who had held out the flag asked where Dido was from.

Sergeant Priddy faced the junior sergeants. "You asked about that girl Dido. She isn't a slave. You ought to know better than that. She was born on Antigua. Although I haven't heard anyone say any good about the place. Her relatives sent her to Bermuda to get an education. Then she moved to London. She's studying at a college or something. They say she's learning Latin."

"Latin? I'm more confused than ever." Wycombe said.

"Why's she following the lady around?" Freeman said.

"A grand lady needs a companion, even when she's a grandmother. Although that works both ways. The old lady's her companion, too."

"Wait – you say she's a lady? A black?"

Priddy nodded. "If your parents are rich enough – yes. The colour of your money counts as much as the colour of your skin. It helps that her father's an officer in the army. Serving among heathens, they tell me."

"Ah. You said that a black could get to vote on Bermuda, if he had enough money," Wycombe said.

"That's right. A man could, but a woman can't," Priddy said.

Freeman was diverted. "You mean you could call yourself a gentleman, sergeant, if you had enough folding money?"

Wycombe grinned. "Priddy doesn't want to be a gentleman, do you, sergeant-major?"

"Damned right I don't," Priddy growled, and they laughed.

Portland, June 16

The soldiers of the battalion prepared for their ceremony and the townsfolk turned out to watch. Few of them had seen a military ceremony like this before. None had seen a British aristocrat before. Most of the black people of Portland, including the sewing girls, had taken the day off to attend.

The invited guests, their backs to the shops and warehouses, were told that they would form one side of the soldiers' square. George stood in the centre of the row. He was holding the pike vertically, with the colours furled around it.

The carriage drew up and Lady Forlaith stepped down, followed by her companion and Mr. Lloyd. They walked to their allotted place, next to George. He said a few words of welcome. Lady Forlaith stepped forward to take the pikestaff. George relinquished his grip and stepped clear.

The band of the marines played the anthem.

The men of the battalion marched along the road, one company after another, past the viscountess and the spectators. Captain Warwick shouted an order and men halted. The captain shouted another order and the men turned to face Lady Forlaith and the guests.

Another order, and the two leading companies wheeled round to form part of the hollow square. The rear companies wheeled to face the leading companies, completing the hollow square.

Sergeant Freeman wore the leather baldric over his shoulder. He stepped forward, accompanied by his colour guard of corporals

Lady Forlaith spoke in clear tones. "The men of this battalion have shown courage and determination to reach this place today. You have chosen freedom over a long life. You have earned the right to bear these colours. I have worked on these colours with my own hands. I present them to you, sergeant, as the representative of this battalion, and ask that you to bear them with honour."

Sergeant Freeman went down on one knee, and together they lifted the foot of the pike into the holster on the baldric. They had practised this the previous evening.

"You have it?" she whispered.

"Yes. Thanks."

Lady Forlaith let go and stepped back.

Sergeant Freeman stood, not without effort. The men of the battalion tensed. But the sergeant retained his balance. He turned to face the battalion.

"Battalion! Present – arms," Captain Warwick said.

The drill was executed flawlessly.

The leading and rear companies wheeled back to take their places in the line. Sergeant Freeman took his place at the head of the column. The band played another tune and the battalion turned and marched off the way they had come.

"That was well done, madam," George said.

Back in the barracks, the enlisted men discussed the ceremony. Most of them were satisfied. They had asked for a grand lady and the viscountess had been grand enough.

Some complained that she had been too grand. "She looked down her nose at us."

Wycombe rejected this. "No more than Sergeant Priddy does. We got what we asked for. She would have been just as grand to a white regiment. Just this once, we got treated the same as them."

Portland, June 17

The viscountess walked out of the hotel, followed by her companion and George, and stepped into the waiting carriage. Together, they drove back to the docks.

She smiled. "I would like to thank you, major, for giving me the opportunity to contribute."

He smiled back. "Thank you, madam. It means a lot to us."

The carriage turned along Commercial Street and then along the steamer wharf. Captain Warwick, Sergeant Wycombe and the honour guard were waiting.

The sergeant gave the command to present arms. Captain Warwick raised his sword in salute. This time, the viscountess touched her hat in reply. She continued on her way, down the ramp to the deck of the ship. She stepped off the gangplank and onto the deck of her ship. The captain stepped forward to welcome her.

Afterwards, in the barracks, Wycombe sought out Sergeant Priddy and described what he had seen.

"You say she saluted the captain?" Priddy said.

"That's what it looked like," Wycombe said.

"She shouldn't have done that. Saluted, I mean. She wasn't in uniform. Shouldn't have done anything at all."

"But she had to do something," Wycombe said. "If she had followed the rules, it would have looked as if she was ignoring us."

"She's part of the battalion, somehow," Freeman said.

New York State, June 18,

Tommy was told to report to the Commandant of Fort Ticonderoga. A private from a southern state escorted her across the courtyard of the fort to the HQ building. The private opened the door to the commandant's office. The commandant was sitting behind a desk.

Tommy stepped forward. "Sir?"

The commandant leaned back in his chair. "Sergeant, we sent a report, via a neutral embassy, that you had been taken prisoner. We have now received a letter in reply, via the embassy.

"Your commanding officer was surprised to learn that

you had been taken prisoner. They seem to have assumed that you had been killed."

Tommy felt a moment's panic. "I can't imagine why, sir." Or – had poor Asher died? Had he suffered a seizure worse than her own?

And – she had refused to establish rapport with anyone. They must have assumed the worst.

She had to tell this Yankee officer something. "Perhaps those Indian scouts made the wrong guess, sir. An' sent a report back."

"That could be it."

"Could I write a letter, sir? To the lieutenant?"

The commandant looked unhappy. "I would have to read it, sergeant."

"Of course, sir."

Lake Ontario, Brant's Ford, June 18

Peter Theyanoguin, the Mohawk regiment's second in command, knocked on the door of the regiment's improvised suburban headquarters. He was shown into what had been Mrs. Teyonhehkwen's morning room.

Hendrick was slouching on the sofa. He looked up, annoyed. "You haven't come here to discuss logistics, have you, Peter?"

"Among other things. Sorry, cousin."

Peter took his place in the armchair.

The girl, Nancy, walked in with a teapot on a tray. She was wearing a dark woollen dress and a white apron. Peter thought she looked neat. And more composed than the last time he had seen her.

Peter grinned. "The veteran has come to talk about battles long ago. Sit down and chat."

She was flustered. "I must not."

Colonel Hendrick helped her out. "Sit down and pour

the tea. Play the hostess."

"Will your mother be angry with me?"

"If Peter visits too often, mother will be angry with *him*. Draw up a chair for yourself."

She put the tray on the table and sat down.

Peter grinned. "Have they been treating you kindly?"

"Yes." She poured tea into the first cup. It was a traditional herbal infusion, not imported black tea. "No. The colonel deceived me. When you said you would take me to your mother, you didn't say your home was army headquarters."

Peter grinned but said nothing.

"We are a poor nation. We have to use our own homes," Hendrick said.

Peter tried a reassuring smile. "What do you intend to do now?"

"I'm working as Mrs. Teyonhehkwen's maid. Or as her companion. A bit of both. She says that if I want, she will give me a work reference. So I could go and work in the big city."

Hendrick grinned at Peter. "There's another choice. The family has a plot of land. My mother suggested that Nancy here should tend it. But she wasn't enthusiastic."

Nancy looked prim. "I'm not *that* traditional."

"My friend Peter is not traditional either. He acts as our adjutant. Or chief of staff."

"What is he chief of?" Nancy said.

"He commands a couple of his cousins, he keeps records, and writes letters to the governor."

"Our uniforms need replacing and we need more ammunition. Boring stuff." That reminded Peter of his task. "Can you read and write?"

"Yes, why?"

"I need someone with good handwriting."

"Is that why you came?" She seemed put out by this.

"Yes. I need everyone I can get. Hendrick is useless.

His handwriting is excellent but very slow. And if he speeds up it's terrible. It's as good as a code, if an outsider tried to read it."

Hendrick changed the subject. "I'm disappointed that the Yankees didn't send the army to garrison Fort Erie. We failed."

Nancy sipped at her tea. "Perhaps they're desperate. They can't spare anyone."

Hendrick frowned. "If that's true, it means we could attack again and they wouldn't chase us out."

Peter was interested. "Detroit? Or another fort further north? The people of Detroit would be much happier as part of Canada."

"Perhaps they would, but it isn't going to happen."

"Sault Ste. Marie, perhaps?"

"Is today the big day?" Peter asked.

"Yes," Hendrick said.

An hour later, Colonel Hendrick received several important guests in his suburban headquarters. One of them was an airship captain with a badly scarred face. The sight unsettled Hendrick. Some of the old warriors had taken warrior scars, but this accidental scarring was far worse.

Another of his guests was Charles Lloyd, a member of a powerful English family and reputed to know everybody of importance in Montreal.

Hendrick led the way down to the basement. He was embarrassed that his headquarters was nothing more than a cramped town-house. He should have found somewhere bigger.

But, from this modest room, he could keep tabs on events along the entire north coast of Lake Erie. A blackboard had been attached to one wall, with a map of the lake painted on it.

Three telegraphists were squeezed along the bench,

facing their needle telegraph instruments. Two were female.

His mother's housemaid handed out cups of tea.

"I'm sorry we're so cramped. But in peacetime this was little more than a clubhouse for the militia officers."

"We've all had to improvise," the airship captain said. "Our headquarters is a wooden shack."

While they waited, he entertained his guests by giving an explanation. "We've been listening to rumours circulating on the Yankee side of the lake. One persistent rumour was of British airships flying over US territory. The journeys covered hundreds of miles in a single night."

The airship captain smiled. "We've heard some of those rumours. Absurd, of course."

"Yes, captain. But I wondered: would our observers be able to spot a US airship if it approached? So I asked for this exercise." He glanced at the clock.

There was a knock at the door upstairs. One of the female telegraphists got up to answer it. She led in a telegraph delivery boy, who handed over an envelope. "For you in person, sir."

"Thank you." Hendrick turned to face his guests. "One thing I can't do is link up to the commercial telegraph. For that last half-mile, the message is carried by hand."

He opened the envelope. "This is from the police sergeant at Nanticoke, on the coast. East of here. I asked him as a special favour to send a telegram. He says that your airship has passed. And he thanks me for organising it. The local people were impressed."

The girl picked up a piece of chalk and marked the reported position on the map.

"But why can't the police sergeant send his message straight here?" the captain said.

"We were given British army equipment," Hendrick

said. He gestured towards the needle telegraph instruments in their wooden cases. "Nanticoke uses the commercial American Morse standard."

"So you don't have telegraph contact with the capital?" the captain asked.

"Not direct contact, no. I have to send a runner to the telegraph office."

"One thing I have never understood." Mr. Lloyd took a sip at his tea. "While we wait, can you tell us how you came to be an independent nation?"

Hendrick glanced at the clock. "I think there's enough time." And he told the story of his ancestor's trip to London.

They waited. One of the girls glanced at the clock.

Then the front door opened with a bang. The Army Air Service captain jumped.

One of Hendrick's soldiers walked in. He wore army boots rather than moccasins. "Beg pardon, sir. This is the routine message from the Telegraph office. Weather reports from Montreal. Steady westerly, they say. And we all know what that means. Headwinds."

Hendrick was annoyed at this brash behaviour in front of his guests. "Thank you, private."

The girl wrote the details of the weather report on their map.

Hendrick handed the message slip to the Air Service captain. "Will this endanger the flight?"

The captain studied the details with interest. "No, colonel, not unless it gets a lot worse than that."

The three telegraphists reached for their telegraph instruments and began sending the weather synopsis on to the coastal stations. Hendrick and his guests waited a few minutes.

Then one of the telegraph needles flicked to and fro as a message came through.

"At last," Hendrick said.

The girl turned and spoke in an undertone. "The first observer, at Long Point – he just says he has seen it."

Hendrick held back a curse. "Idiot. He knows the proper drill. Tell him we need to know compass bearing, distance, and heading."

"Yes, cousin." The girl reached out to her telegraph instrument and tapped out her message.

A message came back promptly. "The airship is a mile east of Long Point, colonel." The girl stood and marked this on map.

"A mile away? Is that plausible?" Mr. Lloyd, asked.

"Certainly. Those airships are quite large, remember," the Air Service captain said.

Over the next half hour, the needle flickered again and again, as the observer gave them updated positions. Then he reported that airship had passed, a mile to the south of Long Point.

The Air Service captain was impressed. Hendrick hid his relief. For months he had promised that his regiment could observe anything that moved on the lake. Now his men were showing that he could keep that promise. Just so long as nobody fouled up.

Port Stanley, military lookout point.

The Mohawk garrison and the local population had turned out on the shore-front to watch. For all of them, this was the biggest event in months.

The farmers had arranged a barbecue, roasting a hog whole. The children had been let off their usual chores.

A girl spotted it first. "There it is! There it is!" She pointed east.

The sergeant looked through his binoculars and sent one of his men running to the telegraph operator.

One boy was disappointed. "It's white. I thought they

painted them black."

"Just goes to show. You can't trust the newspapers," his father said.

They watched avidly as the airship proceeded along the coast.

"It's very noisy," the girl said.

Their excitement heightened when it reached their position. They could make out the serial number on the side. The gondola, slung below the envelope, was open to the elements. The crew were now clearly visible.

The children waved, excited. The crew waved back, which delighted the children.

The Mohawk signaller stepped out of his tiny office, far back from the shore, to take a look. A dozen men had gathered in the street outside his office. He had attracted as much attention as the airship itself.

Then he stepped back inside to send a new message. The spectators took it in turns to peer over his shoulder as he tapped away.

On board the airship, the lookout turned to the commander. "Port Stanley is now on the beam, sir." He had to shout over the noise of the engine.

The commander ducked into the tiny navigator's room and made a note in his logbook. "Very good."

The engineer used a rag to wipe the oil off his hands. "We've used up half out fuel, sir."

The commander was disappointed. "We can't continue to Detroit, then."

"I would not advise it, sir."

"Do you think we can get back?" He realised, too late, that an officer should not admit any doubts.

"The weather prediction was for a steady westerly, sir. That'll take us home with fuel to spare."

"Good."

"We could continue to Detroit, sir. But we'd get home

with our fuel bunkers empty."

The commander was tempted. He shook his head.

"Best not risk it. Besides, we mustn't get too close. They may have rocket defences."

"Yes, sir."

"New course, helmsman. North-west by north."

"North-west by north, sir."

"We'll head inland to the railroad line and then follow it home."

Portland June 18, evening

George Eastman summoned his junior officers to his office. He had put a map on the wall, showing the area from Portland to Sebago Lake.

"The Yankees have an army up north, threatening Quebec. When they launched their attack, they assumed they could send supplies by railroad." The listeners nodded.

"But then we arrived and took the freight depot and the bridges. So now they're sending munitions by road. From Saco to Yarmouth, where they put the stuff on the northbound train. They can only send half of what they did before. I would like to arrange a sally, to stop them. Build a blockhouse to watch over the post-road ... Captain Warwick?"

"We'd need another regiment to do that, sir. Although the very thought of an attack must terrify the Yankees. "

"Yes, of course. But I have received word that a unit of the Maine militia has arrived from the east. The report said two companies. They're positioned on these hills, here, due north of us.

"Now, we could strengthen our defences, wait for them to attack us." He paused, but no-one interrupted.

"But the governor in Quebec is worried that the

Yankees will reach the St. Lawrence. So I have been ordered to take the initiative. To continue the pressure on the enemy, whatever the cost.

"Now, this advance by their militia is a threat to our hold on Portland. I want to attack, drive the militia aside."

"Their deployment threatens that key bridge," Warwick said. "They attacked there last time, broke through our defences."

"Right," George said. "Mr. Warwick, take half of your men. Four companies. Those with the best weapons. Drive the militia off that hilltop ... You will lead the expedition, captain."

"A surprise attack?" Warwick asked.

"No. I want to show the world what these men can do in a stand-up fight. That they can defend this town."

Bermuda, June 19

Mr. Warwick had arranged to receive copies of the most important US newspapers. He was too wise to ask how the papers got past the naval blockade.

He was surprised by the latest edition to reach Bermuda.

He pushed the newspaper across the table towards his wife. "They've reported the viscountess's visit in detail."

Mrs. Warwick took the paper and read them with fascination. Her son was in the news again. "Why all the fuss? A viscountess, travelling alone, is much less important than the governor's wife. Now if her son had been with her ..."

"To the Americans, she's an aristocrat. That's all that matters."

She studied the absurd American reaction. 'US government humiliated.' 'New British regiment.' 'British

Ceremony Planned with Utmost secrecy.' 'Daring visit to field of battle by aristocrat.'

More than one newspaper emphasised that the flags had been presented to a regiment of coloured troops on US soil.

"Well – this visit has taken on the appearance of a propaganda coup," she said.

"Only because their newspapers puffed the matter up," Mr. Warwick said.

"Yes." The Americans were astonished that the British had the self-assurance to send an aristocrat to a war zone.

"I must show these reports to Mrs. Priddy," Mrs. Warwick said.

"Of course, my dear."

"The Yankees are giving this as much attention as a military expedition."

"Yes. But the Canadian newspapers ignored the visit. To them, her ladyship is a poor relation."

Portland, Maine, June 19

The battalion made no attempt at a surprise attack. That would have been impossible.

The troops assembled on Commercial Road, one company at a time. With all of Portland watching, they marched in a long column along the post road. Each company had its own drummer.

Sergeant Freeman and his colour party marched behind the first company. Captain Warwick followed them. An ammunition wagon followed the last company in the line.

The townsfolk watched as the soldiers marched by. There was no anger, only a morbid fascination. Some of the watchers knew that these men were marching to their deaths.

The men of the battalion were subdued. There was no singing today.

They crossed the river and then began climbing the hill.

Warwick realised that this was difficult terrain. There was a patchwork of fields and wooded hills rather than open countryside. But the woods were not too dense. Warwick expected the men to make their way through. And the hills were not too steep.

The first company of troops reached the foot of Leighton Hill. Warwick had never commanded this many men before. He told the first company to form a line, in three ranks, then sent them forward up the hill.

The company advanced through the woods, drums beating, until they reached a clearing. On the far side they could see the Maine militia, also drawn up in a line.

The sergeants told them to straighten their ranks. The Maine militia stood firm, waiting. Captain D'Israeli told the drummer to sound the advance.

Warwick, down below, could hear the shooting. The only thing he could see with his binoculars was trees. All he could do was wait for news and worry. Then runners came down, asking for more ammunition.

"Are they holding steady?"

"Yes, sir."

Warwick sent them off to the ammunition wagon. The second company had now formed line, so he sent them in to support the first company. He knew that the two companies together outnumbered the enemy.

He tried to guess what was happening by the sound alone The first company kept firing and reloading, so they were standing firm. But that meant that the enemy also stood their ground.

The volunteer company's rate of fire was too slow. Much slower than that of militia. What was happening up there?

The sergeant reported to Captain D'Israeli that they were running low on ammunition. "Three rounds for each man, sir."

D'Israeli was shocked at the losses. The enemy militia was still standing firm. "Why can't we get more ammunition? What are they playing at down there? No matter. We can't stop them with bayonets alone. Sound the retreat, sergeant."

"Yes, sir."

Warwick was dismayed when the survivors of the first company reached the foot of the hill. The company had suffered too many casualties.

Warwick told them to get more ammunition from the supply wagon and to take care of the wounded.

The third company had now formed up. They seemed eager, so Warwick sent them forward, to support the second company.

The firing intensified. Runners soon arrived from the second company, begging for more ammunition. There was always a queue at the ammunition wagon.

Warwick was watching the hilltop through his binoculars. The firefight was hidden by the brow of the hill. But then he saw the second company retreating. He knew the third company could not defeat the enemy alone. "I shall lead the fourth company, with the colours."

"Is that wise, sir?" Sergeant-major Priddy said.

"I refuse to sit here while my men go forward, sergeant. Besides, I want to see what the hell's going on up there."

"Yes, sir."

The men of the fourth company climbed the hill, sometimes scrambling on uneven ground. They came clear of the woods. On the far side of the clearing, they could see the long line of the Maine militia, waiting for them. The enemy were standing with a wood at their backs.

Over to the right, the men of the third company were formed in line. The enemy opposite must have suffered casualties too, but they stood firm.

The sergeants shouted at the company to reform their line. They advanced on the Yankees at a steady pace.

Sergeant Freeman and the colour party were at the centre of the line.

The open ground contained bodies in both red and blue. As they approached, the enemy shouted insults at them.

"Company, halt." The men primed their weapons. "Present. - fire."

Wycombe aimed, and fired. He was shocked that only one of their opponents fell. He remembered something that Priddy had told him – you should always aim low.

Captain Warwick shouted at them to reload. Wycombe assumed that they were up against seasoned professionals.

Then the Yankees fired. The man to Wycomb's left fell.

Wycombe sensed that the men were confused. Bewildered. The militiamen in front of them fired again. The company suffered heavy losses.

Then the men realised that their sergeants were as confused as they were. They did not know how to win.

This was the sort of battle that Wycombe had expected, quite unlike World's End. This was a stand-up fight. Men were wounded and fell, screaming.

He could see the enemy flag. But why didn't they charge the enemy?

Wycombe's platoon stood firm and reloaded and fired, just as they had been taught. They continued even when their companions died. But they died free men. This was what they had come for. "Reload!"

They had to fire at the enemy because they had to show that they were steady under fire. "Present – fire!"

The Yankees fired another volley in reply. Sergeant Freeman carrying the flag was killed. The colours fell to the ground. Every man in the honour guard fell, wounded.

Wycombe expected one of the honour guard to pick up the colours, but none of them did. Perhaps they were dead too.

The Yankees cheered – and ran forward.

Wycombe was horrified. He abandoned his place and ran for the colours. "Come on!"

He found the colours. This was their own, the broken chains. He knew what the Yankees would say if they captured the colours- blacks could not fight. He had to save it.

He grabbed the pikestaff and lifted it up. It was their special flag. A private next to him seized the other flag.

The private also knew what the Yankees would say. "Stand fast, stand fast!"

But Wycombe's only concern now was to save his flag from the Yankees. He carried it towards the nearest standing group of men in red. That took him sideways across the battlefield, not forward. His own section followed him.

Everybody else noticed the movement of the colours.

One man after another, they moved sideways to get closer to Wycombe. The captain shouted at them to stand fast, but no-one paid any attention.

Wycombe stepped back. The Yankees continued their

rush. The men of the company fired another ragged volley. The survivors stepped back to keep level with Wycombe. Some were assisting wounded colleagues.

The sergeants gave up the attempt to make them stand fast and stepped back too.

Captain Warwick made no attempt to stop them.

Halfway down the slope, sheltering at the edge of a birch wood, stood a small detachment of D'Israeli's men, kept in reserve.

At the captain's order, they formed a line and primed their muskets.

Warwick and Priddy, retreating with their company, told the retreating men to form a rearguard line behind D'Israeli's men.

"Reload and copy them." Priddy said. Most of the fourth company steadied down and formed a line. But many men just streamed past. "Powder's gone."

The colour-party reached them. Warwick realised that the man carrying the colours was Wycombe. He was still carrying his musket.

"Give the colours to somebody without a rifle. Then rejoin your platoon. Get them to wait to the left of D'Israeli's company."

"Yes, sir."

"But don't risk the colours." He realised that his orders were contradictory.

Then the pursuing Yankees came into sight. They were skirmishers in open order, running through the trees. Warwick guessed that these were professionals, not militia. Had the militia stayed on the hilltop? He judged that there were only thirty of them.

An officer, waving a sword, led them. Warwick noticed that he was plump.

Warwick shouted. "First rank. Present. Fire."

D'Israeli's men fired and stepped back.

"Fourth company. Present. Fire."

Warwick was dismayed. The first volley had little effect. "You aimed too high! Reload."

"Second rank. Present. Aim low. Fire." They achieve higher casualties. "Reload!"

The remainder of the Yankees continued their charge. There was no time for another volley.

The Yankees reached the rearguard line. Suddenly the fighting was hand to hand. But the men of the fourth company were steady. Most had been at World's End. They had done this sort of fighting before.

The Yankee officer was a major. He recognised Warwick, shouted an insult and waved his sword.

Warwick, taken by surprise, fumbled for his revolver. But he was too slow.

Wycombe stepped forward and used his musket to club the major down. Warwick finally pulled his revolver out of its military holster and shot at a sergeant. He missed.

D'Israeli's men, off to one side, fired a disciplined volley.

The Yankees realised they were outnumbered, facing determined opposition, and were leaderless. They pulled back.

Warwick guessed that the men of his company would refuse to advance a second time. He gave the order for them to reload, then continued their retreat.

They reached the foot of the hill. Warwick expected the militia to chase after them. They had the advantage now. He knew that if they attacked, the steady retreat of his men would become a rout.

But the militia did not follow them. Warwick guessed that they had suffered heavy casualties too. He told the men to form a column and withdraw. The ammunition wagon led the way.

The retreat was relatively orderly up to the river crossings, but it was poorly managed by the new sergeants.

Each company should have waited its turn. The ammunition wagon went across the bridge first. But the driver was in a hurry and was careless. The wagon slewed sideways and overturned. The horses panicked too, kicking and rearing. Together, the wagon and the horses blocked the bridge. This unexpected obstacle incited panic in Warwick's force.

Some men attempted to ford the river, discarding their arms and equipment. Soldiers who had crossed the bridge streamed uncontrollably toward Portland.

Only a few men remained by the bridge to act as rearguard. But the militia made no attempt to follow them.

Portland, June 19, dusk

Back in Portland, Major Eastman held a debriefing. The senior, experienced, sergeants stood at the back. The mood was uncomfortable.

Sergeant-major Priddy stepped forward. "The company sergeants have counted up their losses, sir. One hundred dead or missing, another fifty severely wounded. Many of them won't fight again. And fifty will be unfit for duty for a month."

Warwick was appalled. They had lost half of the men who marched out. The arithmetic was simple. They had seven hundred fighting men left.

He turned to the major. "If the Yankees attack now …"

"It'll be dark soon, captain. They won't try it now. And in the morning the men will have steadied down."

"I hope you're right, sir."

"I'll send those Mohawks to guard the bridge itself."

Eastman was grim. "You say that some of the men threw away their weapons? Don't give them new ones. There aren't enough to go round."

"Yes, sir."

"The men brought their colours back? Good. The dishonour would be much worse if they had abandoned the colours."

"Yes, sir."

Eastman was critical of the men who had fought. "It has to be said. They ran away. Will they ever make good soldiers?"

Warwick was defensive. "The men are untrained, sir. In the regular army, they say it takes three years to become a reliable soldier. And today almost all of the men were raw recruits. And -."

"Go on, captain."

"The men were badly led. There were not enough officers or experienced sergeants. It was my fault ... I should have allowed each company to support the others."

"I see."

"But they showed they will hold their ground. The rearguard behaved well. The Yankees know that if they attack, they will meet opposition."

"We ran out of ammunition, sir," D'Israeli said. "We should have arranged proper ammunition-bearers."

There was an uncomfortable pause. None of them had thought of that.

"In the regular army it's done by boys, sir," D'Israeli said.

"I'll ask some of the men without muskets to volunteer, sir." Priddy said.

Eastman was not convinced. "We're going to need more training. At company level rather than platoon level." An unpleasant thought occurred to him. "They've all returned? To town?"

"Yes, sir," Priddy said.

"Good." Eastman remembered a statement of the Duke of Wellington: he did not mind if men ran away in panic, as long as they returned to their colours afterwards.

Portland, June 20

Captain Warwick was having breakfast in the hotel when a waiter brought a message that the junior sergeants were outside and would like to speak to him.

Warwick left the breakfast room and went onto the porch. "Yes, sergeant?"

He was not surprised to see that the deputation had chosen Wycombe as their spokesman.

Wycombe took off his hat and held it in front of him. "We feel that we ought to resign, sir. We couldn't cope yesterday. That cost the lives of more'n a hundred men."

"Out of the question. Who would I replace you with?"

"But - all of us were lost, sir. Clueless. The noise. All that smoke ..."

"Combat is always like that, sergeant. Bewildering. At least next time you'll be prepared. You'll know how baffling it will be.

"It wasn't your fault. It was mine. I sent untrained men into battle." Wycombe looked as if he was about to argue.

"That will be all. Dismissed."

Chapter 10

Fort Malden, June 21

The railroad did not extend as far as the Detroit River. So Colonel Hendrick and Sergeant Chard completed the final stage of their journey by spring cart. Hendrick's Mohawk sergeant, Johnson, took the back seat.

The road emerged from the woods. Chard caught his first glimpse of the fort. It was rectangular, with leaf-shaped bastions at each corner. Colonel Hendrick enjoyed explaining everything that he knew about the place.

"The original fort was destroyed in the war of 1812. Much of the rebuilding was carried out in 1838, during another crisis. The commander was Colonel Townshend.

"Now we have two regiments of infantry, and the Royal Artillery, stationed here against a possible American invasion."

"Then there's the local militia, sir," Johnson said.

"Yes. The idea is that if the Yankees invade, they dare not march on Toronto and leave Fort Malden at their backs."

"I see, sir." Chard looked out over the river. The water was grey. The wind was blowing and the waves had white crests. The far bank was visible only as a dark line. "Is that Detroit over there, sir?"

"No, Detroit is further north. Upriver. The deep-water channel is between us and that island. Guns from the fort could reach the island, so they secure the river." Hendrick urged on his horses and they moved on to the gate.

"Your business, sir?" the sentry said. He tried to avoid

staring at the tattooed sergeant in the back seat.

Hendrick drew up his horses and explained his mission. The sentry saluted and waved them on. "We were told to expect you, sir. The colonel's house is on the left."

Chard looked round. On the western wall, two monstrous coastal artillery guns pointed towards the river.

A platoon was drilling on the parade ground, under the care of a sergeant. Chard realised that all the men, and their sergeant, were black.

"They're from one of the militia companies," Hendrick said. He climbed down from the cart. "Now *they're* motivated."

"They have the most to lose from an attack," Johnson said.

"I see, sir." Chard knew that Fort Malden was the northern end of the Underground Railroad. According to the newspapers, the fort was an embodiment of freedom for those travelling along the Railroad. It acted as a gateway and refuge for the refugees.

Another sentry stood outside the colonel's house. Hendrick walked over and explained is mission. The sentry called for the sergeant, who escorted Hendrick to Colonel Townshend's office. Chard, most uncomfortable, tagged along.

Several officers were sitting round a table. A map lay on it.

Colonel Townshend stood to greet Hendrick. "Pleased to meet you, colonel." He introduced the other officers. The one that Chard remembered was Captain Finch of the Second Essex Coloured Volunteers.

Hendrick smiled. "Pleased to meet you."

"Tea, colonel?" Colonel Townshend said.

"Thank you, sir."

Hendrick sat down. Chard stood by the door.

"Did you see my men outside?" Captain Finch said "Those refugees who succeed in reaching Canada are eager to remain within the country's protective borders."

Hendrick smiled politely. "I see, sir. Quite understandable."

"Many of the refugees joined the militia during periods of conflict. During both the War of 1812 and the 1837 Rebellions, Black Canadians served with distinction at Fort Malden."

Colonel Townshend intervened. "Is it necessary for the sergeant to be here, Hendrick?"

"Yes. Sergeant Chard is our expert on the telegraph," Hendrick said. "You wanted a telegraph wire, colonel?"

Townshend was not happy. "Yes. I want to call for help if I need it. But why did they send you?"

Hendrick smiled. "I organised a wire to my observation posts on the south coast. My men were not very skilled. But, you see, we did it without any cost to the army."

"Ah," Captain Finch said

"So, when the government heard of your request, they remembered that we had improvised our own telegraph service. And so they asked us."

Townshend looked baffled.

"It's a question of accounting, sir," Chard said. "Mr. Hendrick's costs don't show up in the army accounts."

Hendrick nodded. "The Telegraph company won't do it – they say there's no profit in it. The army will provide the telegraph wire, but that's all. The home affairs ministry could pay for the construction. But they could not pay the operators."

"Bureaucratic nonsense," Colonel Townshend said.

Hendrick grinned but said nothing.

Townshend pointed to the map on the table. "The ministry of the interior is worried the Yankees might send a fleet across the river to land *here,* and march on

Toronto ..."

Hendrick nodded. "Strategically sound, really. They tried it before."

"Quite. So the governor approves of a lookout post here. And a telegraph wire linking the lookout post to Hamilton."

"I see, sir," Hendrick said.

"What do you say, colonel? Will you do it?" Townshend said.

"Yes, of course. We need the goodwill of the government -."

"I want this built as quickly as possible," Colonel Townshend said. "If the Yankees attack, I want to be able to call for help."

"Yes, sir. But if speed is important, colonel, you could ask for the Canadian Coloured Corps. They're pioneers, expert in all sorts of construction work -."

The militia captain snarled. "My men won't work with them. The pioneers are regular soldiers and look down on militia units."

Chard was alarmed at this outburst. Officers were not supposed to behave like that. He assumed that the captain was exaggerating. "Well, sir, what if the two teams started from opposite ends? With Colonel Hendrick's men starting from this end?"

"That sounds ideal," Colonel Hendrick said. "But can you to organise this for us, sergeant?"

"Yes, sir. The men have become quite skilled at putting up telegraph poles. But there's no railroad this time. Everything will have to be brought by cart. The wire itself, food for the men, everything. Er - can you keep the work party supplied, sir?

"You can leave that to us, sergeant. Our quartermaster knows his work," Colonel Townshend said.

"It's annoying that if the Yankees attack, the first thing they'll do is cut the wire," Captain Finch said.

Hendrick turned to Chard. "Any ideas, sergeant?"

"I do have a few hundred yards of insulated cable. It might be possible to bury it," Chard said. "Just the stretch between here and the trees."

"Excellent," Colonel Townshend said. "See to it, will you, Hendrick."

Chard could see that Hendrick was angry at this casual remark. "Out of the question, colonel. My men regard themselves as warriors, not construction workers. They regard digging in the fields as women's work. They will dig earthworks, to protect themselves from enemy bullets. But if I ask them to dig a ditch, they will refuse."

Townshend and Hendrick glared at each other.

Chard gulped. He turned to Captain Finch. "Could your men dig that trench, sir? As their contribution to this endeavour?"

"That might work," Finch said.

"And you will supply the telegraph operators, Hendrick," Colonel Townshend said.

Hendrick was surprised. "But why can't you supply the telegraphists?"

Finch was embarrassed. "Most of my men can't read and write. Those who can are busy teaching the rest."

"The general told me said that the Signals Corps couldn't provide the men," Colonel Townshend said. He glanced up at Chard.

"Can we?" Hendrick asked.

"Yes, sir," Chard said. "Your pay-bill doesn't show up in the army accounts. While ours ..."

Colonel Hendrick and Chard walked outside. Sergeant Johnson joined them. Chard was relieved to be away from all those officers.

Hendrick was angry. "It's outrageous. They give this task to us because we are cheap. They pay us little. It will cost them less."

Chard was uncomfortable. "There could be another reason, sir."

"What other reason could there possibly be?"

"They're asking you because they know you can do it. They wouldn't ask you if you'd made a mess of it."

Hendrick was pleased. "True. But now I'm short-staffed. I'll need those ladies after all.

"You won't send them here, sir?" Johnson asked.

"No, I'll keep them at Brant's Ford. The male telegraphists complain of being kept safe. I'll send *them* here."

Maine, June 22

George Eastman's Mohawk scouts reported that the Yankee regulars had finally advanced up from Kennebunk to take the land between the two rivers. They were careful not to come within range of George's men on the Nonesuch River.

Within hours, everyone in Portland had heard the story. The battalion, officers and men alike, were dismayed.

George called his officers together. Sergeant Priddy was present, in his role of Regimental Sergeant Major.

"My scouts have brought back some more information. The Yankees are building earthworks at Eight Corners. When it's complete, they'll probably bring up cannon. Then they'll attack.""

"We can't drive them out. We can't risk another set-piece battle," Warwick said.

"Not against regulars," George said. "Yes, sergeant?"

"The men asked me to speak on their behalf," Sergeant Priddy said. "There's almost three hundred of them without firearms, sir. They ask that we give them weapons."

George was blunt. "That's impossible, sergeant."

"You said, sir, that the only way to get firearms would be to take them from Yankees."

"Did I? Oh, yes."

"They've volunteered to attack the Yankees, sir."

"Attack them? Without firearms?" George was surprised. "It would have to be a night action ..."

"They know the risks, sir."

"It would require very careful planning. The Yankees have the advantage of experience and training. But in the dark - most of that will be lost."

"You'll do it, sir?" Mr. Warwick said.

"Yes ..." George was lost in thought.

"What about the blockhouse they're building?" Mr. Warwick asked.

"We won't go near it. Unless the door is wide open, don't try it. Go after an easy target instead."

June 24, evening

George decided upon an everywhere-at-once night attack on the enemy camp. He wanted everyone to overwhelm the enemy by attacking at exactly the same moment, from all directions.

Everyone involved had been asked memorise his role. The sergeant of each attack group had to draw a map of the roads they would take and the farmhouses they would pass.

Almost everyone in the battalion was involved in one way or another. The armed and experienced men were kept in reserve. George emphasised that their task would be to cover the retreat.

The delays were minor and soon overcome. The attack went ahead on time. The experienced men with firearms, under the command of Captain Warwick, marched across the bridge and formed up in two lines.

George refused to wait in an office, safe in Portland. Instead, he chose to stay with the reserves. "No lights. I don't want to provide a target for marksmen."

The unarmed men walked past them and divided into their individual groups. They wore dark sack-jackets, the buttons smeared with soot.

The groups with the furthest to go were the first to leave. George wished each of them good luck, which seemed to please them.

There was a long wait. George thought he heard some shouting, far to the west. Then he heard shots. Everyone tensed.

Then they could hear the drums summoning the men to arms. George smiled. "That's the Yankee camp. We've ruined their sleep if nothing else."

"Yes, sir," the sergeant said.

The firing went on for over an hour. George wondered whether his men were being slaughtered. Or perhaps the Yankees were shooting wild.

Then one of the raiding parties appeared out of the dark. "Friend, friend!"

They reported they had lost two men. But they were jubilant – they had seized five rifles.

"Did you have any difficulty getting over their wall?"

"They hadn't bothered to build a wall, sir. I reckon they didn't think we would fight."

George grinned. "They know differently now."

Ten minutes later, another group returned, carrying a wounded man.

In small groups, over a period of hours, the men of the raiding parties returned to the bridge. George was impressed by their enthusiasm.

The Yankees, taken by surprise, had made no attempt to stop the raiding parties. In the dark, their advantage of discipline no longer counted.

The reserves had nothing to do. At dawn, George ordered them to retreat across the river. He and Captain Warwick tallied the results. The attackers had seized twenty-three rifles and ten ammunition-pouches.

George was not impressed. He asked about the losses. He discovered that there were ten dead or missing, with seven men brought back seriously injured. That was disturbing, but not as bad as he had feared.

He thought the casualty figure was high, but the survivors were enthusiastic. They thought this a price worth paying.

The raid had provided a boost in morale. Plenty of men without weapons demanded the opportunity to try again.

George was dismayed. He could not afford repeated losses of that kind. But the men were eager. And they were right in one thing - without firearms they were almost useless. So he set about planning a more ambitious attack.

Portland, June 29

Captain Warwick and Sergeant Priddy, followed by fifty men, found the gateway of the abandoned fort on the headland. Its doors had been blown off. They pushed their way inside and tried to make sense of what they saw.

"Remember, sir, the main guns pointed out to sea, to stop the Royal Navy attacking."

"They must be under this rubble, then."

The day before, the battalion had carried out another night attack on the Yankee camp. The men judged it a success.

Warwick knew that Major Eastman had been

disturbed by the casualty figures. He wanted to hold Portland for as long as possible and could not afford heavy casualties. Putting a garrison into this fort might help.

Sergeant Priddy looked round. Bricks and lumps of stone were scattered across the centre of the fort. "It looks as if the powder magazine exploded, sir."

They discovered that the Yankees had blown the huge main guns off their carriages and abandoned them. The smaller guns had been scavenged.

Priddy was saddened at the damage to the guns. "It's enough to make an artilleryman weep."

But Captain Warwick inspected the big guns and thought that one of them could be salvaged.

Sergeant Priddy shook his head. "It's too badly damaged. It'll explode the second or third time you fire it. And likely kill the gun team when it does."

Warwick lowered his voice. "Sergeant, I'm going to propose that we run a bluff. Make the Yankees think this place is fully operational."

"Ah. I see, sir."

"I want you to recruit fifty of those unarmed men as gunners. They'd be more use here than running around in the dark. Form a work team. Build a crane and lift this gun up."

"We'd need to build a gun-carriage first."

"See to it, sergeant."

Fifty volunteers became the permanent garrison of the fort. Warwick diverted a hundred more from other duties to provide temporary work crews.

The garrison raised the flag every morning. They found a small saluting cannon to practice on.

The major approved of Warwick's proposal and insisted that civilians had to be excluded from the fort. He said that if they were running a bluff it would only work if no-one saw the evidence. So sentries patrolled the walls day and night, guarding some ruined guns.

The major kept track of the rumours that began circulating about the fort.

Lifting the scavenged gun onto its new carriage required a huge effort. None of the men had done anything like this before. They had to first erect a temporary crane, which was made up of two tree-trunks. Lifting that into position was itself a major undertaking.

The naval vessel in the harbour provided lifting-tackle but not the manpower.

Portland, June 30

George and Captain Warwick watched from the dockside as a fine mail steamer arrived in the harbour. In more peaceful times it had made the prestigious Southampton to New York run. George could see that the deck was crowded with redcoats.

The first man up the gangplank wore a greatcoat to protect him from the sea breeze. But under it he wore the uniform of the colonel of a Highland regiment.

George saluted. "Colonel MacGregor? We have met before, sir. When we planned that first attack on Portland."

The colonel returned his salute. "A memorable episode, major. I'll wager you never expected to be back here, eh?"

"No, sir."

"I have brought four companies of my regiment with me. The officers commanding them will report direct to me. I hope that will not cause any problems, major."

"Not at all, sir. I am sure they all have more experience than I have. Er – I have a carriage to take you to the hotel."

"How far is it? A mile? I'll walk. I'm tired of being cooped up on that ship."

"Yes, sir."

MacGregor started walking uphill. George and Captain Warwick fell in alongside him.

"When the general heard that the Yankees had advanced towards you, he realised that he had to do something. Either evacuate the place or send reinforcements. And this is the first real success we've had since the snows melted."

"Yes, sir. I've organised a series of night attacks. No more than skirmishing, but it keeps the Yankees on their guard."

"Good, good. I have no intention of pushing the Yankees back, major. Holding on here is the most that we can hope for."

"Yes, sir."

At the fort, Captain Warwick decided that everything was ready.

One team hauled on the ropes that lifted the gun into the air; four more teams pulled on ropes that held it horizontal; another team pulled the new gun-carriage into place underneath it.

The work crews resented having to provide brute labour. They had been told nothing of the purpose of their work. They objected that they were soldiers, not a work-gang

Sergeant Priddy had waved their complaints aside. "Don't be too touchy about your pride. If white marines can do it, so can black infantry. And this is more useful than running around with pikes."

The newly-recruited 'gunners' were told they must not exaggerate the progress they were making.

"Let the gossip spread. I want the Yankees to assume the worst."

Portland, June 30, nightfall

The men who still had no firearms wanted their chance to win one. There was no shortage of volunteers for a third night attack.

Everyone had similar hopes of success. When night fell, George watched the volunteers walk out into the dark. They were grinning. Some of them gave him a wave as they walked past. They regarded this as a game. It was dangerous, but it offered high hopes of glory.

George took his usual place with the reserves. A platoon in skirmish order was deployed forward. He settled down to a long, anxious wait.

So he was concerned when, this time, the shooting started early.

Sergeant Priddy led a special detachment towards the enemy blockhouse. Six men, a detachment of the Royal Marine Artillery, carried three Congreve rockets. Four infantrymen carried the launching trestle. There were six Mohawks scouting ahead. Ten men with muskets brought up the rear. Their task would be to cover their retreat if things went wrong.

"I used to be an artilleryman," Priddy said. "But, to my way of thinking, you can't call a Congreve rocket a piece of artillery. A cannon, now - treat 'er with respect and she'll serve you well."

"Be fair, now," the Royal Marine corporal said. "You have to fire a cannon several times to take out a target. We ought to have a dozen of these things, not three."

Priddy grunted. "Why didn't you bring any more?"

"This is all we've got."

"These rockets are like mules - they kick back. I've heard of 'em turning a circle and coming back at the men who fired it."

"True," the corporal said.

Priddy had to admit that he was lost. He depended totally on the scouts. But they seemed confident. Finally, they reached a road.

The Mohawk private stopped and pointed down the road. "The blockhouse is down there. Maximum musket range."

In the dark, Priddy could see nothing at all. "You're sure?"

"You could go and find out, sergeant," the man said in an injured tone.

"No, thanks." He told the black volunteers to place the trestle on the ground, facing the direction that the scout indicated. He told himself there was no point in aiming the thing. Congreve rockets were notoriously unreliable.

The marine corporal placed the first rocket on the trestle. "That direction? You're sure?"

"The Yankees like straight roads," the Mohawk scout said.

Priddy turned to his men. "Now, if this thing turns an' comes at you, throw yourself flat."

"But that would ruin my jacket, sergeant."

Priddy snorted. "If a Congreve rocket hits you, my lad, It'll do more than ruin your jacket. You can't outrun the thing. So if you see me throw myself flat, you do the same and hope it'll pass over your head."

"Oh, well, sarge, if you do it ..."

"Stand clear." The marine corporal said. He lit the fuse and stepped back a couple of paces.

The rocket ignited. It wagged its tail and then shot off down the road. Everyone watched, fascinated. Then the rocket shot up, almost vertically.

Before anyone could comment, the rocket fizzled and fell back. It hit something with a bang. The rocket began to burn. The light from the fire showed that the rocket had landed on the roof of the blockhouse. But the fire did not spread.

Priddy voiced his irritation. "Why didn't the warhead explode?"

The marine corporal shrugged. "We hit the target with our first shot. Do you expect two miracles?"

Someone inside the blockhouse sounded the alarm. Then the defenders started firing their muskets.

"With a bit of luck they'll come outside, try to put the fire out," Priddy said.

"They aren't that stupid," the corporal said.

"Keep off the road. They can see you now," Priddy said.

The marine gunners ignored the shots. Two of them placed the second rocket on the trestle.

"Stand clear." The corporal lit the fuse.

The rocket raced off, straight towards the blockhouse. For a moment, Priddy thought it was going to hit its target. But then it shot up in the air. Before Priddy could utter a curse, it turned down again and ploughed into the ground, twenty yards short of the door. This time the explosive warhead went off.

Priddy was impressed. "Look at that, now. That rattled their door. Aye, and a few feet further an' it would have blown the door clean off its hinges."

He grinned. "If you did that on purpose, I'll abandon cannons right now."

"No such luck," the corporal said.

The marines place the third rocket on the trestle and the corporal lit the fuse. It shot up, clear over the blockhouse, and then turned in a graceful arc to the right. Priddy wondered whether it would keep on turning until it was aimed straight at him. Instead, it veered off towards Portland.

"I hope it doesn't hit a church or something. The citizens would blame us."

They listened, but there was no explosion.

"I think it fell in the river," the corporal said.

"That second rocket could have weakened the door," one of the black infantrymen said. "We could try to force it – break in."

Priddy shook his head. "If I had a hundred men with me, I'd be tempted. But ten men with muskets – no."

"What do we do then, sergeant?"

"Go back to Portland. I've achieved more with those rockets than I dared hope. Two hits out of three."

Then they heard shooting to the south-west. They all turned in that direction. "Worse than last time," the infantryman said.

"A lot worse," Priddy said.

If the Yankees attack, we'll be trapped," the marine corporal said. "Come on, let's go."

George realised that the Yankees had expected an attack and had prepared an ambush of their own. Judging by the noise, it was vicious fighting out there. There was lots of shooting. "Rifles, not muskets."

"Yes, sir," the sergeant said.

George guessed that the attackers had been taken by surprise. He expected the survivors to come limping back, an hour or so before dawn, if they came back at all. He settled down to wait. Instead, he heard the sound of marching men.

He was alarmed. "Make sure the men are alert, sergeant."

"I'm sure they are, sir." The sergeant sounded reproachful.

"A little reminder won't do any harm."

"Yes, sir."

"Skirmishers forward."

Then the Yankees appeared out of the dark. They spotted the skirmishers. "What are you doing here?"

"It's them. Redcoats!"

"We've found 'em," the Yankee sergeant said. "Form a line, there!" They raised their rifles, aimed, and fired.

George's skirmishers fired a volley of their own. But they were outnumbered and gave ground.

George realised that things were getting serious and that he would need the reserves. "Forward!" He knew that the reserves were men who had fought at World's end.

They advanced past the skirmishers and straightened their line. "First rank, present. Fire."

The men stood firm, aiming and firing coolly. They played their part and covered the retreat of the skirmishers.

George told the skirmishers to reload. Then the reserves withdrew behind the skirmishers.

"Should we withdraw east of the bridge, sir?" the sergeant said.

"If we do that, the raiding party will be trapped. I want to hold on if I can."

In the dark, the Yankees were as confused as the inexperienced defenders. The skirmishers knew what their task was. They fired a volley and retreated, in a disciplined fashion. The ran behind the reserves at the double and reformed their own line in the dark.

"Reload," their sergeant said.

The Yankees could not see this purposeful activity. They shouted insults at the retreating blacks but did not advance any further. Perhaps they thought they had won.

George could hear the trumpets in Portland sounding the assembly. "We'll have more reinforcements here soon."

The Yankees fired one final volley and then withdrew. No-one suggested the battalion should go after them.

George assumed that the raiding party had been wiped out. That meant two hundred men lost. "But we'll remain here for as long as we can, sergeant."

"Yes, sir."

But, over the next hour, a few men trickled back, with stories that the Yankees had been waiting for them.

Then Sergeant Priddy brought back the rocket-team. "We're glad you're holding this end of the bridge, sir. I thought we'd have to walk back the long way."

"Any casualties, sergeant?"

"None, sir."

By dawn, a hundred and fifty men, out of two hundred, had reported back. Some were carrying seriously wounded comrades.

George was saddened and alarmed by this loss. The battalion had gained nothing by it. They could not go on losing men at this rate.

Portland, July 1

The next morning, George made his report to the colonel. "The raiders achieved the same haul as they did the first time, twenty-three rifles and ammunition. But there were fifty dead or missing."

Colonel McGregor listened in silence.

"It is a heavy loss, sir," George said. "But morale is still high. The men feel that they gave as good as they got. They've bloodied the Yankees."

"I see," MacGregor said. "But if we're going to hold on here, we can't afford more losses of this kind."

"Yes, sir," George said. "And I apologise. We were predictable."

He knew that the men without firearms, over a hundred, were still determined to try their luck.

Portland, July 1, Afternoon

Another Royal Navy steamer arrived from Hamilton. It brought an unusual cargo.

"Today's steamer brought your pay," Sergeant Priddy told the other sergeants. It includes a British shilling for each of you."

"A shilling? What's special about that?" Wycombe asked.

"We have a saying, soldiers are men who have taken the Queen's shilling. Well, these are your shillings. One-twentieth of a pound. But you can't spend it here. So the rest of the pay is in dollars.

"We'll hold an assembly tomorrow and hand it out. Make sure each man brings his paybook."

Wycombe was disconcerted. "But what can we do with it?"

Priddy raised an eyebrow. "You could buy me that pint you owe me.. There's bars. This is a port town, so they aren't fussy. An' there's brothels."

Wycombe was angry. "Is that what you think of us? Cheap beer and cheap women?"

Priddy was not offended. "Some soldiers – white soldiers – think exactly that. Every payday, they get roaring drunk. If they don't end up in jail, they think it was a boring night."

"Ah. I see."

"Others, though, save some of their pay. Or send it home. But you can't do that, o'course."

"Home," one man said.

"Why not? Why can't we?" Wycombe said.

"Well – can you?" Priddy was embarrassed. "I thought that slave barracks didn't have a postal address. Or that the overseer would confiscate everything that arrived."

Wycombe was amused at this ignorance. "It isn't that bad. For most of us, it wasn't that bad."

"I'm sorry that it arrived too late for some people," Priddy said.

"We didn't come here for money," one of the other sergeants said.

"Perhaps not. But we've got to pay you. Wouldn't be right if we didn't."

Wycombe was fascinated by the shilling: a small coin bearing the Queen's profile and Latin words.

Someone asked how the British government had obtained US currency. Another man grinned. "Perhaps they forged it."

They examined the notes and coins but they seemed to be genuine.

Portland, July 2, 9am

Wycombe walked to the telegraph office. He had the unaccustomed burden of coins in his pockets. The man behind the counter looked up, surprised.

Wycombe grinned. "Good morning. I want to send a telegram to Miss Montgomery in World's End."

The man was suspicious. "Why?"

"Well - mainly because I can. I've been paid, you see, and I might as well spend it on something. Although - I hope it won't embarrass the lady."

"Let's see it, then."

"Why?"

"You asked whether it would embarrass her. Let's see the message."

"Oh. Right." Wycombe pushed the slip of paper under the grille.

'I hope you are well. I am in good health. The army has paid us at last. So I can afford to send a message down the wire. Sergeant Wycombe, Portland.'

"That looks all right. It isn't as if you were going to see her."

"If I did that, Sergeant Priddy would be *most* annoyed."

"Is he the noisy one?"

Wycombe grinned. "Yes."

Portland, July 2, evening

The men who had failed to win rifles for themselves were still eager to try. They assembled at the eastern end of the bridge. This time, Warwick was in command.

Major Eastman had been reluctant to see further high losses, so he had planned this with care.

This was bigger but less ambitious than the previous attempts. There were more men in reserve to cover the retreat. The major had emphasised that he could not afford excessive casualties.

Warwick led the reserves across the bridge. He had been forbidden to take part in the raid. So he watched as the volunteers marched past and vanish into the dark. The risks were high but the men were determined.

The men in reserve knew that they would probably have a big part in this.

They waited for gunshots. But there was nothing.

Two hours later, the sentry heard something. "Halt! Who goes there?"

Everyone was tense.

"Friend," a voice cried out. "The word is Champlain."

The sentry glanced at Warwick, who nodded. "Advance, friend."

Ten men trudge out of the dark. They were tired and dispirited.

"What happened out there, sergeant?" Warwick

asked.

The sergeant was dispirited. "There were no Yankees to attack. Their camp was empty. They've vanished."

"What? Well - go back to the barracks and make your report, then. The major will want to know."

"Yes, sir."

Warwick suspected a Yankee trap. But, as the night wore on, more men returned, all bringing the same story. They all felt that they had somehow failed.

Warwick told them all to go back to the barracks. "You've done well. Get some rest."

One team, determined to find an answer to the puzzle, had made their way to the River Nonesuch. "That camp of theirs was empty, sir. We reckon they've lit out."

Warwick was baffled by this development. What were the Yankees up to? "That will interest the major. Well done."

Portland, July 3, 9am

An airship was sighted out at sea, due east of Portland. The watchers realised that it was approaching the town, not following the coast. Some men assumed it was a Yankee vessel, but the symbol in the side, 'V+R', was clear enough.

George had received word that the Navy would attempt to make this flight. He knew that the commander would try to land. He had asked whether any men in the battalion had served as ground-crew.

He knew that the airship had flown down during the night, to avoid the strong afternoon headwinds.

Twenty minutes later, a score of volunteers assembled in the field. Only five of them had done this work before. But the rest were eager to learn. They laid out white sheets on the ground to indicate the wind direction.

The airship turned into wind, descended, and then dropped a pair of mooring ropes. The ground crew rushed forward to seize them.

The airship's gondola was now merely two feet above the ground. Several members of the crew jumped down.

The crew were all naval ratings. They advised the volunteers on how to anchor the airship securely. "If it breaks free, it'll be blown right across the Atlantic."

When the airship was secured, George strode forward to greet the commander. "I'm Major Eastman."

The commander stepped down from the gondola. He was of medium height, slightly built, with brown hair. "Good afternoon, major. I'm Lt. Henry Griffin, RN. When the wind turned against us, I thought I wasn't going to make it.

"There's not much that I can achieve here. Airships have a basic weakness, you see. They're no good against a headwind. In most places you'd just wait for the wind to change. But here the wind is pretty constant. Fine if you want to go east, but a hard fight if you want to go west."

"Yes, I see."

"We were watching out for blockade runners but, off the record, it was a waste of time. Even if we had identified a blockade runner, what could we do?"

George was uncomfortable. "Your main task is to impress the Yankees. Make them think we're up to something. I had hoped that you could travel further south. Could you reach Boston? Then turn around and come back here."

"Tricky. I would have to wait for perfect weather."

"Ah. I quite understand, lieutenant. You must not do anything to imperil your craft."

Lt. Griffin listened, fascinated, as the major described the activity the previous evening. "I am determined to find out what the Yankees are doing. I would like you to carry out a reconnaissance."

Lt. Griffin had never done army work before but he agreed at once.

"I want information, Lt. Griffin. Do not take any risks. Find out what they're up to, then bring me that news. Perhaps that news will allow us to plan another attack."

Lt. Griffin nodded. "I understand, sir. Although reconnaissance isn't what we trained for."

An hour before noon, the airship rose into the air and headed west. Lt. Griffin glanced down at the major and his colleagues. The officers seemed prepared to wait all day.

The airship crew could see farmhouses and cultivated land, woods and roads. "There could be anything hiding in those woods, sir."

"Yes, but why would they hide from us?"

They reached the site of the army camp. "Abandoned. No mistaking that, sir."

"No. Let's see where they've gone."

West of the River Nonesuch, it was a different story. The western end of the railroad bridge was fortified. Construction was still under way.

"Emplacements. But no cannon in place yet, sir."

"No. Change of course, helmsman. Turn north. Let's see how thorough they are."

The lookouts found that the Yankees had withdrawn west of river. Every bridge and ford was defended. Each new blockhouse was carefully sited.

"There's no chance of a surprise attack," Lt. Griffin said. "New course, north-east." It was time for him to return and make his report. "Let's have a look at that blockhouse."

The blockhouse, sited at a crossroads, was easy to

spot. The walls were still standing but the building was a hollow shell. The warrant officer sniffed. "If you was to ask me, sir, I would say that they abandoned it and then set light to it to prevent the army from getting ahold of it."

Privately, Griffin agreed. "Back to the landing field. We have to make our report."

The engineer was surprised. "You mean they just abandoned the territory, sir?"

"Yes. It's a victory for those blacks, of a sort. They made the place too hot for the Yankees."

Maine, July 4

Lt. Griffin wanted to take his airship back to its home port. His wife was waiting for him there. But the major asked him to fly another reconnaissance mission. He wanted to give the Yankees an exaggerated idea of what the airship was capable of.

The mission took them inland, towards the post road. The major had explained that this was the main east-west road. He assumed that the US army was using it to send military supplies north.

The airship reached the road, which seemed to be empty.

"Starboard twenty degrees rudder, helmsman," Lt. Griffin said. "I want to follow that road north.

"Twenty degrees starboard, aye," the helmsman said.

They could see routine farm traffic. Then the lookout reported a military convoy crawling north along the road. Lt. Griffin counted twenty wagons. It had a strong militia escort marching alongside it, so both lanes were blocked.

"They must have a healthy respect for those black soldiers, sir," the lookout said.

"Yes."

The soldiers turned to stare at the airship. Then they started shooting up at them. Griffin was annoyed. "Take us up, helmsman. Two thousand feet. They might just hit something important."

"Two thousand feet, aye, sir."

Griffin gave the order to return to Portland. He had to make his report. Then he could go home.

Ogdensburg, July 5

Colonel Hendrick stared across the River St. Lawrence at the US town of Ogdensburg. The artillery based in the town blocked Canadian shipping along the St. Lawrence, so the governor had demanded an amphibious operation to take the town.

A task force had been assembled at Prescott on the north bank of the river. Lord Cardigan, the colonel of the 11th Hussars, had been put in charge. He had no experience of amphibious operations. But, as an aristocrat, he was expected to cope.

His lordship's leadership style consisted of delegating problems to his subordinates. He would then invariably sneer at the ideas before adopting them. He always insisted upon making changes to the proposals. As far as Hendrick could tell, the changes were never improvements.

Cardigan's plan had been for Hendrick's light infantry to attack at dawn – when there just enough light to see by. There was a long tradition of dawn attacks. Colonel Hendrick had to admit that the plan was sensible enough.

The canoes had been delivered to the nearest railroad station. But they had to be transported that last mile by cart. The pioneers had slipped up. They did not have enough carts to carry all the canoes in one go. The pioneers had promised to deliver the last batch this morning.

Hendrick turned to the artillery lieutenant. "What time is it?"

The lieutenant glanced at his pocket-watch. "Almost nine, sir."

"And the canoes still haven't arrived. Cardigan will be furious."

Cardigan did not have a billet here in Prescott. Instead, he had commandeered the house of a landowner, several miles away. He had not bothered to turn up to watch the assault.

The officers of the attack force had gathered outside the farmhouse that they had taken over as their headquarters. It had been built on the riverbank, in full view of observers on the far bank.

They were still waiting for the boats when Cardigan rode over from his cushy billet. Colonel Hendrick thought his hussar uniform made him look absurd.

The earl was tall, with wide shoulders and a narrow waist. He had blond hair and blue eyes.

Now he looked across the river and then down at his officers. "Have you started the attack?"

The colonel's second in command, a major of the hussars, swallowed. "No, sir. The boats haven't arrived yet."

Cardigan glared. "You were supposed to attack at dawn. When I delegate tasks to subordinates, I trust them to get it right."

Hendrick acknowledged that he had a point. An attack at dawn had more chance of success.

Cardigan was still out of temper. And he could vent his temper on anyone. Hendrick had come to dread these encounters.

The earl outranked Hendrick in many ways. He was

English; he was in the regular army; and he was an aristocrat. He despised colonials.

Hendrick was the second most senior present. But that was very different from being second in command.

Hendrick was careful not to make an issue of the insults he received from the earl. Apart from anything else, he had no experience of major assaults.

Cardigan was a snob; but he had received the notion that a Mohawk war-leader was a sort of royalty. He treated Hendrick as an aristocrat. Hendrick did not regard this as a complement.

Hendrick despised the British tradition of buying commissions. But he had to admit to himself that his own situation was similar. Although *he* had been selected for his scholarship.

Cardigan was impatient. "Colonel Hendrick, you are to go immediately those boats arrive."

Hendrick was appalled. "We would have more chance of success in the dark."

Cardigan scowled. "We have waited long enough. Delay gives the enemy time to prepare."

"Yes, sir." He had a quiet word with the artillery commander. "Can you hit the Yankee artillery? I mean, when we're on the way across … can you fire at their artillery? If they open fire on us? Put them off their aim?"

The lieutenant glanced across the river. "Yes, sir. But we can't be accurate at that range. We might hit you by mistake. Ah - did Lord Cardigan ask for this?"

"No. But by all means check with him. Although he isn't interested in details."

The lieutenant backed down. "We would be firing over your heads. If we fall short …"

"That is the least of my worries."

"Very well, sir."

The houses of Ogdensburg village were clearly visible on the far side of the river. Hendrick guessed that the residents probably knew that something was going on. Had they told the authorities?

He was discussing the details of the assault with his subordinates, half an hour later, when the wagons arrived. The boats stacked inside.

Hendrick's men looked the boats over. The devices were flimsy, but seemed undamaged by their journey.

"You've got your muskets? Ammunition? Let's go." His men picked up the boats and ran down to the riverbank. They launched the boats and climbed in.

Hendrick and his men began paddling across. In daylight, they presented an easy target for the enemy artillery.

He could see the Yankee cannons. Men were busy around one of them. The cannons fired. He felt a moment's dread. But the cannonball flew over their heads.

Hendrick knew the artillerymen would adjust their aim and try again. But he just kept paddling.

He expected the British artillery to open up. The lieutenant had promised – hadn't he? But nothing happened.

The Yankee artillery fired again. But the ball fell between two boats. The men were soaked but unhurt. The next salvo swamped a boat by a near miss. It turned over, leaving the crew floundering in the water. Then a direct hit destroyed a boat. There were no survivors.

Then the British artillery opened up. They did not seem to hit anything but Hendrick's men appreciated the activity.

They were getting close to the far shore. Would he be killed before he got there? The Yankee artillery fired again, but he did not see where the shot went.

Their boat grounded on the river-bank. "Go, go, go."

He and his men scrambled out. They spread out along the bank.

Hendrick watched as one of the enemy cannons was repositioned so that it could fire at this new target. His men had only rocks and trees to hide behind. But at least now they could shoot back. He hoped that the enemy gunners would run away. But they were brave and stood by their guns.

The Yankee infantry spread along the earthworks on each side of the cannon. They started firing at Hendrick's men but they did not leave the shelter of the earthworks. Hendrick's men returned their fire and forced the enemy infantry to take cover.

Hendrick told the signaller to use his flags to send a message. "I want our artillery to maintain fire at their artillery."

"They could hit us, sir."

"We'll have to risk it."

A few minutes later, the British cannon fired a round. The cannonball landed short, in the grass. But it bounced, spinning lazily. Everyone watched, fascinated. It was headed straight for the enemy cannon.

He realised with dismay that it was going to fall short. If it had bounced a second time it would have smashed the enemy cannon.

Instead it skidded along the soft ground. He could see that the gunners were splattered with mud.

That was too much for the Yankee gunners. They limbered up and withdrew.

He ordered his men to advance on the village, taking advantage of any cover they could find. The Yankee infantry responded vigorously. His men suffered casualties and made no progress. He realised that if he ordered his men to continue their attack the nation would be wiped out.

Then the first of the boats carrying the heavy infantry arrived. The infantry commander, a captain, made his way to Hendrick's position. The captain was a professional officer, not an aristocrat.

"Colonel, Lord Cardigan has changed his plans."

"Yes, captain?"

"He decided to send us across first."

"Well, the only enemy units are in those fortifications," Hendrick said.

"We'll take care of that. The fortifications are our task, sir."

"When will the colonel come across?"

This is met by a blank stare. Hendrick realised that Lord Cardigan would not come across until resistance had ended. And he should not have asked.

His men watched as the infantry advanced on the Yankee fortification. He told his men to move round to the right to give the attackers covering fire. The defenders' fire slackened. But they did not give up.

Hendrick told the signaller to send a message back for the pioneers to lay the telegraph cable.

Pioneers from the Canadian Coloured Corps towed a raft across the river. Men on the raft unwound the telegraph cable from a drum as they move across.

The raft reached the south bank and the sergeant of pioneers came to report. Hendrick realised that he was the senior officer on this side of the river.

The pioneers hauled the end of the cable ashore. One of his own men, trained by Sergeant Chard, carried the precious telegraph instrument.

The man pointed. "Put the end of the cable by that picket fence."

He threw his coat over the fence, sat down, and set about the task of connecting his instrument to the cable.

The Yankees occasionally fired a bullet or two. Hendrick told his own men to return fire. He pointed to the telegraphist's coat. "That won't stop bullets, you know."

"No, sir. But they can't see me." The signaller grinned. "This is a hell of a lark, sir."

"Shut up and get on with it."

"Done, sir. What message, sir?"

Hendrick abandoned his pride and sat down next to the instrument. "Just send 'test. Please reply'."

The signaller tapped away at the key and then sat back. Hendrick held his breath.

The needle flickered. The signaller grinned. "We're in business, sir."

Hendrick was now in contact with Cardigan. His first instinct was to ask for instructions.

Instead he decided to merely inform Cardigan what he was doing. The colonel could say no if he wanted to.

Hendrick reported that the Yankees were putting up a stout defence. He estimated the American garrison was about 500 men.

But after a fierce battle of about two hours the enemy infantry abandoned the Ogdensburg earthworks. Hendrick told his telegraphist to report that the enemy had retreated south, keeping up a steady fire.

Hendrick wondered how Cardigan would respond to that.

A bigger boat nosed into the riverbank, bearing the first troop of cavalry. The next boat brought more cavalry and the colonel.

Hendrick expected Cardigan to assume command. It would be a relief to put the burden on somebody else.

He stepped forward to greet the earl. "I'm glad to see you, sir. Could you send some men to advance along the road? To warn us in case the Yankees counter-attack.".

"On the run, are they?" Cardigan's eyes gleamed with excitement. He mounted up and waved his sword. "Ride them down. We must not give them a chance to recover." His men cheered. Cardigan led the chase after the retreating Yankees.

Hendrick's men were left gaping. "He's more trouble than the Yankees," the telegraphist said.

"None of that." Hendrick said. He realised he was still in command of the infantry.

The needle flickered again. The operator looked troubled. "That's the operator on the north bank. He's received a telegram from the general. He wants to know whether the town has been taken."

Hendrick was tempted to report Cardigan's incompetence. But that would not be politic. "Send this message. 'The enemy is in retreat and Lord Cardigan is pursuing them. I shall take the town immediately. Signed, Colonel Hendrick'."

He told Sergeant Johnson that he was going into the village.

"But it's too dangerous, sir. All of those Yankees have muskets, sir."

"Shnut up and follow me." Hendrick scrambled across the abandoned earthworks and caught up with the infantry captain at the edge of the town. The street was empty.

"His lordship is chasing the Yankees. Is there any opposition here?"

The captain looked haggard. "No, sir. They left a lot of wounded behind. What do we do about the civilian population? The plan didn't mention that."

He led the way into the centre of the town. The populace came out to meet them. The mayor nudged forward a spokesman.

"Colonel Teyonhehkwen?"

The man had pronounced his name correctly. Hendrick summed the man up. "You're Mohawk, aren't you?"

"One quarter. And - one quarter Seneca."

"That's an interesting combination. How come they haven't shipped you off to the Indian Territory?"

"I have a job and I pay taxes. How about you?" The mayor, aghast, told him to be polite. Both men ignored him.

He tapped the buttons on his sleeve that marked his rank. "I have a job too."

"Is it true that you have an army?"

"It's only a battalion. Under strength. But I can't stay. I have to go back and report to the general."

"All the way to Quebec?" the mayor asked.

"I have a telegraph."

"You have a *telegraph*?" This impressed the mayor more than any army.

"Yes. The army single-needle system."

"How come the Mohawks have their own army?" the half-breed asked.

"That is a story for long winter nights. We haven't time for that now."

"True enough, colonel."

Hendrick was worried that Lord Cardigan would demand that these men give an oath of allegiance – and shoot any who refused. He had to act fast. "I want all of the men of military age to give their parole. You won't take up arms against my troops."

The mayor was truculent. "And what if we want to sneak off and join the army?"

"Well - don't get caught."

The infantry captain said, in an undertone, that lord Cardigan's orders did not mention a parole.

Hendrick was impatient. "He's not here. Until he returns and takes over, I have responsibility."

Montreal July 6

Grace hoped for an interview with the Dowager Viscountess. The old lady was staying in the Hotel Versailles, preparing for her journey home to Britain.

Grace knocked on the door and walked in. She found that Lady Forlaith was sitting in a ladder-back chair, with Mrs. Lloyd standing at her side.

The fortress, on the far side of the river, was quiet. Everyone knew that the Yankees were distracted by events further south. But how long would the calm last?

"Good afternoon, young woman," the old lady said. She was gaunt and intimidating.

"I apologise for intruding, madam, but I have come to request some advice," Grace said. "There is no-one else that I could ask."

"Yes?"

"I would like to be accepted within society. Is that impossible? My army work has given me a bit of money. And the work is – not a trade."

She could make fashionable dresses. She had made a corset for herself, using a pattern that she had found in a ladies' magazine. So it was not as good as the professionally-made garments that these ladies wore. Then she had adjusted her dresses to fit.

The lady frowned. "Do you mean London society? There's no chance of that, my girl." It was clear to Grace that the viscountess did not approve of her ambition.

Mrs. Lloyd sniffed. "So you want to be a lady, do you?"

"It seems that working for Mr. Lloyd has given you ideas above your station, my girl," the old lady said.

Grace refused to back down. "I wish I could meet Queen Victoria."

The dowager snorted in a most unladylike manner. "You might possibly see her in your role as a Talker, but not socially. You would have to be almost royalty to do that."

"I don't suppose your father was a king or a war leader or anything?" Mrs. Lloyd said. "That would change things."

Grace smiled. "You asked me that before. No. The men in my family were all peaceable ... my grandmother was a magistrate. Is that the right word?"

"A magistrate?"

"Among the Abenaki, men are regarded as hot-blooded. War-leaders. Women are calmer. They make better judges. My grandmother tried to arbitrate a peace, with ... But it didn't work."

"Why weren't you there to greet me when I arrived?" the dowager said.

Grace was shy. "I don't know the proper forms of address. And – and - everything. Could you teach me?" She tried to explain. "It matters to me, very much, that I could be accepted socially."

"Accepted? You foolish girl. There's no chance of that."

Mrs. Lloyd intervened. "Isn't that cruel, madam?"

"Would it be kinder to give her hope? No. The high society of Canada are very proud. They barely accept me."

"You, madam?"

"My son has political power. I do not. And your earnings do not matter. Not unless you have thousands in the bank. All you can hope for, on your income, is a life of genteel poverty. Scraping to make ends meet and continual humiliation."

"But -."

"You would only be accepted into society if you married up. A colonel or some such."

"What if I married a - a major?" Grace said.

The old lady gave her a measuring look. "Do you perhaps mean Major Eastman?"

She was mortified. "I didn't say that!"

"Now, the major is a fine fellow. And a good soldier, they tell me. But he despises snobs. And if you're not careful, he'll despise you."

"Oh," Grace said, in a little voice.

"Do you want to enter the Guild?" Mrs. Lloyd said. "Study for a qualification? They accept anyone who completes their studies ... Although you would have to study Newton's Latin."

Grace wanted to study law, not Newton. Although she did not want to offend these women by saying so.

The old lady sighed. "You've got to understand that Mrs. Lloyd and myself are both visitors here. We'll be returning to Britain soon. Mrs. Lloyd's only friends are the wives of other officers or administrators. Neither of us will ever be befriended by the landowning families."

"You seem to be accepted by these scholars," Mrs. Lloyd said. "The intellectual elite, as it were.

"But they despise me as gauche."

"Really? You think so?" Mrs. Lloyd said. "Well, perhaps."

"Then take a few lessons in deportment," the old lady said.

Grace hated the idea. But she nodded her acceptance. "Yes, madam."

"It's a pity she's so dark," Mrs. Lloyd said.

"Oh." This was Grace's biggest fear.

The old lady smiled thinly. "You look like a farm-girl who's spent all summer out in the fields. But don't ever tell anyone that. An Indian girl with an education is rated higher than an illiterate English farm girl."

"Really?" This surprised Grace.

"Oh, yes." And your work in the telegraph room is rated far higher than farm-work."

"Surely, madam, her work with the Engine is rated far higher than sending telegraph messages," Mrs. Lloyd

said.

"Yes, certainly. Although the idea might frighten some people," the old lady said.

Quebec, July 8

Lt. Colonel Green was pleased when he was invited to dinner at General Trevor-Roper's headquarters. He had an urgent request to make.

He had hoped for a convivial evening. Unfortunately, he found that the guests included Lord Cardigan.

He heard the earl grumble about spending a few days with a pack of fools in the infantry.

When they assembled in the ante-room, prior to dinner, Green tried to get a word in private with the general.

But Cardigan refused to take the hint. Green suspected he had already been drinking. The junior officers kept their distance from the general.

The general smiled. "Yes, colonel? You said it was urgent."

"Yes, sir. It is my belief that the Yankees are retreating."

"Absurd," Cardigan said.

Green refused to back down. "Our patrols are advancing further and further south,"

"My patrols can find the Yankees," Cardigan said.

Green ignored the implied insult. "The force that General Scott has left is no more than a veil, to hide what they are doing. In places the veil is so thin that my patrols can push through it."

His men had boasted of their daring and skill. That was true enough. But Green had realised their reports made a consistent pattern. He thought he knew what it meant. Where would General Scott send these men?

Lord Cardigan was sceptical. "They're cowards, that's all. They can't face us."

Green doubted this. But he did not want to contradict his lordship. He turned to the general. They held similar views about Cardigan. "The colonel of infantry tells me that the Yankees haven't launched any attacks for days.

"Either they are very careful withdrawing men, or they're going soft. We can't afford to assume that they're giving up. They could be planning an attack on Portland, sir. Or Montreal."

Trevor-Roper was unhappy. "I cannot order Colonel McGregor in Portland to change his dispositions. He understands the local situation better than I do."

Lord Cardigan showed some interest. "Give him a hint, then. Tell him you've heard a rumour."

Green was annoyed. "It is more than a rumour, sir. Call it information. But -."

"Lord Cardigan is right. It is not a proven fact," Trevor-Roper said. "But I will send word. That's easy, these days. A telegram to St. Johns. Then a fast ship along the coast - thirty-six hours. They're sending ships daily, now."

"It seems miraculous, sir."

"Right. Time for dinner."

Chapter 11

Portland, July 9

Colonel McGregor read the message from the general and decided that it was too vague. His experienced troops, the marines, the highlanders and the Indians were guarding the all-important western approaches. But he knew that the eastern sector was weak. And now, this message from the general … He was worried that the Yankees might try a flanking manoeuvre.

He decided to order two companies of black troops to be transferred east to guard the railway junction. Then he changed his mind. There were two railway bridges across the Royal River. Best send four companies.

He explained this plan to Major Eastman, who worried that their line on the east was being over-extended. But McGregor overruled him. "I want you to march tomorrow, major."

"Yes, sir."

That evening, Wycombe and a couple of colleagues visited the dressmaker's shop. The manager voiced her disapproval of this male intrusion.

Wycombe ignored this. "Beg pardon, ma'am, but I need to speak to Eliza."

"Very well. Eliza, come here."

The girl stepped forward. "Yes, sergeant?"

"Eliza, you have to leave. The mayor dropped a hint to the captain. There's a rumour going round that you've been operating our telegraph instruments. If the Yankees take the town, they could put you in jail."

"But I've never touched one of those devices."

"Doesn't matter. You're the immigrant. Been here less than a year, they could send you south."

"Things won't get that ugly, surely?"

The manager had been listening. "Nothing is certain in times like these."

"What about the other recent arrivals?" Eliza asked.

"I don't know. Nobody's been spreading rumours about anybody else."

Maine, July 10

The battalion marched east, behind their colours. Their drums were beating. Once again, the local populace turned out to watch them go. This time, the mood was less sombre. There would not be a battle today.

Eliza watched them go. She was very unhappy. She had heard that the Indian major had quarrelled with the colonel about this.

She noticed Wycombe. "Come back safely!"

But he merely waved.

"Give 'em a song!" one of the soldiers shouted.

'Then to the east we bore away
To win a name in story
And there where dawns the sun of day
There dawned our sun of glory
The place in my sight
When in the host assigned me
I shared the glory of that fight
Sweet girl I left behind me.'

All the dames of Richmond are fond
And Savannah lips are willing

Very soft the maids of Charleston
And Richmond eyes are so thrilling
Still, although I bask beneath their smile,
Their charms will fail to bind me
And my heart falls back to Freedom
To the girl I left behind me.

Eliza and the other refugees were taken by back roads to Yarmouth railroad station. Their conductor had a word with the guard of a train heading north.

The guard seemed to expect this and put them in his van. He was friendly. "But sit in that corner and stay out of sight. There's nothing to see anyway."

The journey north took them all day. The railroad cut through a forest. Eliza decided that the guard was right. There was nothing to see except trees. There were no towns, not even farmhouses. The guard said that the only habitation was the logging camps.

Then the train stopped at a refuelling point. It was not really a town. Eliza thought it must be the loneliest place in the world.

The guard came to their corner. "You get off here. You can't go any further - the next stop has too many soldiers. They unload the cargo and put it on wagons. Send it over the mountains."

The locomotive engineer and the stoker were on the right side of the train, occupied with refuelling. The refugees were able to get out of the left side of the freight car without being spotted.

Eliza looked round. All she could see, in any direction, was the stationmaster's house, the train, and tree-covered mountains. It was a desolate spot.

The stationmaster was nervous. "Get inside – quick." He knew that this could cost him his job - or worse. "You could be spying on us."

She was indignant. "I'm from Portland. It's full of redcoats. You could say I've been spying on them."

"You come from there? Is it true they've got a regiment of blacks?"

She knew that the volunteers belonged to a battalion, not a regiment. The soldiers were really careful about those terms. But it was just too complicated. "Yes. Almost a thousand men."

"Well - stay out of sight, the lot of you."

After dark, Eliza and the others could see nothing outside. All they could hear was trains travelling south.

"Heavily laden," a man said. "Do you think there's going to be a battle?"

"You mean Portland?"

They looked at each other. "Perhaps we got out just in time."

"Can't we warn them?" Eliza said.

"I reckon they already know. That's why the battalion was sent to guard the railroad bridge."

Maine, July 11, morning

The next day, their guide came to collect them. He was old, his face lined, but he was still sprightly. Eliza was disconcerted to discover that the old man was an Abenaki Indian. He had an army backpack, but a bow was slung over his shoulder. He wore a red uniform smock jacket, but it was smeared with mud and leaf mould.

"What did your sergeant say?" She could imagine what Priddy would say.

He grinned. "We did that on purpose. The red coat was too bright."

The escort was dubious about taking them on. "City folk. Are you fit? Ready for a long hike?" They nodded.

"Let's go, then. No need to say goodbye. The stationmaster will be happier if he doesn't see us go."

He took a small earthenware pot out of his backpack and delighted Eliza by smearing red ochre across his face. "It keeps the insects away. Want some?"

She grinned and took some. The others disapproved. But, by the end of the day, all of them had accepted his offer.

He led them north. The railroad was left behind and they were walking through the woods.

"We have orders to watch and report, not to fight. The general needs to know. So the old men have had to teach the youngsters forest craft."

Maine coast, July 11

Captain Warwick expected the US Army to attack from the west. Instead the northern army on the frontier abandoned its attack and withdrew south.

The men of the battalion became aware of this change when a locomotive hauling a series of boxcars advanced along the Trunk railway.

There had been no trains for days. Everybody turned to watch. The train showed no signs of slowing down, so Wycombe's men put a few bullets through the boiler of the locomotive. The engineers slammed on the brakes. The train slowed and stopped.

Then the doors of the boxcars opened. Hundreds of men poured out. Warwick realised that it was a troop train.

"Form a line, there! Prime your muskets. Present – fire!"

The Yankee soldiers were disciplined professionals. They ignored the clumsy musket-fire and re-formed their ranks. They advanced towards the Redcoats.

Warwick realised that his men could not hold the railway line. It was too open. He gave the command for the battalion to withdraw. "Drummer – sound the retreat."

"Yes, sir."

They retreated south, up the slope of Cumberland Hill.

Major Eastman, a quarter of a mile to the west, realised what was happening and sent a telegram to the Colonel. "The Yankees may ignore us and advance on Portland."

The Major discussed the problem with his Talker, Mr. Laval. "Sir, there's a guild Talker on the Royal Navy cruiser. Mr. Cass."

"Can you ask the cruiser to shell the Yankees?"

Laval nodded. His eyes lost their focus for a moment. "If you wave a red flag, sir, the navy will fire shells."

The telegraph operator interrupted. "The colonel is asking, do you need reinforcements? He's worried that this could be a diversion for the main attack from the west."

The major shook his head. "My men think they can cope."

"Right, sir."

The Yankees sent one company to hold off the blacks while the main force headed towards Portland.

"We can't let them do that. Open fire," Warwick said.

The men had trained well. They maintained a steady rate of fire. The Yankees diverted five companies from their main advance to deal with the blacks. Warwick realised his men were now outnumbered. He told them to retreat over the brow of the hill. They were now within sight of the sea. They could see a warship, close inshore.

"We can't retreat any further." They used the reverse

slope to protect them from enemy fire. The numbers were roughly even and Warwick's men fought the attackers off.

Warwick was pleased. "Stalemate. We can hold them."

Then they saw a second train approach down the line. It slowed to a stop behind the first. Warwick could guess what would happen next.

Once more, the doors were pushed open and hundreds of troops climbed out.

Warwick, through his binoculars, could see wave after wave of Yankee regulars, with colours flying, marching towards Portland.

He asked his signaller to use his flags to send a message. "I want the navy to shell the advancing Yankees. West of my position"

"So it's Portland they want, sir?"

"Yes. I don't think they're just retreating. They want to capture Portland – or its railroad junction."

The Royal Navy cruiser startled them by hurling a brace of shells at the Yankees. For Wycombe, it was uncomfortable to hear the shells go whistling overhead.

Warwick could see that both shells fell short. He told his signaller to send a message. The cruiser fired again. Both shells landed in the middle of the advancing force.

"Why don't they just ignore us?" Wycombe said.

"Because if they did, we would attack *them*. So they've got to deal with us before they attack Portland. If the Yankees overcome us, the marines will have to defend Portland street by street and house by house."

"So we defend Portland just by sitting here and suffering?"

"Yes, that's the size of it."

Wycombe was fond of the people of Portland. There was the black community. And that girl, Eliza. Was she still there? He was glad that their action was defending people – their action was not just strategic.

Captain Warwick told the men to keep down, so that the hill protected them from enemy fire. "Kneel down or lie flat."

The Royal Navy continued to lob shells over the heads of the battalion. That kept the Yankees from advancing.

But then a shell fell short. It landed on the top of the hill but it did not explode.

Wycombe was fascinated. He could see that it was lying in a hole that it had dug for itself. A few men edged closer for a look.

Priddy screamed at them. "Don't touch it! Don't go near it, you fools. It could go of at any moment."

The men backed away. The warship fired again. This time, both shells flew safely overhead.

The Yankees realised that somebody on the hilltop was spotting for the navy. The Yankees diverted most of their army to face the hill. Warwick guessed there were over a thousand of them.

The Yankee infantry formed a line facing the hill. Wycombe guessed they were preparing for a charge. They began walking forward at a steady pace.

The men of the battalion kept up a steady rate of fire. "More ammunition, there."

They discovered the hard way that the Yankees had rifles – they could fire on the battalion from a range that the defenders' muskets could not reach.

Warwick told the navy to change their aim to this new target. To the surviving attackers, this was too much. The advance faltered. They gave up and withdrew.

"They'll be back," Priddy said.

The stretcher-bearers were busy, carrying men to the rear.

Then a third train arrived. "Look, sir!" a man shouted.

A team of Yankees unloaded a cannon from the train. They had no horses, so the men attached trail ropes to it. Ten men pulled it across the open ground towards the hill. Ten more followed, ready to push at the wheels when it hit an obstacle. Sergeant Priddy swore.

Captain Warwick asked for those men with rifles to come forward. "Try and stop them."

The Yankee gunners made no attempt to build a protective earthwork. Warwick's volunteer riflemen opened fire.

"There's no need to rush," Sergeant Priddy said. "Take it slowly. Remember your drill. Aim low."

The gunners were professional enough to ignore the hostile fire. The riflemen scored a few hits but they were unable to stop the artillerymen from serving their gun.

Then the warship sent over a couple of shells. They missed the cannon by a wide margin.

"Damn," Warwick said.

A few minutes later the ship fired again. Everyone turned to listen.

The captain shouted "Down, down!" and dropped flat.

One of the naval shells fell short. This time the shell exploded. Several men were killed by flying shell fragments.

The survivors looked round, dazed. "Stretcher-bearers!" Wycombe said.

Sergeant Priddy told them to dig foxholes to protect themselves. Wycombe passed the order on.

One of his men grumbled. "It's come to a sorry pass when you have to dig a hole to protect yourself from your own guns."

"Shut up and dig. It'll protect you from the Yankees too."

"I came up north to die a heroic death. Facing the enemy. Showing them I was as brave as they were. And what do I do? Dig holes."

The man was already digging so Wycombe let him grumble.

The Royal Navy fired a salvo. The captain shouted

"Down!" Everybody guessed what it meant and dived for their foxholes.

One of the shells fell short. The man nearest to the explosion was killed and several received minor injuries.

"On your feet. Load your muskets." Wycombe said. "And stretcher-bearers."

The men of the battalion developed the habit of falling flat every time the navy sent a couple of shells over.

But, the next time, the captain remained standing. The shells exploded next to the Yankee cannon.

Wycombe climbed to his feet. He was humiliated and angry. "Are you too proud to lay flat? Sir?"

The captain raised an eyebrow. "Shells that fall short sound different. Can't you tell the difference?"

"No, sir."

Sergeant Wycombe felt driven to complain. "More of us are being killed by the navy than by the Yankees!"

The captain was annoyed. "Shall I tell them to stop, sergeant?"

Wycombe considered this. "No, sir. The shelling is the only thing that's stopping the Yankees from reaching us."

Most of the men spent all of the time in their foxholes and only popped up when the Yankees attacked. But they hated the shells.

An hour later, Wycombe came to the captain to report. The captain now had his own foxhole. "The men are asking for permission to charge. They hate this endless delay. And we don't gain anything by delaying, sir."

The captain shook his head. "They would slaughter you. A charge wouldn't achieve anything. You might kill a few, but the survivors would be free to march on Portland."

"It would be better than this – waiting, sir."

"Can you hold out until nightfall? I think they'll give up then."

"They'll give up?" Wycombe said.

"I think they're short of ammunition."

"I see, sir. I'll ask." Wycombe passed the word along the line. The men discussed it amongst themselves.

"Nightfall?" Most of them approved. It gave them a target. Outlasting the Yankees.

The day was drawing on. It would be dark in less than an hour.

The Yankees formed a line, preparing themselves for another charge. "This is their last attempt," Sergeant Priddy said. "There's just enough time for them to defeat us and attack Portland before nightfall."

The Yankee infantry began walking up the hill, their drums beating. To the men of the battalion, they seemed unstoppable. The sergeants told them to load. "Present - fire. Reload."

The Royal Navy fired again and this time both shells landed in the middle of the advancing men. But the Yankees kept on coming.

Wycombe's men had just finished reloading. "Present – fire."

The Yankees cheered and broke into a run. Wycombe realised that, this time, nothing would stop them.

The Yankee charge reached the battalion lines. They were telling like madmen.

Wycombe realised that his musket was empty. Well, he had his bayonet.

The Royal Navy fired again. They could all hear the shell. Wycombe panicked. "It's falling short! Take cover!"

The Yankee sergeant grinned. "Kiss my boots, nigger, and I might let you live."

The shell was about to hit. Wycombe's men knew the

signs and had already fallen flat.

Wycombe heard the white soldier's voice. "Kiss my boots."

Wycombe ignored him. He had no time to answer. All he could think of was the sound of that shell.

The shell landed on the north side of the slope, just a few yards away. The fuse went off and the shell exploded.

Wycombe could see the grass, a few inches from his face. There was a ringing in his ears and he could not hear anything. He realised that meant he was still alive. He sat up and looked round. His companions were still alive. They stared back at him.

The ringing in his ears was diminishing. "Where are those Yankees?"

But the three Yankees were dead. He could see their legs and their feet. The bodies had been cut off at waist height. Everything above that had vanished.

"Oh."

Further along the line, the men of the battalion were defending themselves with bayonets. They refused to give way. For the Yankees, that was their last effort. The survivors realised they were outnumbered and retreated.

"Cease fire. They're out of range," Captain Warwick said.

They learned later that half of the Yankees retreated in good order eastwards, in an attempt to link up with the militia. But the other half of the survivors were leaderless. They withdrew out of rifle range.

The battalion advanced down the hill to the railroad track. The damaged locomotive blocked it.

The telegraphist re-connected his instrument and sent a report to Portland.

"You going to send us after them, sir?" Wycombe asked.

"In the dark? No," Captain Warwick said. "You'd get lost, they'd hunt you down, they might win after all."

"We've won? This is it?"

The captain looked round at the battlefield. "We've won today, sergeant."

Wycombe just felt tired. But he bestirred himself to ask about stretcher parties. The medics were soon busy.

"We need sentries," Captain Warwick said. "And it's time for dinner. When you can cook a meal and they can't, you know who's won."

Sergeant Priddy nominated some men to act as cooks. The survivors found that they were hungry.

The cooks knew their work. One of them added some herbs to the pot. Wycombe had to admit that it smelt good.

Then a pair of Yankees came in out of the dark. The sentries turned their muskets towards the enemy.

"Don't shoot, redcoat. We've come to surrender." Everybody turned to the captain.

"Give 'em a plate and some food," the captain said.

In ones and twos, more Yankees come in to surrender. They explained that they had not eaten for days.

"Our captain said you were short on ammunition," a white corporal said. "Short on everything, he said. But you weren't"

One black sergeant said, in an undertone, "We ought to kick them out."

"Shut up," Captain Warwick said. "If we do that, they'll pick up their rifles and start sniping at us. Besides, the victor should be magnanimous towards the defeated."

"Is this what victory feels like?"

The doctor arrived from Portland and set to work.

The number of Yankees grew. Some were half-carrying wounded comrades. Priddy told the Yankees coming in to wait in line. "Doctor's over there."

The cook told the major that the battalion had brought food supplies for themselves but it was not enough to feed the Yankees as well.

The major was alarmed. "They're hungry enough to fight over it." He told the telegraph operator to send a request to Portland.

The telegraphist bent over his instrument. "Sir, they say they've got the rations but it would take hours to get steam up on a locomotive, sir."

"Hitch up a horse to a buggy? No." The major told sergeant Wycombe to lift the hand cart onto the tracks and go to Portland for more food.

An hour later, Wycombe and his men returned from Portland with a cauldron full of stew. The cooks poured in some boiling water, to warm up and to dilute the stew, and spooned it out. None of the prisoners complained at their rations.

Wycombe reported to the captain. He was just in time to hear Sergeant Priddy come forward with a casualty list. "We have three hundred dead or missing or seriously wounded, sir. That means we have three hundred fighting men left."

Captain Warwick was appalled. "The battalion doesn't exist any more, sir."

"Oh, and over a hundred prisoners." Priddy said.

Portland, July 13

Two days after the battle, the officers of the battalion assembled for their evening meal in a confiscated farmhouse.

The hundred prisoners had been marched to Portland and then sent to New Brunswick by paddle-steamer.

They did not want to discuss the casualty figures so

the topic of conversation turned to strategy.

"Do the Yankees have the resources to attack again?" D'israeli asked.

"Yes, but they would have to bring up more men from the south," Warwick said.

"At least they've abandoned their attack on Quebec," D'israeli said.

"I have something new," Major Eastman said. "The latest New York newspapers make no mention of a new US attack. Instead, they expect the British to repeat our Portland trick elsewhere. But they can't decide where." He grimaced. "The Yankees can't keep anything secret from their newspapers."

"We don't have the resources for another attack. We can barely hold our own," Warwick said.

"Their experts must know that another attack by the British is impossible. But the newspapers don't care," the major said.

"But the rumours embarrass the president," Warwick said.

Chapter 12

Fort Ticonderoga, July 13, after dark

The Yankees had put their most troublesome prisoners into a single site. For some reason that Tommy never understood, she had been classified as a troublemaker. She was still going by the name of Sergeant Alexander Thompson. No-one had discovered her secret.

The British officers were supposed to be strictly segregated from the NCOs. But, for a determined man, those barriers were easy to circumvent.

Tommy had made a suggestion for an escape. The sergeants had approved of the suggestion. But, by the tradition of the camp, they had to submit the request to the Escape Committee.

The sergeants were housed in a separate block. So, after the curfew, Tommy followed the burly militia sergeant in his climb across the roof. The houses had steep roofs and a long drop if you slipped. The sergeant, despite his size, moved silently. Both of them wore moccasins.

They reached the sunlight, which was open an inch. The officer inside, reading a novel, did not look up. The burly sergeant pushed the sunlight open and climbed down. "Good evening, sir."

Tommy followed him.

"I hope this is Escape Committee business, sergeant?" the officer affected to sound unconcerned.

"Yes, sir." There was no risk of them being rejected – everyone was too bored for that.

The officer put away his book and led them along a corridor to a small cramped room. Five men were sitting around a table.

The officer introduced Tommy and the militia sergeant to the Escape Committee. Tommy realised that the committee members were all toffs. Fops. One was a hussar lieutenant. Judging by his accent he was an aristocrat, not a professional officer. His expensive braided jacket was looking tatty.

Tommy guessed that these gentlemen were the sort who insisted upon changing for dinner, even in a POW camp. Not very bright. They irritated Tommy.

The odd man out, sitting at the far end, was Lt. Baden of the Army Air Service. He was a toff too, with the physique of an athlete, but he looked brighter than the rest.

The big sergeant had told Tommy that a clique of officers had formed an 'Escape club'. But the sergeant had said that they had not managed any successful escapes.

"Go ahead, sergeant," the hussar lieutenant said.

"Well, sir, I remembered a previous escape from here. It was in the newspapers. They escaped by boat ..."

"Boat?" the hussar lieutenant said.

"All of the other attempts tried to walk out. They were all caught before they got twenty miles, by local farmers. But if you could travel up the coast ..." Tommy realised that in her nervousness her London accent was reasserting itself.

"Go on, sergeant," Lt. Baden said.

"You see, there's a steam launch in the boathouse. It can carry more men than a rowing boat could. But my guess is that it would take six hours to build up steam."

The Royal Engineers officer perked up. "A boathouse? Steam engine?"

"It's at the foot of the cliff, sir."

Everyone at the table turned to look at the engineer officer. He was the only one who knew anything about stream engines.

"Very well. I promise to look into it."

"Good show," the hussar lieutenant said.

Tommy had to be content with that. The two sergeants made the rooftop journey back to their billet.

Fort Ticonderoga, July 14

The following evening, the Royal Engineer officer prepared to make his way over the wall, a dangerous exercise. But one section of the wall was obscured from the bastions. Only the patrolling sentries could see it.

This was opposite the sergeants' block, so the first part of the engineer officer's journey was over the roof.

Tommy watched as the engineer climbed out of the window, and across to the outer wall. No-one raised the alarm. Now he had to sneak down the cliff without falling.

Tommy waited, anxious. But there was no outcry.

Then the engineer climbed back inside.

He did not explain what he had found. "I have to make my report to the Escape Committee."

Tommy and the big sergeant accompanied the engineer to the officers' block.

There were no chairs for the sergeants. They stood by the door.

"The vessel is seaworthy. The engine is quite small. Local Yankee manufacture, but it seems to be in working order. Somebody must have been taking care of it. The boiler and firebox are quite small too. It will take only two hours to build up steam."

The hussar toff was not impressed. "There's no chance of us getting all the way to Canada. Is it worth the trouble? Half of us will be killed. The rest will be recaptured."

This was received with an uncomfortable silence. Tommy was annoyed at this negative attitude.

The athletic Baden intervened. "The steam-launch would take us halfway along the lake - to within fifty miles of the frontier. We should be able to walk that far. Particularly as the Yankees won't know where to start looking."

Tommy tried to hide her anger. "One measure of success is the number of Yankees we'll have chasing after us. If it's only fifty, we've failed."

"They would send a hundred," Baden said. "If we could avoid capture for two days, they'd send five hundred."

The hussar toff reconsidered. "If we could achieve that, it would be worth doing, then."

The chairman of the committee asked for a show of hands. They agreed, so the chairman asked for volunteers for the attempt. Thirty men did so.

"A mass breakout? You're crazy," Baden said.

The hussar lieutenant invited Tommy to come along. "We need an enlisted man to stoke the boiler for us."

Tommy demurred. "I have to keep these weather records."

"You've found a cushy billet, then?"

Tommy was angry. "Very well, *sir*. I'll stoke for you."

New York State, July 15

They climbed through the narrow window and made their way down to the lakeside. They stood around while the engineer officer tinkered with the engine.

He and Tommy lit the fire and got steam up. They managed to do so in silence.

Up above, in the fort, the sergeants arranged a very noisy argument to attract the guards' attention.

"I don't want to reverse out. Too much noise," the engineer officer said. "We'll have to push her out." Four swimmers offered to do so.

Baden, the Air Service officer, had volunteered to steer. The escapees climbed on board.

The four volunteers lowered themselves into the water and pushed the launch out of the boathouse. The launch drifted a few yards, with the volunteers clinging to the hull.

"That'll do," Baden said, and the swimmers were pulled aboard by their companions

The engineer opened the throttle and the steam reached the pistons. To Tommy, the gentle hiss of escaping steam sounded very loud. The paddle-wheels began to turn and pushed the launch forward. It was very noisy. "Can't you do that quietly?" the hussar officer said.

"Not in a paddle boat," the engineer said. They all glanced up at the fort. But there was no outcry on the shore.

They turned north and headed for Essex county. "Can't we go any faster?" the toff said.

The engineer grinned and opened the throttle further. They built up speed. "We really are overburdened," Baden said. "I hope we don't capsize."

The hussar lieutenant told Tommy to make himself useful by putting more wood on the fire.

"Shut up," the engineer said. "Pressure's high enough. We don't want to run out of fuel half-way."

They kept to the middle of the lake because, as Baden said, it reduced their chances of bumping into anything in the dark.

At sunrise, they found that their vessel was the only one on the lake. But they knew that would not last.

"Some busybody will spot us soon. They'll call for help," the engineer said.

"How can they call for help in this wilderness?" the hussar said.

Tommy felt obliged to speak up. "The railway follows the shore. There's a station every ten miles or so."

"I remember that," Baden said. "Those Indians did their best to sabotage it."

Baden turned the launch towards the shore. They could see that the forest came right down to the water's edge. It was dark and intimidating. "There's a beach, of sorts," Tommy said.

"Can somebody jump into the water fend us off?" Baden said.

The launch grounded on the beach. One after the other, the escapees jumped into the water, exclaimed of the cold, and waded up the beach.

But ten men refused to go ashore. They said the forest was too dangerous and they would prefer to continue northwards on the boat.

The hussar lieutenant was outraged.

"Splitting up will confuse things." Tommy said. "The Yankees may think we all drowned and stop looking."

"Shut up, sergeant," The hussar lieutenant said.

The men on the launch ended the argument by putting the launch into reverse and heading out into the lake.

The twenty men on land turned their backs on the shore and pushed into the forest. A mile inland, they reached the railroad. Tommy had assumed this would be an obstacle. She had expected sentries every hundred yards.

But they found a curved stretch of track that deprived the sentries of a clear view.

"Patrol coming," Baden said. "Back into the woods."

They watched from hiding as a squad of ten Yankees ambled past.

"Slackers," the hussar muttered.

"Shut up," Baden said.

The Yankee patrol disappeared round the corner.

"Now," Baden said.

The escapees managed to slip across unseen. They reached the safety of the forest and headed for the mountains.

They followed the farm tracks, although these often turned in unhelpful directions. This led to arguments. Baden wanted to abandon the track and push through the woods. The hussar lieutenant said that following the track would be quicker than forcing a way through thorns and bracken.

Tommy had heard that many farmhouses had been abandoned. They passed two. Then, that first night, they took shelter in another.

Quebec July 15, evening

The governor in Quebec, Sir Humphrey Waite, summoned Charles Lloyd to his residence. "Take a seat, Lloyd. I want your opinion. You are respected for your ability to bring fresh ideas to a problem."

"Thank you, sir. But what problem is it?"

"Look at these Yankee newspapers. The view in Washington is that the main US attack has been defeated. Their attempt to get their troops out has failed."

Charles read the papers with interest. They were only a day old. Canadian papers often reprinted excerpts of the same stories, with a lag of several days.

He recognised what the governor meant. The American public – and the newspapers – were no longer demanding victory.

"I see, sir. For the politicians in Washington, peace talks are once again possible. Although nobody is saying so out loud."

"That was my impression too," the governor said.

"We can wait for them to make the first move, or we can drop a few hints."

"Bah. We could wait for ever," Sir Humphrey said. "None of those elected politicians has the guts to make the first move."

Charles considered his bargaining counters. What could the British propose and then back down on? "We could ask for an indemnity. Recompense for all the damage they've done."

"Risky. We've done some damage too."

Charles trusted George Eastman's opinion. He asked for a short break so that he could send a message to Portland, via George's Talker, Laval. He sat down, established rapport and explained the problem.

Laval was precise in his reply. 'Mr. Eastman says he wants territory for the Abenaki. Sliced out of Northern Maine. He knows that an independent colony is not practical. Perhaps a county in an enlargement of Quebec?'

'Or Fort Ticonderoga?' Charles asked. He broke contact and waited a couple of minutes.

'Mr. Eastman says the fort is worthless. Do you want to antagonise the Yankees that much? Mr. Eastman suggests it would be more practical to ask for the right bank of the St. Lawrence. This would push the frontier further away from Canadian heartland.'

'Ah. Ogdensburg?' Charles asked.

'Yes. Mr. Eastman also suggests that California must end the bounty for killing Indians.'

Charles was shocked. 'Does that still happen?'

'If it does not, Mr. Lloyd, then there's no harm in asking.'

"True.' Charles wrote these ideas down and took them

to the governor.

The governor examined them with interest. "Territory – Yes. They'll like that back home. But not so much that the Yankees take fright. My principal demand is an immediate ceasefire." He added Charles' suggestions to his own and sent these terms to Washington.

Quebec, July 16,

Charles and his wife took a cab to the railroad station. The governor had asked him to act as courier. Sir Humphrey had made it clear that Charles did not have the authority to discuss the terms.

They found that a crowd had assembled at the station, all eager for a glimpse of him. The Washington newspapers had been reprinted in Quebec. This change in stance by the US government had caused great excitement in Canada.

The southbound train was waiting. Charles said farewell to his wife. Some people in the crowd wished him luck. He climbed aboard and took his seat.

At Champlain station, the frontier crossing point, he was met by an officer of the Lower Canadian volunteers. A crowd had gathered outside the station. The men stood aside to let him pass. A private unfurled a white flag. Together they walked across the barren ground to the US lines.

An officer in blue was waiting for him. "You're the courier?"

He nodded. "Yes. I have the papers here."

"Good. I was told to expect you." The officer led him to a waiting train. "I am to accompany you to Washington."

Charles knew that the journey to Washington would take all day. He would arrive late at night.

Adirondacks, July 16

On the second day, the British escapees continued along abandoned, overgrown, farm tracks. They were trying to make their way west, but the tracks often turned, following the contours.

Then they stumbled across another farmhouse. It was dilapidated, but was still inhabited. Before they could retreat, they were spotted by the homesteader's wife. She called for help. The escapees turned and fled.

They pushed on through the forest. But when they found another farm track they chose the easy option and followed it. Tommy knew they should abandon the paths and strike out cross-country, but knew that any suggestion would be ignored.

The hussar lieutenant said that the farm tracks followed the contours and made an easy climb.

Several hours went by. Then they heard the sounds of men behind them pushing through the undergrowth. "Soldiers. "We've been located," Baden said.

The hussar lieutenant was wheezing because of the climb. "You can't be certain they're Yankees."

Then they heard a shout. "Halt or we'll fire!"

Tommy turned directly uphill, through the woods, and the others followed.

The slope was steep and many men were not used to this. Men began to drop out. Those who did so knew they would probably be captured, but there was no alternative. They had to be abandoned.

Those remaining, the fittest, slowly drew head of their pursuers.

USA, July 16, evening

The journey to Washington did not take as long as Charles expected. They arrived an hour after sunset.

He and his escort transferred to a carriage. He was told that the offices of the State Department were housed in the Treasury Building. He had heard about the grand public buildings of Washington, but the first buildings he passed were boring brick structures.

Then they reached the Treasury Building. This lived up to expectations. It was a neoclassical building with a colonnade. It flanked the White House and faced Capitol Hill.

Charles was led upstairs to a private office. The Secretary of State was waiting.

Charles opened his document case and took out a bulky envelope.

"You will see that the envelope is still sealed. I am not empowered to discuss these terms, sir."

"That is understood, Mr. Lloyd."

"What happens now?"

A junior secretary stepped forward "We've booked a room in a hotel for you. You will stay there until we have prepared our reply."

"Very well."

New York State, July 17

On the third day of the escape, Baden kicked them awake. "The Yankees are already up. Move."

The pursuit continued. That morning, three more men dropped out, exhausted. The survivors occasionally heard the searchers in the distance.

Then they stopped to rest. Most of them were short of breath.

A couple of minutes later, they were surprised when a group of men in scruffy red jackets stepped out of the woods. The hussar lieutenant yelped.

The leader was a sergeant, Thomas Francis. Tommy recognised him.

"Who the devil are you?" the hussar lieutenant said.

"We're scouts from J company, sir. The Royal Americans. I'm sergeant Francis."

"I see," Baden said.

"You mustn't stay here." Francis was blunt. "You must split up. Small groups will be easier to hide. I'll provide guides. You will have to obey them."

The hussar complained at the indignity of taking orders from enlisted men. His companions told him to shut up.

Francis split the escapees into three groups. Tommy was careful to stay with Sergeant Francis. The scouts led them off through the woods. "Single file. And no noise."

The sergeant told them that an airship would be sent to meet them the next day. "If we can win clear of the Yankees, of course."

"Tomorrow?" Tommy said.

"Yes. Assuming the weather holds. It's a very risky manoeuvre."

Montreal, 18, evening

The airship bearing the escapees arrived in Montreal. They were exhausted from their ordeal. They no longer had fear to keep them going. A couple of the men had to be helped down the step from the gondola. The officers then strolled across the grass to the Air Service operations room, leaving Tommy abandoned.

Then she spotted Lieutenant Eathorpe standing on the airfield perimeter.

"Good evening. I've come to collect you." He frowned. "You look terrible. Did they mistreat you?"

"No, sir. It's mainly the last few days. Being hunted."

"Come on, then. I have a cab for you."

"I've never ridden in a cab before."

"I think we can justify it on this occasion, sergeant."

As soon as they arrived as army headquarters, Miss Grace made tea for all of them. Her unspoken price was that she stayed to listen. Then Tommy's questioning began.

"Why didn't you establish rapport?" Lieutenant Eathorpe asked. "Until we got that prisoner report from the US Army, we thought you were dead. We were worried."

She explained her stroke. "But I don't understand why Asher died an' I didn't."

"Mr. Lloyd said he couldn't explain that either. But why didn't you contact me? Or one of the others?"

"Sir – I refuse to make any attempt to establish rapport ever again."

The lieutenant gaped. Tommy could appreciate his dilemma. He must have realised he was out of his depth. "I wish Mr. Lloyd was here."

"There's Mrs. Lloyd, sir," Grace said. "She has all sorts of experience. She served at Osborne House. And – anything she says will be off the record."

The lieutenant brightened. He scribbled a brief note to Mrs. Lloyd. He sent Grace off in a cab. "Tell her that the cab is for her if she wants to come here."

"The sergeant needs a bath," Grace said, and dashed off.

Tommy was alarmed at this. "Impossible. Too risky. Not even a scrub-down."

"A sergeant can demand some privacy, remember," Lieutenant Eathorpe said. "So move it."

Mrs. Lloyd arrived half an hour later. She was concerned for Tommy's health. "I heard about Signaller Asher. Ah - was it instantaneous?"

"Yes, madam," the lieutenant said.

Mrs. Lloyd asked Tommy a couple of questions. She listened, and sat back. "You were foolish to break the safety rules. You're lucky to be alive. Men have killed themselves in this way."

Tommy nodded. "I know. Like poor Asher."

"Yes. But with only a few days' instruction ... The apprentices get four *years*. I'm surprised there's been only one death."

"Yes, madam," the lieutenant said.

Mrs. Lloyd turned back to Tommy. "You're not crippled in any way? I know a man who's spent the last twenty years stuck in a wheelchair due to over-exertion. And another – the whole side of his face just – sagged."

"Nothing like that," Tommy said. "But I refuse to do that ever again."

Lieutenant Eathorpe was blunt. "Mrs. Lloyd, does this count as a refusal to obey a legitimate order?"

Mrs. Lloyd was shocked. "No! Using magic is, is, a specialist task. Above and beyond the call of duty. Like, like – lighting the fuse to a Congreve rocket."

Tommy grinned. "I would be prepared to do that."

"Lieutenant, the sergeant will just have to be given ordinary duties. If you want, I can write a statement to that effect, for your records. My husband can sign it when he gets back."

"Thank you, madam," Lieutenant Eathorpe said. He turned to Tommy. "Well, we need an extra sergeant. You'll be useful here."

The lieutenant escorted Mrs. Lloyd back to her cab, then returned to the office. "Sergeant, that – seizure did you some harm. I want to know what it is."

Damn, she thought. "It's just that it isn't fun any

more. Pretending to be a man. Deceiving everyone. And acting tough. It's just a – chore."

The lieutenant considered this. "Do you want to leave, then? We can probably arrange a medical discharge. Discreetly."

"While the war's going on? No, sir, I won't quit."

Quebec, July 19, Evening.

The train drew into the station at last. Charles could see that a crowd was waiting. He stepped down from the carriage and the crowd hushed.

The governor's aide pushed his way forward. "Stand aside there, stand aside ... Good evening, Mr. Lloyd. If you will come this way?"

He led the way outside to a closed four-horse carriage. He gestured for Charles to go first. Charles climbed the step and discovered that the governor was sitting on the back seat. Charles took the seat next to him.

"Well, Mr. Lloyd? Your telegram was laconic," The governor said.

The aide climbed in, taking the forward seat. The carriage moved forward and Charles sat back in the cushioned seat.

"The Yankees agreed to open negotiations, sir. Although they are outraged at the British conditions. They are prepared to consider redrawing the frontier. Although they hinted we would have to concede some territory. But they refused to consider a ceasefire."

"So they could launch a counter-attack? Go on. There's worse?"

"The Yankees have a precondition: the black battalion in Portland must be disbanded before talks can begin. And the black runaways in the battalion must be sent south."

The aide hissed in alarm. "The emancipation lobby -."

"Quite so," the governor said. "Britain cannot accept that. It would be illegal."

Charles was relieved.

"Did they put that in writing, sir?" the aide said.

"Well – it isn't secret. The newspapers, the morning I left, were full of it."

The governor nodded. "Then my response must be in writing. And if I conceded to this demand, my career would be ruined."

The carriage made its way up the hill to the governor's mansion. "You will dine with us. You will want to change your clothes," the governor said.

Charles would have preferred a bath, but there was not time enough for that. "Yes, sir."

An hour later, Charles walked into the governor's office. All of the men in the room were wearing evening dress. General Trevor-Roper was among the participants.

The governor coughed. "Gentlemen, may I introduce you to Mr. Charles Lloyd, one of my most trusted aides. He has just returned from Washington. Their government is prepared to open negotiations, gentlemen. But they refuse to accept a ceasefire." Everyone turned to stare at Charles.

"They want to keep us on edge," Charles said. He explained the State Department's conditions. The men nodded.

"The documents that Mr. Lloyd drought back merely expand on that," the governor said. "I'm concerned that the negotiators will insist on a clause that they can keep any territory they're holding when the treaty is signed. So we can expect a last-minute attack."

"Although that would allow us to keep Portland," the general said.

"I'm sure that they'll insist that we return Portland," the governor said.

Their precondition about the black battalion is extraordinary," the general said.

"It's the southern senators who object to black soldiers," Charles said.

"We can't send them back. They're British soldiers," the general said. The other men nodded their agreement.

"May I suggest that the battalion should be split up, not disbanded," Charles said. "And we could tell the Yankees that all of the soldiers are, of course, freeborn."

"The Yankees would never swallow that story. Half of those volunteers were runaways," the governor said.

The general grinned. "They've seen heavy fighting. Almost fifty percent casualty rate. So - all of the runaways were among the dead. Determined to prove their courage."

"Ah. Of course," the governor said. "If Washington asks, that's the line I'll feed them. And I shall send a message to London immediately."

Montreal, 21 July

Tommy had been sent back to the Weather team in Montreal. Lieutenant Eathorpe had given her clerical and administrative duties. Miss Grace was overworked, so Tommy filled in, collating the weather reports and distributing the predictions.

Several officers complained that their weather predictions were getting lost en route. Tommy arranged for the telegrams to be addressed to a responsible sergeant, not the CO.

Tommy also assisted Lieutenant Eathorpe with his paperwork. He was occupied full-time, struggling with the weather algorithms. He was disappointed at the Engine's poor success rate and was certain he could improve it.

The work was all vital but, most of the time, Tommy was bored.

Men from the Royal American Regiment visited headquarters every day on routine tasks, but no-one recognised Tommy. She was now in a different regiment, wearing Royal Engineer blue. And, besides, a sergeant associated with a different class of men.

Tommy deliberately tried to imitate the speech of Mr. Lloyd. She did not want to remind anyone of a cockney who spoke in an alto.

Montreal, 21 July

Eliza was lodging with a minister's wife. The Underground Railroad did not reach as far as Montreal, so the small black community had no experience of dealing with runaways.

The minister had hinted that the Missionary Association needed help in Essex County, but Eliza knew that she was not suited for missionary work. She wondered whether the Association needed teachers.

Then Eliza had let slip that she helped stitch the colours of the battalion, and that she had met the viscountess.

The minister's wife had been shocked. "Viscountess Inismore? The dowager?"

"Yes, madam. She told us to call her Lady Forlaith."

"You *talked* with her?"

The minister's wife, it appeared, was a monumental snob. This news was too important for her to keep to herself. "I must visit a friend ..."

The next morning, she climbed the steps of a house in a side-street and knocked on the door. "Mrs. Poole is my particular friend. So mind your manners, Eliza."

"Yes, madam."

"And then there's Mrs. Smith and Mrs. Carpenter."

Eliza held back a sigh. To her it was almost a freak show. Mrs. Poole's daughter opened the door and led them into the parlour. The ladies were all dressed in their best.

Their hostess offered them tea. "I understand why the soldiers wanted a flag, of course, but why did they ask – blacks?"

Eliza knew that the correct military term for 'flag' was 'colours' and they always came in pairs. But folks did not like it when she corrected them. "A white seamstress might have been accused of treason, madam. But nobody cares about us."

An older guest was surprised. "Treason? For a bit of needlework?"

"It was the regimental colours," the minister's wife said. "And then the viscountess presented it to the regiment."

A shiver of excitement ran through the group. "And her ladyship - she sat down with you? In the workshop?"

"Yes, madam. She said she had to contribute. She said that was important.

"At the ceremony, she gave a little speech. She said that she had worked on the colours with her own hands."

Eliza's audience listened in rapt silence. She described her warning and her escape. She did not dwell on the men who had helped her but instead described the Indian village. "They were very kind to me. But it was a stiff climb. And going down the mountain, to the railroad station, was worse. I ached for days." She sipped at her tea. "And Portland is safe. I think I needn't have bothered."

This was met by silence.

She was frightened. "What's wrong? Have the Yankees attacked?" She knew there had been a battle, with heavy casualties. "Has there been *another* battle?" Were they dead?

Mrs. Poole put her cup down. "No, my dear. But the newspapers- the demands made by the politicians ..."

Portland, July 21

The New York newspapers always reached Portland a day late. George had arranged for his own delivery and read them with interest. Today they contained reprints of the Washington papers, with their inside stories of the negotiations. The New York editors added comments of their own, indignant that the southern negotiators had ignored the demands of the northern states. New York wanted an immediate ceasefire and an end to the blockade.

George shared the papers with his secretary, Laval. Then Laval pointed out that the news had reached Portland before the governor in Quebec had made any official announcement of the negotiations.

"Yes, you're right." George knew that meant trouble. "The soldiers will be angry."

The rumours of the negotiations spread like wildfire. At first, everyone in Portland was delighted at the news. Then the soldiers heard the rumours that the battalion would be disbanded.

George was not surprised when RSM Priddy, acting in his official role of spokesman of the enlisted men, made a formal visit to headquarters.

George heard him out and told him to assemble the senior sergeants. "I only want to say this once."

"An hour's time, sir?"

"Very well."

"The assembled sergeants almost filled the room. They were tense. Some were angry

George leaned back in his chair. "At ease. You have heard a lot of rumours. Some of those – but only some - are true." The men stared back, angry or sullen or suspicious.

"First – nobody is going to send you south. But if the battalion stays here, there won't be any negotiations. Some of you might want the fighting to go on forever – no?"

"No, sir," someone growled.

"Good. So the battalion, or what's left of it, will be split up. But you will stay in the army. You will not be paid off." He grinned. "The Yankees were told that every man in the battalion was born free."

"But we did so well, sir. Is this our reward?"

"Listen! A battalion contains a thousand men. When you got your colours, there were that many of you. Now, there are only three or four hundred of you left."

Some of the men, judging by their dour expressions, guessed what was coming next. The grumbling subsided.

"And there's no chance of recruiting any more of you, is there? No-one else will come north to join up. We have black militia companies in Canada but they'll want to defend their homes."

The men accepted this in silence.

"The first battalion of the Sixty-Second, in Montreal, has also suffered many casualties. So 'A' and 'B' companies here in Portland will merge and become 'N' company of first battalion. The other companies will merge to become two independent companies. The first Nova Scotia and the first New Brunswick.

"You will be shipped to Canada, one company at a time, as soon as the Royal Navy can provide the ships."

"Sir - will you take our colours away from us?" The speaker was Wycombe.

George was surprised. "Does it matter so much to you?"

"Yes. The lady gave it to us."

"Very well. The last company to leave will fold up your colours and take them north.

"The general wants you where you'll do the most good. And if the peace talks break down, the Yankees are likely to attack. If that happens, the battalion may be reformed and you'll need those colours again.

"That's all. Dismissed."

Portland, July 22

A mail ship tied up at the wharf. The populace watched as an under-strength company of highlanders disembarked.

They made a brave show of it, with their fife and drums playing as they formed up on the wharf.

A little ceremony had been arranged. The mayor and several other witnesses had assembled on Commercial Street.

A full-strength company of blacks, the new company of the first battalion, marched through the streets towards the docks. They were commanded by Captain D'Israeli.

"What song?" Newbegin said.

"Sing *'the Bonnets'*. And end wi' the de'il," Wycombe said. He had been promoted to company sergeant.

Come fill up my cup, come fill up my can
Come saddle my horses and call out my men
Unhook the west port and let us gae free,
For it's up wi' the bonnets o' bonnie Dundee!

And tremble, false whigs, in the midst of your glee
Ye hae no seen the last o' my bonnets and me!

Dundee he is mounted, he rides doon the street,
But the Provost, douce man, says "Just e'en let it be
For the toun is well rid of that de'il o' Dundee.

The company turned onto the wharf. "Company – halt!" Wycombe said.

"I don't believe they let us sing that," Newbegin muttered.

Wycombe grinned. "It's the Scottish accent. You didn't understand it yourself until they explained it to you."

"I prefer the bit about going free," Smith said.

Some members of the black community had turned up too. Wycombe noted that a couple of the girls were crying. A few of the spectators waved. Would they be offended because he could not wave back?

He spotted Major Eastman, standing with the official witnesses. He had been recalled to Montreal, although no-one knew why.

The highlanders who had disembarked presented arms. A salute, of sorts. A complement.

The mayor walked over. He smiled. "You're not devils, but the town's well quit of you."

"Do you hate us so much, sir?" Captain D'Israeli asked.

The mayor indicated the sergeant's red jacket. "I hate *that*. But ...

"Come back after the war's over, sergeant, and I'll find a job for you. Rather you than those Irish immigrants."

Wycombe was surprised. "I'll remember it, sir."

A naval lieutenant spoke to Captain D'Israeli. The captain gave an order and the company began filing down the gangplank onto the steamer. A few of the spectators waved. The coloured girls were still there, looking sombre. Wycombe decided that the men were not in formation, so he could wave back.

The mayor stayed to witness their embarkation. He was impatient.

Finally, the ship cast off and headed for the harbour entrance.

Captain Warwick turned to the mayor. "Well, sir, can you confirm that the first contingent of black soldiers has left?"

"Yes, captain." He was grudging. He waved a hand to indicate the waiting highlanders. "But nobody said anything about reinforcements."

"Those southern senators don't care about white reinforcements, sir."

He sighed. "True. Let's go to the telegraph office."

There was a crowd at the telegraph office too. Warwick spotted a reporter standing at the back of the crowd. The mayor ignored him.

Warwick followed the mayor inside, to find that the manager and the senior telegraphist were waiting.

No-one in Portland had sent a telegram to Washington before.

The mayor took one of the standard forms and wrote out his telegram. He pushed it across the desk. "There. Do you know where to send it? I don't want it getting lost."

"Yes, sir. They sent me a message, telling me the correct address. The State Department has its own, sir."

"Right. Send that."

Chapter 13

Montreal, July 25

Charles Lloyd had taken a cab to the airfield. He had been given warning that Major Eastman was on his way. The wind was cold so he stood in the shelter of the Army Air Service office building.

The airship turned into wind and descended gracefully until the landing skid of the gondola touched the grass. Eastman jumped down, ignored the ground handling crew, and hurried across the grass to the shelter.

Charles stepped forward. "Good afternoon, major. You're not too tired, I trust? Orders have arrived from London. The governor passed the message to me."

"Yes, I understand, sir."

"I have a cab waiting. But I want a word in private first," Charles said. "Washington has despatched a negotiating team to Brussels. They are due to arrive on the thirtieth. We must hope that the negotiator doesn't drown on the way across."

Eastman winced. "Yes, indeed."

"The British government wants to put the pressure on the US negotiators. They want to imply that Britain is serious about giving full legal rights - and land - to Indians."

"Yes?"

"So they asked me to drum up a delegation to send to London."

"A delegation? Of – Indians?" Eastman was annoyed.

"Yes. An official delegation. Recognised by the British government."

"So you thought of me, you want me to go." Eastman was angry. "But I'm a soldier. I cannot represent these people."

"Then we want you to find a suitable delegate," Charles said.

Montreal, July 26

The ocean-going steam-ship tied up at Montreal docks. The men of the New Company, drawn up on deck, watched as a detail of naval ratings rigged a gangplank.

Captain D'Israeli climbed the gangplank. He realised that the wharf was crowded with people. Then he noticed a lieutenant waiting and walked over.

The lieutenant saluted. "Good afternoon, sir. Accommodation has been arranged for your men."

"Good."

The men of the company followed the captain up the gangplank. They were surprised to see the waiting crowd.

"They turned out to see you boys arrive," a stevedore said.

Sergeant Wycombe was puzzled. What was special about a company of blacks? They were no better than half-trained recruits. He made a guess that there were over a hundred men in the crowd. And – yes, some of them were from the black community.

The stevedore grinned. "Everyone wants to see the soldiers who frightened the Yankees so much."

"But they aren't afraid of us. They despise us."

The man was confused. "Really? Well, the rest of the world thinks they're afraid of your black regiment. And the townsfolk here want to see them."

Captain D'Israeli walked back to the company.

"Sergeant, I want them to look smart. They're on the parade-ground, not a route-march."

"Yes, sir." Sergeant Wycombe turned to his squad. "Straighten up your uniforms. Belts level? Hats on straight? Those senators will be outraged to hear folks saying that they're afraid of us."

Some of the men grinned. Under his orders, they formed up, in ranks of four.

"Let's go, sergeant," the captain said. He marched down the street as if he expected all of Montreal to get out of his way.

Wycombe turned. "Company – by the left, quick march."

They marched through the streets to the barracks. Wycombe discovered the the people *did* get out of their way. They treated a squad of redcoats as just another traffic hazard. The company discovered that a lot of people had turned out to watch them pass.

Wycombe guessed that the crowd was in good humour. A few of the people in the audience, men and women, were black. He wondered whether this town was the end of the underground railroad.

He noticed that the watching blacks were smartly dressed. They were earning enough to buy good clothes.

A few black girls, giggling, threw petals at the men as they passed.

Wycombe went to brush it off his uniform and found it was a rose-petal.

"Flowers! They did that for us."

"They're proud of us." Wycombe realised that the company was famous.

Wycombe turned. "Sing! If they can give you flowers, you can give them a song." He tried to decide which should it be. "Liberty or death."

*Know that freedom's cause is strongest,
Ending but with death!
Freedom countless hosts can shatter,
Freedom thickest walls can batter,
Be this your cry, till life's last breath -
Our liberty or death!"*

The spectators, white as well as black, seemed to like it. They gave a cheer.

The company reached a gateway with elaborate wrought-iron gates. The gates were flung open as they approached. A few white soldiers stood watching, just inside the gateway.

They followed the captain into the parade-ground of the barracks. "Company – halt. Fall out."

"The sergeant here will show you to your quarters," Captain D'Israeli said.

"Yes, sir."

The duty sergeant led them to a large brick building and up a flight of stairs. He showed them the bunks they had been allocated.

Wycombe was pleased. "Real soldiers' barracks. Better than that railroad warehouse."

"That's a true word," Newbegin said.

Wycombe found there were still a few flower-petals clinging to his jacket. He carefully picked them off. He decided he was going to keep them.

"You all right, sarge?" Newbegin asked.

"I've just realised. All this time, we weren't just fighting against the Yankees, we were fighting *for* these people. Defending them."

Newbegin did not understand. "So? That makes a difference?"

"It does to me." He sat down. "I just realised. If the Yankees had won, those black people out there would have been rounded up and driven south."

A young private was shocked. "Oh, surely not."

One of the platoon sergeants frowned. "Perhaps not. But the bounty hunters would probably have grabbed a few."

"Well, they're safe now. They don't have to worry any more," Wycombe said. "And we were part of it."

Montreal, July 26, afternoon

George Eastman went to the barracks and asked the desk sergeant whether there were any off-duty Abenaki soldiers present. "I need to discuss the issue with them. They're in the Royal American Regiment."

"Yes, sir." The desk sergeant pointed the way. "And I think there's ten on fatigue duty. Would you like to speak to them as well?"

"Yes, thank you."

The men assembled in a corner of the mess hall. All of them had adopted the warrior hairstyle of shaving the hair on the side of the head. George found that they were respectful. Too respectful, he thought. They were reluctant to speak up.

George symbolically took off his uniform jacket with its rank badges. "Forget that I am a redcoat. Today I am a warrior." They nodded.

"You have heard of this delegation. Who should go? Who do you suggest?"

"We don't have any war leaders any more. Too old to fight," an older man said.

"We should send an arbitrator," a man at the back said.

The Abenaki warriors looked at each other. "There's Old Melody."

Another man nodded. "She is widely respected."

"Yes." George only knew of her by reputation.

"But will they listen to her in London?"

"We must send someone," George said. "But surely Melody is too old."

A young recruit spoke up. "I left home to enlist earlier in the year. She was hale and hearty then."

Another man suggested Melody's daughter.

George was horrified. "I have heard of her. She's clever, yes. But she is too abrasive. Does Melody have any other relatives?"

"None who are worthy."

"If Melody is fit – ask her to go," the young man said.

Montreal, Army HQ.

George walked back to the Hotel Versailles and went to Grace's little office. He hoped that she had the answer to his problem.

She was writing in a ledger but looked up as he came in. "Good afternoon, major."

"Good afternoon, miss." He summed up the warriors' argument. "They suggested an arbitrator rather than a war-leader. Can we send an invitation to Melody? She seems the best choice. But we may have to find someone who can accompany her."

Grace was embarrassed. She looked down at her lap. "I have an admission to make, major. I am Melody's grand-daughter. But when I defied my mother, I had to leave the Community."

This was a revelation for George. He was thunderstruck. "I see. But is she healthy enough to travel?"

"I believe so, sir."

"I shall have to write to her, then."

That evening, George went to see Charles Lloyd. He explained his choice. But Charles was baffled. So he had to explain the notion of female delegates.

"Things just keep getting worse. That girl Grace is Melody's grand-daughter."

"So she comes from a distinguished family?" Mr. Lloyd asked.

"Oh, yes. Much more important than me."

"Really? She's good at keeping secrets, then."

"Well, that explains Grace's attitude. I thought she came from an important family. But it wasn't a military one."

George decided that Melody was the best candidate. No male delegate would be accepted by men of other families.

"I shall have to ask Miss Grace to write a message to Melody's village."

Mr. Lloyd was dubious. "Do your people have a tradition of female ambassadors?"

"Well, not ambassadors. Only as magistrates. But the people back home respect her."

"Would the fighting men accept a treaty that Melody had signed?

"Yes. This whole mission is entirely symbolic. Am I right? You want to annoy the Yankees – put them off-balance. The British negotiators won't ask our representative to make any decisions. But, for the Abenaki, sending a female negotiator has deep symbolism.

"It's the civilised thing to do. For the British to honour their female negotiator, rather than a warrior, would be powerful message."

"I see. I'll speak to the governor."

Quebec, August 4

Grace had received a telegram from a bemused station-master at Sainte-Sabine. George and Mr. Lloyd accompanied Grace on the train journey to Quebec.

Then they waited at the railroad station for the train from the east.

The train slowed to a halt. A porter shouted that this was the train from Sainte-Sabine.

They watched as the old woman descended from the second-class carriage. She was accompanied by an Abenaki soldier.

The woman was wearing a cheap, but neat, brown woollen dress, adjusted to fit. George guessed that she was a skilled needlewoman. Her hair was covered by a traditional woollen hood, richly embroidered.

The train captain stepped down, looked round, and spotted George. He walked over. "Major Eastman? I was told to ensure that this – lady reached here. Travelling on a government pass. I wondered whether I was being set up. But it looks as if it was real."

"Yes, it is. Thank you."

"I don't suppose you could tell me what it's all about?"

"No. It's a state secret. But you'll probably read about it in the newspapers soon enough."

"This is her bag, sir." He indicated a carpet bag.

"Only one?"

"Yes, sir."

Grace stepped forward to greet her grandmother. Melody hugged her. "You have embarrassed us all, child."

Melody turned to George. "Eastman? Your mother was born a Contoocook, I believe."

"Yes, madam."

"An old woman cannot travel alone. I need a young companion." She turned to Grace. "Will you volunteer for the task, girl?"

Judging by her demeanour, Grace was reluctant.

"We have a cab waiting, madam," Mr. Lloyd said. "We have an appointment with the governor."

But the old woman refused to get into the stuffy cab.

Instead, she insisted upon walking to the governor's residence. "Is it far?"

George pointed. "The top of the hill, madam."

She squinted. "Not far at all, then."

George, embarrassed, turned to Mr. Lloyd. "You could take the cab, sir ..."

"While these ladies show their stamina? I have more pride than that."

Melody was sprightly despite her years and maintained a good pace as she climbed the hill. She chatted with Grace, who had no trouble keeping up.

The sentry at the gate raised his eyebrows at the ill-matched group, then saluted George.

"Major Eastman? "I was told to expect you, sir."

"Excellent." George returned the man's salute and they walked across the bailey of the castle. He pointed. "This building is the governor's residence."

The doorkeeper betrayed no surprise at all. He opened the door wide. "Good evening, sir."

The women were fascinated at the interior of the home. "All that furniture," Melody said. "And so much space."

The governor's secretary escorted them to the governor's office. Sir Humphrey stood to greet his guests.

Charles introduced the governor to the ladies. Grace bobbed a curtsey. George explained their role.

The governor shook his head. "No. Women cannot take part in serious negotiations in London. You will have to make the trip, Eastman."

George was surprised. "But I'm a soldier, sir. An officer. I cannot act as representative of a civilian group. It's a conflict of interest."

The governor was annoyed. "Major, I can order an army officer to act as spokesman for these people."

George realised that he was very angry. Unless he was

very careful he might say something that he would later regret. "You may order me to do that sir, but you cannot order the Abenaki people to accept anything that I say in their name."

The women listened in dismay. Grace translated this in an undertone for her grandmother, who shook her head.

"I can see your point, major," Mr. Lloyd said. "Can nothing be done?"

Grace turned back to her grandmother. "But - can we accept the Iroquois method, grandmother?"

Melody started. "Why, yes, child." She turned to George. "Young man, we elect you as war leader of the Abenaki."

George was thunderstruck. "What?"

The governor was annoyed. "What's that? What's going on, Eastman?"

"The Iroquois have this absurd tradition, sir. When the old war-chief dies, the hereditary matriarchs select the new one. But *these* women can't do that to *me*."

The governor smirked. "It is perfectly acceptable to me, major."

"But -." George drew breath. "I insist that these ladies accompany me. As my, ah, counsellors. I need someone to tell me the opinions of my people."

"Do you think that is necessary? Hum. I suppose you'll need a bit of pomp. Very well."

"One other thing, sir. Something I heard at school. In the revolutionary war, the Iroquois sent a spokesman to London. He was introduced to King George. I was wondering whether that fellow's descendant could be asked to go."

"Iroquois? Those savages?"

"They can do diplomacy as well as war," George said. "And that old warrior was a great success with King George."

"They're trying to be civilised these days," Mr. Lloyd said.

"It might impress the State Department, sir," George said. "They frighten each other with stories of the Mohawks."

"I'll think about it," the governor said.

Upper Canada August 6

The New Company had been put on a train and sent to upper Canada. They were told that they were being sent to Fort Malden.

The fort was almost two hundred miles from the rail terminus, so they had to march. This took them several days. But they were used to that.

They learned, as they marched through the region, that it had a strong black community. Essex County was famous as the end of the Underground Railroad.

The farm workers turned out to watch the company go by. There was no cheering: these people were used to the sight of soldiers marching to and fro.

Wycombe's first impression of Fort Malden was low-lying and gloomy. "Well, I heard of this place, but I never expected to see it."

"And now we have to defend it," Newbegin said.

"Yeah. I would never have expected that."

They were met by a sergeant from the Essex Coloured Militia Company. He showed them their barrack room. "This place is half empty. Plenty of room for you. "

"We get all this room? Great," Sergeant Wycombe said.

The sergeant's expression was sour. "It isn't great for me. This room's empty because we're undermanned. We're glad to see you. If the Yankees attack, take us by surprise, they could break in."

"You think that's likely? An attack, I mean?"

The sergeant scowled. "They're bound to try something."

Wycombe could not place the sergeant's accent. "Were you born free, sergeant?"

"Yeah. I was born in Canada. My parents travelled north together."

"I see."

When Sergeant Wycombe met the militia sergeant again, at dinner, he realised that the militia men were resentful of the new arrivals. "But why?"

The militia sergeant grinned. "You have combat experience. We don't. I hear there was heavy fighting around Portland. All we've done is watching and waiting. And drills."

"We could have done with more practice before we fought that first battle," Wycombe said.

"Will you stay here after the war?" a militia private asked.

Wycombe shook his head. "I'm superstitious. Don't speak of the war ending until the Yankees put their signature on that bit of paper."

The sergeant grinned. "Right."

After dinner, the militia sergeant took Wycombe up to the sentry-walk. "Across the river - see the far bank? That's Michigan."

"Do you get any refugees?"

"Lord, yes. Thirty a day, sometimes. The missionaries try to find homes for 'em."

Everybody was afraid that the Yankees would try something tricky before the treaty was signed. Would they attack the peninsula?

"They've attacked here before. In 1812, they took the place and burned it to the ground," the militia sergeant

said.

"Most of their attacks have been further east, " Newbegin said.

"Perhaps the other Portland companies will be sent there," Wycombe said.

Montreal, August 6

Charles and his wife and child accompanied old Melody, Grace and Major Eastman as they walked up the hill to the Mont Royal landing field. The waiting airship loomed over them.

The day before, a new message had arrived from London. The negotiations were about to begin. The government was eager to put pressure on Americans. They wanted the governor to send the delegation immediately.

So George had been forced to ask old Melody and Grace to leave at once.

The two women travelled light, but their bags contained several diplomatic gifts. Melody had brought traditional leather skirts and leggings, all richly decorated.

There was just enough time for the party to sit for photographs for the newspapers. The governor was eager for the Yankees to know about this stratagem.

Charles' daughter was fascinated by these strangers. She was very quiet.

Melody glanced at the child in Charles's arms. She said something in Abenaki.

Grace smiled and translated for her. "My grandmother says that this is a story that you will tell to *your* grandchildren."

Charles doubted whether his daughter understood this, but something amused her.

Then the airship's engines started up and conversation became impossible.

The passengers climbed on board. A crewman handed up their bags.

"Godspeed," Charles said. His daughter waved. The airship lifted off and turned east, destined for Halifax.

Canada, Quebec, August 6

Colonel Hendrick had received a summons to the general's headquarters. The general sat behind his desk, while his aide stood at the old man's shoulder, with a look of prim disapproval on his face.

Usually these visits were as unpleasant as a trip to the headmaster's office. But, this time, the general was courteous.

"Sit down, colonel, sit down."

"Thank you, sir."

"You seem to have a knack for irregular actions, young man. For finding unusual answers for problems, for achieving results with few resources."

"Thank you, sir." He wondered what was coming next.

"The Yankees must be planing some trickery."

"Yes, sir."

"I want you to plan an expedition to keep the Yankees on their guard."

"I see, sir."

"However, this is to be a low-priority affair. I can only spare a small number of experienced regulars. So most of the troops will come from the militia companies."

"I see, sir. That will make it more – interesting." Hendrick knew that he could not organise such an expedition on his own.

"Sir, I would like to ask you for an experienced adjutant or staff sergeant. A man who understands the forms to fill in."

"No head for paperwork, eh? Very well. The general turned to his aide. "Please find a man with suitable experience."

"Yes, sir." His look of prim disapproval did not change.

"There's Detroit," the general said. "We took it in 1812."

Hendrick had thought of that too. If he could take Detroit, his glory would be assured. He shook his head. "It's stronger than it was in 1812."

Halifax, August 7, morning

The next morning, George and the ladies assembled in the breakfast room of the hotel. All of the other guests had finished their meals and left. The airship had reached Halifax the previous evening an hour late. The airfield station manager had escorted them to the town's best hotel for the night.

The group was subdued. There was a long voyage in prospect.

Then a boy in the uniform of the telegraph company walked in. "Major Eastman? Message from Quebec, sir."

"Thank you." George opened the envelope and read the message. He was dismayed.

"What is it, major?" Grace said.

"Ah – madam, there has been a change of plans. To save time, the governor wants us to cross the Atlantic by air."

Grace was shocked. "The Atlantic? By air? Is that possible? What happens now, major?"

"The Royal Navy has a base here. I assume that they have received a telegram too."

"Look," Grace said in an undertone.

A naval officer had walked into the breakfast room. George watched as he spoke to the waiter. The officer was of medium build and had brown hair. George recognised him: Lieutenant Henry Griffin. George recalled the lieutenant saying that his wife was with him in Halifax.

The waiter pointed. Griffin turned and walked over.

George stood. "Good morning, lieutenant."

"Good morning, sir." The lieutenant was not happy. "We have an airship stationed at Halifax, watching for blockade runners. The commander has to be a naval officer, you understand. No army officers had the navigation experience."

"Yes, I understand."

George guessed that Griffin was outraged, but trying to contain it.

"Why is my precious airship being taken out of the combat area? We can go *eastward* easily enough, but it's impossible to *fly back* against the prevailing wind. The only way to get back here will be to dismantle my airship and put it on board a cargo ship.

"If the fighting breaks out again, my airship will be useless!"

George understood the lieutenant's problem at once. He set out to placate the man and explain. He turned to Grace. "Can the lieutenant join us, madam?"

"Is it for me to say? Oh, yes, of course. Please sit down, lieutenant."

"Thank you, madam."

"This flight is a diplomatic gesture," George said. "It may affect the peace negotiations. Speed is essential."

"It wasn't my idea," Grace said. "But when you get a polite request from Osborne House, you can't say no."

"That's where your orders come from?" Lieutenant Griffin was shocked. He turned to George.

"I think it's actually Lord Palmerston."

"Well, in either case, a poor naval officer can only concur."

"Yes."

"We will leave at 6pm. I shall have to visit the telegraph office and send a message to the weather people. If their prediction is favourable ..."

Grace smiled. "I quite understand, lieutenant. The best person to contact would be Mr. Lloyd."

"You know him? Thank you for the tip, madam."

Halifax, August 7, afternoon

The trio packed their bags and took a cab to the landing field. There was a two- storey hostelry on the edge of the airfield. George inspected it and discovered that the building had a partitioned parlour-snug, suitable for ladies or families.

George was tempted by the bar, but decided to stay with the ladies, to deter unwanted attention.

The window looked out over the airfield. In the far corner of the field they could see the naval vessel, held down by an array of tethers.

Their quiet was disturbed when an Army airship approached the airfield from the north. This was so unusual that everyone went out onto the veranda to watch it land.

The airship had only one passenger, a fussy man wearing a suit and a top hat. One of the airmen climbed down after him and accepted a bulky carpetbag from another crew-member. The passenger scuttled across the airfield to the hostelry, holding his hat in place. The crewman with his bag followed at a leisurely pace.

The passenger noticed George and the two women on the veranda and walked across. He took off his hat. "Good afternoon. Are you the Abenaki delegation?" He smiled. "My name is Brant, David Brant. I'm the Mohawk delegate. Can you imagine that? The governor said that an Iroquois delegate would impress the Yankees far more than an Abenaki one. Not that I claim to be very impressive, you understand."

"The name of your people may be enough, sir," George said.

Brant was cheerful. "Our brave warriors were clamouring to be chosen. Then they heard that the delegation would travel by airship and suddenly they decided that I was the best candidate after all.

"Then they heard they would be travelling with the famous lady Melody." He bowed.

"You are impertinent," Melody said.

Brant grinned. "They should have sent our noble war-chief, but he's off on campaign."

"He's acquired a reputation," George said. "Come inside. Would you like something to drink? Tea? Coffee? Or something stronger?"

"Oh, tea. I have a letter of introduction for Lieutenant Griffin."

But when the lieutenant joined them he said that he had already received a telegram. "I am delighted to meet you, sir."

The travellers took over a corner of the partitioned parlour- snug. For a couple of hours, they had it to themselves. Brant explained that his bag contained a few diplomatic gifts. "A leather frock-coat, seventy years old, can you imagine that?"

Then a lady walked in. She was thin and looked consumptive. George guessed that she was a Talker and what she was about to say. He stood and Brant followed his example.

The lady walked over to Grace. "Miss Abenaki? I'm Mrs. Griffin. I used to take the weather observations in

New York. Now I take the observations here."

Grace smiled. "Ah, I see. You contacted Bermuda? Today? I used to run the reports in Montreal, you see."

"Yes. They promised to run a special report for us. They don't like it, but they agreed that this was a special case."

Grace nodded. "The Engine in Montreal isn't equipped for Atlantic weather predictions."

George was annoyed at Grace's lack of manners and gave her a look. She wanted to be a lady, after all.

She took the hint. "Oh. Please, sit down, madam."

"You've worked with the Engine? I envy you that," Mrs. Griffin said.

Lieutenant Griffin walked in. "I thought I'd find you here, madam."

He sat next to his wife. Edith glanced at the clock. From her handbag she produced a bulky pocketbook. "I have a contact in Quebec. "Henry?"

"Of course, dear." He pulled a notebook and stub of pencil out of his jacket pocket. Then he produced a pocket-watch.

Mrs. Griffin pulled one of the visiting cards from her notebook. She stared at the far wall. "Synopsis. There's a hurricane moving across the Atlantic towards the Azores. It is expected to dissipate over the next three days. Halifax. Wind, south-west, force four, decreasing. Four octans. Visibility good."

George was alarmed. "A hurricane? Isn't that dangerous?"

Mrs. Griffin put her pocketbook away. "Well, those hurricanes are powerful, but they're only a hundred miles across."

Lieutenant Griffin looked up. "That prediction's good enough. The hurricane shouldn't bother us. We'll pass well to the north of it. But I'm supposed to wait for a telegram. That helps to preserve the secrecy."

George nodded.

"Major, I shall go whether I received a telegram or not. But people might ask why I'm risking such important passengers."

George was cheerful. "Oh, we're expendable, lieutenant."

"Well, yes." The lieutenant sipped at his drink.

Then the telegraph messenger boy arrived. "For you, Lieutenant Griffin, sir."

He handed an envelope to the lieutenant, who opened it and glanced at the contents. "Yes. This message confirms the weather forecast."

He apologised to the ladies and went to speak to his Leading seaman artificer. George went outside to watch as the crew completed the task of preparing the airship.

Mrs. Griffin remained in the parlour. "I must be careful not to interfere in any way. Miss Abenaki - my father is a diplomat. Mr. Abernethy. He's been transferred to London. If you meet – tell him that I am well."

"Yes, of course, madam."

The crew ran the propellers at full speed. "They always do that at the start of a flight," Mrs. Griffin said. "Time for you to go."

George tried to hide his unease. Three crewmen walked in and took their bags. Mrs. Griffin led the passengers across the field to the gondola. She kept her distance and watched while they filed on board.

George discovered that the main gondola was dominated by a steam engine that hissed in an ominous fashion. One of the crew led them down below. He explained that the women would share a cabin.

The lieutenant stepped down and walked across the grass to say goodbye to his wife.

She stepped back and the lieutenant climbed back on board. He gave the order for the ground crew to cast off.

"Slow ahead. Starboard ten rudder." The airship rose gracefully into the air. "Get those mooring lines flaked down."

After a few minutes the bustle of their departure decreased. One of the crewmen explained to the passengers that he was also the cook. "It'll be a long voyage. Three days, the skipper said. But don't worry, ladies and gents. I'm held to be a good cook."

Nova Scotia, 6pm

George asked for permission to go back on deck. He realised that the airship was steadily gaining height.

"Course east-south-east," Lt. Griffin said.

"East- south-east, aye," the helmsman said.

George watched as the land receded behind them. There was no going back now – the wind was too strong.

Lt. Griffin took a careful compass bearing of the headland. He dashed down to the navigator's desk to mark their position on his chart. "We're making good progress, major.

"Engineer, close down the main engine." He turned to George. "The main engine is fuel-hungry. We can't carry enough fuel to keep all three engines going for three days."

George hid his dismay. "I see."

The engineer closed the throttle and the engine fell silent. He doused the fuel in the firebox.

"But the wind is in our favour, all the way across."

"Time for dinner, sir," the cook said.

At dinner, Lt. Griffin explained that he had decided to take them higher to find stronger winds.

"You seem to enjoy this challenge," Grace said.

"Oh, yes. And I rarely get the opportunity to try it."

North Atlantic, August 8

Just before dawn, Lt. Griffin climbed onto the promenade deck, sextant in hand. The leading seaman followed with a stopwatch. When the sun was high enough, the lieutenant took a morning sun-sight, while the seaman timed it to the second. George watched, fascinated.

The lieutenant went down below to plot their position on the chart.

The ladies emerged from their cabin. Lt. Griffin asked Grace to take on the task of monitoring the weather instruments. "I have special instructions from the Board of Trade. They rarely get observations of this part of the Atlantic. It'll help them to improve their algorithms."

"Of course, sir."

Montreal, August 8

General Reginald Trevor-Roper had asked his aide to find a talented sergeant to assist the colonel to plan his raid.

But that was too much trouble. Colonels always complained when they were deprived of their best men. Instead, the aide looked round for sergeants who were under-employed.

He listened to the rumours circulating around headquarters. He heard that Tommy, in the signals team, was considered to be at a loose end. But he was also regarded as hard-working and useful.

Most important, the Signals Service did not have a jealous colonel to watch over them.

The aide made his choice. He paid a visit to Lt. Eathorpe.

He explained that Sergeant Alexander Thompson, in Eathorpe's unit, was considered to be under-employed. He was over-qualified for the work he was doing. But he was also regarded as diligent. Just the fellow to help out that uncouth Colonel Hendrick.

Lt. Eathorpe was horrified. But it appeared that he had no choice.

Maine, Portland, August 8, evening

The last black independent company had left for Montreal. Their place had been taken by a company of marines from Bermuda.

Colonel MacGregor called a council of war. The officers had chairs, while the senior sergeants stood at the back. "I have received a message from General Trevor-Roper in Quebec. The general wants us to put the pressure on the Yankees. To pre-empt them before they can do something underhand to us."

"I see, sir," the captain of marines said. "We could attack the road again."

"There's Kennebunk," the colonel said.

"A nautical operation?" the captain of Marines said.

Sergeant Joseph Thayendanega, standing at the back, knew what that meant. The men in Portland had learned that the Yankees were assembling stores in Kennebunk, by the railroad, five miles upriver.

"They are clearly preparing for an attack," the colonel said. "The question is, are they planning to attack soon, or is this a contingency in case the talks fail?

"Perhaps we could send a party shore and attack the stores," The captain of marines asked said. "We have some men from the Bermudian militia here. Some of them have experience of pilot boats – small seagoing boats – but not of rivers."

The colonel nodded. "And the Mohawk soldiers have experience of rivers."

Joseph was annoyed. He had no experience of boats. But these white men regarded all Indians as experts.

The naval lieutenant raised a hand. "I managed to find an official pilot book, published by the Yankees." He stood and drew a sketch on the blackboard.

"The river flows into the Ocean at Goochs Beach, which lies to the west of the mouth …"

"Could we find it in the dark?" the marine captain asked.

The lieutenant added a detail to his map. "There's a large conspicuous house, here. The river mouth is to the west of it." He squinted at the book. "Walker's Point. About two miles from Dock Square.

"The entire navigable length of the river is five miles. Kenebunkport is on the east bank of the river, one mile upstream, *here*. The stretch from the mouth of the river to Dock Square is very busy due to commercial boat traffic.

"Make sure you stay well aware of your surroundings, and check all around you for boats. Ships anchor in the river. Don't bump into them."

"Do you think the crews might spot us?"

"Personally, sir, I think it's more likely you'll ram one of those ships in the dark. Above Dock Square, there's the dockyards." He glanced at his notes.

"The upper section of the Kennebunk River, above the boatyards, has very little boat traffic of any kind. I doubt if anything larger than a ship's longboat could get up there."

"We can find suitable boats here, in Portland," the colonel said.

"Yes, sir. Kennebunk is on the west bank of the river, north of the Railroad Bridge."

"The Railroad Bridge is five miles from the mouth.

And the river becomes unnavigable north of there."

"Thank you, lieutenant," the colonel said. He turned to the captain. "Your men will disembark just above Kennebunk Landing and march inland to that military depot."

"Yes, sir."

"Sergeant, your task is to proceed further upriver and create a diversion for us."

"Yes, sir."

Canada, Montreal, August 9

Lieutenant Eathorpe summoned Tommy to his office. "You have received orders that you are attached to the Mohawk battalion as a staff sergeant."

"I see, sir." Tommy was shocked.

Lt. Eathorpe was annoyed. "Sergeant, this is outrageous. I'll tell the colonel that I can't spare you."

Tommy smiled. "I'm sure you and Sergeant Chard can cope without me, sir."

"Yes, but it's dangerous. You might not come back. I should never have recruited you."

Tommy was offended. "I refuse to let you keep me safe. I'm a soldier. I'll fight."

The lieutenant gave him a stare. "Very well, sergeant. You are ordered to report to Brant's Landing immediately. Ah- staff-sergeant. It's a promotion. Quite a complement, really. Good luck."

Tommy was anxious about the nature of the problem. So he went to Sergeant Chard for advice.

"Staff Sergeant? Don't worry. It's the same work that you're doing now. Except that you'll be doing it for eight hundred men rather than eight."

Tommy did not find that comforting. "But I've been

sent to Brant's Ford. They're savages."

"They're trying hard to be soldiers. An' it's your task to help 'em." And staff sergeant - It's a promotion for you."

"That's what Mr. Eathorpe said."

"Yes. Staff sergeants hold seniority over sergeants who are members of a battalion or company, and are paid correspondingly increased wages. You'll probably earn every penny."

"Thanks, sergeant."

The insignia was the monarch's crown above three downward pointing chevrons. So Tommy had to spend an hour sewing the new insignia on his jacket.

Maine, August 9, Sunset

The paddle steamer made its way along the coast and paused at the river mouth, out of range of any shore guns, just long enough to lower the boats. The steamer had been doing this for the last three days. Everyone hoped that the Yankees were bored of the sight.

"Hopefully, they won't see the small boats," Joseph told his men.

Six naval long boats were lowered into the water. The marines climbed down into the boats, set out the oars, and headed for the shore.

Then it was Joseph's turn. The mixed team of Mohawks, Hurons and Bermudians had four boats, smaller and lighter than the ones the marines were using. The boats were equipped with masts and sails but they had agreed that sails would make them too conspicuous. As they headed for the shore, they could see the silhouette of the large house.

They followed the marines as they made their way to the river entrance. The ocean swell was unpleasant and the crews were eager to reach the shelter of the river.

Then they realised that one of the big rowing boats had gone aground on the Arundel sandbank. The crew had to unload the boat, push it into deeper water, and load up again. The Bermudian doing the steering was careful to alter course to the left of marines. They rounded the end of the sandbank and turned right.

Joseph could see the shore to his left now. Would the Yankees hear them? Or were the Yankees waiting for them? But no-one shouted a challenge.

The swell was still unpleasant. They were relieved when they reached the shelter of the river.

The people of Kennebunkport were asleep. Only a couple of lights showed. A black object loomed up at them in the dark. One of the Mohawks yelped in surprise.

"Shuddup," Joseph said. The object was only an anchored ship, blotting out the sky. But no lights showed. Joseph realised the crew must be asleep.

The next obstacle was Kennebunk Landing, a short stretch of the Kennebunk River where the shipyards were located. It was an internationally famous shipbuilding area, or so the Bermudians said, and the home of more than twenty shipbuilding firms. They passed four newly-completed ships moored in mid-river. But tonight all was quiet.

They made their way past the town and continued on their way.

The marines in their big boats pulled over to the west bank and disembarked. Their task was to march inland to the military store.

The Mohawks ignored them and continued on their way. The river narrowed. Then, on a bend, the lead boat ran aground. The men groaned.

"We'll have to turn back. Or go ashore and walk."

"Let's think things through," Joseph said. "This is the

east bank. So the main channel must be further west."

Four of the Mohawks slipped overboard. "Ugh. Soft mud." They managed to push the boat free.

The Mohawks floundered in the mud, but they managed to pull themselves back on board.

They continued to row up the river towards the railroad bridge. They were more cautious now. One of the Mohawks sat in the bows, occasionally prodding the river bottom to find the deepest channel.

Finally. the Mohawk pointed. "There it is. The railroad bridge." His voice seemed very loud.

"Shut - up. Take us over to the east bank." The helmsman turned right and one after the other the boats grounded on the east bank.

"How many sentries? Only one?" On Lake Champlain, there would be a blockhouse and twenty men. Joseph tapped a man on the shoulder and pointed.

The man nodded and slipped away. He returned five minutes later. "All clear. I hit him behind the ear and then tied him up."

"Good. Well done."

The Mohawks were supposed to set light to the bridge. Sergeant Joseph carried a small barrel of pitch.

They climbed the embankment up to the railroad track. One man looked over towards the west. All was quiet. "I wonder how the marines are getting on."

"Shut up and concentrate on what you're doing."

Joseph opened the stopper on the barrel and poured the pitch over a section of the bridge timbers.

"Right. That's it. Stand clear." With exaggerated caution, he struck a light and applied it to the pitch. They watched the flames spread. The fire took hold.

"Let's go." They ran back to their boats. "Now let's see if we can get away."

There was a shout to the west. Their fire had been spotted.

They scrambled aboard their boats and pushed away from the shore. Sergeant Joseph was impatient. "Come on, let's go."

The Mohawks heard an explosion. "That was south of Kennebunk. North of the landing," a Bermudian said.

They listened as the Yankees in their camp sounded the alarm. Drums beat to quarters.

Then a bugle sounded in the town. "Some men billeted there too," Joseph said.

Then, up ahead, the firing started. "The Yankees have counter-attacked," a Bermudian said.

Joseph said nothing. He had just realised that a Yankee advance against the marines might cut him off from the sea. He wanted to tell his men to row faster. But unless they took care, they would just run aground in the mud.

Judging by the firing, the marines were retreating back to their boats. They were fighting the whole way.

Then the firing stopped. "The marines have got away."

"Let's hope so."

A few minutes later, the Mohawks passed the landing site. "In oars. Not a sound."

Joseph could make out one of the big naval rowing boats on the beach. The marines had been forced to leave it behind. "Heavy losses. Not enough men," Joseph whispered.

He expected the Yankees on the shore to notice them and open fire. But they were concentrating on the abandoned longboat. He began to hope they would slip past unnoticed. Then one of the men in the fourth boat splashed his oars in the water.

The Yankees shouted the alarm. They fired a few shots but they all went wild.

"Out oars. Give way." Joseph knew that the boats had to get past Kennebunkport. They heard more shooting up ahead. He realised with dismay that the enemy there was awake and waiting for them.

The Mohawks, trailing behind the main force, heard the shooting intensify. They approached the town.

"Keep low in your boat. I don't want you to be silhouetted against the sky."

They heard a lot of splashing and screaming up ahead. "What was that?"

"One of the long-boats must have overturned." Joseph guessed that the marines were taking heavy losses.

The town was now a blaze of lights. Every householder must have woken up and lit a lamp.

"We can't get past that," Joseph said.

The men looked at him. "What choice is there?"

"Go ashore. Walk back to Portland."

"That would take days. They'd be hunting for us all the way."

"Walk across the headland. Steal a boat," a Bermudian said.

"No. Carry these boats," a Mohawk said.

"You're crazy." Joseph tried to remember the map. The distance across the headland was about a mile, two at the most. But these boats were heavy. He doubted that his men could do it.

They steered for the shore, just above the town. They got ashore without being seen and dragged their boats up the beach. They emptied the gear out of the boats. All of the oars had to be carried. Six men had muskets.

There were enough men to carry all of the boats, eight men to each boat. They lifted the upturned boats onto their shoulders and started walking. The men with other gear tagged along behind. Joseph chose a route that took them north of the town.

The boats were heavy and they had to rest frequently. Joseph tried to be patient. They could not rush things.

They reached a road, put down the boats, and had an argument. Joseph said the road would take them too far north. They should cross it and head south.

He persuaded them to agree. They passed an isolated house. But it remained silent as they trudged past.

"There's someone in there. He'll call for help as soon as we're past," a Bermudian said.

"He's a civilian. Let him be," Joseph said.

"Only a mile to go."

The large house on the headland came into view. "I know where we are now. We have to keep to the east of it."

One of the men suggested they hole up there. Joseph scorned this. "The place is a trap. If we went in, we'd never get out."

They heard hooves and the jingle of harness, ahead of them. They put the boats down again.

"Yankee horse artillery," Joseph said. "They want to trap us here." They stopped to rest and heard a couple of gun teams gallop towards them.

"Should we abandon the boats?"

"We've come this far."

"If they've brought cavalry with them ..."

"We can't see the gunners. So they probably can't see us. We have to make less noise than them."

"Is there a beach to the west of the house?" Joseph said

"Yes."

"Keep your head down and keep moving."

"There they are," one of the men shouted.

The gun team stopped. Somebody shouted an order. Joseph was angry. "Damn. Now we're trapped."

He told them to change course and head for the beach to the west of the house. He recalled that it was called Sandy Cove. That was a good omen, surely?

They reached the edge of the grass and dragged the boats down the slope. Joseph was worried that the boats would be damaged.

Then, to the north of them, the artillery opened up.
"What are they shooting at?"
"Us?"
"No. That fine house," Joseph said
"But we aren't in it."
"Just keep moving. And don't make any noise."

They discovered there was a beach, of sorts. They launched their boats. One of them was damaged and taking in water but the crew was confident that they could bale out.

"Let's go." They rowed past the house. The Yankee artillery fired a few more rounds. The rowers watched as the large, conspicuous house got trashed.

"Pity, that. Such a nice house."

Once clear of the headland, they set course for Portland. The Bermudians were confident that they cover the distance in a day.

The Marines, in the four remaining longboats, got back to the steamship. They climbed on board and the marine captain reported to the naval commander.

"We took heavy casualties at the supply depot. We were forced to leave one boat behind. Another boat was overturned, with loss of life, at Kennebunkport. And another is half-empty.

"You destroyed the weapon store?"

"Yes, sir."

"You achieved your target, then."

They waited for the Mohawks in their shallow boats but at sunrise they had to give up.

The British officers decided that the attack was a success but costly. "Pity about the Bermudians."

Chapter 14

North Atlantic, August 10

At dawn, Griffin took his usual sun-sights. The patchy cloud made this difficult. He began the task of calculating their position.

His passengers were having breakfast but he kept to his task. His result surprised him.

He went into the saloon. "Good morning. We've made good time. We've just reached Irish coast. The coast should be visible through the clouds. We've covered more ground than I expected."

"Will we land, then, lieutenant?" the major asked.

"I regret that we're too high. It would be a struggle to bring us down quickly. We shall have to make for Dublin. If I bring you down there, you can take another airship across the Irish Sea."

"Why not continue?" Miss Grace asked.

"Well ..."

"Are you out of fuel?" the major asked

"No, sir. We have fuel in reserve. And the wind is still favourable."

Griffin decided to continue. Or try to. He told the artificer to start up their main engine. He kept his face impassive. If the engine would not start they would be in real trouble.

But, when the artificer spun the flywheel, the engine behaved and burst into life.

Grace got out her notebook and sent a message to Charles Lloyd. He promised that he would send a message to colleagues in London.

They crossed the Irish Sea, descending slowly as they did so. They continued across England at a steady pace. The tops of the clouds were brilliant white but they cast the ground below into shadow. The lieutenant worried about poor visibility.

By the time they reached Hendon airfield, to the north of London, they were only a thousand feet up.

Grace sent another message to Charles, who replied that he had already made arrangements for someone to meet them.

The airship made a careful approach and the crew dropped their mooring lines. The ground crew secured the airship.

The passengers were finally able to disembark. At the edge of the airfield, a group was waiting for them. The crewmen carried their bags as they tramped across the grass.

One of the ladies waiting for them had strong white hair. George and Grace recognised Lady Forlaith, the Dowager Viscountess Inismore.

"I am delighted to see you again, Lady Forlaith," Grace said.

Lady Forlaith introduced her male companion as the diplomat Mr. Abernethy. He was tall and thin and wearing an elegant suit.

Grace introduced her grandmother to the viscountess. The old lady bobbed a curtsey.

Lady Forlaith smiled and held out her hand. "So you got into the social world after all, Miss Abenaki."

"I didn't expect this, madam."

"No. We have decided that you ladies will stay with me at my son's London house." She smiled. "When my son heard that you had been invited by her Majesty, he agreed at once."

"Major, Mr. Brant, I have obtained rooms for you at a hotel," Mr. Abernethy said.

London August 11, morning

Carlton House Terrace, in the West End of London, was the residence of the Minister for Foreign Affairs. The terraces, four storeys in height above a basement, were designed in a classical style, with a Corinthian columned façade overlooking St James's Park.

The conference room was at the rear. George was not interested in architectural styles. But, from the full-height windows, he could see across the expanse of St. James's Park. Mr. Abernethy had told him that Downing Street was hidden by the trees of the park. Beyond the trees, George could see the towers of the Houses of Parliament, including the half-complete clock-tower. He would have liked to study the view. But the powerful men around him ignored it. To them, it was an everyday occurrence.

He turned and took his seat. Seven men sat round the table. The Foreign Secretary was Lord Malmesbury. Mr. Abernethy was the only familiar face. George found the procedure intimidating. Which, he thought, was the whole point.

Mr. Brant, sitting at his side, seemed unruffled by this pomp. The ladies had been excluded. The senior diplomats were polite to George and Mr. Brant. But they had refused to negotiate with women.

George tried to explain that these women would be listened to back home. Any agreement made by a warrior would not be accepted by community until women had discussed it.

"You do not have to ask for their comments, sir. You merely have to keep them informed of your negotiations."

Mr. Abernethy nodded. He accepted the concept.

The Foreign Secretary waved this aside. "I want you to travel to Brussels this evening. And, in the morning, let this Yankee spokesman know that we have you here."

George did not like that at all. "Very well, sir."

Mr. Brant watched this in silence.

"A couple of reporters want to speak to you," Mr. Abernethy said. "The story of your arrival is in the newspapers. They want more. All this must be very trying for you."

"Yes," Mr. Brant said. "But a distant relative of mine came to London and was introduced to King George. So I ask myself what he would have done."

"Nonsense," Lord Malmesbury said. "A Mohawk? Here?"

"If it did happen, there would be a record of it," Mr. Abernethy said. He looked intrigued.

When Mr. Abernethy introduced them to the newspaper reporters, they wanted to meet ignorant savages. They were disappointed to meet educated gentlemen in suits. Mr. Brant repeated his story about his relative. But they did not believe him.

Canada, Brant's Ford, August 11

Tommy packed his bags and took the train to Upper Canada. In the neat little town of Brant's Ford he walked to the quiet suburb that Chard had described. Tommy's mother would have regarded this genteel location as paradise.

Tommy drew a breath and knocked on the door of the house.

The situation was just as bizarre as Chard had said. A young maid with Indian features, but wearing a prim black dress and a pinafore, opened the door.

"Sergeant Thompson? Yes, come in." Her

pronunciation was better than Tommy's carefully-maintained rough cockney.

"If you will come this way, sergeant ..." Her tone implied that a maid was equal in status to a soldier.

Tommy decided that Colonel Hendrick was very young for the task, full of self-confidence. And, Tommy thought, far too handsome.

"So you're the Staff Sergeant that I asked for."

"Yes, sir." He quoted what Chard had told him. "Certain senior sergeants are assigned to administrative, supervisory, or other specialist duties as part of the staff of a regiment."

"I had hoped for Sergeant Chard."

"His, er, specialist experience is needed elsewhere, sir. Unless it's telegraph wires, sir?"

"No. There's no telegraph where we're going."

Tommy wondered what that meant. "I, er, have a reputation for being able to adapt to new challenges, sir."

"Well, I hope you're right."

Tommy explained that, in the British Army, a staff sergeant outranked the other sergeants. As a member of the colonel's personal staff, he was responsible for all the organisation, administration and discipline for the Field Force

"Yes, that's what I want." He smiled.

The more Tommy learned to the situation, the more bizarre it seemed. Most of the Mohawk militia officers who visited headquarters were less literate than Tommy. They knew less about how the British army worked than Tommy did.

The government schools were wretched. No wonder the colonel needed help.

Yet the colonel kept in contact with Fort Malden and his militia units along the coast via his own telegraph network. All of the telegraph operators were Mohawks, because the British army refused to provide any. Tommy could easily understand *that* piece of folly.

All of the operators were Hendrick's cousins, to some degree, and most of those here in Brant's Ford were women. They all wore neat blue jackets.

And half the troops, out in the peninsula, were savages with tattoos or ritual scars. The colonel was amused at Tommy's initial reaction and said they weren't as frightening as they looked. His offhand manner towards enlisted men was disconcerting to a British army soldier.

Tommy had little experience of this role and had to learn on the job. Mostly it involved paperwork, letters to the quartermaster or the colonel at Fort Malden. Tommy's world was one of lists. Tasks that had to be done. Equipment that had to be assembled.

All of this meant working alongside the colonel.

Tommy had to send a request to headquarters, asking for a paddle steamer to meet them when the Field Force reached Port Elgin. The colonel had signed it, of course.

Headquarters replied that a paddle steamer big enough to accommodate the entire ask force would be ready when they arrived. The colonel was dubious at this confidence. Tommy had shared that concern.

Tommy found that she was attracted to the colonel. That was very annoying. It was a pity that he was already spoken for.

Brussels, August 12, morning

Paul Abernethy, Major Eastman and Mr. Brant stood in the corridor outside the meeting room. They were all wearing civilian suits.

"In a minute, we'll go in and meet the US representatives," Paul said. "The senior one is a Southern Democrat. He ran for the governorship of Mississippi on the issue of the Compromise of 1850, which he opposed. You know about the Compromise?"

"Oh, yes," the major said. "We got a lot more refugees after that."

"I was forgetting that Canada would be affected. Mr. Davies was defeated by fellow Senator. That left him without political office, but Davies continued his political activity. He took part in a convention on states' rights, held at Jackson, Mississippi, in January 1852 ..."

"I see," the major said, trying to hide his boredom.

"Well, he seems eager to complete the debate here and return home. I don't know why."

"The elections," Mr. Brant said. "The presidential election of November 1852."

"He hopes to be president?" Paul was shocked.

"No, no. But if he campaigns on behalf of the right candidate, he could be rewarded with ministerial office."

"Oh, I *see*. Yes."

Paul walked into the meeting room, followed by the major and Mr. Brant. "Good morning, Mr. Davies."

"Good morning, Abernethy." Representative Davies stood with his back to the table. This was expensive and highly polished. He glanced once at Paul's companions and then ignored them.

Paul was not impressed by what he saw. The delegate was plump, with magnificent sideburns. He sported a gold watch-chain. He was a career politician rather than a career diplomat. Paul had detested him on sight.

"Before we begin, Abernethy, I wish to repeat our demand that your black regiment must be disbanded."

"I believe that has been done, sir. The last unit should have been withdrawn from Portland ten days ago. You should have received independent confirmation of this from Washington. Although there are black troops in Upper Canada."

Davies waved this aside. "I don't care about Canada. Just so long as those blacks are no longer on US soil." He sniffed. "Although we want our runaways returned."

Paul heard the major straighten up. He guessed that Davies had said that for the record book, not because he expected a favourable reply.

He had been instructed as to the correct response to give. "No man in that battalion is a runaway, sir. Most of them come from New Brunswick or Nova Scotia. They're Tories – their ancestors fled north after the Revolution."

Davies did not look impressed by this story.

"I have been told that more than five hundred men of the battalion fought and died. Perhaps those are your runaways."

Davies was not pleased. "They fought?"

"Yes, they fought," Major Eastman said.

Davies changed the subject. "Then there's your demand that the governor of California stops offering a bounty for Indians. That is a state matter, not a federal one. So it cannot be a matter for discussion here."

"I understand," Paul said.

"The governor was embarrassed, though," Davies said. "I hear that your Indians sent some women to speak for them. And you're listening to 'em." His tone was mocking.

Paul was annoyed. "We also have a Mohawk delegate. They are waiting here to see you."

Davies was shocked. "Those savages have a fearsome reputation."

"And yet – they also have diplomats. Sir, may I introduce -."

"No!" Davies took a step backwards. Everyone in the room turned to stare.

Davies deliberately turned his shoulder towards them.

"You really intend to give land to them? And you expect them to remain loyal after you've given them all they want?"

Mr. Abernethy smiled. "We expect that fear of the United States will keep them loyal."

Major Eastman ignored the representative and spoke to Paul. "May I ask whether you have heard of the Indian Territory, sir?"

"Indeed I have, sir. It is sad to reflect that on occasion the British government has treated its subjects just as badly."

Mr. Brant intervened. "I assure you, Mr. Abernethy, that our brave warriors are prepared to defend Her Majesty's frontiers at any time."

"No more of this." Davies stalked off.

"Oh dear. Did I overdo it?" Mr. Brant asked.

"I think you got it exactly right," Paul said.

"You're a Brant, sure enough," Major Eastman said.

London, August 12, afternoon

Grace and her grandmother were staying in Inismore House in prestigious Mayfair. But the mood in the household was uncomfortable. Lady Forlaith's daughter-in-law resented the presence of her mother-in-law and her strange guests. She said that as these uncouth strangers did not have evening dresses, they could not possibly attend the family's evening meals.

Lady Forlaith was offended. She even offered to pay for the dresses. But Grace did not mind. She and her grandmother were perfectly happy to eat their dinner in their bedroom rather than in the dining room with the family and their proud guests.

Then Grace told Lady Forlaith that she wanted to see the Court of Chancery. "I read about it. In Mr. Dickens' book."

"Well - Chancery cases are held in Westminster Hall,"

Lady Forlaith said. "Although if a case is being held today they won't let us in."

"Let's go and see, madam," Grace said.

Lady Forlaith was eager to escape from the house so she gave in. She called for her carriage to be brought to the front door. "I have to borrow my son's horses. But he doesn't mind."

She lent the ladies fashionable shawls to wear over their shoulders. "No lady wears a coat these days."

When they reached the hall, next to the Houses of Parliament, the constable informed them that nothing special was going on, so they were allowed inside.

Grace was awed by the great stone hall.

"Look up, my dear," Lady Forlaith said.

"Oh! Look at that ceiling," Melody said.

"Very few trials take up the whole hall, you understand. Although King Charles was tried here," Lady Forlaith said.

A double row of trestle tables had been set up along the length of the hall, where people were selling books. Grace, glimpsing at the titles, guessed that they were law books. Lady Forlaith walked past them and led her guests the length of the hall.

At the far end was a wooden screen, twelve feet high. The carving was delicate.

"Most court hearings take place through here, in one of the small rooms partitioned off by this screen."

"So small?" Grace was delighted. "We could do *that* in a long-house."

London, August 12, evening

The ladies returned to Inismore House feeling that they had enjoyed a pleasant day out. But the atmosphere was as uncomfortable as ever. All of the ladies gathered in the morning room. Grace and her grandmother kept to themselves in one corner.

Then a housemaid brought the news that Mr. Abernethy was downstairs and was asking to speak to the ladies. Lady Forlaith was pleased. "Yes, yes, send the gentleman up at once."

He gave a little bow. "I have strange news for you, madam. The Native American delegation has been invited to Osborne House. In three days' time."

Grace was shocked. "Do they mean it?"

He smiled. "Oh, yes."

"But what can we wear?"

There was a scramble to get suitable clothes. "We can't possibly make them in time." Lady Forlaith had been to court and knew the rules. Mr. Abernethy said they should defer to the dowager's experience.

Then Mr. Brant and Major Eastman turned up. "We got your message, Mr. Abernethy, but you weren't at home. You wanted to see us, sir?"

"Yes, you've been invited to Osborne House."

Lady Forlaith advised Mr. Brant to wear the buckskin frock coat that he had brought as a diplomatic gift.

He had doubts about this advice. "The garment is too primitive, madam. It is uncouth. And old - it was a gift to my grandfather from the governor."

Mr. Abernethy was pleased. "Then it's a gift from the king's representative. Was that George the third? So it's got a story behind it."

Lady Forlaith agreed. "They will be disappointed if you look - ordinary. Her majesty enjoys the exotic. It's either the leather coat or you wear feathers in your hair."

Mr. Brant pouted. "The coat, then, madam."

"With a silk top hat?" Mr. Abernethy suggested.

Grace was in a panic. She could not get a court dress made in time.

Melody remarked to Lady Forlaith that they had

brought decorated wraparound dresses as gifts.

Lady Forlaith was intrigued. "It sounds ideal. Embroidered? I must see them."

London, August 13, morning

A scholar visited Mr. Brant at his hotel to explain that he had discovered a picture of Old Joseph Brant in the National Portrait Gallery. He invited Mr. Brant to visit the gallery and inspect the picture of the Old warrior. The ladies were bored, so they all decided to go.

Mr. Abernethy advised Mr. Brant to wear his buckskin frock coat. George wore his regimentals.

Mr. Brant was a bit of a showman. He enjoyed strolling across Trafalgar Square, in coat and top hat, through the crowds. People had somehow learned of their visit and had turned up to watch.

He climbed the steps and explained who he was to the man at the desk. One of the curators had arranged an impromptu exhibition of Indian visitors over the last 150 years.

In pride of place was a portrait of Old Joseph Brant, with his head shaved, wearing a feather head-dress. He stared haughtily from the picture.

"He would have disapproved of me," Mr. Brant said, in a mournful tone.

George smiled. "You're not doing too badly, sir."

"Is he your grandfather, Mr. Brant?" the curator asked. He sounded awed.

"No, no. He was not an ancestor. My mother was descended from his sister."

Mr. Abernethy found time to ask George about their negotiating position. Should the British negotiators concede their claim for land?

George was taken by surprise. He spoke more sharply than he intended. "I am not an expert, sir. I know nothing about negotiation. I didn't have much of an education."

"But you are widely-read, major. You grew up there." He smiled. "I'm supposed to be the negotiator. But I need alternative sources of information."

"Oh, in that case ... Best ask Mr. Brant and Miss Grace. They also had a feel for the Yankees."

"Don't ask for towns, only uninhabited areas," Mr. Brant said.

"Wealthy men have political influence in the republic," Grace said. "Poor men do not."

"That is true everywhere," Mr. Abernethy said.

"The US is a bit different, sir," George said. "The Maine logging interests are companies, not individuals. But, you see, during the last campaign, they forced the governor to keep their militia in the east to protect those forests."

"They ignored the people of Maine? The voters?"

Mr. Brant nodded. "Then there was '38. Those logging interests nearly started a war to grab the forests of New Brunswick."

"They're that powerful? I see," Mr. Abernethy said. We had hoped to gain Fort Ticonderoga. But they will not let our troops travel there."

George shrugged. "The place has no military value, sir. It's a trap. I read how the Yankees lost it."

"It has value as a bargaining counter, major. We asked whether we could send soldiers along the lake by boat. They said yes. But they would allow soldiers to step ashore to walk across to the fort."

Grace was amused. "But that logic would allow an airship to approach."

"So it would. That's worth bearing in mind. As a bargaining counter," Mr. Abernethy said.

408

Brussels, August 14

Paul Abernethy spent a lot of time shuttling between Brussels and London by airship. His task was to advise the Foreign Secretary.

Lord Malmesbury favoured a swirling moustache rather than the fashionable sideburns.

The Senior US representative, Mr. Davies, was very proud of his magnificent sideburns. Paul detested him.

They sat on opposite sides of the table. Mr. Davies started by demanding that the Canadian troops withdraw from Portland.

Paul conceded that this would be done. "We have no intention of maintaining a position in Portland."

Mr. Davies gestured to the secretary at his side, who made a note.

"If the British have to give up Portland, we want gains elsewhere," Lord Malmesbury said. "We want to enlarge Quebec, to push the frontier away from our vulnerable major cities.

"This includes our claim to a section of territory to the south of Quebec. We are eager to strengthen our frontiers."

"No. Out of the question," Davies said. "I thought we had made that clear. We will not abandon any cities, or any territory of value. I insist that the US will not abandon the forests at the eastern end of the state."

"Our claim does not include any cities," Lord Malmesbury said. "What about Maine, Abernethy?"

"That is correct, my lord." Paul was not surprised by Davies' demand. Major Eastman had predicted this. "The present eastern border – with its valuable forests - is acceptable to us."

"It is the frontier with Quebec that concerns us," Lord

Malmesbury said. "The territory we want has been chosen for strategic reasons, not commercial ones."

The minister was particularly eager for his claim to a strip of the south bank of St. Lawrence. "The territory in question is only ten miles wide, Mr. Davies."

"But this contains the town of Ogdensburg." Davies was outraged. "No. We cannot allow the Colony of Quebec to expand south. Any of your colonies, come to that."

Paul rephrased his description. "None of this land is inhabited. Or valuable."

"No inhabitants?"

"Apart from Ogdensburg, already in our possession, the only inhabitants are the indigenous population."

"Is that so?" Davies called a break in order to discussed this with his companions.

When he returned, he was smirking. "Yo say you've got Indians living there? We cannot allow your colony to expand south The US government would, however, agree to giving this territory to an Indian nation."

"What?" Lord Malmesbury said.

"A new colony in this area, run by the people already living there. Although if the experiment failed, if law and order collapsed, the US would have to intervene to restore order." He smiled.

The minister was about to agree. Paul, alarmed, asked for a word in private.

The minister was annoyed. "Yes, Abernethy?"

"It's a trap, sir. Mr. Eastman said that his people didn't ask for freedom, because they knew the US Army would invade as soon as our militia was disbanded."

"They plan to break their word? What you suggest is monstrous."

"Davies assumes that the Indians would be unable to maintain law and order. The US would have an excuse to intervene. Quite within the rules. Monstrous, yes. But is it monstrous enough for us to re-start this war?"

"We must ask for a second opinion, Abernethy. Why isn't that fellow Eastman here?"

Isle of Wight, August 15

George had wanted Mr. Abernethy to accompany the delegates to Osborne House. But his presence was required in Brussels. This increased George's anxiety. He had come to depend upon the diplomat.

George and his companions travelled to Portsmouth by train, in the company of Lady Forlaith.

At Portsmouth they caught a glimpse of the capacious harbour, the gigantic men-of-war, and the stone forts protecting it all.

They boarded a steam ferry, the *Fire Queen*. Lady Forlaith wanted to sit in the lounge. The other ladies joined her, but George preferred to stay on deck.

He was impressed most of all by the narrow entrance, where the ships entering and leaving had to somehow dodge each other. Grace escaped from the lounge to join him. The first part of the journey was south-east, to avoid the Hamilton Sandbank. Gradually, the view opened up. Warships were anchored here too.

"Is that the Isle of Wight?" Grace asked.

"That line on the horizon, yes. It can't be anything else."

Then their ship turned west, avoiding the anchored warships. They were now steaming parallel to the island shore. "One of those grand houses must be Osborne House. But I don't know which one." They passed another transatlantic steamer heading for Southampton, just arrived from Quebec.

Their journey took over an hour. As their destination drew closer, their anxiety mounted.

"There should be a carriage waiting for us at the pier," Lady Forlaith said.

Mr. Brant opened his carpet bag and drew out his leather frock-coat. He held it up, admiring it, and then asked George to help him put it on.

When they disembarked, they found an open carriage at the pier. A footman in a red uniform was waiting for them.

Lady Forlaith informed the footman of her mission. He gave a slight bow and opened the carriage door.

"Her majesty prefers open carriages," Lady Forlaith said.

"Yes, I dislike enclosed places myself," Melody said.

The carriage took them up the hill, through a formal archway and then along a private road.

"There's a carriage circle. We'll go round that. But the house had two entrances," Lady Forlaith said. "The grand main doorway there is reserved for royal guests. We're not royalty, so we will not use it."

The grand doorway was marked by a pair of stone pillars. The coachman ignored it and took them a few yards further round the carriage circle to the secondary entrance. This was flanked by a pair of lamp posts.

The footman opened the carriage door for them. They climbed down and Mr. Brant adjusted his frock-coat. George took the hint and checked his uniform jacket.

The palace door opened and a woman stepped out. "Good afternoon, Lady Forlaith," the lady in waiting said.

"Good afternoon, my dear."

"If you will come this way, please ..." She led them along the grand Marble Corridor. "You will wish to refresh yourselves," the lady in waiting said.

"We need to change our dresses," Grace said.

"Quite."

Twenty minutes later, the lady in waiting led them

into the withdrawing room. This was empty. But she gave them no time to look round.

"This way." She opened one of the French windows and stepped out onto terrace. She turned left and continued onto the lawn. The grass was damp.

A canopy had been set up on the middle of the lawn. George could see a table positioned under it. The Queen was sitting at the table, with Prince Albert sitting at her side. He smiled at the newcomers. Half a dozen servants stood behind the royal pair.

"So all the stories are true," George said.

"Hush," Lady Forlaith said.

The lady in waiting bobbed a curtsey. "The dowager Viscountess Inismore and her companions to see you, madam."

Lady Forlaith stepped forward and gave a deep curtsey.

The Queen did not look pleased. "You took a grave risk in going to Portland, Lady Forlaith."

"I felt that I had to do my duty, madam."

"Indeed."

George wondered whether the Queen was jealous. He noticed the red government despatch-boxes under the table at the Queen's feet. Lady Forlaith stood and began the introductions.

"Your Majesty, may I introduce you to Major Eastman, commander of the Black Regiment. I first met him in Montreal."

George stepped forward and bowed as Lady Forlaith had instructed him.

The Queen favoured George with a smile. "You are welcome, major."

"Thank you, your majesty."

"So you commanded the Black Regiment."

He forbore to mention that he had only commanded a single battalion. It was unwise to contradict a monarch.

"While it lasted, madam." He stepped back.

Lady Forlaith turned. "Madam, may I introduce to you Mr. David Brant, of the Mohawk nation?"

Mr. Brant stepped forward. His bow was graceful.

"Do the Mohawks truly have a nation of their own, Mr. Brant?"

"Yes, your majesty. That was the promise that your grandfather gave us."

The Queen smiled. "I believe that a relative of yours was introduced to our grandfather, Mr. Brant."

"Yes, your majesty. He was my great-uncle."

The Queen gestured towards the despatch boxes. "We believe that our representative to Brussels has requested that the United States should concede some territory. That was one of our negotiating points. However, we are concerned. The Republic's delegate has instead proposed the creation of two new colonies, rather than enlarging the territory of our existing colonies."

This was news to George. Did the Queen want his opinion? He fought down panic. "Perhaps they are hoping that you will lose interest in this new territory, your Majesty. So when they invade, you will not complain." He explained the fate of the Cherokee, exiled to the Indian Territory.

"And you fear you may meet the same fate? I see."

Mr. Brant came to George's rescue. "The territory is of little value, your Majesty. The Republic may believe that you will decide that it is not worth defending."

The Queen nodded.

George stepped back. Lady Forlaith led Melody forward and introduced her. The old woman managed to perform her curtsey with dignity. The Queen complemented the old lady on her dress.

Grace came last. She was introduced as Melody's trusted companion.

"I admire the decoration of your dress. Is it your own

work?"

"Alas, no. madam. It is a heirloom, a present from my aunt. I have not had the time. I have spent the last few months working as a telegraphist."

The Queen recoiled. "A - telegraph operator? Isn't that rather – plebeian?"

George hastened to intervene. "Miss Grace has also worked on the Analytical Engine. The weather predictions then have to be sent to everyone who needs them."

"The Engine, yes." The Queen was uneasy. "We trust that you have no desire to emulate Lady Lovelace?"

"No, no, madam."

Mr. Brant remained affable. He neatly changed the subject by explaining the origins of his coat.

"So it is not a Mohawk pattern?"

"No, madam." He entertained the Queen by describing the legal fiction of the Mohawk nation.

The Queen showed some interest. "And the governor says that unwinding this fiction is beyond his powers? Then we must let it continue."

"Yes, madam." He was disappointed. "We have our own army too."

"And is it true that women choose your general?"

Mr. Brant smiled. "Why, madam, don't you choose the British army's generals?"

The Queen was taken aback. Prince Albert was amused. "Such decisions are made only after listening to her Majesty's most trusted advisers."

"Quite so," the Queen said.

They were careful to withdraw as soon as her Majesty looked bored.

Mr. Brant remarked to George that he had wanted to speak to the Queen about the government school at Brant's Ford. The place was badly run, living conditions were terrible and money was wasted.

Grace overheard this. "Doesn't the legal fiction apply to schools too? Aren't they the nation's schools?"

Mr. Brant perked up. "The governor doesn't think so. But it's worth a try."

They withdrew to the terrace. George was angry at what the Queen had told him. "A nation of our own - this is a farce! It's impossible. The Yankees are laughing at us."

"A colony?" Melody asked. "What would we have to do?"

"Calm down, Major," Grace said. "What would a colony require? Clerks – paperwork? Large, expensive buildings?"

"I don't know," George said. "You'd need public buildings. A governor's mansion ... meeting house ...?"

"We can't afford all that," Grace said.

"What are the diplomats talking about, while we're stuck here?"

"We have to go back there tomorrow," Brant said.

Before their journey home, they had luncheon with the Queen in the grand dining room. The doors were left open. Her Majesty liked fresh air.

George was surprised that there were only three courses. Lady Forlaith explained in an undertone that the mid-day meal had less prestige than the formal evening meal.

Brant's Ford, August 15

Tommy knocked on the door to the colonel's office and walked in. Her admiration of Colonel Hendrick increased steadily. He was creating a strike force out of odds and ends of military units.

The colonel's original idea had been to assemble his

troops at Brant's Ford before marching them off north.

Tommy had disapproved. Using her best 'veteran soldier' manner, she had argued that this would waste too much time. The young major, Peter Theyanoguin, had added his arguments to hers.

So the colonel had given in. Two companies of the first battalion of the Sixty-Second Regiment had arrived by rail the day before and were now marching north.

Tomorrow, a detachment of horse artillery was due to arrive.

The two black companies from Fort Malden would march due north. But, to save time, they would take the coast road without visiting Brant's Ford.

Only the Iroquois companies had assembled outside the little town. They had rations and ammunition, and carts to carry them. Tommy and Peter Theyanoguin had worked together to achieve that. He had been surprised to learn that a request to the appropriate sergeant would often achieve more than a formal letter to an officer.

Hendrick looked up from his desk. "Yes, sergeant?"

She was attracted to him. He was elegant, and quite dashing, even if his uniform was home-made. He had led two daring attacks and now he was preparing another. His savage relatives somehow added to his appeal.

She knew that her attraction was really quite absurd. And he was already spoken for. But - that girl seemed more interested in the major than the colonel. A man would not have noticed that. Tommy had spotted it at once. But these thoughts were dangerous. She reminded herself that she must think of herself as Tommy. Always Tommy.

"There are the latest newspapers, sir."

He sighed. "Right. What lies are they telling about us?"

"They're worried about Detroit."

"Good." But he ignored the papers. "You are from England? From London, yes?"

She knew that to these Indians, 'England' meant 'London'. Those who had been to school had read Dickens' description of London. And the young scholars then had told the stories to all their relatives. So even the illiterate ones had heard of London's squalor. Tommy's background met all the clichés.

"Yes. I grew up in the East End. In Whitechapel." The colonel looked fascinated. "Outsiders – even other Londoners - don't understand Whitechapel. The main streets - the post roads - are respectable. The houses have many rooms, big rooms. They even have a few servants. The side streets are respectable too. There are fewer rooms to each house, the rooms are smaller, but that's all. But the back streets, the alleyways - they have several people sharing a room. Several families, sometimes, to a room."

"Ah," the colonel said. "The West End - does that have back alleys?"

She smiled. "It has stables. For the horses and carriages of the rich. The servants live above the stables."

"Ah."

She knew that she should not say any more. But she could tell him part of the truth. "My family moved from a side street to a shop in the main road. My father was ambitious. He wanted to give me an education. But then they died of cholera. All of the men who owed money to my father kept silent. The men who had lent him money demanded their money back. The stock was sold to pay them. Soon there was nothing left. For me, it was the back alleys - or the army."

"Did you make the right choice?" Judging by his expression, he knew it was wrong to ask that.

"Yes, sir." She enjoyed being a sergeant. Especially a

sergeant with a technical skill, respected, but with no squaddies to keep in line.

Tommy decided to get back to her subject. "And there's these newspapers, sir." She pointed to the top one. "It's an inside page, but still ..."

Hendrick, with the permission of the governor, had leaked the news that they were planning a raid, but not its target.

A journalist had turned up from the local newspaper. Hendrick had swallowed his distaste and given the man an interview.

Hendrick was most gratified when the Yankee newspapers published the story. "Yes. Their worst dread is an attack on Detroit."

Tommy was alarmed. "It's too strong for us, sir."

He sighed. "I know. We've got to keep dropping hints, though. And tomorrow, sergeant?"

"We're ready to go, sir. My work here is done."

Hendrick told his friend Peter that he would have to stay behind. "We're the only two who have a college education *and* combat experience. If both of us fail to return, some other poor devil will have to gain combat experience, just so he can lead our people.

"Or the British might decide to put one of their officers in charge here."

Peter accepted this with bad grace. "I don't like this mission, Hendrick. The only reason they would put an Iroquois in command is because they regard this as a suicide mission."

"Oh, it isn't as bad as that. But they expect this to fail. The whole thing will become an embarrassing flop. If a professional officer was in charge, his career would be ruined." He smiled. "But I have already risen as far as I can go."

"Well, I suppose that's true."

Brussels, August 16

The Minister for Foreign Affairs, Lord Malmesbury, was prepared to agree to some of Davies' requests in order to get the document signed. He wanted to show *some* benefit from the negotiations.

Mr. Abernethy still held the view that Davies' proposal was a trap.

George agreed. "What they are suggesting is monstrous, sir."

"Yes, major. But is it monstrous enough for us to restart this war?"

The minister led the way back to the table. Mr. Abernethy and George followed. There were only two chairs for the British delegates.

Davies had insisted that only accredited diplomats could have chairs, and George was not a diplomat. Mr. Abernethy had suggested George could have a stool to sit on, but Davies had said no.

The minister and Mr. Abernethy sat. George went down on one knee at the minister's side. Davies ignored him.

"Good morning, Mr. Davies. We are prepared to consider your proposal. That these territories are stand-alone colonies. However, each territory would be graced by her Majesty's representative."

"Her – oh, you mean a governor. Appointed by you."

"Appointed by her Majesty, yes," Mr. Abernethy said.

"However, we want the land west of the Saint John River," the minister said.

Davies made a pretence of examining the map. "It is essential that Fort Kent will remain US territory."

The minister glanced at George, who nodded.

"Agreed," the minister said. "Then there's the St.

Lawrence."

"That may be possible," Davies said. "But – there must be no troops stationed there."

The minister was annoyed. "We must build forts to defend this territory."

Davies conferred with his companions. "We cannot allow forts so close to the US border."

To George, it looked like deadlock. He asked for permission to withdraw so they could discuss the issue. "It's important, sir."

"Nonsense, major," the minister said. "Speak up."

"Building a fortress would be most unwise, sir."

He received a stare from the minister. "How is that?"

"The purpose of this new territory is to force the US Army to move its artillery ten miles away from our existing fortresses. Building new fortresses would merely provide their artillery with new targets."

"I see. Thank you," the minister said

"We should insist, though, on the right to build lookout posts."

His listeners looked baffled. Davies tried to pretend he had not heard.

"These posts would be equipped with telegraph equipment, you understand, linking the posts to Toronto. To warn them of any unusual behaviour."

"Ah." The minister nodded. "We would have to obtain confirmation, of course, but on those terms ..."

"Agreed," Davies said.

Davies sat back. "And the US also demands that your weather office in Montreal must send their weather predictions south by telegram."

Mr. Abernethy exchanged glances with the minister. Both were surprised.

But George knew how vital those weather predictions were. It was only natural that the US wanted them too.

And the Board of Trade would distribute its predictions to anyone who might need them.

Mr. Abernethy recovered. "Certainly, sir. We will do that as soon as the war ends."

Davies leaned forward in his chair. "No. Washington wants it now."

"To help you in your war effort? No. I reject this out of hand," the minister said.

"I must insist," Davies said. "You have that infernal machine in Montreal. That gives you an unfair advantage."

"Abernethy?" the minister said.

"We promise to discuss your request with our colleagues in London, sir."

"Beg pardon, sir," George said. "I suggest a bargain: Montreal would send its daily analysis if an observer in New York could send weather reports to Montreal every six hours. We would come out ahead."

"How so?" the minister said.

"Lieutenant Eathorpe in Montreal is desperate for that information, sir. The Atlantic seaboard is the biggest gap in his observations." He smiled at Davies.

"I see," the minister said.

"That would improve the accuracy of the lieutenant's predictions. That would make our airships safer, sir."

Davies had pretended he had not heard. Mr. Abernethy summarised George's suggestion. "Would Washington agree to those terms, sir? If those conditions gave us an advantage?"

"No, no. I am certain that we would gain the most, even on those terms."

Mr. Abernethy glanced at George, who shrugged.

The minister tired of this. "Perhaps we should reconvene in the morning."

London, August 16, Evening

There was a travellers' hostelry Battersea airfield. Mr. Brant stood at a window. He had been told that Mr. Abernethy and Major Eastman were returning to London by airship and he wanted to greet them. He had worried that a cab driver would be reluctant to take orders from an 'Indian', but he had found that a top hat and an assured manner worked wonders.

He watched as the airship from Brussels flew up the river, descended and landed safely. Mr. Abernethy and George stepped down from the gondola and hurried across the field towards him.

"Good evening. I have a cab here for you, sir."

"Thank you," Mr. Abernethy said. They climbed into the cab. "That fellow Davies has made a bizarre request. But he conceded the south bank of the St. Lawrence. Just like that."

"They quibbled over Ogdensburg," Eastman said.

"It sounds as if they gave in too easily," Mr. Brant said. "No white men have settled there. Why? It's probably a fever-infested swamp."

George saw a different problem. "Is the British minister taking this proposal seriously, sir?"

"What do you mean, major?"

"Well - would the British government accept Davies' condition that new colony is run by the people living there?"

Mr. Abernethy shrugged. "Her Majesty's Government wants to look good to British public. Any concessions that we can force out of the Yankees would help, no matter how flimsy they are."

"I see, sir."

"Even if this gift of territory is only an irritation, we want it to last as long as possible."

Chapter 15

Lower Canada, August 16

The second company of the disbanded battalion had been sent to Fort Longueuil, opposite Montreal, in case the Yankees attempted a last-minute assault. But only the pessimists still expected them to.

The men spent most of their time doing drills. They were bored. Yet they were within range of the Yankee artillery, who sometimes fired a few shells as a reminder that the war was not over.

Charles Lloyd paid a visit to company headquarters, which disrupted their routine. "Captain D'Israeli, I have received a most unusual request. So I decided to have a word you."

"Yes, Mr. Lloyd?"

"You see, the government expects the peace treaty to be signed soon. They're planning for a parade through London. Ending at Buckingham Palace. They want thirty men of your company to take part."

"Yes, that's certainly unusual." Captain D'Israeli said.

"Would like to lead the platoon to London? Captain Warwick thinks this is a chance to get your career moving again."

He was unhappy. "But that's staff-work. I want a field command."

"I don't know how these things work." Charles said. "But you'll get to meet Queen Victoria. You might even be introduced to her. It's the chance of a lifetime."

"I see."

"The government wants to tweak the nose of the senior negotiator," Charles said. "By the time you arrive, his title could be American ambassador.

"The negotiations are almost complete. The fighting on the east coast, and any place linked by telegraph, will stop twelve days after the treaty is signed. Fighting on the lakes will stop twenty-five days after the treaty is signed."

"So this parade could take place before the fighting stops?"

"Yes."

That changed things. "There's no chance of more combat experience, then."

"No."

"The squad would need an intelligent sergeant." Captain D'Israeli decided to invite Sergeant Newbegin.

The sergeant arrived promptly. His uniform was in good order. He glanced at Charles, in his civilian suit. He tried to keep his face impassive, but he was curious. "Yes, sir?"

"At ease, sergeant," Captain D'Israeli said.

"Sergeant, we want thirty volunteers," Charles said. "They must be well-behaved. They must be good on the parade ground. And they must look good in their uniforms."

"Sir? That's a strange list."

"You see, the government expects the peace treaty to be signed soon. They're planning for a parade in London. Outside Buckingham Palace. They want thirty of you people to take part."

Newbegin was astonished. "I'm not superstitious, sir. But - aren't you counting your chickens, begging your pardon, sir?"

Privately, Charles agreed, but he was not going to admit it to an enlisted man. "The government also wants me to find a group of thirty Indians. Mainly Mohawks, of course. The Londoners would never forgive us if we didn't send any Mohawks. Major Eastman will lead those."

"I see." he shook his head. "No, sir. That's not my sort of thing at all. Might I suggest Sergeant Wycombe?"

Essex County August 16, evening

Company Sergeant Wycombe and Platoon Sergeant Smith had been invited to the home of a local black shopkeeper. In truth, Wycombe had invited himself, by dropping heavy hints. This community fascinated him.

Six people were sitting in the parlour. The shopkeeper, Mr. Hope, was accompanied by his wife and two half-grown children. The room contained so much furniture that there was barely room for the guests.

Wycombe was uncomfortable at their hearty welcome. He was clearly the honoured guest. They had even produced their best coffee set.

Mrs. Hope was wearing a store dress with a very tight waist. She had to be wearing a corset.

To Wycombe, it was all so *ordinary*.

"I hope you understand, sergeant, that few of us own our farms," Mr. Hope said. "Most of the residents of our community work as labourers on others' farms. Others attend the school, and work in sawmills, grist-mills, and other local industries."

"Yes, I understand." If he survived the war, would he end up scratching a living as a field hand? Working in a mill had a better sound to it.

He tried to change the subject. "I admire your dress, madam."

Mrs. Hope smiled, but said nothing. Her husband grumbled. "It cost me a fortune."

Smith laughed.

"You must be all right if the worst you have to worry about is the cost of your wife's dress," Wycombe said.

"True," Mr. Hope said. "But my children don't understand."

"That must be a good thing, surely."

"I suppose. I'm too old to join the militia. They offered me a post as quartermaster-sergeant, but I said no. So they made me chaplain instead."

"Warrant officer," his wife said with pride.

The son pouted. "I don't want to join the militia. I want to join the Sixty-second."

Wycombe knew there was small chance of that. "If you joined the militia, you'd be defending your family."

The girl pouted. "They won't let me join."

"That is folly, girl," Mrs, Hope said.

Wycombe did not know what to say. He was rescued by Sergeant Smith. "If the fighting starts out again, they'll need telegraphists."

"The telegraph company won't recruit blacks," the girl said.

Wycombe had an answer to that. "The telegraph company uses the American System. The British army uses its own single-needle equipment. They say they're short of trained operators. So if someone was already prepared …"

The son of the house perked up at this description of technology.

His father shook his head. "They refused to train militiamen as telegraphists. Said they couldn't spare any men for the task."

"So they gave it to Mohawks. Crazy," his son said.

To distract them, Wycombe told them about the visit of the viscountess to Portland to present their colours. It worked. Not just the mother, but the whole family was fascinated by the tale.

"The colours should have been presented by the governor, but the risk was too great. If the Yankees had attacked …"

"What did she wear?" Mrs. Hope said.

"It looked to be just an ordinary day dress. I'm no judge of fine fabrics."

"And she stitched the flag herself?"

"She did a bit, so she could say she had taken part. She thought that was important."

Smith intervened. "I'm surprised that the British gave these farms to blacks."

Mrs. Hope gave a whoop of laughter and then, embarrassed, stared down at the floor. Her children were grinning.

"What did I say?" Smith said.

"Everyone says that when the Yankees invade, they'll come along this road -." the boy began.

"If, not when," his sister said.

"If, sure. But they'll burn all the farmhouses. So the British thought, why not give the land to ..."

"So they weren't being generous after all," Smith said.

"No," Mr. Hope said.

"So buying this land was a gamble," Wycombe said.

"I preferred to be a shopkeeper," Mr. Hope said.

They were interrupted by somebody pounding on the door. Mr. Hope jumped. Wycombe judged that he was afraid for his family, not himself. But his daughter, unconcerned, jumped up and ran off to open the door.

There was a murmur of low voices. "You'd better come this way," the girl said.

The man she let in was wearing signals blue. "Sir, sergeant, sir! Message for you."

Sergeant Wycombe remembered old Priddy's little lecture about never calling a sergeant 'sir'. But that could wait until later. "Calm down. What is it, signaller?"

"Message for you, sergeant. Secret. Sent in Iroquois, can you imagine that? I had to ask them whether they really meant it. They said they did. I translated it into English. Here."

Sergeant Wycombe took the scrap of paper and read the message. "Good God." He handed it to Smith.

Mr. Hope frowned. "Not bad news, I hope?" He was anxious.

"Can you keep a secret? You being in the army and all." Sergeant Wycombe handed him the slip of paper.

The other members of the family were wildly curious.

Smith grinned. "Can you keep a secret? No boasting, just to look important?"

Mr. Hope looked at his son. "He's a good lad."

"They're sending thirty men of the battalion to London. For a parade. They want me to volunteer."

"That's not for me," Smith said. "A parade, with all of London watching? I'd rather face a cavalry charge than take part in a parade."

Wycombe grinned. "I want to go. Sounds like fun."

Mr. Hope stared at him. "But you're under orders to march. Everyone knows that."

Wycombe waved the bit of paper. "Some people think this is more important."

"Then you'd better leave at once," Mr. Hope said.

London, August 17

George could not forget the idea of a colony for his people. He knew that Grace and her grandmother were fascinated about the practical details. Even if there was no chance of this imaginary colony coming into existence.

So when he heard that Mr. Abernethy was visiting the ladies, he hurried across London to join the conversation.

"Surely setting up a colony would cost a great deal of money," Grace said.

"Yes, how the British would pay for it, sir?" George

said.

Mr Abernethy smiled. "Well, normally, the British would invite in settlers to new colony. Their taxes would cover the costs."

"But the Yankee proposal forbids that. Besides - Mr Abernethy, this land is worthless. Any homesteader would be forced out after a couple of years ... Although I suppose the government could set up a logging franchise."

Mr Abernethy was surprised. "You would agree to that? Don't you want to preserve the forests?"

"Yes. But we understand that the government needs to make a profit. We have agreed that logging is the least-bad option. We want sustainable logging."

These grand buildings - what would they cost?" Grace said.

Mr. Abernethy smiled. "The Yankees didn't start building the Washington capitol until 50 years after independence. You can wait equally long."

"I see."

"And the Yankees' money ran out halfway through," Mr. Abernethy said. "It isn't completed, even today. The Yankees had to make do with an existing building."

Grace was disappointed. "But all we've got is a long-house!"

Mr. Abernethy shrugged "I wouldn't want a classical style residence with marble columns. Dragging all that up the mountain would cost a fortune.

"I've heard that a New York millionaire built a 'log cabin' in the Adirondacks," Grace said.

"I've seen it. A folly," George said.

"If it's pompous enough for a millionaire, then it's pompous enough for Her Majesty's Government. And it could be built from local products."

Halifax, August 21, Afternoon

The Parade Team, with Sergeant Wycombe, had embarked on a coastal steamer and travelled to Halifax in Nova Scotia. This was a naval base, overlooked by the masonry Citadel. The soldiers were impressed by the anchored warships that had come in for refuelling.

In charge of the Indian contingent was a Mohawk, Sergeant Joseph Thayendanega.

He remarked that he had seen warships before. "Bermuda was full of them."

But the men were given no time to look around. A junior officer was waiting for them on the dockside. He came on board as soon as the gangplank was rigged.

"Captain D'israeli? You are late, sir. The transatlantic liner is waiting for you. You are to get your men on board at once."

"Very well." The captain turned to his sergeants. "Are your men ready? Excellent."

Upper Canada, Port Elgin, August 22

The Mohawk companies, marching along the dusty road, joined the other units of the Task Force camped outside Port Elgin. The sergeants gave the necessary directions and they pitched camp.

Over the past few months they had become used to British army tents. Pitching them had become routine.

Tommy learned that Major Pride of the First Battalion, Royal American Regiment, was staying in the town's hotel. She passed this information on to Colonel Hendrick.

"Excellent. You will accompany me, sergeant."
"Yes, sir."
"Good afternoon, sir," the major said. "But I should

explain that the two black companies haven't arrived yet."

Tommy tried to hide her dismay. This would upset her neat timetable.

"Have we got transportation, though, Major?" Hendrick said.

When the governor had promised that a paddle steamer, big enough to accommodate the entire task force, would be ready when they arrived, Tommy had been sceptical.

The major nodded. "Yes, sir, our transportation turned up. Would you care to see it?"

"It's here? Good," Hendrick said.

The major led the way through the small town of weatherboard houses. Canoes were drawn up on the beach. Two sailing boats were tied up to a rickety wooden pier. Three squat paddle-steamers lay at anchor.

Tommy was relieved and rather surprised. "Which one's ours, sir?"

The major shrugged. "Unfortunately, none of the lake steamers was big enough. So the authorities had to requisition three steamers - all the ships available."

So they had no excuse for delay. Tommy's fear was that the black companies would not reach Port Elgin in time.

"I have some refreshments in my billet, colonel," Major Pride said. He led the way back through the town. "They call it a hotel, but -."

A horseman caught up with them. He was a despatch-rider in a red jacket. He was black. Tommy could guess where he was from.

"Colonel? Despatches from Captain Warwick, sir. Commanding the independent black companies. That road is mortal bad, sir."

The colonel took the proffered envelope and opened it. He looked up. "Captain Warwick reports that the two companies will arrive a day behind schedule."

"Will that upset your timetable?" Major Pride said.

The colonel glanced at Tommy, who shook her head. "Our schedule has some slack in it, major."

Hendrick turned back to Major Pride "This delay is unexpected. If there was one large ship, we'd have a problem. But, with three steamers here, that delay doesn't matter. The units here can start at once. As soon as those ships have steam up."

Nova Scotia, St. John's, August 27

The mail steamer turned into wind a couple of miles outside the harbour entrance. A small sailing boat was waiting for them. The wind was slight, for which the captain was grateful.

The captain, standing on the bridge, bent over the voice-pipe. "Slow ahead, Mr. Campbell, if you please."

The engines slowed until the ship was moving forward just enough to counterbalance the wind and the current.

The captain watched, impatient, as the sailing boat edged closer. He did not want this clumsy boat to damage his paintwork.

"What news?" the skipper of the sailing boat shouted.

The captain picked up his speaking trumpet. "It's peace. The Yankees have signed a treaty. It comes into effect as soon as the Yankees send a telegram to their troops. I've got a sealed packet for you, to be delivered to the governor. Don't drop it in the ocean."

"You're not coming into harbour?"

This foolishness irritated the captain. "No. I've got to continue on to New York."

"But we could telegraph them from the town. The wire's up again."

"Do you think they would believe a word we said? I've

got another sealed packet for the State Department. Signed by the negotiator. They sent three, by separate ships, to be on the safe side."

The skipper of the sailing boat took the sealed, waterproof packet. "God-speed, then." He gave orders for his crew to head back to harbour.

The captain waited until the sailing boat was clear and then bent over the voice-pipe. "Full speed ahead, Mr. Campbell, if you please."

The mail steamer picked up speed and continued on to New York. The captain expected to arrive there on the 30th.

London, August 28th

The men of the Parade Team disembarked at Southampton and were put on the train to London. They were bored after being cooped up for so long. The sky was overcast and a light rain was falling.

The train slowed as it approached London. They went past thousands of small terraced houses. The size of the town impressed all of them.

The train stopped and Captain D'israeli stepped down from the carriage. He recognised Major Eastman waiting on the platform. "Good afternoon, sir."

"Good afternoon, captain. But your men must hurry. We have to march through the centre of London to reach our destination. I have a wagon here for your kit."

Sergeant Thayendanega was dismayed to hear that they were being billeted in the Tower of London. "But it's a prison."

The men formed up in a column and marched off. The drivers and pedestrians stood aside to watch them past. They seemed used to marching soldiers.

When they got the 'Tower' they found that it was really a sprawling castle, several hundred years old. The castle contained within its walls an ordnance factory and a barracks.

The warders were armed with halberds, eight feet long. Sergeant Wycombe had never expected to see one.

One of the warders stepped forward to greet the major. The man had a gaudy red and gold uniform but Wycombe could recognise a sergeant when he saw one.

"Are you the squad sent here for the parade, sir?"

"Yes, that's right," the major said.

"Accommodation has been arranged. If you will follow this person, sir."

The warder handed them over to a sergeant of the Royal Fusiliers who led them through two sets of stone gateways. They had to march under a portcullis.

"This is Water Lane, sir. We turn left here, under the Lanthorn Tower. That's the White Tower, to the left.

"We'll put your men in the Waterloo Barracks. It was built to accommodate 1,000 men, so we can find some spare room for you. It's new. They built it in 1845, when the Duke of Wellington laid the foundation stone."

"I see," Major Eastman said.

"There are separate quarters for the officers, sir. Over there, to the north-east of the White Tower."

"Very well, sergeant."

The Wellington Barracks was three storeys tall. The men were led upstairs and shown their bunks. The other soldiers in the room were participating in the parade too. "There are several starting points. They all converge on the Palace. This is the furthest starting point, so you'll have to march further than anyone else."

One of the warders offered to give the men an impromptu tour. He was as fascinated about the Americans as they were about him. "The inner tower was built 800 years ago. The outer walls were built in

1300."

"And the cells?" Joseph asked.

"Oh, this place was never intended as a prison. The cells were merely rooms in the old stone towers."

"And you, sergeant? Your unit, I mean?"

He grinned. "The Guard was formed in 1485 by Henry the Seventh."

"I thought there was a moat," a private said.

"Well, there was, but it was drained in 1841. You walked across the ditch on your way in."

That evening, in the Officers' mess, a steward brought a visiting card to Captain D'Israeli. He nodded and the steward escorted him past the officers' mess to a small ante-room. Several ladies were chatting to officers. In one corner, the Viscountess and her companion were waiting to meet him.

She smiled. "Good evening, captain. I am delighted to see you again."

"Thank you, madam."

"I have tried to keep track of your battalion. I was fascinated by that prior condition of the negotiators."

"Nobody seems to understand it, madam. It was intended as an insult."

She smiled. "Many insults have rebounded on their creators."

"Yes, madam."

Mackinac Island August 28, dawn

Hendrick was on the bridge of the paddle steamer as it approached the harbour. The skipper had allowed him up there on the understanding that he did not interfere.

The men had assembled on deck, their muskets loaded. Ahead of their own vessel was the smaller steamer with the contingent of blacks.

A hill loomed over the town. Halfway up the hill was their target, Fort Mackinack. The walls had been painted white to make them more impressive. The approach was so steep that the road contained a couple of switchbacks. His contacts had told him that the garrison was very small.

Hendrick had wanted to put his men into small boats so they could row ashore unseen. It had worked last time. But the skipper had said that the island was surrounded by dangerous rocks, with only one safe entrance. It would be safer to sail straight into the harbour and take everyone by surprise.

The British major had been appalled. But the audacity of the idea had appealed to Hendrick and he had given his approval. It had taken the ships half the night to get into position for a dawn attack.

Hendrick had wanted to be on the lead ship but everyone had told him that the commanding officer was not supposed to do that sort of thing.

The leading steamer came alongside the pier. Before the crewmen could tie up, two of the blacks ran across the paddle-box and jumped ashore. Others followed them.

"Idiots," the skipper said. "Reckless."

That was true, of course, but Hendrick approved. He had told them that every minute counted. It appeared that they had taken his orders to heart.

The skipper cursed. "Slow ahead."

"What's wrong?" Hendrick said.

"I had planned to come in astern of the *Duchess of Devonshire*. But there's a rowing boat tied up there."

Hendrick glanced at the delicate craft. "Skipper, there's a war on. My men are risking their lives. We can afford to sacrifice a small boat."

The skipper sighed. "Port ten, helmsman."

The steamer approached the pier. The small wooden boat was crushed like an eggshell.

Up ahead, the crew of the *Duchess of Devonshire* had rigged a gangplank. The party of ten sappers, with a small barrel of gunpowder, made their way across to the dock. They and their escort of thirty blacks made off at a trot through the town

The crew of Hendrick's vessel tied up and rigged their own gangplank. Hendrick stepped ashore.

Sergeant Johnson, in charge of his escort, hurried after. "We're to escort you, sir."

"Very well." He turned to look at the town. The street was empty.

The company of the Royal Americans came down the gangplank. They formed ranks under the eye of their sergeant and marched off.

Hendrick's own company of Mohawks were the reserve and came last. He wanted to lead them, but Sergeant Johnson said no.

"You're too valuable, sir. You're the only leader we've got."

The English Staff Sergeant, Tommy, tried to hide a smile but failed.

"Off you go, then. I'll follow."

The third steamer was approaching the dock. It had the remaining three companies. But, by the time they got ashore, the battle would be won or lost.

Hendrick's men hurried through the town and started up the hill. Staff Sergeant Tommy accompanied Hendrick. The sergeant was armed with nothing more than a notebook. Hendrick noted with approval that a sword-bayonet was attached to the sergeant's belt.

They reached the first switchback and made a sharp right turn.

Some of the black soldiers had abandoned the road and were making their way up the rocky slope. Hendrick wondered why they had chosen the difficult option.

Anxiety made Hendrick talkative. "This is only a diversion, really. We mustn't linger here. If we don't succeed at the first attempt, I won't try again. Just move on to our main destination. I don't want the Yankees to trap us here."

"I see, sir," the staff sergeant said.

The hill was so steep that the cliff on his left protected him from musket-fire above. He was safe. Then he looked up and realised that one of the bastions of the fort jutted out over the cliff. Anyone peeping out through the crenellations would have a clear shot down the length of the road. So *that* was why the road was so straight. And that was why the blacks had abandoned the road.

There was even a cannon up there. If it was loaded with grapeshot ... But it pointed out to sea.

He shouted to Sergeant Johnson. "Have you a marksman who can take out that cannon crew?"

"Cannon's not manned, sir."

Hendrick squinted and saw that his sergeant was correct. He had gambled on a dawn attack to take the defenders by surprise. But they should be alert by now. Where were they?

If there was a marksman on that bastion, he could decimate Hendrick's force. But he dared not say so.

"Stiff climb, eh, sergeant? There's another fort at the top of the hill. It was built by the British during the revolutionary war. They called it Fort George. The US Army took possession of it in 1815. They renamed it Fort Holmes. But then they abandoned it. The earthworks and buildings just eroded away. Or so my informants say. I hope they're right."

"Why, sir?" The staff sergeant was panting.

"If we take Fort Mackinack, then the garrison of the higher fort can fire shells into it -." He heard an explosion up above. "What - ."

Then he remembered the plan. "That's the sappers blowing the doors off their hinges. At least, I hope it is." The hill was too steep for talking.

They reached the wall of the bastion. There was still no sign of the defenders. The road made a sharp left turn, doubling back on itself.

They came into sight of the gateway to find the men of the Royal Americans milling around outside. They blocked the road. His own men came to a halt.

"What's going on?"

"Narrow gateway, sir," the staff sergeant said.

Hendrick was annoyed. "Let me through." Sergeant Johnson looked alarmed. "Very well, come with me, sergeant."

The sergeant told ten men to follow him. Hendrick ignored them.

As he drew closer, he saw that the heavy wooden doors had been split open. The crack was quite narrow. The men were filing through, one at a time.

So that part of the plan had gone all right. He realised for the first time that there was no sound of defiance from the fort.

Had they won? "Let me through. Stand aside, there."

He stepped inside to find himself in a courtyard. He noted that three bodies had been laid out on the cobblestones. All wore red jackets.

Sitting in the centre of the courtyard, their hands over their heads, were ten men in blue jackets.

"What's this? Who are they?" Hendrick said.

Captain Warwick turned to face him. "Good morning, sir. This is the garrison. Or, rather, the ordnance sergeant here was responsible for the upkeep of the fort."

"And the casualties?"

"My men got over the wall, realised it was undefended, and went to open the gates. That was when the sappers let off their barrel of gunpowder."

"I see," Hendrick said. He was appalled.

"My men are upset, sir," Warwick said.

"Yes, but – are you saying that if I'd just strolled up here and knocked on the door, they would have let me in?" So his dread, on the way up, had been unnecessary.

"That's about it, sir."

The staff-sergeant coughed. "That has happened before, sir. Soldiers firing on men on their own side. It's part of war, sir."

"Yes. I see."

"Might I suggest, sir, that we commend the black troops? They did very well."

"What do you expect me to say? That they were heroes? No. They did what I asked them to do."

"Well, telling them that would please them, sir," Warwick said.

"I'll make a note of it," the staff sergeant said.

Hendrick looked round. "This changes things." He turned to the staff sergeant. "Find a messenger. From the Royal Americans. I would like Major Pride of the infantry to join me at his earliest convenience. But - there is no need for him to send his troops up here."

"Yes, sir."

Major Pride joined them and they held a council of war in the officers' quarters. The dust-covers had been taken off the furniture. Hendrick told the staff sergeant to take notes.

"Major, I want to press on. Our task is to create as much confusion as possible. So I want to leave a company here, to garrison the fort. I would prefer to leave one of your companies.

"Very well, sir."

"If the fort is attacked by superior numbers, after

we've gone, the garrison commander is to surrender. I don't want unnecessary deaths."

The major looked unhappy. "That might look like cowardice."

The staff sergeant coughed. "Might I suggest, sir, that the garrison should only surrender if the enemy gets over the walls in significant numbers?"

Hendrick turned to the major, who nodded. "Very well." The staff sergeant made a note.

Hendrick glanced round. "I want the remaining force to continue on its way tomorrow."

"Are you so eager to attack, sir?" the major said.

"Our orders are to distract and alarm the enemy. We've got them off balance. I want to exploit that."

Brant's Ford. August 28

Peter Theyanoguin had made another visit to the neat suburban house that served as the battalion's headquarters. He was talking to the girl from Fort Erie, Nancy.

A courier had brought news that Colonel Hendrick had reached Port Elgin. The two black companies had caught up. The entire force, in three ships, had all sailed north. Since then – nothing.

There was a knock at the door. Peter wondered who it was.

One of the housemaids opened the door and then escorted a messenger from the telegraph company into the room.

"From Quebec, sir," the telegraph boy said. "For Major Peter Theyanoguin. In person. You have to sign for it, sir." The boy was impressed.

Everyone stopped to stare. Now that the colonel had departed, their workload had diminished.

"Yes, that's me." He signed the receipt and tore open the envelope. "It's from the governor. A peace treaty has been signed -."

"What's wrong? That's wonderful news," Nancy said.

"Yes, but 'Fighting must cease as soon as the commanding officer receives a telegram or ...' The governor has ordered us to send a courier to tell the colonel."

"Of course," Nancy said. "Will you tell the colonel to call off the attack?"

He bit his lip. He had been envious when Hendrick had gone off to war. His friend would be making life-or-death decisions. Now he had a decision of his own. "No. I can't tell Hendrick what to do."

She looked alarmed. "No, sir. But it's our duty to, er, give him the information he needs to make his own decisions."

He brightened up. "True. But none of our telegraph wires runs in that direction. I'll have to send a horse courier."

"Yes, sir."

"And when the messenger gets to Port Elgin ..." Peter's doubts returned. Were there any ships left in Port Elgin?

London September 2

At first light, a courier brought news to Major Eastman in the Fusiliers' building that the Board of Trade had prophesied fair weather for the parade. He passed this news on to his men. He knew they would be relieved.

The men billeted in the Waterloo Barracks formed up in Water Lane. Their uniforms were clean, their buttons – and boots – were polished.

The fusiliers were at the west end of the lane, closest

to the gatehouse. The Mohawks and Major Eastman were wearing glengarry bonnets and had obtained feathers to attach to the badges. The major had told them that the people of London would be heartbroken if the Mohawks weren't wearing feathers.

The contingent of blacks was led by Captain D'Israeli. He glanced at his pocket-watch.

The Tower warders opened the gate. The captain of the fusiliers shouted an order. "Atten-shun! By the left – quick march."

Major Eastman waited for the fusiliers to get clear and then ordered his own men to advance. He led his men out of the castle.

Captain D'Israeli waited a moment, glanced at Wycombe, and then gave his own order. The men marched out, under the arch of the gate and into the sunlight.

Wycombe had been told that the parade would be led by the regiment of grenadier Guards. The guards had a band. The black unit was half a mile behind them, but Wycombe could hear the band's big drum. And, occasionally, when the cheering died down a little, they could hear bells.

The first part of the route took them up to the Bank of England and then through the City of London. Huge crowds had assembled on each side of the road. But their enthusiasm was impersonal. None of these people had been in fear of their lives. For Wycombe, this was nothing like Montreal.

The marching blacks reached a group of people who burst out cheering as they approached. Wycombe realised that the cheering men were black. Until then, he had not known there were any blacks in London.

Wycombe was sorry that he could not acknowledge their cheers. But, just in time, the captain gave the order.

"Eyes - left."

Wycombe had learned that in the British army, only the person in charge of the party was to salute.

The route took them right across the city. Many of the buildings had balconies, which were packed with cheering people.

Mr. Brant was led up the stairs of Buckingham Palace and across a grand room with antique furniture. There were three sets of windows, each leading to its own balcony. The Queen and Prince Albert stood at the central balcony.

Mr. Brant noticed Miss Grace standing on the left-hand balcony. The British Foreign Minister was standing further back. He turned as Brant walked in.

"Ah. Mr. Brant." He walked forward, then indicated the new US ambassador. "Mr. ambassador, may I introduce to you Mr. Brant, of the Mohawk nation."

Brant smiled. "I am delighted to see you, sir." He did not make the mistake of holding out his hand.

The ambassador returned the smile. "I am pleased to meet a true American."

Brant was irritated. "We are both Americans." He smiled. "We both have the blood of three continents in our veins."

The Ambassador was not amused.

Prince Albert turned and gave him a warning frown.

The team marched past Trafalgar Square, with its half-completed column. Then the followed Major Eastman along Whitehall towards the Big Ben tower. At the last minute they turned right, between two tall buildings. Soon, there was a park on their right.

Then, up ahead, tiny in the distance, Wycombe could see the stone edifice of the palace. The crowds here were more exuberant. They could hear the guards' drum more clearly now.

As the squad drew closer, Wycombe could see that the iron gates of the palace were open. But the marching column ignored them. They wheeled right, between a stone statue and the palace gates. Wycombe risked one glance to his left. The people on the balcony were tiny. He turned his attention to maintaining his distance from the men in front. He could not afford to mess up now.

Now the captain had to salute the Queen. "Squad – halt!"

Wycombe hoped he wouldn't drop his sword. There had to be three hundred people watching.

But the captain had been practising. He brought the sword up with a flourish so that the ornamental hilt was level with his mouth.

Then, in a single flowing movement, he lowered the sword swiftly to the right side so that his right arm was straight, the edge of the sword was to the left and the point 12 inches from the ground, in front of his right shoulder. The hilt was just behind his right thigh.

The captain brought the sword back to the vertical.

"Squad, by the left – quick march." Wycombe was relieved. They had done all right.

The troops followed the route to Hyde Park. The iron gates had been pushed wide. A uniformed orderly at the gate instructed the various units to head for different sectors of the park.

"Royal Americans? Over there. The far corner." The parade was formally over. Wycombe was relieved that there had been no mishaps.

Tables and booths had been set up around the edge of the park. The captain explained that some ladies had volunteered to give refreshments to the marchers. Wycombe assumed that the portions were merely symbolic.

At the table reserved for the Royal American units,

three women handed out drinks and dainty biscuits. One of the women wore the uniform of a maid.

Wycombe realised that one of the ladies was Lady Forlaith, the dowager viscountess.

The other men recognised her too and were suddenly very polite. This was the closest any of them had ever been to her.

The lady smiled. "Tea, major, captain?"

"Thank you, madam." The maid poured out the drink.

Wycombe was so surprised that he spoke up. "Should you be here, madam? Begging your pardon."

Lady Forlaith did not seem to mind. "This was the only way for me to meet you dear boys. I could not go to the barracks ..."

"Oh! Of course not, madam. But ..."

"This is informal and therefore acceptable." She smiled. "Although perhaps a bit eccentric."

Wycombe understood. Lady Forlaith was already regarded as eccentric.

"I was shocked when I heard that only thirty of you were coming."

He smiled. "The army is too stingy to send all of us, madam. There's over three hundred of us on the strength."

"Just the same ..."

"They died free, madam. That was why they travelled north and signed up."

"I suppose so." Her tone was mournful.

He tried to think of something to say. "We've found that we're fighting for something. Defending the black community in Canada."

"Excellent."

"But we were all disappointed when the battalion was disbanded."

"Oh, that always happens. When a war is over, they disband the new regiments or new battalions. So this would have happened anyway. It just happened a bit sooner."

"Yes, madam. We still have the colours you gave us. Do you want them back?"

"Dear me, no. That was a gift. Those girls in Portland made it. Keep it for your Veterans' Association annual meetings. Or something like that."

This notion surprised him. "I suppose we can call ourselves veterans now, madam."

"Yes, certainly. A unit that has lost so many men ... I am so sorry that so many died," Lady Forlaith said. "I am glad that the dying is over."

"Yes, madam."

Chapter 16

Canada, Sault Ste. Marie, Sept 2

The Field Force had re-embarked on their paddle-steamers. A day later they disembarked at Echo Bay.

The last leg, within sight of the Michigan shore, had been on foot.

The town of Sault Ste. Marie was a straggle of wooden houses, parallel to the waterfront. Colonel Hendrick was not impressed.

The slightly-built Londoner, Tommy, was still attached as staff sergeant. Hendrick had come to rely on the English staff sergeant, whose book-keeping skills, initiative and experience of the British army had proved to be very useful.

But there was something not quite right about him. He was of slight build, with a high voice. But he was also hard as nails. All of Hendrick's men respected him. Even the old-fashioned ones with face tattoos.

The evening of their arrival, they held a council of war in the mayor's house. Hendrick was accompanied by Sergeant Johnson, one of those who sported traditional face tattoos. When the man smiled, the tattoos distorted. The sight made Tommy queasy, so he could guess what effect it would have on the Yankees.

The second man was Major Pride of the infantry. He commanded six companies of the Sixty-Second regiment, including the two companies of blacks. The third man was the lieutenant of artillery.

Next was Captain Waite of the Upper Canadian Militia. Hendrick tended to despise the white militia, who trained less than his own men. But he had not seen them in battle, so he reserved judgement.

The militia captain was unhappy at this planned aggression. Hendrick understood why. Once the fighting started, it could spread and involve the entire territory – including the captain's home.

Also present were the Chief of the local Ojibwa tribe and his middle-aged female interpreter.

"All they have is cavalry," the interpreter said. "Men on horses. All the men in Detroit who were fit to travel."

"Mounted infantry. Dragoons." Captain Waite said.

"Yes. The infantry will take three days to get here," the interpreter said.

"They will come here? Not Mackinack?" Major Pride said.

"Here," the interpreter said.

"How does he know?" Pride asked. "Does he have scouts everywhere?"

"Possibly. Or perhaps he just listens at keyholes," Hendrick said. "We will speak to the Yankees in the morning."

He had been surprised when the British major had allowed him to be the spokesman.

But Major Pride was ready to explain. "You have the gift of the gab, sir. And I don't."

He had, though, made very clear the limits of their bargaining points.

The English staff sergeant asked to accompany them to the debate.

"No," Hendrick said. "We need you here to organise things. I want them to see my colour sergeant and his tattoos. You're far too civilised."

Tommy tried to keep his face straight but did not quite succeed. "Yes, sir."

Michigan, Sault Ste. Marie, September 3

They had rowed across to the Michigan side of the river under a flag of truce. The southern town was not much bigger than the Canadian one. The Yankees received them in a large house in the centre of the town.

This route had taken them past the fort. The outer palisades were made of tree-trunks. Hendrick had tried not to stare.

They all sat round a table. Facing Hendrick was the Colonel of the Michigan militia. Hendrick had learned that he was a local politician. The fellow's main concern was his career. Perhaps he resented having to ride all this way in a hurry. "I don't believe this. You've sent an army to this backwater."

The town mayor was silent. Hendrick guessed that he was honest, an amateur politician rather than a professional one, and cared for his community.

Sitting each side of Hendrick were the British Major of infantry and the Captain of Canadian Militia. Hendrick's sergeant stood behind them, his face impassive.

"Our two nations are at war," Hendrick said. "Perhaps you and the governor forgot that. My task is to remind you."

"This is crazy. You won't get away with it. I know for a fact that you have less than a full battalion with you. I've already sent a courier, asking for help. Then we'll crush you."

Hendrick nodded. The US Army marching north was exactly what he wanted. Some men would say that he had already achieved all that the governor in Ontario expected. It would be unwise to say that, of course.

"We are following the rules. When the war started, the militias on both sides agreed that if they were going to attack, they would give notice. All very honourable. So I am giving notice now."

"Why have you come?" the colonel demanded. "The real reason."

Hendrick shrugged. "To protect our canal."

"It's for canoes!"

"All *you* have is a porterage."

"You don't have enough men to attack us. Except carry out - Indian raids." He sneered.

The mayor blanched. The thought of Indian raids probably gave him nightmares.

Hendrick kept his tone neutral. "We don't have enough regulars, no. But we have a couple of Volunteer companies. And enough regular artillery to knock a hole in your blockhouse." He turned to the mayor. "I give my word that my men will comply with the rules of war."

The mayor nodded. "Thank you, sir."

The Yankee colonel missed this by-play. "Half of those regulars are blacks. They won't fight."

Hendrick smiled. He enjoyed this. "They fought at Portland. They're battle-hardened veterans. They've probably seen more of combat than all of your men put together."

The mayor was more unhappy than ever. "They were the ones mentioned in the peace talks?"

Hendrick nodded.

The colonel tried to recover control of the situation. "But if you Redcoats break the truce, we will go onto the attack and invade Canada."

He smiled. "Really? You don't have the resources. We know that the garrison was withdrawn when the war started -."

"It's got a garrison of volunteers now." The colonel tried to sound confident.

"You might be able to withstand a siege. But you can't attack. And if the Washington government sends a couple of regiments of regulars to push us out – that is exactly what the British want." He enjoyed the expression of dismay on the white man's face.

"Are those Ojibwas fighting with you?"

"No, no. they're just here as observers. Don't worry, they distrust the Iroquois just as much as they distrust you."

"And how far do you intend to attack?" the colonel asked.

Hendrick should have ignored the question. But he could not resist. "Don't worry. We aren't going to conquer Michigan. We're going to restrict our activities to islands. This island, Drummond Island."

"This isn't an island."

"No? You had to cross a bridge to get here."

They rowed back to the Canadian side of the river and returned to the mayor's house. Captain Waite of the Canadian militia was unhappy. "Is it necessary to go ahead with this, sir? With the peace negotiations and all? You've created your diversion. You've got the Yankee infantry marching north."

Major Pride glared. Soldiers were not supposed to stop fighting just because peace talks were under way.

"I want to take Detroit. Chief Tecumseh did it in 1812."

Tommy was surprised. "Detroit's garrison outnumbers us, sir."

"Half of that garrison is marching north. I plan to take this fort, put my men back on those steamers, and take Detroit before those Yankees can get back home."

That sounded crazy to Tommy. But it explained the colonel's actions.

Port Elgin, September 4

The Mohawk messenger from Brant's Ford, Lieutenant Hardy, was not used to riding. He was tired and saddle-sore. He reached the town of Port Elgin late in the afternoon and asked for directions to the police station.

He asked the police inspector for a ship to take him after the colonel. A *fast* ship.

"They've signed a peace treaty, inspector. I don't want the colonel to break it."

He expected trouble. Some of these whites did not recognise the legality of the Mohawk army or the authority of its officers.

But the inspector was eager to help. His objections were not what the messenger expected.

"Lieutenant, no ships are available. Colonel Hendrick has taken them all."

Hardy fought down panic. "But if the colonel attacks after the deadline, he could start another war."

The inspector shook his head. "The only things in Port Elgin that can float are sailing boats and canoes." The lieutenant was horrified.

"And a couple of bateaux, open sailing boats," the police sergeant put in.

The lieutenant thought about it. He asked to speak to the mayor.

"I plan to continue on by bateaux. But one of the steamers might return. They are much faster."

"Better to wait, lieutenant."

"I cannot bear to sit here and do nothing." Then he asked the mayor to make out a copy of his orders. "And I want you to certify that it was a true copy. So if a steamer comes in, you can give the captain this copy and send him back."

The mayor was dubious. He asked the inspector.

"What if this story of a peace treaty is lies?"

"I doubt that, sir. But don't worry. You're being asked to swear that this is an accurate copy. Not that it's true."

Sault Ste. Marie, September 12

They agreed that their only chance of success was to attack at night. The colonel had asked Major Pride to work out the details. The major had promptly delegated most of the work to Tommy. The planning had been intense. Tommy had prepared lists and timetables. Everything had been checked and double-checked.

They used a mixture of canoes, obtained locally, and British folding boats.

The colonel had told Tommy he was convinced that the fort was under-garrisoned. "They would have been better to build a blockhouse. With a roof to keep us out. But no. I think we can get in over the walls."

Tommy had found the necessary ladders. Major Pride had told him to find a way to stow them in canoes.

The artillerymen intended to ferry a single cannon across, in sections, with the barrel on two British army folding boats fastened together.

The colonel had asked Tommy to check the details.

"You can ferry it across?" Tommy asked.

"We will need five boats. This is routine for gunners," the lieutenant said. "Mind your manners, sergeant."

He glared at Tommy. Then his eyes lost their focus, his eyes rolled up and he collapsed.

Everybody gaped. "What -." Tommy said.

The lieutenant lay on the ground, his limbs convulsing. Everyone stared, appalled. No-one knew what to do.

"Shouldn't we 'old him down?" a gunner asked.

"That would hurt him more. Hurt us too."

The spasms ceased. The lieutenant lay face up. "Turn him face down. He could choke," Tommy said.

They did so. "He could smother himself," the artillery sergeant said.

"Then turn his head to one side. And call for the doctor."

The figure on the ground twitched. He groaned.

"Someone will 'ave to tell the colonel," the artillery sergeant said.

Tommy sighed. "I'll do that,".

He found the colonel talking to Major Pride of the Sixty-Second. "Bad news, sergeant?"

"Yes, sir." Tommy explained in concise terms.

The colonel was shocked. This was not the crisis he was expecting. "Why did this have to happen now?"

Major Pride frowned. "Is he faking it? To avoid this battle?"

Tommy was offended. "I believe that his pain is genuine, sir."

"What do we do now?" the colonel asked, to himself.

"He says he'll be back on his feet in a few hours, sir. He wants to lead his men this evening. But at the moment he can't stand. It would take four men to carry him."

"Out of the question. Is his sergeant competent?"

"Well, yes, sir. He has years of experience. But – he's not suited for independent command. He works best when there's someone looming over his shoulder."

"Then go and loom over his shoulder."

"But I'm needed here, sir."

"You were needed for the planning,". Major Pride said. "That is completed, so you can be assigned to other chores."

Tommy wanted to stay with Hendrick, but saying so would be a mistake.

The colonel subjected him to a glare. Tommy saluted and left.

The artillery sergeant, understandably, resented his presence. "You can't teach me anything about guns."

"Yes, yes. But do you want to argue with *him*?" Tommy said.

"We should have an officer in charge here."

"Do you want a battlefield commission, sergeant?"

There was nothing that the sergeant wanted less. He shut up.

After nightfall, the men assembled on the bank. Everyone understood the need to keep quiet.

The gunners tied two of the boats together and then assembled a cradle on them. The artillery sergeant assured Tommy that it would work. The boats had been designed for this task. Tommy assumed the whole contraption would collapse, sending the barrel to the bottom.

Tommy watched with dread as the barrel was winched up and then lowered onto its cradle. But the gunners knew their business. The two boats settled lower into the water under the huge weight, but they remained stable.

Everything had to be done in silence and without showing any lights.

The balls and the gunpowder were loaded into three other boats.

Tommy reported to the colonel. "The artillery is ready, sir."

"It's time to go," the colonel said. He told his men to climb into their boats. He clearly thought this was great fun. The risk that the current might sweep them past Sault Ste. Marie and out into the lake only made it more interesting. He grinned in the dark.

Tommy was attracted to him. It was a pity that he was already spoken for.

The colonel climbed into his boat and gave the command in a whisper. His men began paddling across the river

Tommy returned to the artillery team. "It's time to go, sergeant."

The rowers were clumsy, splashing the water, but no-one raised the alarm. At last, Tommy's boat grounded on the shore.

The artillerymen had landed further downstream than the colonel's Mohawks. They got to work. They had brought a hoist in one of the boats. They used the hoist to lift the barrel of the cannon back onto its wheeled carriage.

"Quiet, there," the gunner sergeant said.

They were joined by a company of blacks from the Sixty-Second regiment. They had served in Portland and had experience of night work.

"The plan is to attack the gate," Captain Warwick said.

Tommy wanted to tell him to shut up. But sergeants weren't allowed to do that.

Tommy had been ordered to stay with the cannon. The artillerymen dragged it across the island and into place.

"Load 'er. Quiet, now," the gunner sergeant said.

"They must know we're here," a gunner said.

"Shut up," the sergeant said. "Stand back. Fire."

The first shot missed, hitting the wall instead of the gate.

The sergeant was unperturbed. "Reload."

The Yankee sentries, aware of the danger at last, began taking pot-shots at the gunners. But, in the dark, they were shooting blind.

Tommy heard an outburst of shouting. On the far side of the fort, the Mohawks were using their ladders to climb the wall. Hopefully, they had achieved surprise.

That distracted attention from the team at the gate.

A bugle sounded inside the fort. "A bit late for that," Mr. Warwick said.

"Yes, sir."

The artillerymen kept reloading and firing. Three direct hits smashed the left-hand gate.

"That's enough for us," Captain Warwick said. "Follow me!" His men rushed forward.

Tommy expected the black soldiers to suffer heavy casualties. But the gate appeared to be undefended. The attackers burst through the smashed gate and into the fort.

Colonel Hendrick had wanted to be in the thick of things. He was asking his men to risk their lives.

He wanted to be the first man into the fort. But his junior officers said he was too important to take risks. His sergeant said that he did not need to prove how brave he was. So he stood back, out of musket range, and watched as his men climbed the ladders.

The first attempt to take the walls was repulsed. One of the ladders was pushed over. Two men fell to their deaths. The survivors fled back to where he was watching.

He heard the cannon firing at the gate. He told his men to try again. "You shall follow me."

Sergeant Johnson complained. "Sir, you mustn't -."

Hendrick scowled and the fellow shut up.

"This time, I'll lead the way up the ladder."

"At least let me go first, sir," Johnson said.

"No." So Johnson followed behind.

He let the sergeant push the ladder into place. "Hold it steady." He reached the top and got over the parapet. A Yankee sergeant rushed along the sentry-walk.

A Mohawk down below fired his musket. A luck would have it, the ball hit the sergeant and not the colonel.

Sergeant Johnson climbed over the parapet, pushed his commander aside and ran screaming at his enemies.

The last of the defenders fled along the sentry-walk. Johnson sergeant ran down the steps.

Hendrick hurried after him. The defenders, on this side of the fort, were too few to hold him back. He realised the battle was won. Men were still fighting but he was was victorious.

Someone in the dark fired a musket. It hit him in his left side and knocked him off his feet. Then the pain came. Men gathered round.

"Boss!" Johnson said.

"Help me up." There was not much blood. It could not be too bad.

"We'll find a stretcher, boss. Lie still."

Hendrick swore at him and climbed to his feet. The wound in his side was painful but he was determined to keep on going.

There was more shouting. The black redcoats came running from the other direction.

They recognised Hendrick and cheered.

The garrison commander realised the battle was lost and asked to surrender.

Tommy abandoned her post by the cannon and entered the fort, trailing behind the blacks.

She was just in time to witness Colonel Hendrick accepting the commander's sword. But he was swaying on his feet.

Tommy was shocked. "Get a surgeon. *Now*, dammit."

Three of Hendrick's men went running off. She persuaded the colonel to sit down.

The town doctor examined him. He stepped back and told the onlookers that the wound was fatal. "Internal bleeding. He'll be dead by morning."

Tommy suspected that a surgeon experienced in

gunshot wounds might have saved him, but there were none.

Tommy was shocked. This was the second time a handsome young officer had died. She decided to avoid handsome men in future.

The lieutenant in Montreal was sweet on her too. Despite knowing her sordid history. Perhaps that was the answer. He was safe and boring.

Major Pride turned up, leading his company of regulars, and took over. "Who's the senior Mohawk officer?" He behaved as if Hendrick was already dead.

"Sergeant, what's the casualty list?"

Tommy was close to tears. But she must hide it. These men depended upon Tommy.

"Help me to my feet," Hendrick said. Tommy was reluctant to touch him. But she and Sergeant Johnson stepped forward and pulled him to his feet.

"Give me that sword." Major Pride handed it over.

Hendrick leaned on the sword. "I claim this land for Queen – Victoria. And – my people."

"You can't do that!" the Yankee commander said.

"I was appointed by the governor. He was appointed by Queen Victoria. Of course, real life is a bit different."

Major Pride was shocked. "You've just given the negotiators a lot of trouble."

"That is not my problem," Hendrick said.

About the author

He studied the history of science at Britain's Open University, which was one of the pioneers of distance learning. He lives an hour's travel from London.
For his employer, he writes technical guidance and publicity material, published on the internet, but most readers will not be interested in those.
He uses research for these novels as an excuse to make regular visits to the City of London – and further afield. He visited New York in November 2014 and the Adirondacks in March 2015.
His hobbies have included sailing yachts and flying sailplanes. He is interested in hiking and cross-country skiing. Writing is his oldest hobby.

He is a member of the British Science Fiction Association.

*

The cover, depicting a sergeant of the Essex County militia, was prepared by Christa Hook.

Lightning Source UK Ltd.
Milton Keynes UK
UKHW02f1657050418
320581UK00006B/164/P